YEARS LATER,
LONG AFTER THE WAR,
DUANE COULDN'T
HOLD BACK...

"I really have to know."

"Know what?"

"Well, do you remember that first raid on Truk? The sweep?"

Fred held up his disfigured hand, and touched his side. "I'm still carrying a piece of my plane. How could I forget?"

"Look," said Duane. "I saw Jack leave the target in a perfectly flyable aircraft."

"Yeah?"

"Did he ditch just to be with you?"

Fred stared numbly at Duane... "Jack and I were a lot more than just wingmen."

WING-MEN

ENSAN CASE

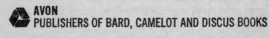

AVON
PUBLISHERS OF BARD, CAMELOT AND DISCUS BOOKS

There actually was an Air Group Twenty in existence during the time period covered by this book, and it may or may not have participated in the historical actions described herein. The Air Group Twenty of this book, however, is totally fictitious, as is the carrier *Constitution*. The characters which people this story, with obvious exceptions, bear no resemblance to real persons, living or dead.

WINGMEN is an original publication of Avon Books. This work has never before appeared in book form.

AVON BOOKS
A division of
The Hearst Corporation
959 Eighth Avenue
New York, New York 10019

Copyright © 1979 by Ensan Case
Published by arrangement with the author
Library of Congress Catalog Card Number: 79-65534
ISBN: 0-380-47647-9

First Avon Printing, November, 1979

AVON TRADEMARK REG. U.S. PAT. OFF. AND IN
OTHER COUNTRIES, MARCA REGISTRADA, HECHO EN
U.S.A.

Printed in the U.S.A.

DEDICATION AND THANKS.

For T. P., with love.
Thanks to silly Dick Newhafer
and his first Tallyho.

Contents

I	VF-20	3
II	*Ironsides*	63
II—A	Interim: Pearl	129
III	Combat One: Marcus	157
III—A	Interim: Leave	181
IV	Combat One: Wake	191
IV—A	Interim: Decisions	217
V	Combat Two: Tarawa	235
V—A	Interim: The Affair	273
VI	Combat Two: Kwajalein	305
VI—A	Interim: Consideration	337
VII	Combat Three: Truk	355
VIII	Scrapbook	389
IX	Epilogue	401

By the first half of 1943, both Japanese and American air groups were coming to rely on pilots who had received their training since the war began. The story of the burgeoning strength of the United States Navy, the resul* of the great disparity in comparative economic might of the respective nations, was well known by the Japanese at the time and is fully documented today. Behind the scenes, however, of this dramatic increase in power lies a seldom-told tale of another important facet of that growth: the training of the men to man the ships, to fly the new aircraft, and to maintain and repair those ships and aircraft. It is a tribute to the American economic system with its classless qualities that when the great fleets began to meet in combat during that and the following years the pilots in the blue aircraft with the white stars were better trained, better equipped and flew more reliable aircraft, while the men flying under the rising sun could claim but one advantage: their willingness to face death.

> (J.E. Hardigan, Commander, USN (ret.),
> *A Setting of Many Suns: The Destruction of the Imperial Navy* [The Naval Institute Press, 1962], p. 126.)

Part I

VF-20

1

The girl moaned softly and massaged Fred Trusteau's shoulders with her fingertips. This young man had already lasted four times longer than any of the previous three men who had made love to her, and she was now feeling something entirely new and wonderfully salacious. Their bodies rose and wove, rose and wove, meeting in a precise fit that made her marvel and think that he must have done this many times before. It was so much better this time. She was having her first orgasm.

Fred thrust softly and relaxed, thrust and relaxed, over and over, amazed at how the strength was being sapped from his body by this necessary but emotionally neutral act. The warm wetness and the sounds they made would not go away, so he tried to forget about them and think of other things.

He knew that the other guys in the squadron would give their last ten bucks to be in this darkened room in the clean-sheeted bed with this attractive girl. He also knew that he and the girl had been seen entering the boarding house by at least one other couple, a young fighter pilot and a nurse. Probably they had waited to see if the lights would go out in the girl's room. The word would quickly get back to the squadron that Fred had scored big. Part of the price of acceptance would have been paid.

The warm Honolulu trade winds rustled the curtains at the open window. Fred looked across the small, cluttered room, and like a child recalling a new and delightful toy, he reminded himself that he was a Hellcat pilot. In the morning a big blue fighter would again be put into his hands. The novelty of that adventure hadn't worn off, even though it had been at least two weeks since the almost-daily flights had begun. Tomorrow the guns would be loaded with color-coded tracers, and the firing runs against the towed sleeve would begin. This would be the closest he had ever come to the awful reality of fighting. Often in the past year he had wondered just how it felt to touch the firing button that sent the tracers blazing into an enemy plane, and then to see the frail aluminum craft explode or burst into flame, shedding chunks of metal and oily smoke before disappearing into the clouds below. That another young pilot much like himself might be dying horribly in that blazing coffin meant little; in one of the training films they'd been shown, taken from the wing camera of a fighter in action, the pilot of the doomed aircraft had tried to exit. The class had watched him climb with amazing agility from the shattered cockpit to the wing root, where he clung for a second before he, too, was exploded by hundreds of hot slugs. Then he had tumbled away like a grotesque ragdoll. The entire class had erupted into clapping and cheering, and Fred had cheered as loudly as the rest.

The girl let out a mingled cry like a sob and a laugh, and she dug her nails into Fred's back. Good, he thought, leave something for the guys to see in the shower tomorrow. She began to move more quickly now, almost desperately, and Fred knew she was climaxing. He concentrated, trying to bring on his own, but he only felt emptiness. Par for the course, he thought, without bitterness.

He had worked hard to arrange this evening, making certain that the other men in the squadron would hear about it. He wouldn't exactly brag, but neither would he deny it when the men made him the butt of suggestive, good-natured ribaldry. If what he was doing now would make his fellow pilots like him more or show him more consideration, then so be it. The time and the money he had spent on the girl would be worth it.

Now she gave a short cry and arched her back, lifting Fred with her. Then she froze in one position until she settled at last into a trembling state of aftershock. Fred extracted himself and rolled off her body. Only their feet still touched. The girl's eyes were closed, and she was breathing deeply and quickly through her open mouth. For a moment Fred watched her, then he rolled out of bed.

Fred took a cigarette and matches from the pocket of his uniform shirt and lighted up. He sat down on the edge of the bed and smoked, occasionally looking over at the girl. She lay quietly, apparently asleep. He suddenly noticed he was covered with sweat and figured the girl was, too, but he didn't reach out to check.

When he'd finished with his smoke, he ground it out in the ashtray and padded naked across the room to the tiny bathroom, retrieving his shorts on the way. He turned on the bathroom light and closed the door. He was surprised at the good feeling that privacy—real privacy—afforded him. There were no other men in the shower with him, no one using the toilet across the room, no one shaving at the sink. He turned on the water and stepped into the tub, pulling the curtain closed behind him.

The female paraphernalia of shampoos, razor, and bath oils that crowded the corners of the tub amused him. He washed himself clean, then dried off on the only towel he could find. Pink and fluffy, it smelled like the girl. He hung the towel back where he had found it, straightened the bathroom a little, then went back into the bedroom.

When he was dressed, the naked girl turned over and watched him tie his shoes. "Was it good for you, too?" she asked. Her voice had a dreamy, sleepy quality.

Fred finished tying his shoe and let his foot fall to the floor. "Sure," he said.

"You're leaving now?"

She was, he thought, really a nice girl. He hoped she didn't think he was a love-'em-and-leave-'em type, or feel any guilt about what they had done.

"Afraid so." He touched her arm. "We'll be flying early tomorrow and I should get some sleep."

"What ship are you on?"

"We don't have a ship yet."

"Why?"

"I'm a pilot with Fighter Squadron Eight, part of Air Group Number Eight. They'll assign us to an aircraft carrier when they have one ready for us."

"What's it like?"

"What?"

"Flying."

Fred thought for a moment, then stood up. "I don't know," he said. "I think it's about the best thing in the world."

"You're kidding," she said smilingly. She stretched sensuously, then curled into a satisfied little bundle. Fred covered her with the sheet.

"Nope," he said. "It's the best." He crossed the room and opened the door into the hallway. "Good night," he said without looking back and closed the door softly behind him.

2

Lieutenant Commander Jack Hardigan was the new skipper of VF-20, the fighter squadron of Air Group Twenty, soon to embark aboard the carrier *Constitution*. Jack Hardigan was also more interested in flying his shiny new Hellcat than in coping with the mess he was confronted with now. The new aircraft had arrived over a month ago, at about the time he had received final command of the squadron, and he had yet to log more than twenty hours of flight time in them. For this he could thank the former squadron commander, who had just departed for the continent to form a new air group at whose head he would fly. The old commander had preferred making speeches and giving pep talks, in which he would say things like, "It's an ugly fucking job, but the sooner we get out there and blast the slanty-eyed bastards to hell, the sooner this fucking war'll be over," and "They're the best goddamn pilots in the fleet and I love 'em for it"—to doing paperwork. So Jack had inherited quite a backlog of it. Jack had not been fooled by the oratory of VF-20's former commander. He knew the man wished the war would never end and was having the time of his life. He didn't in fact love his pilots any more than he loved any one of the innumerable prostitutes he had bedded in his enthusiastic pursuit of a colorful reputation. Images, reflected Jack, were everything to some people.

The latest VF-20 crisis entailed fitness reports on the pilots, due on CAG's—the Air Group Commander's—desk not later than the third week in June, which would give him time to review them, make changes, and sign them into the respective jackets. Jack could easily finish this minor task in about an hour. CAG, however, another pompous little man who had hated all fighter pilots since Midway (80 percent of his torpedo squadron had been destroyed there and he had needed a goat), would undoubtedly send half the completed reports back with little notes that read, "Unsat, do over." He would then rant and rave like a wounded chicken when the week was over and the reports were due but unfinished. Denied leave, Jack would then forego everything else, regardless of priority, and stay up all night to finish the goddamn reports. The crisis would end, only to be taken up by another, more horrendous crisis—and that would keep Jack on the ground and out of town until the *next* crisis. Life in Air Group Twenty was not exactly a bed of roses.

Jack sighed and shuffled the stack of fitness forms in front of him, dismayed at their number. Thirty-two pilots needed to be graded. He had done eight of them because those eight were the division leaders. The rest were done by the division leaders themselves, men who could fly well enough but knew absolutely nothing about the English language—a few, he was convinced, spoke no English at all, just a smattering of flying slang and profanity, equally mixed. The reports these officers and gentlemen had composed would have to be completely re-written.

Jack sorted the forms into two stacks, one for the pilots he had known for a while and one for the new men. Counting himself, only fourteen of the thirty-three pilots had any operational experience, and only eight of those fourteen had been in combat. Nineteen of the men were brand-new. All but one of them were ensigns. Jack found himself wishing that gaining experience in the ugly game of war for at least some of the new men would mean something other than the finality of death.

Jack glanced at the clock and took the first form from the stack. It was 9:45. The yeoman and office staff had long since left and he was alone in the building. Outside, in the warm Hawaiian night, a low-flying Avenger (he recognized the sound of its engine) droned overhead, then receded into the darkness. In town and at the Officer's Club, his pilots were blowing hundreds of dollars on booze and broads, for no other reason except that all the other pilots were doing the same thing. War provided a marvelous opportunity for them to prove their manhood. But when the time came to manhandle an overladen aircraft off a pitching carrier deck, only a few would retain that cavalier attitude. Some would die without ever seeing the enemy.

"Ensign Jacobs is a fine pilot and always scores above

average in shooting." Jack winced at the fractured line and rewrote it. "Ensign Jacobs displays a natural flying ability enhanced by the ability to profit quickly trom the advice and instruction of more experienced aviators. He has consistently scored in the twenty to twenty-five percentile group in air-to-air gunnery exercise." Jack pictured Jacobs in his mind; he was just a kid. He had probably soloed only once or twice by the time Jack had fought and survived the engagement at Midway.

Midway. It always came back to those few hundred square miles of ocean. Funny, thought Jack, how such an island could exert such an influence for so long. He wondered if other pilots who had fought there—and most of those around at the time had—felt the same as he did. He tended to think of his life as having started at Midway, that the war until then had been something of a lark—a little scary perhaps, but still in the high adventure category. He had been flying off the *Hornet* and had gone with Colonel Doolittle to Tokyo. Thus he had missed the Coral Sea engagement, which no doubt had served as the starting, or stopping, point for a lot of other flyers. *Yorktown*'s and *Lexington*'s groups had been decimated at Coral Sea. But that was the point: Things like that happened to other groups, never to yours.

Jack was blooded at Midway. Drinking buddies and roommates died horribly before his eyes—or simply vanished into the depths of the Pacific Ocean. Midway was three days of terror and exhaustion, a life-changing combination if ever there was one. And Jack had most certainly changed.

It was almost midnight before Jack reached a stopping point on the forms. He had corrected the grammar and spelling on all the reports for the new pilots, and he would finish the rest the following night. Leaving the fitness forms, he skimmed through the other items on his hot list.

Item two concerned a new ensign named Carruthers who had joined the squadron three weeks before and was now accused of rape by a local girl. The investigation into this affair would take another week at least. Then would come the court-martial, which would take three weeks to get started. CAG had informed him in strictest confidence that the air group would ship aboard and sail with the fleet in less time than that, although how he had managed to obtain that piece of information, Jack would never know. Then CAG had ordered Jack to have the offending pilot detached to the naval base (since he was spending his time in the BOQ under house arrest anyway) and then locate another pilot in the islands to replace him—as though Jack, a new lieutenant commander, had friends on Admiral Nimitz's staff. Jack had already decided to make a stab at it, then call it quits; he had enough to do without attempting the impossible.

Item three concerned three new pilots who had never arrived. They were two weeks overdue now. Jack had mentioned it to CAG about a week ago in a memo. He'd offered the opinion that since the squadron was already more or less up to full strength, perhaps they should do nothing. Since he felt sure that CAG would find his opinion unacceptable, he had already requested assistance from the naval base personnel office in locating them. It was obviously an administrative error. Three new pilots coming back from post-flight-training leave would never jump ship, all at the same time. Jack was more concerned with the effect on the squadron than with finding the "missing" men, because now he had a man without a wingman to train with. He had partially solved the problem by sending his pilots to the Naval Hospital at Pearl Harbor three at a time and rotating the odd man through the other divisions for training. That odd, new man probably knew more about the other pilots in the squadron and the F6F-3 Hellcat, Jack reflected ruefully, than he did.

He straightened the papers on his desk, temporarily satisfied that everything was under control. He snapped out the lamp and darkness engulfed him. He pulled open the blackout curtains. Straining to see in the dim moonlight, he could just make out the concrete revetments, the runway, and the hulking shapes of parked aircraft. He sat for a few minutes, feeling very lonely. He'd always heard that those in command were lonely people, but he'd discounted it. Now he craved someone to talk to, someone with whom he could share his thoughts, and he realized that he had felt this way before, often. He'd always written it off before by telling himself he was merely horny. Now he wasn't so sure. It'll be better when we go to sea, he thought. But he sat in the darkness for another ten minutes wondering about it.

3

The squadron insignia for VF-8 made a clever play on words and was nonsensically sordid. A grinning skeleton sat on the wing of a Wildcat, wearing a flapping flight helmet and dealing aces and eights from a deck of cards. One of the aces was severing the head of a surprised Japanese pilot, who sat in the exposed cockpit of a cartoon airplane. Over the skeleton's head were the words "Deal's Deadly Dealers" and below it was written "Fighting Eight." When Fred Trusteau first saw it, he thought it a joke. He soon discovered otherwise.

The insignia was painted on a piece of sheet aluminum. The original wooden one had been tossed out of the *Enterprise* prior to the Eastern Solomons engagement, in one of the frequent efforts to rid the ship of nonessential flammables. Fred wondered if the paint would burn, and he imagined himself heaving the metal sheet over the side of the ship. It hung now in front of the longish classroom used by the group as it re-formed and trained at Kaneohe near Honolulu. Under the skeleton's baleful gaze, the squadron received its daily training in defensive flying, attack techniques, air navigation, shipboard procedures, and survival.

The skipper of Fighting Eight was not a large man by any standard other than the size of his gut. Lieutenant Commander Deal was fast approaching the age at which he would have to be removed from air combat status because of his slower reactions.

At thirty-seven, he had the dubious distinction of being the oldest squadron commander in the fleet. He was in fact older than the Air Group Commander, and would have been moved up and out long ago had it not been for the battles at Midway, the Eastern Solomons, and Santa Cruz, eighteen months in all of continuous wartime operating, which had cut down considerably on competition for command aviation billets. Now, however, time was catching up with Lieutenant Commander Deal. Whole classes of new pilots were arriving in the islands.

Deal swaggered into the ready room this morning and theatrically took the floor from his executive officer, who had been briefing the pilots on the morning's exercises. He wore a forty-five automatic in a holster under his left arm, and his khaki uniform showed that it had been slept in for the past two nights. There were small darkened stains on the front of the trousers, but they were almost indistinguishable among the accumulated stains. Deal was too occupied or too lazy to put out his laundry for the stewards. The man nauseated Fred.

"Good morning, gentlemen," Deal said to the pilots on the left side of the room. These were all veterans and had flown in combat at least once. Seven or eight of them claimed kills. "And for the flying turkeys," he said, addressing the right half of the room, carefully segregated by a cleared aisle, "I have an announcement to make. One of you bastards is going to leave my squadron today."

He paused to let this information sink in. Fred glanced around at the men near him, including one miserable j.g. who had been with the unit for over six months and hadn't flown a single combat mission. "I have been directed," Deal said slowly, acidly, "to ask for a volunteer—" He split the word into three precise syllables, as if he were talking to complete idiots. "—to transfer to a real chicken outfit." He paused for effect.

"Well, now," Deal continued, after a moment of silence. "Don't you all speak at once. I have nothing better to do than stand here and look at your pretty young faces."

One of the men in the front row tentatively raised his hand and started to ask which air group it was, but stopped when most of the assembled pilots suddenly turned in their seats. Two men were standing: Fred Trusteau and the miserable j.g.

Fred watched the look on Deal's face as the older man realized that at least two members of his squadron didn't care where they went, just so long as they went. Deal scratched nervously under his armpit where the holster chafed him and said with as much venom as he could muster, "Come with me, you bastards."

Deal's office was a chaos of flight gear, flight manuals for the new Hellcats, and stacks of assorted and uncompleted paperwork. He left the two men standing as he cleared a pile of personnel jackets from his swivel chair and sat in it. There were no other chairs empty enough to sit in, so Fred and the j.g. remained standing. Deal rummaged in the pile of officer jackets and came up with theirs.

"Well, Trusteau," he said, "I can't say I'm surprised you found things a little too rough in the Dealers. We don't want quitters anyway." He opened Fred's folder and began flipping through the entries. "But you, Silver. We'll make a man out of you yet." He snapped the folder closed with a small swoosh of air. "You stay."

"Will that be all, sir?" asked Silver helplessly.

"Get out of here," said Deal.

As Silver turned to go, Fred grabbed him lightly by the arm and held out his hand. He looked the j.g. in the eyes. "It's been nice," he said. "Good luck."

"Thanks," said Silver. He made scarcely a sound as he left the office and closed the door behind him.

When he had first been assigned to VF-8, Fred had really wanted to like Lieutenant Commander Deal. His first impression of Deal had been that the man had strength and control; that is, strength of personal character and control of the people and events around him. But after two days in Deal's squadron, Fred felt entirely different. Deal divided his pilots into two groups and spent more time with the veterans. He heaped contempt on the inexperienced men and urged his better pilots to do the same. Of course they're the better pilots, Fred thought. What did Deal expect from the newcomers? There weren't any Jap carriers in Lake Michigan. He soon realized that Deal was narrow and childish. His control of people amounted to a grown-up form of bullying.

Deal was busy writing. Without looking up, he said, "Trusteau"—(pronouncing the name "trust-oh," which was incorrect)—"your attitude stinks like hell." He put down his pen. Fred saw that he had been working on an officer's fitness report. "I believe in letting a man know where he stands with me, and I'm telling you now. Straighten up your attitude toward your superiors and things will go a lot better for you."

"Yes, sir," said Fred.

"Your flying ability isn't in question. But this grab-assing around isn't the real thing, either. When you meet your first Jap pilot out there, you better pray like hell your friends'll stick up for you, or that Jap'll blow your ass out of the sky so fast you won't have time to wipe it." It was a long speech for Deal. But Fred watched him steadily. "I hope your next skipper knows what the hell to do with you," the older man said. He shoved the personnel folder across the desk and Fred took it. "Now get the hell out of my squadron."

Fred held the folder, wishing he could tell Deal exactly what he thought: that Deal was an asshole.

"Sir," he said, "if I may. What outfit am I headed for?"

Deal scrounged through the papers on his desk. He found a half-smoked cigar, which he lit. "VF-20, other side of the island," he said. Clouds of blue-gray smoke engulfed him. "Biggest bunch of yo-yos this side of Bora Bora. The yeoman's cutting the orders now."

"Thanks," said Fred. He knew that now he'd have to rebuild his image from scratch, but that it would be worth it to get out of this squadron. He turned to go, then stopped at the door. "It's been nice," he said. "Good luck." He left.

"Fuck it all," said Lieutenant Commander Deal.

"Trust-oh?" Lieutenant Commander Hardigan was leafing through the contents of Fred's personnel jacket only an hour or so after Deal had finished with it.

"True-stow," said Fred. He sat in a nice padded armchair, marveling at the difference between the two squadron commanders' offices. Even the ashtrays were clean in this one. Jack Hardigan wore a laundered, freshly pressed khaki uniform with a black tie. His dark hair was neatly trimmed and combed to one side.

"Do they call you Fred?"

"Yes, sir, when the occasion suits it."

"In this squadron, the occasion suits it." Jack smiled and leaned back in his chair. "So you came here from Deal's Deadly Dealers?" He was surprised at how fast the personnel office had hustled him up a replacement pilot. It told him that Air Group Twenty was indeed probably due to embark and sail sooner than Air Group Eight, a vital bit of intelligence.

"Yes, sir. I hear I was transferred to replace a guy in the brig."

"House arrest only. Don't believe everything you hear." Jack glanced down at his desk. The jacket lay open to the hastily written fitness report. "Lieutenant Commander Deal says your attitude and cooperativeness aren't up to par. What do you have to say about that?"

Fred looked sincerely puzzled. "I don't think he liked me very much. I never quite understood him." He wondered if his little act was successful and was relieved when the squadron commander tore the fitness report out of the folder, wadded it into a tight little ball, and dispatched it into a wastebasket behind the desk.

"Jerry Deal and his boys are the worst bunch of crazies this side of Tongatabu."

Fred smiled. "That's funny. He said almost the same thing about VF-20."

"Let me guess how he put it. The worst bunch of screw-ups this side of Vella Lavella?"

"Yo-yos this side of Bora Bora."

Jack sighed and stretched, then put his hands behind his head. Suddenly he looked very serious. "Jerry Deal loses more pilots than any other skipper," he said. "He teaches them to go charging off after anything in the air without thinking about the consequences. They get into fixes they can't get out of, and the guys they're supposed to protect get clobbered. I've seen it happen." He thought for a moment. "Don't repeat that to anyone." Fred nodded. "I teach cohesion," Jack went on. "Clearly stated objectives and control to achieve those objectives, with sections sticking together like glue and divisions doing what they're told. I teach radio discipline. Last year we almost lost the *Enterprise* because the pilots jammed the circuits with bullshit, and they couldn't vector us onto the incoming Jap planes." Jack shut his eyes for a moment, remembering that violent day.

There was a lull. Fred spoke first. "Any word as to when we'll be sailing?"

"Only scuttlebutt, but it shouldn't be too long. *Ironsides* has been in Pearl over a month," Jack said, using *Constitution*'s nickname.

"Good," said Fred. Then, to offset the implication that he was overeager for killing: "I've seen all of Hawaii. A change of scenery might be nice."

"You're not alone. Most of the guys are anxious to leave, even though they don't say as much."

Aircraft engines sputtered and roared to life outside the building, and Fred looked toward the window.

"Well," said Jack, "back to work. Have you moved to this side of the island yet?"

"Not yet, Skipper."

Jack pressed a button on his desk, and a harried-looking enlisted man in working whites opened the door. Jack told him to get a driver and a vehicle for Fred and to have a room prepared at the BOQ with the rest of the squadron. The enlisted man disappeared.

"Take the rest of the day off to get settled," Jack said. "Tomorrow's Sunday and we don't fly. Monday morning we do. Check in with the XO and he'll assign you to a plane and fill you in on details." Jack stood; the interview was over. "Nice having you in the squadron." They shook hands.

"Yes, sir," said Fred. When he reached the door, he looked back at the squadron commander. He felt good about him and expected a smile or at least a nod. But Jack Hardigan was already hard at work.

4

Ensign Fred Trusteau was unofficially but overwhelmingly accepted into the squadron of Fighting Twenty on the Saturday night of his arrival. His initiation concerned a cherry stem and a girl.

After driving across the island of Oahu to retrieve his uniforms and toilet gear, Fred checked into the BOQ near the air station and got a small but well-furnished room for two with a view of Pearl Harbor—if you leaned far enough out the window. It was just after four and nobody was around, so Fred went out for a walk in the hot sunshine, happy to have the good fortune of a few hours to himself. The little air base was smaller than the Kaneohe station but large enough to have its own base exchange. His last liquor ration had been wasted on people he hadn't felt like drinking with, but now that he was a member of VF-20 he had another ration to enjoy. Thanking his lucky stars for this precipitous turn of events, he bought two bottles of overpriced Scotch and headed back to the BOQ, having been out for about an hour. There, he found that a party was underway in the room next to his. He considered the alternatives and decided to take the plunge.

Feeling very much like an intruder, Fred pushed open the door and stepped inside. Twelve sweaty faces turned to look and silence fell with unnatural swiftness. "Good afternoon," said Fred. He pulled the two bottles of Scotch from the paper bag and held them up. "I'm the new kid from down the block and I brought something for the party." A roar of approval went up and a boozy, reeling pilot with a beefy face staggered over to Fred and threw an arm around his shoulders.

"Name's Fred Trusteau," said Fred.

"Fuck the introductions," said the drunken pilot, "let's crack them bottles." The bottles disappeared into the crowd, and Fred was given a place to sit on a bunk between a gangly man with a big nose and a stocky, black-haired man with small features and tufts of black hair peeking out the top of his T-shirt. When Fred was seated, the stocky man shoved a half-filled water glass into his hands and said, "That was such a nice thing to do, I could just kiss you," and he gave Fred a scratchy peck on the cheek. Fred decided the pilot was juiced beyond rational thinking—no small accomplishment for less than an hour's drinking.

"I'm Frank Hammerstein," said the thin man. "Looks like you made a hit with the squadron."

"Fred Trusteau. But will they still love me tomorrow?"

Frank laughed and raised his glass in a salute, and they drank together.

Looking around the room, Fred could see several lieutenants, a bunch of j.g.'s, and the usual collection of ensigns. The experienced pilots mixed easily with the new ones, and Fred decided he would like flying with this group. They were certainly friendly enough after hours.

"In case you're wondering," said Frank Hammerstein, talking loudly to override the babble of voices, "this is our Saturday afternoon strategy conference."

"Conference?"

"We do this every Saturday night, while we try to decide on what we're going to do the rest of the weekend."

"You mean on Sunday."

"Yeah, but sometimes we get too far along and end up right here all Saturday night."

"Sounds like fun." Fred emptied his glass. "How do you get a refill?" he asked.

"Just wait," said Frank. "A bottle'll be around in a minute." A moment later a bottle of gin appeared in Frank's hands. He poured both of them a few fingers and passed the bottle to the stocky man with the hairy neck, who raised it to his lips, chugged a few swallows, and fell back into the bunk. The bottle continued to the left and disappeared into the haze of cigarette smoke and the crowd of brown khaki uniforms.

"Hope you like gin," said Frank.

"I never refuse a drink from a friend," said Fred. The gin was not particulary good, but Fred drank it anyway. He was nearly finished with it when the door burst open and a j.g. staggered in, dragging a girl with him.

"Hey, fellas," he said, "I've got something to show you. You won't believe this when you see it." The hot smoky air of the room visibly affected him, and he leaned on the girl. Fred looked at his watch. It was only 5:20. The j.g. must have set some kind of speed record getting into town, getting drunk, picking up the girl, and bringing her back here—all in a little over an hour. No one in VF-8, not even Deadly Deal himself, could do that.

The girl was probably a prostitute. She wore a shiny black dress that hit her legs at the knees and had a loose, low-cut top. A large island flower was pinned over her left ear, and she wore more make-up than Fred had seen on any two people at the same time. She was not, he decided, beautiful; but to most of these men she might look it.

"This lady," the j.g. was trying to say, amid pealing laughter and derisive punches, "this lady can—" He lost his train of thought and stood there, leaning on her shoulder and staring, glassy-eyed. Someone handed him a bottle and he drank. Wiping his mouth with the back of his hand, he tried again. "This lady can—can—"

"I bet she can," someone called out, and everyone else in the room dissolved into hooting laughter. The j.g. took another drink and kneeled to set the bottle on the floor. When he tried to stand up again, he couldn't. He slowly sagged to the floor and lay down at the feet of his fellow pilots.

"What is it, honey?" someone asked. A hand reached out and caressed the girl's knee, slid up her leg, and pulled up the shiny skirt. The girl switched her dress and tried to move away, but the other pilots had moved in and surrounded her.

"What can you do that's got poor Fritzi here so excited?" A dark brown shoe prodded the inert form on the floor. It stirred and moaned.

"I guess I'd better go." The girl spoke in a classic, dumb-blonde falsetto.

The red-faced pilot who'd greeted Fred at the door ambled up to the girl and draped himself over her. "Did poor old Fritzi here give you any money, honey?" His voice oozed with concern.

"Well," said the girl, looking at the floor.

"Well," said the man, "I think he did." With a very agile thumb and forefinger he plucked a folded ten-dollar bill from her cleavage.

"That's mine," said the girl, and she snatched it back.

At her feet, Fritzi moaned again and struggled to his hands and knees. His head swung ponderously back and forth. He spoke, and the room quieted to take in his words. "She can tie. A knot. In a cherry stem. Without using her. Hands." He struggled to his feet. A small red bottle dropped from his shirt to the floor. His face ashen, he ran for the door and was gone.

"What the hell does she use if she doesn't use her hands?" someone asked.

Fred slapped Frank Hammerstein on the knee and climbed to his feet. "I know what she uses and I can do it, too." Thirteen faces turned to look at him. "And I can do it faster than she can." The liquor in his belly was giving him amazing courage.

"Ten bucks on the broad," someone said immediately.

"Well," said Fred, "is there a cherry in the house?" Someone gave the girl a gentle shove and she fell into Fred's arms. The entire room erupted into howling laughter.

"Captain Fitzsimmons picked some up on the way over here," said the girl, and she bent to pick up the little red bottle. The party now was in hysterics over Fritzi's new rank, and it was some time before the room could be shouted into silence.

Then the contest could start. It was decided, of course, that the girl would go first. A man with a watch quickly emptied a chair of its occupant and she sat in it. A cherry was taken from the jar, the stem removed, and the self-proclaimed official held it up. "Where do you want it, sweetheart?" he asked. She held her hands behind her back and opened her mouth. The official slipped the stem between her teeth (which Fred noticed were slightly bucked), and she worked her lower jaw animatedly for a few moments. Then the stem, tied in a knot, re-emerged from her teeth. The official held it up to the light and said, "Well, I'll be goddamned." The pilots applauded mightily.

"How long did it take her?" asked Fred. He took a cherry from the jar and ate the fruit, leaving the stem.

"Minute, ten seconds," said the man with the watch.

Fred held the stem between his teeth like a toothpick, clasped his hands behind his back, and waited for the start signal. Money fell to the floor in little piles.

"Ready?" asked the timekeeper.

"Roger-doger," mumbled Fred.

"Go."

Fred sucked the stem into his mouth, biting it three times with his front teeth as he did so. Wedging one end of the stem between a molar and an incisor on the left side of his mouth, he bent it where he'd bitten it, looped it through with his tongue and pulled the knot as tight as he could. He turned to the timekeeper, opened his mouth, and said, "Ahh."

The official leaned close and reached carefully between Fred's teeth. He emerged with the cherry stem, tied in a disjointed granny knot. The crowd roared and the little stacks of money were split up.

"What was my time?" asked Fred.

"Forty-seven seconds. No contest." The timekeeper shouted for silence and took Fred by the hand. He pulled up the girl with his other hand and held her close to Fred. "This contest," he said loudly, "has proved beyond a doubt that a cherry doesn't stand a chance in this squadron." Laughter and applause. "Insofar as this beautiful lady has been paid for her services and has not as yet produced—" More applause. "—and insofar as these two cherry stem knot tiers were obviously made for each other, it is my official decision that she be assigned to him for payment in full of her contract." Wild applause and cheering.

Fred looked at the girl, wondering why he did dumb things like this.

The red-faced drunk, whom Fred now saw was a full lieutenant, fell on the two of them and nuzzled up close to Fred's ear. "I'm really proud of you, kid," he said. "Bang her a good one for the guys."

"Sure," said Fred, "you bet." He took the girl by the hand; they forced their way through the crowd to the door. On the way someone handed him a quarter-full bottle of bourbon. The noise receded as the door was abruptly closed behind them.

"Boy," said the girl, "am I glad to get out of there."

"Me, too," said Fred. He opened the door to his room, allowing her to pass through first. He turned on the light, though it wasn't really necessary.

"That's some trick. Where'd you pick it up?" She sat on the edge of Fred's bed and tested it with both hands.

"The Golden Serpent," said Fred. He closed the door and turned the lock.

"San Diego?"

"That's the one."

"Stanley, the bartender." She took off a shoe and placed it carefully under the edge of the bed.

"Yeah. Stanley." Fred sat down beside her.

"I mean, it's a small world, isn't it?" She laughed easily.

"Look," said Fred, "I didn't know they would do this—"

"Forget it," said the girl. "Unhook me?" She turned her back to Fred. He did so. She wriggled and the dress fell from her shoulders. "Thanks."

Fred stood, a little too quickly.

"The way I see it," she went on, "a deal's a deal."

Fred looked at her carefully now, a little surprised at how fast she had undressed.

"Besides, I think you're kind of cute." She smiled and lay back on the bed.

Seeing no way out now, Fred reached for the light switch.

"Who was that guy?" asked Rogers.

"Name's Trusteau," said Frank Hammerstein. "Came over from Fighting Eight at Kaneohe."

"What I want to know is how he tied that knot," said the timekeeper, a j.g. who, unlike the other j.g.'s, had never been in combat, having attended flight school after graduation from the academy and six months in the line navy.

"Beats the shit out of me," the red-faced, drunken lieutenant replied. He had been lucid enough to size up the newcomer as a talented trivia artist, and he had made twenty bucks by betting two-to-one on Fred. "I wonder what the hell else she can do with her tongue," he mused.

"Well, what the hell're we gonna do tonight?" asked Duggin, the stocky, hairy-necked man.

"I know what one of us is doing," said Frank. He had pressed his ear against the wall over the bed and was listening. He waved for silence and then they could all hear it: Thud; squeak. Thud; squeak. It was the bed in the next room, gyrating rhythmically against the wall.

"Hotdamn," said Brogan, "he's banging her." Two other pilots pushed their way to the wall and pressed their ears to it.

"He's sure got rhythm," said one.

"How long you think he'll last?" asked the timekeeper.

"Five minutes."

"Three at the most."

"Ten bucks says he lasts five minutes."

"You're on." The money began to pile up on the floor and more ears were pressed to the wall.

"Hold it," said the timekeeper, "he's speeding up." The noise was louder now. Thud; squeak. Thud; boom; squeak. It accelerated until the thuds and squeaks were almost continuous, then abruptly stopped.

"Hotdamn," said the drunken lieutenant. He reached for the money.

"Wait a second," said Hammerstein. "He's starting again." From the other side of the wall: Thud; squeak. Thud; squeak. Thud; squeak.

"Seven minutes," someone said. "He's really hanging in there." More bills fluttered to the floor. Bets were taken. Everyone waited.

A short eternity passed in near silence. The only sounds were the sloshing of booze in bottles and the steady thud-squeaking of sex in the next room. One more time the sounds sped up and stopped, only to be resumed a few seconds later. More bills hit the floor. Five minutes passed and the sounds became continuous—almost frenzied—lasted for another minute, then stopped altogether.

"Seventeen minutes," someone whispered, awe-struck. The money was split up swiftly, most getting none, a few getting most of it. They heard the door to the next room open and someone walk into the hall. The drunken lieutenant opened the door and poked his head out.

"Well?" he said.

"Well what?" said Fred. He was wearing only shorts.

"How the hell was it?"

"I don't know. All right, I guess." Fred wanted to say something sharp and witty but couldn't muster the strength.

"You're all right," said the lieutenant, and he went back to the party, leaving Fred alone in the hall. Outside it was getting dark. Fred walked down to the head, turned on the shower, and washed away the smell of sweat and sex.

The next day, Sunday, he made another friend when he introduced himself to Fitzsimmons and paid him back the ten bucks Fitzsimmons had been unable to collect for himself. Fred didn't mind that part because, as he told himself, it was well worth it.

5

"Tower Control, this is Dumpy One with flight of three SBDs. Request taxi clearance."

"Hold at flight line until ordered, Dumpy One. Unidentified Avenger on the flight line. Identify yourself."

"Alpha Tango Five Seven, Control, Alpha Tango Five Seven. Ready to roll."

"Wait one, Five Seven."

"Control, this is Banger Seven, flight of two F6Fs. Request taxi clearance."

"Dumpy One, you are cleared to roll with your three buzzards. Watch for cross traffic."

"Roger, Control."

"Banger Seven, get your clearance individually if you don't mind. You will be cleared for taxi after, repeat, after Avenger Five Seven."

"Roger, Control." Duane Higgins leaned far over in his cockpit and looked at the aircraft next to his. The young pilot there, Trusteau, made a circle with his thumb and forefinger and nodded broadly, then jutted his thumb toward the control tower.

The kid was on the ball, Duane thought; he had heard the entire exchange and knew now to request his own clearance. Butting in on the already crowded control frequency was not necessary. The controller continued directing the Monday

morning traffic jam on the concrete strip, and Higgins leaned
back into his seat to wait for their turn. All around them the
aircraft of Air Group Twenty taxied through the parking areas,
became airborne, and circled off to their rendezvous and
training areas. Among all these pilots, thought Duane, the one
who needed the flight time the most wasn't there, and he wished
he could do something about it.

Duane was a dedicated skipper watcher. He figured he felt as
deeply for Jack Hardigan as he did for any man or woman alive.
He never considered using the word "love" to describe the
emotion—love being what mothers felt for sons and vice versa,
what occasionally fathers felt for sons, and what infrequently
and with great caution one felt toward a younger member of the
opposite sex. The last thing he remembered loving was a dog,
when he was twelve or thirteen, and he had come to realize it
only after the animal was hit by a car and left to die in the street.

Ahead on the taxi strip the last of the three Dauntlesses
moved onto the airstrip and roared off. The plump Avenger (not
of our air group, Higgins thought, wondering why he was here)
rolled to the holding line and braked to a stop. Trusteau pulled
up close behind him. The controller was ordering the Avenger to
hold, and then Duane saw why: One of the Dauntlesses was
coming back down with a smoking, sputtering engine to the strip
it had just left. A goddamn deathtrap, Higgins thought. It was a
wonder there hadn't been more accidents. With a sort of
left-handed logic, Duane wished they were back at sea where
minor emergencies were a hundred times more deadly. At least
there he felt at home, regardless of the danger.

Duane Higgins and Jack Hardigan had been together since
the last part of 1941, when the younger man, then an ensign, was
first assigned to the *Hornet*'s air group and flew wing on division
leader Hardigan. Incredibly, during those first twelve months of
war, when the few available air groups were shifted around like
pawns, split up, reassigned, worked over by the enemy, and
fragmented all over the South Pacific, the two had managed to
hang together like husband and wife, or more accurately, like
twin brothers. When the *Hornet*, like twenty or so of her sister
ships and hundreds of aircraft and crews, was sacrificed for the
stinking little island of Guadalcanal, Jack and Duane had finally
been separated. Duane went to the *Enterprise* as a replacement
pilot. Jack went to the States, the lucky stiff, to help form a new
air group.

Despite the closeness between these two, they had not
corresponded while they were apart. Attachment for another

man is not something two grown men easily admit, so Duane was flabbergasted and secretly overjoyed when the orders came for his transfer to Jack's squadron. Though they had never talked about it, Duane was somehow sure Jack had arranged it. Regardless, he was now Executive Officer of Fighting Twenty, well qualified for the job, and having the time of his life.

"Avenger Five Seven, you are cleared for takeoff."

"Roger, Control. Five Seven out."

"Control, this is Banger One Three, F6 at the hold line. Request clearance for takeoff."

"Wait one, Banger One Three."

Ahead of the two Hellcats, the Avenger, obviously heavily loaded, roared down the runway and struggled into the air. Duane applied a little throttle, released his brakes, and pulled up behind Trusteau. He wished the skipper was in the other plane—they had had such good times together when they were wingmen. Everyone knew the skipper hadn't been in the air enough since the new aircraft arrived—everyone but CAG, who was a jerk anyway, who didn't know his ass from a hole in the ground, and who would one day depend on Jack Hardigan for his life and wish like hell he had let him spend more time in the air when it really mattered. . . .

"Banger One Three, you are cleared to roll. Banger Seven, move to the hold line."

"Roger, Control." Fred released his brakes and added a touch of throttle; then he pulled onto the end of the runway and turned left to make his run. Still moving, he scanned his instruments quickly and rolled his head once to check for low flyers. ("Never trust the control tower," his first instructor had said, "check for yourself.") Then he smoothly pushed the throttle all the way forward and the rubber-marked concrete runway slid under the nose of the Hellcat with increasing speed. Fred relaxed his body and let the acceleration press him into the seat. These first few moments before takeoff were the most thrilling. Being so close to the ground, moving so fast with so much power at your fingertips, with the danger of destruction so immediate—it never failed to take his breath away and fill him with exhilaration. With half the runway still before him, Fred drew back the stick and hopped the fighter into the air, easing back slightly on the throttle and pushing the landing gear lever into the "up" position. Gaining altitude quickly, he rubbernecked once more for encroaching aircraft and began the turn which would take him in five minutes to the rendezvous point over the beach.

*   *   *

Duane's first impressions of the new pilot were almost uniformly good. Having been around planes and pilots for a number of years, he could size up a flyer in a short time with a fair amount of accuracy. New pilots were generally unpredictable, though. A short period of time with combat-experienced pilots could turn an uncertain young kid into a topnotch pilot, or a promising flyer into a complete bust. Still, there were things about Fred Trusteau that he liked to see in the men who flew with him: nonheroic self-assurance, a calm attitude, the promise of being able to handle whatever came along without a lot of bullshit.

Higgins watched the leading Hellcat take to the air and begin its right turn, then he began his run. First impressions were one thing, actual ability something entirely different. He smiled as he pulled his Hellcat into the air, recalling the stories already circulating in the squadron regarding Trusteau's first Saturday night "strategy conference." Some of the guys were calling him "Trusty" now.

Duane started a right turn and headed for the rendezvous point. He hoped that Trusty Trusteau's flying abilities were as well developed as his screwing abilities.

Fred reached the rendezvous point over the beach and went into a gentle right-hand turn at ten thousand feet. The weather this morning was excellent: scattered cumulus below eight thousand feet, ceiling and visibility unlimited above. It was a common tropical condition which aviators lyrically referred to as "scat-cum-cavu." Below, the lush green jungle crowded a white beach that was brushed by long foaming combers. The deep blue Pacific stretched away into infinity. Fred switched to the operating frequency on the radio and waited, enjoying the view.

"Banger One Three, this is Banger Leader, radio check."

Fred touched his throat mike and replied, "Banger Leader, this is Banger One Three, loud and clear." It sounded like the Exec was just off his wing, but there was no sign of the other fighter. Fred circled once more, straining to see in the direction he had flown from, but still saw no other aircraft. Checking his clock, he determined that fifteen minutes had passed since he left the airfield and that the Exec was now five minutes or more overdue. Fred knew exactly what was going on. Lieutenant Commander Deal had tried the same thing barely four weeks ago. He wasn't about to get caught twice.

Fred pushed the throttle all the way forward and headed up, directly into the morning sun. He hoped he wasn't too late. When he reached fifteen thousand feet, he leveled off, throttled back, and began searching for Banger Leader's blue Hellcat.

"Banger One Three, this is Banger Leader. Sorry for the delay, got held up at the strip. Are you still at the rendezvous point?"

"That's affirmative. Estimate your time of arrival."

"Five minutes or so, One Three. Hold your horses."

"Roger, Banger Leader. Nice day for flying, wouldn't you say?"

"That's a firm worm, One Three. Just dandy." Fred knew he was in time but went up another thousand feet just in case. The rendezvous point was below him now, directly down sun, a mile closer to the earth. And now, Fred deduced, Banger Leader would say something like—

"One Three, I'll explain what we're going to do when I get there. I'm going to make a few runs on you, and you're going to try to get away and get on my tail. Got that, One Three?"

Fred smiled to himself. "Roger, Banger Leader. I'm ready when you are." And then Fred spotted the Exec's plane. It was circling in from the ocean side, at maybe twelve thousand feet. Gotcha, thought Fred.

"I don't see you yet, Banger Leader," lied Fred, and he pushed the stick over to begin his run. If he was lucky, he could make one pass and get away below into the clouds. He could no more outfight the Exec in a matched dogfight than he could run a four-minute mile, but he would at least have the satisfaction of knowing he had bounced the better pilot.

"Just stay where you are, One Three, I'll find you." The Exec was making a shallow dive through the rendezvous area; his speed was high, but he was still in a position to jump anything that appeared in front of him. Fred watched his altimeter unwind through thirteen thousand and checked his gun switches to make sure they were off. The square wingtips and round nose of Banger Leader's Hellcat grew in his gunsight, and Fred corrected a little to the right to keep him on target. He was suddenly aware of a pounding sensation; it was his heart. He wondered briefly what he would say as he passed. The target filled the gunsight ring. Fred squeezed the trigger on the cap of the stick and held the Exec's fighter in the gunsight for four more long seconds.

"Bang, you're dead," he said, and in the fraction of a second when the two aircraft passed, he saw the other plane flip into a violent right-hand wingover and head down.

Then he heard a startled voice say: "Shit!"

Duane had his first indication that something was wrong when he came up to the rendezvous point in a fast shallow dive and found nothing. Still, the new pilot could have wandered off, and Duane took his fighter into a gentle right-hand turn for a last look around before he headed up and away. He had just completed his turn and had his hand on the throat mike to call the errant wingman when that chilly little voice went "Bang, you're dead." Then he knew he'd been bounced like a goddamn trainee, and his flying and fighting instincts took over.

When the little black dots quit dancing before his eyes and he was back in the clear, with Trusteau somewhere below him, Higgins realized with a touch of grudging admiration that Fred had used the same tactic on him that he and Jack had used on the Zeros at Guadalcanal: It was a fast attack out of the sun from above that gave their slower fighters' weight a speed advantage, and a break away below before the more skillful Japanese pilots could force them into a dogfight.

"Good run, One Three," Higgins said, scanning the tops of the clouds for Trusteau's plane.

"Thank you, Banger Leader," came the reply.

"Let that be your first lesson, One Three. Never assume your enemy's going to be where you want him to be."

"Roger, Banger Leader." Higgins caught a fleeting glimpse of a dark form dodging through the clouds below and rolled into his first attack. Now he'd show the little bastard what real flying was.

Fred raised his goggles up over his eyes and wiped the sweat from his brow. His eyes burned from perspiration and the glare of the sun; his neck and shoulders ached from the constant rubbernecking and the strain of flying upside down and sideways most of the morning. It had been just as he had expected: Higgins had shot him down about a dozen times. After an hour, though, Fred had caught on to most of his moves and could escape for maybe two minutes before the Exec found his way on to his tail and clung there as though tied on. He had never seen anyone fly like that before, not even Deadly Deal.

"Banger Leader, estimate thirty-five minutes' fuel remaining."

"Very well, One Three. That was a good workout. Take us back to the strip."

"Roger." Fred caught a glimpse of a mountain peak in the distance, estimated their position, and headed inland.

"Negative, One Three. That isn't the established return route." The Exec's plane had glided in on his left wing and was waggling back and forth.

Fred looked across the space between the two aircraft and saw the Exec remove his oxygen mask. The older man made the sign for "follow me." Then he rolled off to the left. Fred sighed and followed him, wanting only to get back on the ground and stretch his legs. The two Hellcats cut through the scattered clouds and leveled off at three thousand feet.

"Tallyho. Targets at eleven o'clock low." Fred looked and saw a five- or six-story building in the jungle just off the beach. "It's the noon hour, One Three. We should catch a few bandits on the beach." The two aircraft slowed and dropped to a thousand feet, turned gently in to parallel the sand and breakers. Then Fred understood.

The building was probably a hospital; a dozen or so girls in bathing suits were lounging around on the beach or splashing at the water's edge. Several waved as the two fighters passed over.

"Wouldn't mind meeting a couple of those in close-in combat." The Exec banked to get a better look.

"Message understood, Banger Leader." Even up here, thought Fred. "Twenty-five minutes' fuel remaining."

"All right, One Three." Higgins sounded miffed. "Think you can find you way back?"

"Affirmative, Banger Leader," Fred said, already beginning his turn toward the heading of the airstrip. They made the flight in ten minutes, neither offering a single word of conversation. Fred landed with ten minutes' of fuel in his tanks; this was a totally unacceptable margin of safety for him. Duane landed with fifteen minutes' worth, which was twelve minutes more than he had had when he landed aboard the *Enterprise*, a hunted, damaged carrier in the middle of a hostile ocean, after the *Hornet* was hit. He could thus afford to be a little blasé about the whole thing, and even enjoy a bird's-eye view of a little nooky while the needles were hovering around "empty." Fred Trusteau wondered what it was that caused most men to do such ignorant things when it came to women.

6

"Pass."

An explosive thunderclap rattled the building. Torrents of tropical rain fell outside the windows, pounded on the wooden roof, seeped in under the outside door of the ready room. Fred looked at his cards briefly, then folded them into a neat little pack which he set down carefully in front of him.

"Pass."

Three soaking wet officers burst through the door and stood for a second, dripping, cursing at the fates that had caused them to step from the Navy bus moments before the downpour began. Fred looked at Hammerstein, his bridge partner, and watched him study his hand. He probably didn't have anything worth bidding. Fred hoped the hand would be passed out....

"Pass."

Higgins poked his head through the door at the other end of the room, surveyed the scene, and said, "That does it for flying today, fellas. Smith, get a haircut." Higgins disappeared, banging the door shut behind him.

One of the wet pilots wrung the water out of his garrison cap. "Goddamn rain," he said.

"One heart."

Damn, thought Fred, now Bagley will come in with a spade bid and Levi will go to two hearts and we'll play a nothing hand.

"Look, guys," said Fred, "Frank over there has at least ten

points and three or four of your hearts. You sure you want to play this one out?"

Hammerstein looked up in surprise. "How'd you know that?"

"Well?" Fred prodded.

Levi rolled his eyes and tossed his cards into the center of the table.

"You watch the way he sorts his cards," said Bagley, gathering the cards into a deck and starting to shuffle.

"Hey, listen to this," said a pilot who had his feet propped up on the chair in front of him. "Says here, 'On board an escort carrier en route to landings in North Africa, brave fighter pilots pass the time in their ready room by engaging in a songfest.'" The man was reading from a tattered copy of *National Geographic,* and he paused between some words and mispronounced others. Bagley dealt the cards. "'Later in the same day, these men flew off in their fast and sturdy aircraft to engage enemy forces around the port of Dakar, no doubt carrying in their hearts the ambition and desire to help make a world where they could sing their songs under peaceful skies, and not in the ready room of a ship bound for enemy waters and combat.'"

"Horseshit," said one of the wet pilots.

"Come on, guys," said the reader. "Let's have a songfest."

"Horseshit," said the wet pilot.

"You got something against peaceful sentiments?" asked the reader.

"Pass," said Bagley, folding his hand without enthusiasm. Fred finished arranging his cards and counted up his points. It came to twenty-three—the biggest hand he ever remembered having.

The door at the other end of the room opened now, and the Skipper came in, carrying a clipboard with a thick bundle of papers on it. Unlike the listless pilots in the room, he wore a tie and his black hair was neatly trimmed and combed, his trousers had a sharp crease, and his shoes gleamed. A chorus of voices produced a ragged "Afternoon, Skipper."

"Scuttlebutt has it that you're gonna learn to fly one of these days, Skipper," said Brogan, one of the old timers.

"Only if the sun comes out," said Jack Hardigan, stopping beside Hammerstein and patting him on the shoulder. "Your call just went through, Frank," he said pleasantly.

"Jesus Christ," said Frank. He slapped his cards down on the table and headed for the door. "Thanks, Skipper," he called, his voice echoing down the hall.

Fred closed his eyes and sighed. "I knew it was too good to be true," he said. "I get the first good hand of the game and now we can't play it."

Jack leaned down and picked up Hammerstein's cards. Fanning them with one large hand, he scanned them once, closed them up, and said, "Pass."

"Oh, boy," said Fred.

"Pass," said Levi.

"Four hearts," said Fred.

"Pass," said Bagley.

"Six hearts," said the skipper, still standing, and reading from a page somewhere near the middle of the stack on the clipboard.

"Pass," said Levi.

"Pass," said Fred.

"Pass," said Bagley, tossing out the first card.

Without a word Jack turned Hammerstein's cards over, spread them with a single movement of his left hand, and started back across the room. Halfway to the door, he stopped and turned. "You guys doing anything tonight?"

Levi and Bagley shrugged.

Fred said, "Not me, Skipper."

"Twenty hundred. My room at the BOQ. Bring your own booze." He reached the door and disappeared.

"I'll be damned," said Fred.

"He's a good bridge player," said Levi.

Tricks began falling and were raked into Fred's corner of the table.

"Bridge," snorted Lieutenant Brogan from across the room. "You ladies ought to play acey-deucy. Now there's a man's game."

"He wouldn't say that with the skipper in the room," said Bagley.

"Neither would I," said Fred. He busied himself with the play, winning all but the last trick. "Penny a point?" he asked.

Duane Higgins met Jack Hardigan in the hallway outside the ready room and followed him into the squadron office. He made himself comfortable in the padded armchair and lit a cigarette. Jack sat down and buzzed for the yeoman, who appeared moments later, looking as harried as ever.

"What's the good word?" Higgins asked the yeoman, a little man with glasses, named, predictably, Sweeney. Sweeney handed a stack of correspondence to the skipper.

"Nothing much happening these days, sir," he said to Duane.

"Typed error-free with two copies," said Jack, giving a hand-written letter to the yeoman. "Then knock off for the day."

"Yes, sir," said Sweeney, and he started for the door. Then he stopped and said: "Scuttlebutt has it the *Enterprise* is headed for a yard period in the States. Most likely Bremerton."

This was a good piece of information. Not overly dramatic (like the previous week's rumor that Nimitz was heading for Tokyo again with all his carriers) or improbable (like the more recent one that said the Army was testing a fighter that could hit four hundred miles per hour in straight and level). The thinking man would conclude that if the brass could release a heavy carrier for a yard period, then the next big push would not be for a while yet.

"No word on *Ironsides*?" asked Higgins. Jack appeared to be working diligently but was actually listening closely to what the yeoman had to say.

"They've got one of the main boilers torn all to pieces and the requisitions for fresh meat haven't even been begun yet. We couldn't sail in less than two weeks if we had to."

"Very interesting," said Higgins, looking absently into his own cloud of smoke. Sweeney left and closed the door behind him. "Jack," said Higgins.

"What's on your mind?" asked Jack, scratching away with a thick fountain pen.

"Oh, nothing much." A smoke ring slipped out of Duane's mouth and drifted through the air over Jack's head.

"There must be something."

"I was just wondering when the hell you're going to get in some serious flight time on the new birds."

"Duane." Jack stopped writing and looked at his Executive Officer, whom he never called by his first name in front of other people. "This entire air group has just been reorganized. We just got new fighters. New flight crews. New pilots. One is under arrest and three are missing. Fitness reports are due tomorrow. That's just the tip of the iceberg. Don't hound me about flying. When I get things squared away, I'll put some more time in. Until then, don't worry, okay?" Jack began writing again. Outside, the rain slackened and the lightning and thunder moved off over the mountains.

"Okay. I'm sorry I brought it up." Duane swung one leg over the arm of the chair and began tapping his foot maddeningly against the side of the desk.

"Duane," said Jack, "is there anything else you want to discuss? I'm kind of busy."

"I was just wondering if you might like to take an evening off, you know, maybe hit the beach, like we used to."

"As a matter of fact, I *was* planning on leaving a little earlier tonight."

Duane's face brightened and he swung forward in his seat. "I know this place downtown," he said, "and it's strictly off limits to the Army pukes. They got a floor show where this broad really peels it off."

"I was planning on a few games of bridge with three men in the BOQ. You're welcome to come along if you like."

Higgins dropped his foot to the floor and stood up heavily. "No thanks, Jack. I don't feel like cards."

"By the way."

"Yeah."

"How's Trusteau in the air?"

"Good. A little cautious maybe, but he's good. Maybe if he had a little instruction from the top dog in the group..."

"Mrs. Hawkins is throwing a party next Saturday evening. I want six couples besides myself to go along. Arrange that for me, will you?"

"Sure, Skipper," Duane reached the door.

"Duane?"

"Yeah, Skipper?"

"CAG's coming through in the morning. Update the training sked on the bulletin board and take down the acey-deucy skeds, okay?"

"Sure, Skipper. Anything else?"

"Not at the moment, Duane. See you in the morning."

The door opened suddenly, bumping Duane's foot, and Sweeney came through. Excusing himself to the lieutenant, the yeoman huddled over the skipper's desk, and the two men launched into an earnest discussion of the Squadron War Diary. Duane shook his head a little sadly and left.

7

Fred Trusteau had learned by the age of ten, and by necessity, that intelligence can compensate for a lack of brute strength and a bully mentality, both of which uncannily occurred in all those people who were bigger than he. His own unstated Law of the Jungle told him it was best to simply avoid these unpleasant people as much as possible, to become instead more intelligent, and if possible to reveal his superior mentality only when it wouldn't incite the bullies to retaliation. Usually, though, Fred would not reveal it in front of those to whom it mattered the most—his teachers.

He had had this problem quite recently. The teacher was an instructor in Primary Flight Training, in which Fred received eighty hours of flight time in that classic craft known lovingly as the Ryan Yellow Peril. He had wanted almost desperately to be closer to the man, but the teacher had other students as well and hardly noticed Fred. When he was off duty, he drove home to a wife and three kids, leaving Fred in a barracks full of noisy flight students, many of them bullies, who spent their spare time telling dirty, untrue stories and gaping at poorly composed pictures of girls with cleavage showing. Fred had survived that lonely period with flying colors by being smarter than almost all the other students. That, at least, was gratifying.

Fred had picked up on bridge in January of 1942, when most of the war news—after you scraped aside the stories about

37

all-American heroes fighting against overwhelming odds and taking half the enemy fleet down with them—was bad. He had just entered the world of flying at the level known as Flight Preparatory Training, a college-campus affair with classes in physics, aerodynamics, air navigation, and Naval Orientation at San Francisco State College. ("The aircraft carrier is a supporting vessel designed to provide assistance to the capital ships of the fleet in the areas of scouting and reconnaissance and possibly protection from enemy submarines," said the Naval Orientation instructor, a doddering, retired captain who would have failed Fred had Fred spoken what was on his mind. Always full of discretion, he put it instead into the required term paper on sea power: "The Japanese failed at Pearl Harbor because the planes which did the scouting were unable to force the American battleships into the`open sea, where the resulting engagement may have been disastrous to them.")

Bridge gave the intelligent player limitless opportunities to triumph over the big guys; only, alas, the big guys never played the game. The hottest thing for the other fliers in spare-time activities, aside from female conquest, was acey-deucy, a cup-pounding, dice-flying, pure-chance derivation of backgammon which Fred learned in ten minutes but never seemed to win. He searched around wherever he went for other bridge players. They were few and far between, so he was looking forward to the game with the skipper and Levi and Bagley with more than a little anticipation. He even showered and shaved before going.

Fred showed up early at the skipper's private room and tried to be at ease with his commanding officer while the older man put on his shirt and combed his hair. Fred glanced around at the slightly cluttered space, mildly embarrassed about catching the Skipper in what amounted to a condition of undress. Jack appeared not to notice.

"You finish up at Pensacola?" asked Jack from the door of the small bathroom, where he was combing his hair.

"No, sir, Corpus Christi." Fred was looking at a heavy volume on a small coffee table. The book was entitled "VF-20 War Diary." He wondered if it would be too nosy to open it and see what was inside.

"Texas?"

"Yes, sir, on the Gulf coast. I flew through Pensacola once, though, on my way to carquals in Lake Michigan."

"Lake Michigan?" Jack was half-amused that a revolution in flight-training procedures had taken place since he went through the program. This young man was a result of that upheaval.

"There was never anything to do there," said Fred, overcoming his hesitation and hefting the big volume into his lap. He opened the book.

"Where?" asked Jack, turning his back to Fred as he undid his trousers and tucked in his shirttails.

"Corpus Christi. The town's five miles from the air station and all it's got is a filling station and a hardware store."

Jack laughed. "Sounds like Pensacola in 1935." He came into the room looking his usual fresh and dapper self. "Find that interesting?" he asked, indicating the War Diary on Fred's lap. He reached behind the open bathroom door and pulled out a card table.

"Yes," said Fred, "yes, sir, I sure do."

The first entry read: "*2 March 1943*: This unit activated as part of Air Group Twenty this date during ceremonies at North Island Naval Air Station, NavBase, San Diego, California. Lieutenant Commander Arthur E. Blasshill commanding."

Meanwhile Jack had sprung the legs of the table open and set it upright in the middle of the room.

"This is a new squadron," said Fred.

"Almost new," said Jack. He slid the table over to the edge of the bed and reached for a chair from in front of a small desk. "But it's old enough to have its share of organizational problems." The skipper eased himself down into the chair.

"What kinds of problems?" asked Fred; then he was sorry he had. He was intruding on the skipper's private domain.

Jack laughed. "We don't have anybody to write the War Diary." He began snapping and ruffling a deck of cards. "Come on," he said, "let's get our signals down."

Fred put the War Diary on the coffee table and sat on the bed, swinging his legs around and under the card table. The table was low but not especially uncomfortable. And there was something exciting about sitting where the skipper slept.

Jack dealt out a sample hand, and they began practicing their bidding sequences.

Bagley and Levi arrived ten minutes late, each carrying a chair. Bagley brought a bottle of Scotch, and Levi had a radio crystal set in a wooden case. It reminded Fred of the one his adopted father would listen to, back when FDR first became president. Levi set it up on the dresser and tuned in a Hawaiian station. The lilting, dreamy music filled the room. They dealt the first hand.

"Well, Trusty," said Bagley, "what's it going to be this hand?"

"Trusty?" asked Jack.

"Ol' Seventeen-minute Trusteau," said Levi.

"Seventeen minute?" asked the skipper.

"Hey," said Fred, slightly embarrassed, "we came here to play cards, okay?"

"Skipper," said Bagley, "did you know Trusty here can tie a knot in a cherry stem without using his fingers?"

The skipper's eyes glanced once around the table, resting for a split second on Fred's face. In that brief moment Jack caught and understood hesitation, defensiveness. "No," he said, "I didn't, and I don't really care. At the moment I'm only interested in what he can do with a bridge hand." His eyes jumped back to Fred and he saw relief. Interesting, he thought.

Fred and Jack won the first rubber handily, but no one made mention of a change in partners. The second rubber was started with the same teams, but not before the skipper left the table and went into the bathroom, closing the door behind him. The three pilots began sorting their hands.

"He was at Midway, you know," said Levi, a little smugly.

"The skipper?" asked Fred.

"And the 'Canal. They say he's got three or four Jap planes to his credit."

"I never knew that," said Fred.

"The skipper doesn't talk about his victories much," said Bagley.

The bathroom door opened and Jack returned, carrying two small shot glasses and a pair of water glasses, which he distributed around the table. Bagley poured from the bottle of Scotch, and they began the second rubber. It proceeded like the first, while the radio quietly gave out soothing music, and the coolness of the night came in through the open window. But Fred was playing with a new partner: The Skipper seemed a different person now, a man with a history of dangerous and laudatory acts to his credit. Fred felt himself privileged to be playing cards with a man who had been at Midway, a man who was obviously better than he.

At 11:30, still in the same teams, they finished the third rubber and decided to call it quits for the evening. Fred glowed from the Skipper's company as much as from the Scotch. Bagley and Levi took their chairs and the radio and departed, but Fred hung back for a moment. When they were alone, Fred asked again about the War Diary. He wasn't that great a writer; he felt like a school kid trying to impress a glamorous teacher.

"What about the War Diary?" asked Jack.

"You said you didn't have anyone to write it."

"The guy under house arrest was handling it before now."

"I wouldn't mind doing it. I mean if you don't have someone else picked..."

Jack walked over to the coffee table and came back with the Diary. He handed it to Fred and said, "Here. Look it over tonight and see me in the morning when you get a chance."

"Sure," said Fred. "Well, sir, see you in the morning." He didn't really want to leave. He enjoyed being in the Skipper's company.

"That's classified material. Don't let just anyone see it."

"Yes, sir," said Fred. He stepped through the open door.

"Night, Trusty," said the skipper, and he started to close the door.

"Please," said Fred, "I prefer Fred."

"Seventeen-minute Fred," said the skipper, and he laughed and closed the door. Fred sighed with pleasure, feeling the bulk of the War Diary in his arms. But there was a confused sort of sadness, too. He headed for his room.

When he was alone, Jack carried the empty glasses into the bathroom and left them on the sink. He went back into the room and collapsed the card table. Then he realized that he'd really had a very nice time this evening. He was a much too private person, he decided. He didn't open up to people and enjoy life often enough. But still, there was something different about tonight.

Stowing the card table behind the door, Jack went over and turned down the bed. He began to undress.

It was the new kid. Only he couldn't call him a kid. Trusteau had an awareness, a maturity that belied his twenty-one years. He carried a surface polish that had already earned him nicknames and complete acceptance in the squadron—an accomplishment few could claim. But underneath, he was more complex, Jack decided, and he didn't reveal that complexity to everybody.

Jack folded his trousers and hung them on a hanger in the small closet. He draped his shirt over the back of a chair and smoothed a rag over the shine on his shoes; they looked good enough for another day's wear without repolishing.

At one time or another, Jack had, of course, passed judgment on every pilot in his squadron. Many of his decisions had been merely to wait and see until combat could prove the worth and abilities of each. It was something he had to do regardless of his personal feelings toward any of the men. Now, brushing his teeth, Jack decided that he was comfortable with Fred Trusteau, and that the squadron would benefit from having him as a member. That was as far as it would go. All his instincts told him that he couldn't come to form anything more than a professional attachment for any of his pilots.

Turning the light off in the bathroom, Jack pulled a briefcase from under the bed and removed a clothbound training manual entitled, "Flight Manual: Flying the Chance Vought Corsair." He propped himself up in bed to read about a new carrier-borne fighter that supposedly outfought anything in the air but landed like a pogo stick. It was after one o'clock when he turned out the lights and went quickly to sleep.

Fred Trusteau stayed up later than usual that night. He was reading the War Diary.

"*19 March 1943*: Edward R. Castel, Lt., USN, DFC, DSM, failed to return from routine training flight near San Clemente Island this A.M. Aircraft involved in search operation included Divisions One, Five, and Six from this squadron and patrol craft of PatRon 34 based North Island NAS. Search continued until approximately 1800 hours local time and broken off due to darkness. Officially listed as missing and presumed dead."

After reading through the twenty or so pages of the Diary, Fred decided that writing it would be a snap and give him good reasons for seeing the skipper often. He finished reading around midnight and slid it quietly under the bed. His sleeping roommate snored soundly away, but Fred didn't feel tired. He turned off the desk lamp and went outside. A huge summer moon had risen while he was reading the Diary.

Finding a small bench near the street, Fred sat down and leaned back, drinking in the fresh tropical air. He was thinking for some reason that it would really be great if the skipper came out and sat down beside him. They could light cigarettes and talk for a while, kept company by the moon and the blazing stars.

After ten minutes of solitude, with the moon providing enough light to see by, a figure lurched up the street and spied Fred sitting on the bench. When the figure came closer, Fred saw that it was Lieutenant Brogan. Without invitation, the lieutenant fell down on the bench, fumbled for a cigarette, and accepted a light from Fred.

"You know, Trusty, you're all right," Brogan said. Booze and sweat wafted through the air to Fred's nose, but he didn't find it an especially unpleasant odor.

"Thanks," said Fred. He had never learned the lieutenant's first name and wasn't about to call him "Lieutenant" under these conditions.

"You know?" said Brogan, "I had *friends* once." He slurred his words just like a movie-comedy drunk.

"Yeah?"

"Let me tell ya, Trusty. They were the best. Yeah," said Brogan, his unseeing eyes fastened on a spot on the ground in front of Fred's shoes. "One of 'em, his name was Billy." Brogan struggled to get the words out. "He got shot down."

"I'm sorry," said Fred. "Where?"

Brogan thought for a moment. "I forget," he said. "There's this other guy, I forget his name. We used to be the acey-deucy champs of the whole fuckin' air group." The drunk smiled and laughed a little, perhaps remembering some good times. "He came back one day, you know? And landed all right, but then he wouldn't get out of his plane, and then they went to see what was wrong, and you know what?"

"What?"

"He was shot all to pieces, this great big hole right in his guts, the goddamn cockpit—this full of blood." He indicated the depth of the blood with his hands. "And goddamn it if they didn't assign that plane to me the next day—and it always stunk like hell, all that blood and all. They just couldn't get the stink out, not that they tried that hard and all. That old crate is still flying around out there somewhere." Brogan waved an arm through the air, trying to indicate "out there" for Fred.

"Where did that happen?" asked Fred.

"Beats the shit," said Brogan. He belched quietly. "Out of me." He clutched at his crotch and struggled to his feet. "Gotta take a leak," he said, but before he left he tousled Fred's hair and said, "You're all right, Trusty, but I gotta tell you." He shook a finger in the air. "Don't get too friendly." He turned away from Fred as though he'd already forgotten him and disappeared up the short walk and the small flight of stairs leading into the dark BOQ.

"You bet," said Fred.

He sat on the bench in the dark for another fifteen minutes, half expecting Brogan to come back out and tell him about his friends. But no one came to join him. Finally he gave up and went to bed.

8

FROM: Commander Air Group Twenty
TO: Mister Hardigan
SUBJ: Attached Officer Fitness Reports

1. These fitness reports are unsat and therefore not acceptable.

2. Do over.

Buster Jennings, Commander, USN

It was typical of CAG, thought Jack Hardigan, the way he worked subtle insults into otherwise harmless memos like this one. Officially, it is quite proper to address a lieutenant commander as "Mister," but it is avoided so as not to imply junior officer status. CAG always called Jack "Mister," even in written memos when it was almost as easy to write "Lt. Comdr." And the closing. Even casual correspondence requires an "R"—short for "Respectfully"—when it is addressed to an officer of lesser rank. Jack pulled up a plain white note pad and uncapped his fat red fountain pen.

FROM: Lieutenant Commander Jack Hardigan, Commanding Officer VF-20
TO: CAG-20

SUBJ: Attached CAG memo

1. The attached reworked fitness reports are resubmitted as per prior instructions.

Respectfully,

Jack Hardigan, VF-20

Jack attached the new note to the stack of fitness reports and slid the packet into his "Hold" tray. In a couple of days, just before the weekend, when CAG would be gone until Monday morning, Jack would forward them into his "Out" tray. They would arrive at CAG's desk and sit there for a few days until he found them. It would then be too late to send them back again and the entire matter would be forgotten.

FROM: Commander Air Group Twenty
TO: Mister Hardigan
SUBJ: Attached Memo regarding nonarrival of three (3) new pilots assigned to VF-20

1. Why the hell wasn't I kept informed of this condition earlier?

2. What are you doing to rectify the situation?

3. This matter is IMPORTANT. Reply ASAP.

Buster Jennings, Commander, USN

FROM: Lieutenant Commander Jack Hardigan, Commanding Officer VF-20
TO: CAG-20
SUBJ: Attached CAG Memo

1. Original memo regarding this condition was forwarded to CAG two (2) weeks prior to attached memo.

2. Personnel Officer, NavSta Pearl Harbor and Personnel Office, NAS Ford Island have been informed and are currently working on the problem. Their estimation of situation concludes that all three were diverted to another command possibly in the States without proper procedures being followed. They have prom-

ised an answer and replacements as they become
available.

3. It should be noted that replacement of one (1) pilot was
provided for Ens. Carruthers who was recently
detached pending outcome of court-martial investigation of rape charges.

Respectfully,

Jack Hardigan, VF-20

Correspondence from CAG invariably came in spurts,
usually on Friday morning, which probably meant that the son
of a bitch worked late on Thursday clearing his desk so he could
leave early on Friday. Rumor had it that he was screwing a local
product named Suzy, who had been a dancer at one of those
fancy luaus thrown for the brass at the Moana, and that he was
brown-nosing his way into the circles of higher-ups on Admiral
Nimitz's operations staff. The man was insufferable. Even his
golf game was bad.

FROM: Commander Air Group Twenty
TO: All Squadron Commanders
SUBJ: Officer Personnel Jackets, Photographs of Offi-
       cers

1. All squadron commanders are reminded that regulations require the inclusion in every officer's personnel
jacket of a three (3)-by-five (5) photograph of that
officer in a dress uniform.

2. Squadron commanders are requested to comply with
this regulation ASAP.

Respectfully,

Buster Jennings, Commander, USN

Jack Hardigan read through the memo once, then wadded it
up, and threw it away. His first inclination was to ignore it
completely. Then he decided that it would be best not to give the
bastard free ammunition; it really wouldn't be all that difficult to
take care of. He drafted a note to Duane Higgins saying that the
pilots were, without exception, to bring with them on the

following morning a white cover and their dress white blouse with awards. The purpose of this, he said, would be head and shoulders pictures for personnel jackets. Also, Schaeffer was to bring his camera and two rolls of film.

Jack was beginning to feel more comfortable with his job. He was catching up on the paperwork, the new pilots were working their way into the fabric of the squadron, major problems with the new aircraft had been few. He had a gut instinct that the squadron was shaping up the way it should. He made a note to develop a briefing or two on shipboard organization and procedures, but decided to wait until he had met with CAG and the *Constitution*'s executive officer so that he could obtain a copy of the ship's operational manual. Scanning his desk, Jack decided everything could wait for a few hours. He wanted to get in a little flight time, so he gathered up several more CAG memos and shoved them into the "In" box, tidied up the pencils and paper clips, and carefully pushed his chair up to the desk.

Jack was in the ready room, picking up his flight gear, when Fred Trusteau found him.

"There you are, sir," said Fred, coming through the door. He was carrying the War Diary under one arm.

"Yes," said Jack, "here I am." He pulled on a yellow Mae West.

"I read the War Diary last night. You said to see you this morning sometime."

"You think you can handle it? When we get into combat—" He realized suddenly that yes, all this would end one day soon, and they would go back to the war, with himself responsible for their lives. "When we get back into action, it might take up a bit of your spare time." He buckled the throat mike and left the loose end dangling.

"Yes, sir, I understand. I still want to do it."

He was so sincere, so polite, thought Jack. "Spell 'receive.' "

"*I* before *e* except after *c*."

"The job is yours."

"Thank you, sir."

"Check with Yeoman Sweeney for old training schedules and bring it all up to date. I want an entry for every day. And don't thank me for extra work."

"Yes, sir. Was there anything else you wanted?"

Jack picked up an inflatable seat raft and headed for the door. "You flying today?"

"This afternoon. Some gunnery with a target sleeve."

"Good. Until then, get busy with the Diary."

"Yes, sir." Jack left him, still standing with the War Diary under his arm, and walked through the aircraft maintenance area, past his squadron's Hellcats getting gassed and oiled, torn down and put back together, loaded and armed. He climbed into the plane with the number two painted on the fuselage aft of the cockpit and on the forward panels of the landing gear doors, and allowed an affable chief to help strap him in. Fifteen minutes later he was back in his own element: the sky.

Jack knew the waters and skies around Oahu as well as he had known the back yard of his boyhood home in Portland, Maine. He had flown into and out of Ford Island in Pearl Harbor more times than he could count, both during wartime and before it. At that time the Navy had kept half of its carrier strength, meager though it was, in the Atlantic Ocean. He had been there, in the Atlantic, when *Hornet* was first commissioned in October, 1941, two months before the war began, and he had seen the awful destruction wrought in the Navy's greatest anchorage a month after it had occurred. Since that time, during the desperate months immediately following Pearl Harbor, when the *Hornet*'s sister carriers succumbed one by one to brutal attacks by the Japanese, Jack had watched Pearl Harbor clean itself up, raise its sunken battlewagons, and go right on fighting.

The second from the last battleship to be raised from the mud was the *Oklahoma*. It was below him, up the channel that leads from the harbor mouth. He circled in from the seaward side, fascinated as always by the Lilliputian-like workings around and on the capsized ship. First, giant wooden frames (they reminded him of the Tinker Toy he had played with as a child) had grown up around the red keel that had faced up toward the sky. Then, cables had been stretched from the shore at Ford Island—one hundred yards distant—to the landward edge of the ship's main deck, over the top of the frames. Then, in a logical though gargantuan effort, they had simply pulled the huge hulk into an upright position. During the weeks that VF-20 had been on Oahu, the main deck and mangled upper works, with the big guns the only recognizable portion, had risen from the murky waters. Now the ship was upright, though resting on its bottom. From a great height, the blackened ruins of her superstructure were invisible, and she looked like any other ship at anchor, waiting for the tide of war to carry her back to dangerous waters.

Jack circled the harbor once, noting the ships gathered there.

He found the new *Constitution* berthed on the opposite side of
Ford Island. Clusters of destroyers dotted the western
anchorage. Cruisers and deadly-looking new battleships were
everywhere. Two carriers he had never seen before were
anchored near the *Constitution*. It was a marked contrast to the
days of 1942, when the *Hornet* went into battle accompanied by
two old, heavy cruisers and a small group of destroyers.

Below him, a small, bi-winged seaplane buzzed in and landed
on the Ford Island airstrip, its shadow racing with it across the
ground, catching up the instant the craft touched down. Far to
his right the black specks of fighter planes (probably Army, he
thought, from Bellows) tangled in slow-motion aerobatics; a
single slow-flying SBD approached from his left at the same
approximate altitude. The skies these days were as crowded as
the harbor below. Jack pushed the throttle forward and headed
up, turning to the left to cross the SBD and head out to sea.

When he was alone like this, Jack rarely thought about his
job. To him, flying was the best way to escape the harassments of
being commanding officer. Up here, they couldn't touch him.
He thought about the coming weekend party at Mrs. Hawkins's
place and decided he didn't really want to go but that it would be
a ghastly social insult to refuse. Mrs. Hawkins was the widow of
a former shipmate killed at Guadalcanal. He had been a search
pilot on the cruiser *Vincennes*, the loss of which had gone
unmentioned in the newspapers and radio programs. He
wondered if Mrs. Hawkins was fully aware of the circumstances
of her husband's death. She certainly never mentioned him
anymore.

Jack turned right, paralleling the coast, which brought him
to the vicinity of a training area his squadron often used. There
were no other aircraft visible, no chatter from the radio. He felt
completely alone—a good and rare feeling. He began to think
about the Japanese, the war, himself. They were all tied together
somehow, and that was important, if only for the reason that he
had never thought about himself before the war came along.

He knew, almost from instinct, that he didn't personally hate
the Japanese. A sort of professional hatred was a part of the job
of fighting, but that didn't mitigate the respect he felt for their
pilots. Without exception, they were professional and devoted
and fought with a tenacity of purpose that he hoped his own
pilots would display. He remembered the two Vals he had killed
at Santa Cruz. One had flamed immediately, but the pilot had
held his course toward the *Hornet* and the rear seat gunner had

made no move to parachute. The other Val, on the wing of the first, flew on as though nothing had happened, holding its place in the formation despite the other plane's being slashed from the sky. That one had finally exploded into small pieces after a short burst. As Jack and Duane Higgins had circled outside the range of the flak while the Vals attacked *Hornet*, a damaged, smoking Zero had tried an attack from above and had been destroyed by Higgins. Jack would never forget those hours of combat.

He reached the limit of the practice area and turned inland. To the north the afternoon thunderstorms were gathering; it was time to head back. He checked his fuel and instruments and found nothing amiss.

His thoughts on the Japanese pilots forced him to think about his own pilots. Somehow he always felt lonely when he was among them. They were thin-skinned, loud-mouthed, shallow individuals. More and more he felt out of place in their company. He wondered if the training program as it existed picked individuals who were thin-skinned, loud-mouthed, and shallow, or if they became that way after they became Naval Aviators. The question was moot. They were all he had to work with and there was little chance to change them.

When he reached the airfield, Jack requested permission to land and was told to wait for a flight of Hellcats to take off. He circled to the north and watched four of his fighters take to the air; when they switched to their operating frequencies he recognized the voices of Duane Higgins and Ensign Hodges, Lt. (j.g.) Fitzsimmons and Ensign Trusteau. Higgins was calling himself "Banger Leader."

"Banger Leader," said Jack, "this is Banger Leader Leader."

"Skipper," said Higgins, "that you?"

"Roger, Banger Leader."

"Didn't know you were up here, Skipper."

"Take care of my boys, now, you hear?"

"Sure thing, Banger Leader Leader. See you on the ground."

Jack turned into his final approach and lowered his landing gear. The four Hellcats joined into a finger-four formation and disappeared into the clouds. Why did I say that? he thought. Did I really mean it? He brought his Hellcat down to the ground—now it was back to fitness reports, missing pilots, rape cases, and CAG.

Fred heard the skipper's voice talking with the Exec and a strange, wonderful, surging feeling washed over him. He wished the skipper would stay up there with them and maybe come out with them to the firing range. Fred could show him how well he flew, what a good shot he was. He felt that if the skipper asked him to take on the whole Japanese air fleet, he would do it single-handedly and without hesitation. He would do anything for Jack Hardigan. But before he forced his mind back to the serious business at hand, Fred wondered if the skipper felt anything at all for him. He couldn't answer the question, and a sad, lonely feeling clung to him all afternoon.

9

"I'm glad you could make it this time," Jack Hardigan said. He poured Scotch into two old-fashioned glasses, added soda and ice, and handed one to Duane Higgins.

"Thought it might be a nice change of pace," Duane said and accepted the drink. He looked across the room at his date, a bosomy, bleached blonde, about thirty years old, who was inching her way closer and closer to the man next to her on the couch. She was the relatively well-off, widowed owner of a sugar cane farm, and Duane had asked her because he thought she would display some degree of class. Now it appeared she couldn't keep her hands off the other pilots. What was especially galling, though, was that she was getting very friendly with Lieutenant Brogan.

Jack turned around and leaned back on the padded bar. The two men surveyed the room. It was abnormally large, with a giant living-rock wall down the long side. A cluster of plush sofas and chairs, accented with potted trees and floor lamps, stood near glass doors leading to a veranda with a magnificent view of a tropical valley. Opposite the bar, near the rock wall, was a dark, polished grand piano with a golden candelabra above the keyboard. One of the guests, a bomber pilot from the same air group, sat at the piano with his date, tinkling out nice melodies.

"Nice bunch of people you picked," said Jack.

"I tried to be selective," Duane said. "I knew you figured on a high-class affair."

"Mrs. Hawkins likes pilots. She doesn't really care how classy they are." Jack was a little irritated at Duane for choosing three of the other six couples from outside the squadron; he liked to meet his pilots on a social basis occasionally, and this was a perfect chance for some intermingling. But Duane had picked his own friends, including the commanding officer of a bombing squadron who had flown fighters first but had transferred because he thought he could do a better job than the current crop of dive bomber pilots. Jack thought him an annoying blowhard.

"Excuse me, Skipper," said Higgins, and he headed for the sofa where his date was linking arms with Lieutenant Brogan. Jack thought it humorous that Duane could trust neither of them. He watched the Exec flop into the couch beside the girl, pull her head over to him, and plant a kiss on her lips. Brogan lost interest at once and began fondling the knee of another woman in the chair next to the couch.

"You find them amusing, too." Eleanor Hawkins glided up from behind Jack and slipped her arm around his waist. She was an attractive woman of about thirty-five, wearing a frilly, pale yellow dress with transparent sleeves and knee-length skirt. Jack put down his drink and placed his arm around her shoulders.

"They're like little kids sometimes," he said, "fighting over the toys."

"And you're the responsible father trying to keep peace in the family."

"They don't call me the old man for nothing." Jack took his arm away and looked at the wall above the bar. A look of concern came over Eleanor's face and she leaned on the bar, close to him.

"What's the matter, Jack? Aren't you having a good time?"

"Sure," he said automatically, but his voice showed a decided lack of enthusiasm.

"Come on," she said, "I've seen happier faces at a funeral."
Jack thought for a moment. "I was thinking about the war."

"The war touches everybody at one time or another."

"I was thinking that we've been going at them for a year and a half and there's no end in sight. I have the funny feeling things are just starting to get interesting."

"That's a strange way of putting it."

"I guess I'm a strange man."

"I'll say. I put on the sexiest dress I could find and you haven't made a pass all evening."

Jack looked at Eleanor closely, a little surprised. He had had no idea she expected him to make a pass. "I didn't know we were playing football," he said.

She smiled. "I love all kinds of sports," she said. She stirred her drink with a swizzle stick, then suddenly dropped the little glass rod on the bar. "Come on," she said. "We're ignoring our guests." She tugged at his arm and he followed, vaguely aware of her using the word "our." They crossed the room and sank into a love seat. The skipper of the bombing squadron was relating his story of how he had decided to become a dive bomber pilot.

"I'm telling you I was there," he was saying. "They couldn't find anything else to go after so they went down on this Jap can. Fourteen flying jarheads. I had a division, and we were flying cover at twenty thousand. They had fourteen shots at that can, and then we went down to strafe and she wasn't even scratched. Fourteen misses. Just like that. Then we get back to Henderson and these clowns were claiming four hits and a bunch of near-misses and saying they had sunk a light cruiser. Made me sick. I said to myself, I can do a damn sight better than that, and the next day I took one of those orange crates up the Slot, and I swear to God I got one of those transports on my first run. That was last November. Jack was there."

Everyone turned to look at Jack for confirmation. Jack shrugged. He had been in Norfolk, Virginia at the time, but felt no need to refute the man's story.

"Anyway, I been teaching these buzzards how to fly ever since." The man leaned forward and lowered his voice conspiratorially. "And I'll tell you something else. When I get through with them, they're going to do as well as the Japs did at Santa Cruz. Four of the bastards," he held up four fingers, "four of them Val babies got through and two made hits. And those Kates. Three of them got through and two made hits. I tell you, if we could guarantee that kind of hit percentage, this war would be over in six months."

"If the Japanese are that good," said one of the women, "why didn't they win the war in six months?"

"Is it true," asked another, "that they lock their pilots in their airplanes so they can't get out when they're sent on a mission?"

"I heard that if they miss when they try to drop bombs on one of our ships, they're supposed to crash into it and sink it."

"What was that Marine's name who crashed that Jap battleship at Midway?"

"Henderson?"

"Fleming, and it was only a cruiser."

"Whatever it was, you sure wouldn't catch me pulling a Jap stunt like that."

Jack smoked and listened to the pilots and their dates discuss the war and the enemy and the Navy. Frequently, he disagreed but he never pressed the point. Shallow, pushy individuals, he thought, saying things just to hear themselves talk. And these are the men burdened with the weightiest responsibilities. Eleanor Hawkins, holding his hand, closed her eyes and let her the head rest on his shoulder. The evening drifted to an uncertain close.

"Well," said Duane, stretching expansively and looking at his watch, "I guess I should be getting you back." He stood and pulled his date up from the sofa.

"Guess that means us, too." Lieutenant Schuster gently dislodged head of the woman dozing on his shoulder and they stood to go. Eleanor sat up and let loose of Jack's hand.

"Brogan?" asked Duane. "You coming?"

"Sure," said Brogan. "Everybody got a ride?" All the couples were standing, trying to work out without words who was to drive back with whom; one of the two cars they had used to get out here could not be left behind for the skipper to drive back later.

"That's all right," said Eleanor. "I'll drive Jack to the base a little later." She smiled up at him.

"That settles it." Higgins looked at Jack with a knowing smile and winked. "We had a nice time, Eleanor."

"We enjoyed having you."

There's that "we" again, thought Jack. Eleanor walked the guests to the front door and Jack lowered himself back into the love seat, not knowing whether he wanted to stay there with Eleanor or head back to the BOQ and his bothersome pilots. But the matter had evidently been decided without his consultation, for better or for worse. He lit a cigarette and tried to get comfortable. He felt sleepy.

Car engines started outside the house. The front door closed and they were alone. Jack closed his eyes. When he opened them again, Eleanor was back, kicking off her shoes, sitting on the rug at his feet and resting an arm across his knees.

"Jack, is something wrong?"

Jack looked up at the wall of living stone. "I know what that wall needs," he said. "A fireplace."

"In Hawaii? Come on." Jack said nothing and presently

Eleanor spoke again. "Jack. I'm wealthy, attractive, and single."

"Widowed."

"It's still a winning combination."

Jack thought for a moment and said, "I considered you and Stan to be two of my closest friends."

"Stan is gone. Now we can be more than just friends. Stan would understand."

"I'm not worried about that."

"Are you worried about making me a widow twice?"

Jack's eyebrows arched in surprise at her offhand reference to marriage. "You never talk about Stan any more," he said.

"He's been gone for over a year. What's there to say?"

"A year ago next August."

"But he shipped out several months before that." Eleanor took her arm off his knees and massaged the back of his calf with her hands. "Where did you first meet Stan?"

"On the *Lexington* in '36. We were both boot ensigns." Jack smiled. "The *Lex* is gone now, too."

"Jack, how was Stan's ship lost?"

She was certainly direct tonight, Jack thought to himself. Yet something in Eleanor's tone told him she was more interested in listening to him talk than in hearing how her husband died.

"I see intelligence reports. Talk to people who were there. A lot of what happened was never released to the papers."

"Tell me," she said.

"It was a surface engagement. Not a very long one, but in half an hour we lost four heavy cruisers and they didn't lose a ship. Savo Island they call it now." Jack's cigarette had burned out, and he dropped it into an ashtray on the carpet near the end of the love seat.

"I'm sure they had their reasons for not telling the papers. There's such a thing as public morale."

"We're going to win this war. I've never doubted that. But how long will it take? How much will it cost?"

"You worry about things you can't do anything about." Eleanor stood up. She sat down next to Jack and placed a hand on his thigh. She waited.

Jack kissed her then, but only because he knew she wanted him to. His hand caressed her ribs. His thumb touched her breast. He ran his hand down her leg, along the outside of her thigh. This is for you, not for me, he was saying to himself. It does nothing for me. Suddenly he stopped, pulled away. He knew she had felt his reluctance.

"The war touches everybody," she said.

He searched her face, then looked away. "And it affects everyone differently," he said.

"I may have to look for someone else, Jack," she said seriously.

"That's your decision, Eleanor." Jack pulled her two hands into his lap and covered them with one of his. He glanced at his watch.

"I guess it's time you got back to the squadron," she said.

Fred Trusteau was sitting on the little concrete bench outside the door of the BOQ when a car carrying two people stopped at the curb opposite him. The engine was left running, but the couple (the woman was driving) sat inside talking quietly for several moments. The two kissed lightly, suddenly, and the man left the car on the far side and waited while it pulled away. Fred realized in a second that it was the skipper walking toward him. A twinge of emotion he couldn't identify cut through him. But he didn't have time to think about it.

"Mind if I join you?" asked the skipper.

"Not at all, sir," said Fred, moving down to give him room.

"How come you're sitting out here all by yourself?" Jack fished in his pocket for a cigarette, then accepted one from the pack Fred offered him.

"Just enjoying the fresh air." Fred offered Jack a light and was pleased when the skipper cupped his hands around his own to shield the flame. The brief contact sent shivers up and down his spine.

"How's the Diary coming?"

"Just fine, sir. No problems there at all."

"Good." Jack collected his thoughts, trying to think of something to talk about that wasn't connected to flying or the management of men. "I guess I didn't tell you, but I sure enjoyed the bridge game we had last week."

Fred laughed. "We won. It was a new experience for me. We'll have to do it again sometime."

"You can count on it."

They stopped talking. Jack drew deeply on his cigarette and expelled the smoke. The night air was deliciously cool after the stifling humidity of the day.

"Fred," said Jack suddenly, leaning closer and putting his arm behind Fred on the back of the bench, "do you mind if I ask you a personal question?"

"Not at all. Fire away." It felt good to be called by his name.

"It may not seem important, but when you're—" Jack

wanted to say "commanding officer" but changed it at the last moment—"in my position, you don't always hear what's going on, what's really happening with the men in the squadron. I was just wondering why they call you what they do."

"Trusty?" Fred laughed a little. "I don't care for it."

"And the Seventeen-minute thing. What do they mean by that?"

Fred scuffed at the ground, looked away, leaned over, ground out his cigarette on the sidewalk, and dropped the butt into his shirt pocket.

He's embarrassed, thought Jack, watching closely.

"You know, sir, when you're with these guys you get trapped into doing things that you don't really feel like doing. Sometimes I get the feeling only a few of the guys here are really acting the way they would normally, and the rest are just along for the ride. Do you know what I mean?"

"You don't want to tell me, do you?"

Fred sighed. "They call me Trusty because I can tie a knot in a cherry stem without using my hands."

"You can?"

"It's just a bar trick I picked up somewhere on the way to becoming an aviator. I'll show you sometime."

"What about the seventeen minutes?"

"I'm not completely sure, but if it's what I think it is, it's pretty personal and no one's business but my own."

Jack shrugged and flicked his smoldering butt in a long arc through the air and into the street. The little shower of sparks at the end of its flight reminded him of the bounding tracers of a predawn attack on the Japanese airstrip at Buka. He had lost a wingman there and burned two planes on the ground.

"You know, Fred," he said, after a moment, "we all wear the same uniform and do the same things most of the time. If you were an enlisted man, you'd go to bed at night at the same time and get up in the morning at the same time as everyone else. In the military, especially during wartime, it's tough to be a good navy man and still retain some portion of your real self." How had Eleanor Hawkins phrased it? "The war changes everyone it touches, but if you're able to make that change a good one, then..." Then what? "I guess you're a better man for it." It felt strangely good to say something like that, even to an ensign. He felt that out of all the pilots of VF-20, Fred would probably understand it and keep it to himself.

"You know, Skipper," said Fred, "I'm glad as hell they transferred me to this group."

Jack laughed and clapped Fred on the knee. He stood up, stretched hugely, and said, "I don't know about you but I'm going to hit the sack. It's been a long week."

"That sounds like a good idea," said Fred, and the two turned toward the darkened BOQ.

As they trudged up the steps, the skipper threw his arm around Fred's shoulder and said, "Fred, I'm glad as hell you like it here."

"What's the matter, darling?" the woman asked.

Duane Higgins stood at the window and watched as Jack and Fred left the bench and headed up the walk. The woman in the bed kept calling him "darling" and "honey," and it irritated him mightily. And it was perplexing to see that Jack had not spent the night, or even an hour, with Eleanor Hawkins. He must have been crazy not to have seen how hot she was for it. Everyone else could see it.

"There's nothing wrong." He let the curtain fall into place and turned back to the narrow bed. He sat down on the edge and pulled the sheet back to uncover her body.

"You devil, you," she said.

Duane ran his tongue around one of her nipples, gloried in his own excitement, and thought, I don't know about Jack but I'll be damned if I'll ever outgrow the need for a good piece of ass.

One night during the week following his conversation with the skipper outside the BOQ, Fred had a wet dream. It was memorable only because he hadn't had one since he was sixteen years old. In the dream, he was at home in San Jose, in his father's hardware store. Strangely enough, he was playing bridge on the front counter where he had worked during the summers. His ejaculation came for no apparent reason, as one of the players casually bid six hearts. The irresistible surging overwhelmed and, moments later, woke him. Since most of Fred's dreams were hard to understand and frequently even bizarre, he rarely remembered them long after he had them. A week later, during a briefing in which the skipper announced the first sailing date, Fred remembered the dream and who the player was who had bid six hearts. In a totally unnerving flash of insight he realized his feelings for the commanding officer were a lot more than admiration.

10

8 July 1943: Squadron VF-20 today participated in Operation Boondoggle, a training exercise involving all of Air Group 20 as well as elements of the Hawaiian Area Air Defense Force (Army) flying from Bellows Field. In this operation, the entire Air Group effected a predawn rendezvous fifteen miles south of the island of Oahu, carried out a mock attack on the aforementioned Bellows Field, and correctly intercepted a moving Point Option north of the island. During the attack, fighters of this squadron carried out an offensive sweep of the airfield prior to the arrival of the torpedo and dive bomber squadrons, which then carried out simultaneous high- and low-level attacks with good coordination. Army P-47s engaged members of this squadron but were notably unsuccessful in carrying out attacks on the other two squadrons. Despite early difficulties in the predawn rendezvous, the training mission has been judged a success.

14 July 1943: A four-plane division of Chance Vought F4U Corsairs arrived today from U.S.S. *Bunker Hill*, with accompanying orders attaching the aircraft to VF-20 for an indefinite period of time. One division of Curtiss SB2C Helldivers arrived also for attachment to VB-20. The official purpose behind the attachment of these aircraft to date has not been specified.

20 July 1943: Aircraft Number 20-F-18 piloted by Ensign Luden Hodges, USN, crashed into the sea today near the center of gunnery area Bravo-8. Reasons for the crash are unknown, although the pilot of the tow aircraft reported that Ensign Hodges failed to pull out of an overhead firing run from seven thousand feet. Search aircraft included those aircraft engaged in the exercise and a single aircraft from PatRon 37, NAS Ford Island. No trace of Ensign Hodges or his aircraft have been found. He is officially listed as missing and presumed dead.

21 July 1943: Official orders have been received placing the air group on alert and specifying an Embarkation/Sailing date of 28 July 1943, for purposes of training and flight-testing of the new aircraft. Duration of the cruise and location of the training area to be utilized has not been released.

24 July 1943: VF-20 organizational changes brought about by the loss of Ensign Hodges are as follows: Ensign Frederick Trusteau, USN, is assigned to fly wing on Squadron Commander Lieutenant Commander Jack Hardigan, USN.

Part II

Ironsides

11

"All right, gentlemen, this cruise is going to be something none of us has ever been on before: a wartime training cruise. Mister Higgins and I spent a couple of hours yesterday with the skippers and execs and the air group commander, together with the *Ironsides* air officer and captain, to get our signals down straight."

Fred Trusteau hardened his face into a show-nothing mask and considered the skipper through half-closed eyes. Jack Hardigan leaned back against the edge of the large table in front of the ready room, tapping a pointer carelessly against his left shoe. His voice seemed to fill the room and surround Fred with its resonance.

"The purpose of this mission is to operate the ships and aircraft of the task force under wartime conditions where the threat of enemy intervention isn't expected. They haven't told us where this area will be, but I think we can assume that it'll be between Pearl and the west coast. As to how long the cruise will last, your guess is as good as mine." The skipper braced his palms on the edge of the table, casually splayed his long legs toward the quiet, seated pilots. Had he noticed, Fred would have been surprised at their seriousness, but his attention was on the man in front, for reasons no one save him could know.

"VF-20's secondary mission is the testing and qualification of the Chance Vought Corsair as a ship-borne interceptor. When we finish here, I want to see the guys I picked to fly the Corsairs aboard and we'll work out the details." Jack pointed toward the blackboard, on which was chalked a diagram of a carrier task force. Great pie-shaped wedges emanated from the center of the circular formation of ships. He said: "The ship will keep a minimum four-plane CAP on duty during all daylight hours. Mister Higgins will post the duty rotation for even and odd days by tomorrow morning and keep it current on board. Don't rely on your memory as to when you'll pull the duty. Check a couple of times every day. *Ironsides* will also be employing standard antisubmarine searches, close in and extended, so don't think the bomber jockeys are getting off easy."

A battle was raging in Fred's mind as he considered the man with the pointer at the front of the ready room. He had given up trying to concentrate and retain the information that the skipper was giving out—information that could quite conceivably save his life. He was instead trying to sort out the first incredible rush of sensations that had nearly smothered him only minutes before. When the skipper had first taken the floor to begin the briefing, he had, for no reason at all, remembered the dream. In a way, it was as if a switch had been thrown, and a light had come on, revealing with perfect clarity what had heretofore been hidden in darkness, struggling to get out. And now that it was out, Fred wasn't at all sure he wanted it that way.

The skipper was speaking: "The ship will go to General Quarters every morning before dawn and remain at stations until the launching of the morning CAP or whenever the captain decides to secure. We can also expect a couple of unscheduled GQs during each day and at least three a week after dark. There'll be some major battle problems, maybe involving another carrier, but at this point they're still unscheduled. From what I hear, most of the ships in the group will be brand-new so this is a training exercise all around. There's even going to be a makee-learn admiral aboard getting his sea legs and learning port from starboard."

"Peachy," said Lieutenant Brogan, "no flight gear in the wardroom."

"Now boys," said Lieutenant Schuster, "start with the fork on the outside." Laughter scattered through the room and some of the tension was broken.

"Tomorrow morning at this time Mister Schuster will conduct a half-hour seminar on wardroom etiquette."

"Me, Skipper?"

"You're the only Schuster we've got. Tomorrow this time."

"Sure, Skipper."

Fred decided he liked the way the skipper trimmed his sideburns in the middle of his ears and kept a neat quarter-inch of skin around them. He would let his sideburns grow out some and ask the barber to trim them that way.

"This admiral's name is Berkey and he's an air officer from way back. He's going to be looking primarily at big strike coordination and radio procedure. CAP vectoring is another of his interests. What I'm trying to get across is radio discipline. It's important that you not come up on the circuit unless you have something important to say, and for most of you that's nothing. And the first person I hear calling the *Ironsides* or any other ship by anything other than its designated call sign won't see a promotion for a long, long time."

Fred studied the skipper's hands as he talked, noting a small black bruise on his right thumbnail. His hands were big, like Fred's stepfather's had been, but the skipper kept his nails trimmed and cleaned. And his stepfather could never have handled himself the way the skipper did now. His stepfather had not been either approachable or self-assured. It took me all these years to appreciate that, thought Fred. But why is it important?

"The squadron will form up on the twenty-eighth at about 0700 at fifteen thousand feet. Rendezvous point is point Zebra, due southeast of the airfield and one mile off the beach. Formation is squadron in echelon right, divisions in finger four. I'm telling you this now so that in case there's an early sailing announcement, we can skip a briefing and get into the air without delay. And another thing: Beginning tomorrow morning, every pilot, without exception, will pack up his gear in regulation luggage with his name on it and leave it on his bunk, ready to go. Sailing dates are always subject to change and often as not they're moved forward. And clear all your personal junk out of the ready room here. When we leave, everything here will go with you in the aircraft, and I don't want to see anything except regulation flying gear."

"Ah shoot, Skipper," said one of the veterans, "my girl wanted to see the ship."

"No ukeleles, no tennis rackets, and no booze. If you can't get it into a seabag and a B-4, it doesn't go with us."

"How about my golf clubs, Skipper?" asked Lieutenant Brogan.

"Only admirals can have golf clubs aboard." Jack looked

down at a piece of paper on the table and read silently for a few seconds. "One other thing. We'll be bunking in four- and six-man staterooms for the most part. They've decided it's best that the occupants of each compartment be taken from all three squadrons, so you'll probably have a bomber jockey in the rack over you.

"Why's that, Skipper?" asked a young ensign.

Duane Higgins broke in and said primly, "It's to promote better social relations between the pilots of the air group," and a scattering of laughter ran through the room.

"Think about it," said Jack. He had been leaning against the front edge of the table. Now he easily hefted himself into a sitting position on top of it. Fred watched his every movement. Jack continued: "With the ship in enemy waters, with subs taking pot shots at her, you don't want all your important men in one spot. A single torpedo could kill them all at one time."

"That's why the captain and the admiral don't share a stateroom," said Brogan.

"And it's also to promote better social relations between the pilots of the air group." Jack smiled and scanned his pilots. "Are there any questions you need answers to?" Heads turned and looked but no hands were raised. "Mister Higgins has the stateroom assignments, so look him up sometime before you get aboard. If I don't get the chance to talk to you again, assemble in the ready room on board as soon as you get there. Okay?" He scanned the room one more time. "Let's do some flying." Jack slid off the table while the room dissolved into stretching, talking men, but Fred stayed seated and watched the skipper. He liked the way the older man had kept his body in shape, the way his clothes enhanced his trimness. He was wearing a pair of gabardine slacks instead of the usual starched wash khaki. The top button was closed under his tie. His shoes gleamed. He was a very handsome man.

"You asleep, Trusty?" Hammerstein towered over him and tousled his hair.

"Just thinking, Frank." Fred stood up and stretched. In the front of the room, the three lieutenants the skipper had picked to work with the Corsairs had clustered around him.

"About girls no doubt." Fred laughed.

"Yeah," he said. "Girls."

"For the benefit of the less experienced members of the squadron, we will now attempt to demonstrate proper wardroom etiquette." Lieutenant Schuster stood in the front of the ready room, facing the seated ensigns and a few j.g.'s. Under his arm was a blue, bound copy of *The Division Officer's Guide,* which he now held up for all to see. "Our reference work will be Emily Post's favorite manual, one which is both near and dear to our hearts." Some of the ensigns snickered.

Schuster walked to the door leading to the outside of the building and opened it. Four pilots came in, all wearing their round, officer's combination caps. Across the front of each man's chest was pinned a wide strip of paper with words written on it. Lieutenant Bradley's chest said "XO." Frank Hammerstein's said "Engineer." Duane Higgins' read "Guns." Lieutenant (j.g.) Bracker was "Aviator."

"These are four typical officers from the complement of an aircraft carrier," said Schuster. "They have just entered the wardroom for the evening meal, which is called dinner."

Fred sat uncomfortably in his chair and tried to get into the spirit of Schuster's ridiculous lecture. But his mind kept wandering back to what he had realized exactly twenty-four hours earlier as he sat in this same chair and watched while the Skipper talked. The thoughts and feelings were no less real when Jack Hardigan was out of his sight; if anything, they were stronger. He had lain awake most of the night exploring them. The pilots in front masquerading as fools had no effect on him whatever.

"Gee, fellas," said Bracker the aviator, "what's for supper?" The other three men walked sullenly to the far end of the table, where they sat and huddled together, hands in pockets.

"Stupid Aviator," said Higgins loudly.

Lieutenant Brogan came through the door now, wearing a blue baseball cap with piles of gold braid on the bill. His chest was covered with clattering medals and rows and rows of ribbons.

The three men at the end of the table all spoke sweetly in unison. "Good evening to you, Captain."

Brogan walked into the aviator on purpose, knocking his hat off. "Stupid Aviator," he muttered.

"Good evening, Captain," said Bracker.

"Never speak to the captain unless spoken to by him," said Schuster. The captain joined the men at the far end of the table. XO pulled out a chair at the end and offered to seat him. Engineer and Guns pulled out their chairs and sat down. Aviator did the same.

"Ha, ha," said the captain, "got you, you dingbat. I'm not sitting down yet."

"Never take your seat," said Schuster, "until the captain does so." XO took his seat beside the captain and Schuster said: "Notice how the order of seating allows the most important officers to sit at the head of the table and those of lesser rank and position are seated further away from them." Aviator was by himself at the opposite end. All but aviator now removed their hats and put them face up on the table in front of them.

The captain leaned over and spoke to XO. "Tell that stupid aviator to take off his hat."

XO leaned over and said to engineer: "Tell that stupid aviator to take off his hat."

Engineer leaned over and said to Guns: "Tell that stupid aviator to take off his hat."

Guns turned to face aviator and said loudly: "Hey, you, Jerk, take off your hat."

"Never wear your cover in the wardroom," said Schuster.

The captain elbowed XO and said: "Hey, did I tell you guys about this broad I knocked up in Honolulu? Cheloobies," he said, indicating the size with his hands, "they were like watermelons."

Aviator took out his wallet and opened it up to reveal a small snapshot. "Did I ever show you guys a picture of my baby daughter?"

"Stupid Aviator," said the captain, and the three officers beside him nodded in agreement.

"Never discuss women with your fellow officers while in the wardroom."

"You know, your highness," said Guns, "if we could just get rid of some of those silly airplanes, I think we could put an eight-inch mount up on the forecastle."

"That's a good idea," said Engineer.

"Sure was a nice day for flying," said aviator.

"Who is that asshole on the end?" asked the captain.

"Just one of the flyboys," said XO. "You know how they are."

"Never talk shop while in the wardroom. Politics is also a forbidden subject. This leaves the officers and gentlemen free to discuss such exciting topics as art, the weather, and poetry."

"There was a young lady from Dallas," said the captain, "who used dynamite for a phallus. They found her vagina in South Carolina, and her asshole in Buckingham Palace." The "actors" roared with laughter and elbowed each other broadly.

"Always laugh at the captain's jokes," said Schuster. "That one isn't in the manual, but it's a pretty good idea."

"Oh, darn," said aviator, "I dropped my soup spoon."

The Captain stood up, pounded the table with his fist and shouted, "Who's the motherfucking son of a bitch who said that? There'll be no fucking cursing in my wardroom!"

"Swearing in the wardroom is the mark of a brutish and insensitive cad," said Schuster.

Guns produced a white handkerchief which he fluttered through the air toward Aviator. "You insensitive cad, you," he said.

The five seated pilots pulled folded pieces of paper from pockets and hats. "If you are ever late for a sitting," read Brogan, "and arrive after the meal has been served, approach the captain, apologize for your lateness, and politely request permission to be seated."

"Never," read Hammerstein, "never, never put your feet up on the wardroom furnishings."

"Always start with the outside fork," read Higgins.

"The uniform for the evening meal is the dress uniform for the appropriate clime," read Bracker. He looked up. "Jesus, is that right?"

"Depends on the captain," said Schuster. "Please continue."

"If you must leave before the captain finishes eating, wait until coffee is served, then politely ask the captain if you may be excused." Higgins read, then wadded up his piece of paper, and tossed it over his shoulder. "What a crock of shit," he said.

"Do not tarry in the wardroom during working hours or after a meal," offered Brogan, stumbling over the word "tarry." "This gives the steward the chance to perform cleaning duties and prepare for the next meal."

"Thank you, gentlemen," said Schuster. "This concludes my presentation on wardroom etiquette. Are there any questions?" He looked around the room. One ensign was nodding off. No one appeared terribly interested.

"Hey," said Duggin, at the back of the room near the door. "I think the skipper's coming." Brogan turned around and began taking off his medals.

Jack Hardigan came into the room. Fred took a sharp breath, turned his head, closed his eyes. "Forget the speech, Mister Schuster," Jack said. "*Ironsides* sails in one hour and we take off in two." He disappeared back through the door. Fred exhaled slowly and opened his eyes.

Duane Higgins was already on his feet, removing the "XO" paper, and forcing his way through the room to the door Jack had just gone through. When he reached it, he turned and spoke loudly to the whole room. "Don't just sit there, guys, get moving." He opened the door, was gone.

Fred climbed wearily to his feet and thought, it'll be better when we get to sea, I'm sure it will. He found his yellow Mae West and pulled it on. It has to be better, he thought.

The United States Navy's dramatic increase in carrier strength during 1943 is best illustrated by some simple figures: At the end of 1942 and one year of war, only two of the Navy's six original fleet carriers, the *Enterprise* and the *Saratoga*, were still on the surface of the Pacific Ocean. Both had suffered severe battle damage, were manned by exhausted crews, and had depleted, weary air groups.

On the first day of July, 1943, the Pacific Fleet's carrier strength included four *Essex*-class and five *Independence*-class ships in commission, of which three and four respectively were approaching combat readiness. By the end of the same year, Admiral Nimitz had assembled at Pearl Harbor six *Essex*- and six *Independence*-class ships, plus *Enterprise* and *Saratoga*, all combat ready and fully manned with highly-trained, competent crewmen and pilots. This veritable explosion in naval strength is an economic achievement unparalleled in modern or ancient history.

(J.E. Hardigan, Commander, USN (ret.),
*A Setting of Many Suns: The Destruction
of the Imperial Navy* [The Naval Institute
Press, 1962]. p. 280.)

12

Jack Hardigan was filled with a gut-level gratification. On either side of him the other three Corsairs buzzed along contentedly, holding a precise and unmoving formation. Behind him and to the right stretched the thirty-four Hellcats in four-plane, lopsided Vs. By leaning as far over as he could and looking down, he could catch a glimpse of the leading Dauntless divisions. The sight of so many aircraft on a coordinated mission never failed to fill him with chilly feelings of evenly mixed awe and wonder. As a squadron commander, the feeling was stronger than ever: He knew about the organization that had brought all these machines together at this point in time, made sure they could all fly, trained the pilots to fly them, and assembled them into such clean formations at this altitude. But the gratification was for another reason.

"Banger Leader to Banger One Seven."

"Roger, Banger Leader."

"Any stragglers, One Seven?"

"Nary a one, Banger Leader."

"Roger, One Seven." Jack was inwardly thankful for a good executive officer. Only an hour ago, Higgins had reorganized nearly every division for the flight to the *Constitution* when the ship's air officer had radioed that the four Corsairs would be brought aboard all at one time and after all other aircraft had landed. This made it necessary for those four to form their own division. Duane shuffled the pilots around and filled the resulting gaps. The hour they had had before it was necessary to begin the forty-five minute journey to the carrier had been well spent and the launching was begun on time.

What satisfied Jack the most was the incredible flapping around the dive bomber and torpedo squadrons had gone through to get ready—if indeed they were ready. He had seen one busload of harried pilots heading for the BOQ to pack their personal belongings, just as the one truck he had sent arrived with his pilots' gear all packed and ready. They had even had time to round up four volunteer pilots from another air group to fly the four extra Hellcats to the *Constitution*. An Avenger would fly them back to the island later in the afternoon and return before dark. Everyone benefited from this arrangement: The ship and the air group had the extra aircraft and the other pilots got in some flight time in the new fighters and valuable carrier landing experience. Jack smiled to himself, thinking how nice it was to be well organized.

It was, as usual, a beautiful day for flying. He had concluded long ago that the clear skies and deep blue waters of the Pacific were capable of lulling the most experienced pilot into a sense of false security; the ocean's vastness could overwhelm the negligent or inattentive. A malfunctioning homing device and an unnoticed crosswind could cause a single plane or a flight of aircraft to miss their tiny carrier by ten miles—a miniscule error by navigation standards—and send them off into wastes of sky and water. They would eventually realize their mistake but would be unable to fight the inexorable mathematics of fuel consumption or the approach of darkness. And wartime necessities may dictate that the carrier remain in silence to protect her location, or even forbid the detachment of ships or additional aircraft to search for the lost pilots. The most you can hope for, Jack thought, is that it doesn't happen to you.

"Red Rocket Leader, this is Rocket Two Four." One of the Dauntlesses.

"Roger, Two Four."

"I'm running rough and hot. Oil pressure fluctuating."

"We're closer to the roost than from where we came from, Two Four. Think you can make it?"

"Negative, Rocket Leader." It was a kid's voice. Young. Very scared. "She's getting worse every second."

"Stay in formation as long as you can, Two Four. If you have to put her down, I'll leave someone here to keep you company until we can pick you up."

"Roger, Rocket Leader." It had to happen, thought Jack. Out of the almost one hundred aircraft in the group, at least one had to develop trouble. Why couldn't it have been while they were still over the strip?

"Oh, Jesus, she's gone. Just like that. I'm putting her down, Rocket Leader."

"Roger, Two Four. Three Two, follow him down and get a good fix. Drop your raft if necessary. We'll get you out of there, Two Four." Maybe, thought Jack. If your wingman gets a good fix on your location. If you make it out of the plane before it sinks. If the ship can contact Pearl in time to get a plane out before dark. If a squall doesn't swamp your raft.

"Banger One Seven, this is Banger Leader. Everything all right?"

"Couldn't be better, Banger Leader. Quit your worrying."

Some minor but unexpected turbulence buffeted the Corsairs, bouncing them around briefly before the pilots could compensate. They were so different, these new birds, from the Grummans he was used to flying. Maybe that contributed to his uneasiness. Jack looked across the intervening distance into Lieutenant Bradley's cockpit; the pilot, who had his goggles pushed up and oxygen mask dangling, smiled confidently and gave a thumbs-up.

The engineer who designed these planes, Brogan had said, must have had a wild hair up his ass, and Jack could understand what he meant. Most aircraft critics said the Corsair was graceful in appearance, but Jack had to disagree. The wide, thin wings dipped sharply away from the fuselage. It was called an inverted gull wing configuration, but from head on it was more reminiscent of a bat than a gull. Jack had no idea what aerodynamic advantages were gained by this setup, although it did allow for a larger propeller. This was because the landing gear kept the nose of the plane higher than normal when on the deck. But the higher nose position made taxiing more difficult because forward visibility was cut—a condition compounded by the fact that the cockpit was located near the center of the fuselage, almost aft of the wing. Jack also found the position of the horizontal stabilizer curious; it extended well aft of the vertical. He was intrigued by aircraft design and sometimes wished he had been an engineer. But basically he would rather fly the damn things than design them. Despite its unusual appearance, the Corsair had amazing power and speed. It handled like a dream throughout the range of power settings and attitudes. We've come a long way, he thought, since the Buffalo.

Far below him, an irregularity on the surface of the ocean caught his eye. Jack tipped the fighter to get a better look. A tiny toy ship was there, a destroyer by the look of it; it was making a foaming bow wave and leaving a broad wake fanning out behind it. The disturbed water gradually reassumed its slatelike surface. The destroyer was headed in their direction, almost precisely, and Jack figured it was making speed to join the *Constitution*'s group. As he watched, the speeding ship abruptly changed course, turning to starboard, its feathery wake sweeping into a giant question mark of white foam. Odd, he thought. Then he remembered the pilot who had just gone down and wished he could be that lucky when the time came. The carrier could only be minutes ahead now.

Ten minutes after the destroyer was sighted the *Constitution*'s escorting ships hove into view, then the carrier herself, a tiny rectangle of gray surrounded by the parallel wakes of destroyers and cruisers. It was a good sight, and for a moment, in his mind, Jack was back with the *Hornet*, among friends, on the way to Tokyo, surrounded and absorbed by the strength and security of throbbing steel, pulsating power. It's great, he thought, just great to be home.

Fred watched Higgins' Hellcat bank sharply to the left and head down. He counted aloud to fifteen and followed him, using stick and rudder to swing ninety degrees exactly and cut his altitude in half. Glancing over his right shoulder, he saw Fitzsimmons make his turn and settle into the new course. Looking to his left, he saw task group ships heading directly for him. He felt somehow lucky: He would be the second pilot aboard *Ironsides*, preceded only by the exec, who was flying in the place of the skipper. The skipper, he thought; too bad. It must be some honor to be the first aboard a ship on her first operational cruise. Now Higgins would have the privilege.

Ahead and to the left of him, Higgins made his second left turn to take him on a course down the port side of the carrier. Hoping he wasn't too close to the leading plane, Fred made his turn and leveled off behind the exec's aircraft. The exec dropped his landing gear and tail hook. Fred dropped his. Behind him, he knew, in an aerial game of follow-the-leader, the remaining Hellcats of VF-20 were engaging in the same ritual, and behind them, the thirty-five Dauntlesses of VB-20 were doing the same. After the dive bombers would come the Avengers of VT-20, now circling high overhead. Finally, ignominiously bringing up the rear, were the four Corsairs, led by Jack Hardigan, and the four Curtiss Helldivers.

Ahead of Fred, the exec's Hellcat passed over a slender light cruiser bristling with gun mounts. As Fred approached it, he noticed groups of sailors lining the rails, watching. He released the latch on his canopy and slid it back, surprised at the rush of cool air and the roar of engine noise. He pulled his goggles down over his eyes, then waved to the sailors on the cruiser. A few waved back, probably thinking what a lucky stiff he was to be having such a good time up there in the air. In reality, Fred was beginning to sweat his first landing on the *Constitution*.

During the last part of his formal flight training, Fred had made his first landing on a ship underway. At the end of that phase, the officer in charge of the flight school had addressed the assembled students and said, among a host of patriotic platitudes and we're-depending-on-you's, that there were tens of thousands of pilots in the world but only a few who had been trained to make a landing on a carrier deck. He said that the average Army pilot wouldn't even know how to go about doing it and would be scared out of his pants if he had to try. What he neglected to say was that most Navy pilots had no idea how to go about it the first time either and were also scared out of their pants when the time came to try it.

Much later, sitting in the Officer's Club bar in San Diego, Fred had overheard a group of pilots trading sea stories about their bad landings. One had said that he had been making landings, hundreds of them, for over a year, when one day he just got rattled and was waved off six times before producing a satisfactory approach. When he got the cut and caught a wire, his right tire blew out, the landing gear collapsed, and he ended in the starboard catwalk hanging straight down, looking at the blue water a hundred feet below him. Another complained about the turbulence caused by the *Saratoga*'s massive island structure, saying that once he got a wave-off from the landing signals officer while landing and had poured on the coal, but a downdraft caused him to catch a wire anyway, with full power on. He, too, had ended up in the catwalk with a five-inch gun barrel in the cockpit with him. He could laugh about it only in retrospect. Then the group had solemnly drunk a toast to a good old boy who had pancaked—whatever that was—right in front of the plane guard destroyer and had been run over by the ship that was supposed to save his life. Fred had noticed that pilots always seemed to be drunk when they told such stories.

Ahead of him, the exec lowered his flaps and began circling left of his final approach. Fred was just off the port bow of the *Constitution*, passing down her port side. From this close, she looked much bigger. Crowds of people jammed the narrow catwalks ringing the flight deck. Fred wondered how many of them were spectators and how many were supposed to be there. He would find out in about a minute. The great vessel, with its five-inch gun mounts, its hulking island topped by a jumble of rotating radar antennae, its flat expanse of flight deck, passed quickly by him. Then it was time for his own final approach.

As he circled in, Fred found the LSO's windscreen and the landing cables, then the tiny figure of the landing officer himself, with his two brightly colored paddles. They called this imaginary, three-dimensional highway, which terminated on the after end of the flight deck, the groove. The LSO was in sight throughout the short trip. Fred just had time to see that the deck was still empty; that Higgins had taken a wave-off. Fred would be the first to report aboard.

You're high and to the left, said the paddles. Now you're good. A little fast. Your right wing is high. You're good. You're good. Cut.

Fred pulled the throttle all the way out, saw the deck rush up to meet him, felt the first rough contact of aircraft and ship. Then the arresting gear grabbed him and slammed the Hellcat to a stop, throwing Fred forward against the restraining straps. Fred looked up now, astonished at being where he was with so little difficulty. He slipped his goggles up on his head. The sweat poured down his face, and he knew instinctively that he would enjoy doing this for a living.

The ready room was in the island. Fred remembered as much from the briefing given by the skipper. He was thankful for this much information, even if it wasn't very specific, because he would otherwise have had to search literally hundreds of steel-gray compartments, any one of which could have been the ready room for VF-20. Fred was about to find out the hard way, just how big an aircraft carrier was.

He climbed from the Hellcat carrying his plotting board and the miscellaneous accouterments of his flight gear. Behind him a multitude of figures in colored jerseys descended on his aircraft and began to push it down the deck toward the bow of the ship. Fred was suddenly out of the familiar surroundings of his aircraft and smack in the middle of uncertain, almost alien, territory. Not wishing to appear stupid even though he knew that most sailors considered ensigns to be quite stupid, he headed for the only man who didn't appear occupied and asked him where the ready room was.

"Huh?" said the man, almost shouting to overcome the sound of the twenty-five knots of wind that threatened to carry away everything Fred was holding on to.

"Where are the ready rooms?" Fred shouted. Overhead another Hellcat took a wave-off and snarled down the length of the flight deck, tail hook dangling.

"Beats me," said the sailor. He wore a close-fitting cowl the same color as his jersey, and it covered his entire head except for the face.

Fred decided that further talk was futile and left the man standing there. He headed for the only open hatch he could see, stepped inside, and was instantly gratified to be out of the wind. He looked around, saw nothing that he could recognize, then bravely went forward. It was, he decided, better than standing there helplessly until someone wandered by. When he turned the first corner he came to, he collided with an admiral.

"Pardon me, sir," said Fred, noticing the single gold star on each collar tab.

"That's all right, son," said the admiral. He was a fiftyish man with a friendly face and an emaciatedly thin body, on which his uniform hung like a well-pressed rag.

"I was just heading for the ready room," said Fred. He picked up a black grease pencil dropped in the collision. "You wouldn't know where to find it, would you, sir?"

"As a matter of fact," said the admiral, "I don't have the foggiest idea. Here, let me help you." The wizened little man took the grease pencil and tucked it into a pocket on Fred's left arm.

"Thank you, sir."

"I was just heading topside to watch the air group come aboard. Would you care to join me?"

"Why, uh, yes, sir, I guess I would." Fred turned aside in the narrow passageway, to let the admiral by, still slightly awed by the man's rank and his obvious friendliness.

"You must have been the first one aboard," said the admiral over his shoulder. The two hurried down the corridor Fred had just traversed, turned into a narrow flight of steel steps with a single handrail, and headed up.

"Yes, sir, I was. The first one was actually the exec but he took a wave-off, and then I came in." They reached the first level above the flight deck, circled around, and headed up again.

"Well, let me be the first to welcome you aboard the *Ironsides*. She's a fine ship, don't you think?"

"Yes, sir, I think she is."

"How many ships have you been aboard, son?"

Another deck, another ladder.

Fred was getting tired of climbing. "I never kept track, sir, but I think about two."

The admiral laughed. When they reached a final level, he pulled open a watertight door that led outside. The two men stepped through and onto a narrow steel ledge with a chest-high wall. Fred looked down on the flight deck in time to see a Hellcat (it looked like Hughes) catch the last wire and plunge to a halt. "Nice view from up here, sir," he said.

"It certainly is, son. It's so good we discourage spectators from coming up and getting in the way." The admiral leaned against the retaining wall and looked out over the flight deck, which was three decks down. His loose uniform flapped in the wind. Fred put his plotting board down on the deck and moved up next to the admiral.

"I guess I haven't been very polite, sir. My name's Ensign Trusteau."

A Hellcat came down the groove, plopped onto the deck, and screeched to a halt. Blue-jerseyed sailors scrambled across the deck to release the tail hook.

"Ensign Trusteau. What the hell's your first name?"

"Fred, sir. Frederick."

"Well, Fred, I'm Clarence Berkey. You can call me Admiral." Below them the deck crew manhandled the Hellcat's wings into the folded position and began to roll it down the deck. "Jesus H. Christ, that's a slow bunch of plane pushers," said the admiral. "I've seen faster crews on a Chinese junk."

"Maybe they're just inexperienced," replied Fred. He'd thought the plane pushers were pretty fast; the organized confusion that reigned on the deck below would look impressive to any but the most experienced.

"You take that situation over there," said the admiral, pointing to the port corner of the flight deck forward, where Fred's aircraft and two others were sitting, wings folded and wheels chocked. "They should have put the first one on the elevator and sent it down. When the rest of the group gets aboard and they have to put up a CAP, they'll have to shuffle all these goddamn air planes like Chinese checkers." Fred looked for and found the forward elevator, in the center of the flight deck.

"But that would leave a hole in the deck," he said, "and they'd have to work around it."

"Not that elevator, Fred. There's another one over there on the edge of the flight deck, right about in the middle. It's a new invention. They call it the deck edge elevator. It's revolutionizing plane pushing."

"That's very interesting," said Fred, hoping he didn't sound stupid. It *was* very interesting. Another fighter landed, snagging the wire while still airborne, and crashing to the deck like a falling stone.

"That LSO's bringing them in too high. What was his name?" The admiral pulled a battered little leather notebook from a back pocket, thumbed through its handwritten pages and came to a name. "Lieutenant Harden. Got to talk to him."

"Pardon me, sir, but are you the force commander?"

The admiral laughed. "Not me, son. I'm on vacation."

"You must be the—" What was it the skipper called him?

"The makee-learn admiral. I don't have a care in the world right now, Fred. I just observe and make notes and once in a long while I get up the energy to make a suggestion that everyone oohs and ahhs over but never accepts. Some day before long, though, you watch, I'll be making the decisions and they'll be the same as the suggestions and everyone'll say, 'Gee. Admiral, that sure is a smart decision.'" He laughed again, sounding very pleased with himself.

Another fighter landed. There were six Hellcats on deck now, including one sitting on the deck edge elevator. Fred saw Higgins climb from the nearest one and head for the island. "I think I better be getting down to the ready room, sir. They might want me for the first CAP."

"Well, I hope you find it all right. You know, I heard a story once about a pilot who tried to find the head on a carrier. They didn't see him for three months." Admiral Berkey laughed. The creases in his forehead and around his eyes smoothed out briefly. For the first time Fred noticed the gold wings pinned over his left pocket and understood how the admiral could look sad, worried, and happy all at the same time. The admiral was a pilot and felt things like a pilot. He was worried when young men did dangerous things, such as landing a bucking fighter on a moving carrier deck. The admiral liked Fred because he liked pilots.

"It's been a privilege to talk to you, sir," said Fred. Admiral Berkey smiled, grunted, and turned back to watch another Hellcat land. Fred left and wandered around the island with his plotting board and flight gear until he found the ready room.

13

"Sloppy, gentlemen," said Commander Buster Jennings, commanding officer of Air Group Twenty. "It was goddamn sloppy." CAG was referring to the air group landing ten hours earlier. He was speaking with the squadron commanders. The four men were crowded into CAG's none-too-spacious stateroom with its single bunk, tiny fold-down desk, and chair. Two of the squadron leaders sat on the bed. Jennings had the chair. Jack Hardigan stood uncomfortably against the outer bulkhead and wished CAG would wind it up so he could go to bed and get some sleep. "Hardigan, your boys got more wave-offs than either of the other squadrons. Didn't you train those clowns?"

"Come on, Skipper," said Bloomington, the C.O. of VB-20, whose popular name was "Boom." "You know it was that LSO. This is his first cruise. He was waving everyone off."

"If I want excuses," said Jennings, "I'll ask for them. On the whole, our appearance this morning was deplorable. There'd better be a lot of goddamn improvement, or someone will pay with his ass." He shuffled through an amazingly thick pile of papers and thought of another attack. "I hear from the crew chiefs that some maintenance gear and a whole cartload of wing tanks got left behind. Who's responsible for *that* screw up?"

The three squadron commanders looked at each other and shrugged.

"You know, Skipper," said Woody Heywood, the torpedo

skipper, "the only guys really prepared were Jack's boys. The rest of us did the Chinese fire drill number." He shrugged again, nonchalantly. "But we're all here."

"Like hell we are," said Jennings.

"If you mean Ensign Prebble," said Boom, "he got picked up by a can this morning. They'll highline him and his crewman tomorrow morning."

"No, sir, I wasn't referring to *that* foul-up. I meant that our prepared skipper of the fighters lost three of his pilots over a month ago and hasn't found them yet." Jack shifted his weight to relieve the tingling in his right leg.

"Geez, Jack," said Woody, "I'm sorry to hear that. They die of the clap?"

"They're really lost," said Jack. "Missing in inaction."

"I don't think humor at this time is very appropriate," said Jennings. "Mister Hardigan, I want a written report regarding the final disposition of those pilots on my desk by tomorrow afternoon. Is that understood?"

"Aye, aye, sir."

"Mister Bloomington, I want to see that Ensign what's-his-name in my office as soon as he gets aboard tomorrow."

"Mister Prebble?"

"Yes, as soon as he gets aboard." A blue-covered flight manual dislodged itself from the sliding pile of papers and fell to the deck with a thud. "Oh, yes, while I think of it. Tomorrow evening at this time I want to see Mister Hardigan and Mister Bloomington regarding the training programs for the new aircraft. Come fully prepared. I won't have you wasting my time." He looked directly at Jack as he said that. "And the first battle problem briefing will be Sunday night." Jack wanted to say something to CAG about the times when he was scheduling all these meetings, since they would conflict with the show time of the evening movie in the wardroom. He wasn't that fond of movies but it just wasn't fair. He was about to speak up, but Boom beat him to it.

"Geez, Skipper," he said, "couldn't we find another time for these briefings? I mean the wardroom movie starts at eight."

"What's more important, Mister Bloomington, the goddamn movie or this training cruise? And use military time if you don't mind."

"Aye, aye, sir." Boom sighed audibly and rolled his eyes.

"Well, sir," said Woody, yawning and stretching, "it's been a long day."

"Good," said Jennings, "then I'll start with you. Bring in your training charts and we'll go over them tonight."

Silence hung awkwardly for a long moment before Woody spoke. "Whatever you say, sir."

"You two can go." Jennings nodded to Jack and Boom.

Boom stood up. "Good night, sir," he said, stepping over CAG's legs and following Jack through the door. The two men found their way down the red-lighted passageway toward their own staterooms, dodging the unfamiliar obstacles that cluttered their path. The ship's movement through the waters of the Pacific was only slightly perceptible.

"What a son of a bitch," said Boom. "He's really got your number, hasn't he?"

"Hell," said Jack, "he just likes to hear himself talk. He doesn't really bother me." He *does* bother me, he thought; I can't stand the bastard.

They reached the door to Boom's stateroom and stopped. Boom stretched. "You interested in a cup of coffee?"

"No, thanks," said Jack.

"I don't mean the wardroom variety of coffee," said Boom. "I mean my own special blend."

Jack knew he meant liquor, but he didn't feel like it. "No, really. A little fresh air and then I'll hit the hay."

"How're those Corsairs turning out?"

"Little early to tell right now. They say the tail hooks are giving trouble, and the chiefs are bitching about inaccurate manuals. And they land funny." He understated the problem; the Corsair he had flown aboard that day had the tightest, bounciest landing gear oleo he had ever encountered.

"That's about the same with those Curtiss jobs. The controls are all wacky, especially near the red line."

"You'll get the bugs worked out."

"Yeah, I suppose so." Boom gave Jack a mock punch in the gut. "Well, tiger, I'll see you in the morning."

"Sure. Good night."

"Night." Boom Bloomington disappeared into his stateroom and the door closed.

Alone in the dark passageway, Jack stood for a moment, savoring the sounds and smells of the carrier at night, trying to feel at home the way he should. The air was not hot, but it was stuffy and warm, helped little by the continuous circulation of fresh air through blowers topside. Jack walked down the close corridor, passing several doors opening on unlighted rooms. He could hear an occasional heavy snorer or muted voices discussing the ship or the war or girls. Almost everyone was sleeping.

Blundering somewhat, he managed to find a ladder leading topside (they'd built this ship so differently from the *Hornet* or the *Enterprise* or the *Lex*) and climbed two decks to the echoing, plane-jammed hangar deck. Fresh night air poured through the huge, unlighted enclosure and eddied around the silent aircraft. Jack headed aft toward the deck edge elevator, which he found so intriguing in its simple elegance. He passed a carefully shielded group of mechanics, working on and cursing a Dauntless engine. The elevator was in the down position, with fold-up life nets bordering the edges. Jack let his eyes adjust to the dim light of the stars before he stepped over the loose chain that hung across the opening in the ship's side and walked out onto the elevator. He was there in the wind and sea smell for almost a minute before he realized that he wasn't alone.

It was Fred Trusteau. "Fred," Jack said.

"Skipper."

"How come you're not in the rack?"

"I guess I'm just too charged up, Skipper. It was a pretty exciting day."

"Sure was." They moved closer together so their words wouldn't be carried away by the pressure of the wind and stood looking out into the blackness of the tropical night. A large, irregular shape which Jack knew to be a heavy cruiser lurked an indefinite distance away. It blotted out the stars that blazed all the way to the horizon.

"Nice out tonight," said Fred. He shoved his hands in his pockets. He looked cold.

"It's always nice out here," said Jack. The wind pressed against their bodies like a living force. Jack pulled off his garrison cap and shoved it into his hip pocket. "Well," he said, trying to think of something to say.

"I talked with Admiral Berkey today," said Fred.

"Is that right? And what did the admiral have to say?"

Fred laughed. "He told me all about deck edge elevators."

"Admiral Berkey was the C.O. of the *Langley* back before the war. He knows all the old-timers. Nice guy."

"You've met him before?"

"I'm one of the old-timers." They huddled in silence for several seconds. "You just made me realize how long I've been in the Navy."

"How long would that be, sir?"

"Too long." He thought for a second, realizing that Fred deserved a better answer than that. "Almost nine years. The last year and a half seems like a hundred all by itself."

"Do you plan on staying in when the war's over?"

How can he ask a question like that, thought Jack. How did he know I was just thinking about—

"The end of the war's too far away to consider that right now," Jack said.

That was the truth. But having a boss like Buster Jennings made the prospect of civilian life seem more and more desirable.

Fred rolled his head, looking up at the incredible splendor of the stars. "I've never seen so many stars before. I had no idea it would be this way."

"You've never been to sea before?"

"Does the ferry to Santa Catalina count?"

"Only if you make the trip during a typhoon."

"Well, just seeing this almost makes it all worth it," said Fred.

How many of my pilots ever stopped to consider the stars? thought Jack. Some of these guys are going to die without ever realizing how magnificent the stars are.

Fred fumbled in his pocket and came up with a nearly empty cigarette pack. He offered one to Jack.

"We shouldn't. Not here. Might show a light."

Fred replaced the pack and buttoned the flap on his pocket. "Live and learn," he said.

"That's what I'm here for." Jack smiled, knowing it couldn't be seen in the dark.

"Speaking of learning," said Fred.

"Yes?"

"Well, Skipper, I'm your wingman and we haven't flown together even once."

"That's right, I guess we haven't." Jack was thinking, Damn you, Buster Jennings and damn you, Art Blasshill for not giving me the time for what's most important: training these men to survive the enemy.

"I really think—I mean I really would like to, the first chance you get."

Jack was silent for a moment. "Don't worry. We'll have plenty of time later." I hope, he thought.

"That'd be great, Skipper."

"Mister Higgins says you're pretty sure of yourself in the air."

"He's being very generous."

"Perhaps." Jack took a deep breath, a last look around. "I guess it's about that time." He turned to go.

"Can I go with you?" Fred almost blurted it, then added quickly, "I haven't learned to find officer's country by myself yet."

Jack laughed. "Neither have I. But I think between the two of us we'll manage."

They stepped over the safety chain and crossed the hangar, picking their way through the parked aircraft. On the second level down, Jack asked Fred for the cigarette he'd offered before, and Fred gave it to him. They said good night outside of Jack's stateroom. Then Fred was alone.

Fred walked slowly down the passageway toward his six-man cabin, savoring the almost imperceptible roll of the ship and the hot-oil smell of the vast machinery humming and throbbing all around him. He wasn't exactly sure where his stateroom was, but he knew that if he just followed this corridor, sooner or later he'd find it. He stopped for a drink at a water fountain and realized then that his knees were shaking and his hands trembling. He'd gone topside half an hour earlier to try to stop thinking about the skipper. Now it was all back again, hanging over him like a thick, smothering cloak.

He tried three different doors before finding his own. All the bunks but his were occupied by shapeless bundles of sleeping men. The euphoric glow from talking with the skipper was gone now. He undressed in the dark and took his hurtful, helpless feelings to bed.

14

"Banger One, vector two eight five, angels five."

"Roger, Turkey Trot." (Turkey Trot, thought Fred. How ridiculous.)

"Request altitude confirmation, Banger One."

"On contact, Turkey Trot, on contact." (Pushy bastard. Fred listened to the FDO and Higgins exchange information and said nothing.)

"Target course one zero zero, speed one six zero. Please confirm."

"Roger, Turkey Trot. Wait one. This one's yours, One Three."

Fred looked into the cockpit of Higgins' Hellcat and gave him a thumbs-up. Applying power and pulling back on the stick to gain altitude. Fred started a climbing turn that would bring him to eight thousand feet on a heading of two eight five. They had been doing these simple interceptions of the antisubmarine patrol for the last two hours. The novelty of the feat was beginning to wear off, even when the FDO was wrong, which was frequently.

"Tallyho, Turkey Trot. Beginning attack." The Dauntless was at approximately three thousand feet, idled back, and cruising along in as leisurely a pace as was possible in the middle of the ocean, a thousand miles from the nearest friendly base. The FDO needed to bone up on his tactical operations, thought

Fred. He should know that an ASW sweep wouldn't be at five thousand feet. Fred began his attack from high and to the right, glancing around to make sure the exec was still with him, then rolling into a deflection shot made easy by the steady course of the Dauntless. When the target was still small in the gunsight, Fred squeezed off an imaginary burst and pulled up and away. The Dauntless waggled its wings and continued on its way.

"Turkey Trot, this is Banger One. Interception completed. Altitude angels three, course one zero zero, speed one six zero."

"Sorry about the altitude, Banger."

"No problem, Turkey Trot. Returning to station." Fred started back in the direction he had come and realized as he did so that Higgins was no longer with him. He rubbernecked, seeing only empty sky and the rapidly retreating Dauntless. He was about to call for the exec when his voice broke in over the radio.

"Turkey Trot, this is Banger Leader. I have smoke in the cockpit. Request immediate clearance for landing.

"Banger Leader, estimate your position."

"Quadrant One, dropping through angels six at this time. I will make a right turn onto final approach."

"Roger, Banger Leader, you have a clear deck. Bring her on in."

"Thank you, Turkey Trot." Higgins used a calm, everyday voice, as if a fire in the cockpit were a common occurrence. Fred pushed over to get below the scattered small clouds blocking his view of the task force and tried to find Higgins' aircraft. Five miles away, the ships of the force turned in unison, their white wakes more visible than their gray hulls.

"Banger One Three, you are now Banger One. Remain on station."

"Roger, Turkey Trot." Fred looked once more at the force, satisfied that he could find it again without trouble. The ships were already straightening out their turns and steadying on a new course, obviously into the wind, to allow the exec to land. Fred climbed back to ten thousand feet, passing through the milky gray interior of a cloud before emerging into dazzling sunshine above. He waited. Checked his instruments. Circled. Looked and caught a glimpse of *Ironsides* through the clouds. Waited some more. Heard the FDO direct the other pair of Hellcats orbiting on the other side of the force, into an interception of a returning patrol bomber. The routine workings of the task force were being carried on without incident.

"Turkey Trot, this is Banger One. Did Banger Leader make it back all right?"

"Wait one, Banger One." Fred promised himself to find out who the FDO was so that he could see what kind of man could be callous enough to ignore a potentially fatal situation in one of the fighters he was directing. "Banger One, that's affirmative on your last. Returning to base course and speed at this time."

"Turkey Trot, will Banger Leader be replaced?"

"Wait one, Banger One." This guy, thought Fred, must be sitting in a black hole with only his radarscope, a grease pencil, and a radio mike. He doesn't know a goddamn thing about anything.

"Banger One, that's a negative on your last. Remain on station until normal relief arrives." Fred checked his panel clock and saw that that was half an hour away. He yawned and tried to get comfortable in the cramped cockpit. He began daydreaming about the skipper.

Fred had gone back to the deck edge elevator the following night and waited to see if the skipper would show up, but he hadn't. He had gone to him every chance he got during the day, but the skipper was always talking with the Corsair pilots or the Exec or the Air Group Commander or a crew chief or another pilot with more important business. Fred watched him closely, though, admiring the way he talked, made decisions, carried himself with an unhurried sureness. He makes me look like a bumbling twelve-year-old, Fred thought, and that's when he's on the ground. God knows what he can do in the air.... Fred imagined for a moment that they were in the heat of combat, and he was shooting a murderous Zeke off the skipper's tail, fending off others trying to finish off his damaged Hellcat, protecting him on the way back to the carrier, and being acclaimed a hero and saying, Geez, Skipper, it was nothing, while Jack Hardigan shook his hand, put his arm around his shoulder, held him—

"Banger One, vector two three zero, angels five, bogey not showing IFF."

"Roger, Turkey Trot."

Another Dauntless was returning from an extended sub patrol. Fred turned to the right and increased power, gaining altitude to intercept from above.

"Banger Two, unidentified aircraft approaching home base. Vector two seven zero, angels five. Assume quadrant one position and assist in interception."

"Turkey Trot, Banger Two, Roger."

What is this? thought Fred. They think there's a hostile

aircraft out here? Oh, Jesus, what do I do? "Turkey Trot, Banger One. Estimate range of target."

"Ten miles and closing, Banger One. We are launching additional CAP."

They're serious, thought Fred. This can't be for real. There aren't any Japanese ships or planes this side of Hawaii....

"Banger One, bogey is losing altitude, still closing. Report on contact."

"Roger, Turkey Trot. I am charging my guns." Fred flicked the gun switches and the lights came on that told him the six heavy-caliber machine guns in the wings were armed and ready. His right index finger caressed the trigger button on the top of the stick. The circular gunsight glowed faintly in the bright sunlight. Fred looked for his target. He could feel his heart pounding and the blood rushing in his ears. He pulled his goggles down over his eyes and pushed the stick over for additional speed. And he found the target.

"Tallyho, Turkey Trot, bogey in sight. Altitude about four thousand. I am attacking." What do I do if this isn't one of ours? Can I shoot it down?

"Identify bogey, Banger One. Please identify."

He was closer now, turning to approach from above and to the right. I just made a pass like this, he thought. It was easy. I could kill this plane in a single burst. The target grew, and Fred could make out two engines, a silver-colored body, twin tails. There were no markings on the wings.

"It isn't one of ours, Turkey Trot. Twin engine, twin tails, silver color. I see no markings, Turkey Trot. Please advise."

"Wait one, Banger One."

Oh, Jesus, Fred thought, this guy is unreal. The twin-tailed aircraft grew in the gunsight and was almost in range, dropping closer to the surface of the water. Two minutes, thought Fred, and he'll spot the force. Fred was behind him and above him. He was also very close, but the other plane seemed not to notice.

"Banger One, put a burst in the water in front and to one side, repeat, in front and to one side. We don't want to kill a friendly. Make him turn his aircraft."

"Roger, Turkey Trot." Here goes, thought Fred, for better or worse. He banked slightly to throw off his aim and squeezed the trigger.

The report of the guns was always surprising. The plane vibrated powerfully. He thanked the heavens above he wasn't in the path of these guns. The tracers reached out; between each of these tracers were dozens and dozens of hot slugs, which churned up the surface of the blue ocean, kicking wide, lopsided fountains of spray into the air. Fred released the trigger and lined up the target in the gunsight, ready to kill this time. The silver plane turned quickly to the right and continued to lose altitude. Grimly, Fred followed, reducing speed to keep from getting too close. He was already so near that he would have to make an effort to miss.

"Cease fire, Banger One, cease fire." The target began to circle to the right now and Fred followed. "Keep target under your guns, Banger One. Do not fire." Fred glanced around quickly, spotted two Hellcats circling several thousand feet above him. If this plane's a Jap, he thought, he's a goner. He looked back at the target. Curiously, it had lowered its landing gear.

"Banger One, target is an Army aircraft off course. Repeat, target is a friendly. Wait for instructions."

Fred pushed his goggles up and reached out to deactivate his guns. Then he brought his Hellcat alongside the silver plane and looked inside its cockpit. He could make out a face looking back, breaking into a smile. A hand waved. You poor stupid bastard, Fred thought. If you only knew how close I came to—

"Banger One, assume a course of three three zero and maintain altitude until notified."

"Roger, Turkey Trot."

"Banger Two, return to station."

"Roger, Turkey Trot." Fred recognized Fitzsimmons's voice and looked up in time to see the two Hellcats wheel about in formation and head for the task force. And Fred escorted the errant Army plane out of the area, climbing to a higher altitude only when they were safely out of sight of the ships. When he returned, he found that two more fighters had taken over his CAP station. He was taken aboard where everyone pounded him on the back and asked him questions and admired his sure hand in the air. Everyone except the skipper.

"Come on, fella, tell us how you did it. Did the bastard try to get away?"

It's the story of my life since joining the Navy, thought Fred. A dozen sweating men packed into an oversized closet, all smoking to beat hell. The hairy-necked ensign named Duggin kept punching Fred in the ribs with his elbow.

"Hell, if that was me up there, I'da shot first and asked questions later."

"I hear there was a broad in the copilot's seat. That right, Trusty?"

"Just like a broad to get lost in the middle of nowhere."
Everyone laughed except Fred.

"I didn't see the copilot's seat," said Fred. He needed air. He
wanted to go to bed. He had the first CAP in the morning, and it
was already past ten. His problem was the location of the bull
session: his own stateroom.

Duggin lit another cigarette from the butt of his previous
one, then offered the pack to Fred. Fred refused.

"I went out with this female pilot once," said Ensign Rogers.

"Only once?" someone asked.

"I tried to hold her hand, and the next thing I knew she had
me in a full nelson. Couldn't walk for a week afterward."

"That's bullshit. There aren't any female pilots."

"Like hell there aren't. They ferry planes from the factories to
the west coast."

"You're full of shit."

"Hey, Trusty, aren't there lady pilots?"

"Yes," said Fred, "there are."

"See, dumbo, I told you so."

"Knock it off, you guys." Hughes stood up in the middle of
the compartment. "The voting for Miss Fighting Twenty has
reached a deadlock. No one can decide who has the best ass." He
held up two fold-out pages with pictures of women in bathing
suits. The first was lying on her stomach with one leg bent
playfully. The other was standing and coyly looking over her left
shoulder into the camera. Big deal, thought Fred.

"This one was submitted by the men of Division Three and
this one by Division Five," Hughes continued. "After a careful
vote the decision is all tied up, so we decided to let an impartial
outsider with considerable experience in the field pick the one
with the best ass." He held the two pinups out so Fred could see
them clearly. "Trusty, the decision is yours."

You gotta be kidding, Fred thought.

"Come on," said Duggin, "the blonde's a knockout. The
other's a bag. What do you say, Trusty?"

"Why don't you let the skipper pick?" Fred asked.

"Naw, we want you, Trusty."

Goddamn, I hate that name, he thought.

A man's head appeared in the doorway and peered through
the smoke. Fred noticed him and thought he recognized the face.

"Is Fred Trusteau in here somewhere?" the man asked. It was
Admiral Berkey.

"Attention on deck," someone said. The pilots struggled to
their feet and silence fell with choking suddenness.

"Don't get up on account of me, fellas," said the Admiral,

standing just inside the door—it was impossible to get any further in. "Just take it easy." He began to inspect the faces of the pilots as they self-consciously took their seats again. "There you are, Fred," he said at last. The other men raised their eyebrows in surprise or nudged their neighbors. Fred Trusteau was on a first-name basis with the admiral.

"Good to see you again, sir," said Fred, still standing.

"I just wanted to congratulate you on the way you handled yourself in the air this morning, Fred. It was right commendable."

"Thank you, sir," said Fred. He was very embarrassed.

"And we found out what airplane that was, too."

"Sir?"

"It was an army trainer. Not yet marked. Some hotshot Army pilot thought he could navigate to Hawaii with a general aboard. Got lost along the way and ran into us. Scared the pants off him, you did, Fred."

"I wasn't trying to, sir."

"I was in radio listening to that pilot. He was almost in tears."

"That's nice, sir."

"And someone's going to catch hell for allowing an improperly marked airplane into a combat zone." A few of the pilots laughed discreetly. "Well, I just thought you'd like to know how it all worked out." The admiral turned to go.

"I did, sir, and thanks again."

"Good night, son, and keep up the good work." The admiral left.

"Yes, sir," said Fred.

There was a moment of silence.

"I don't believe it," someone said.

"He's chummy with the goddamn brass."

"An Army general. I bet he shit in his pants."

"You're something else, Trusty."

"Sure," said Fred. He sat down heavily.

"Come on, Trusty, now you *gotta* pick the best ass."

The two pinups appeared before him again. Fred thought for a moment, trying not to look at the girls. "Put that one up first. For a week. Then put the other one up for a week. Okay?"

"That's all right with me," said Hughes.

"Why didn't we think of that?" asked Duggin.

"You have to have a brain to think of something like that, that's why."

"Did I ever tell you guys about this broad I went out with?"

said Hughes. "She had one big tit and one small one."

"You're full of shit."

"I'm not kidding. She had half a falsie on."

Fred looked at his watch and climbed to his feet.

"Where you going, Trusty?" Duggin asked.

"To take a leak. You want to come along?"

Duggin laughed. "No thanks. Maybe next time."

Fred forced his way through the crowd and into the darkened passageway. It took him five minutes to reach the deck edge elevator.

"You've got it pretty well planned out," said CAG, "but there's going to have to be a few changes."

"Changes?" asked Jack. I knew it, he thought, the son of a bitch couldn't leave well enough alone. "What kind of changes?"

"I need two aircraft a day to tow antiaircraft sleeves for the ships' guns."

"Isn't that usually handled by the Avengers?"

"Generally, yes, but they've got their hands full with the ASW patrols, and they haven't had the opportunity to train with ship targets before this. So I want to use the Hellcats."

"My men need the training, too."

"Put your experienced pilots on the duty. Let the new ones work out by themselves."

"Most of my division leaders are working with the Corsairs."

"I believe you're arguing with me, Mister Hardigan."

"No, sir, I'm not. I'm just trying to stick up for my men, that's all."

Jennings looked intently at Jack for several seconds, then turned his attention back to the overladen desk. "The flight schedule for the Corsairs isn't heavy enough. I want them in the air every day, without fail," he said.

"The crew chiefs say the main problems with the Corsairs are in maintenance and repair. They're having trouble with the tail hook assembly. They may not be able to get them into the air every day."

"Mister Hardigan, those chiefs need motivation, something *you* are supposed to supply. Why don't you get busy motivating people instead of finding excuses for not flying?"

"Sir, are you saying that I'm not making an effort to fly every day?"

"Mister Hardigan, I'm saying that you're fighting me tooth

and nail on every major operational policy for your squadron.
I'm starting to think that your attitude could use some
improvement."

Jack leaned back and tried to calm down. Rage was boiling
up inside him, and he was having a hard time controlling it.

"Very well, sir," he said. "I'll rework the training schedules as
you suggest. I'll have them ready tomorrow morning."

"No, you won't."

"Sir?"

"You'll have them ready for me tonight."

"Tonight?"

"You heard me, Mister Hardigan. This training cruise isn't
going to last forever."

Eight years of training is preventing me from punching you in
the mouth, thought Jack. He reached across the desk and picked
up the papers. "Aye, aye, sir. Will there be anything else?"

"I asked for a report on the outcome of the search for those
three pilots. Where is it?"

Please, God, thought Jack, help me make it through this day.
"Sir, we've sent the dispatches and we're awaiting the replies.
That's all I can say."

"Find out more, Mister. And find out fast. I'm tired of
waiting. Is that clear enough for you?"

"Yes, sir." Jack stood and walked from the Air Group
Commander's stateroom without looking back. He closed the
door quietly. When he reached the squadron office, he let
himself in with the key, then slammed the door as hard as he
could; some papers were dislodged from the desk that occupied
most of the little compartment. He bent to pick them up. One
was a note to him from Sweeney, the yeoman.

TO: Lt. Comdr. Hardigan
FROM: YN2 Sweeney
SUBJ: Radio Traffic/replacement pilots

Sir: Message arrived yesterday evening saying that two
     (2) replacement pilots for those lost in paperwork
     mess will arrive the day after tomorrow via highline
     during normal refueling by oiler.

     Very Respectfully,

     Sweeney.

*   *   *

Jack checked the date and saw that it read yesterday. He knew, though, that Sweeney had put it there less than an hour ago. He had been in the office earlier and had not seen it. If only he'd had it five minutes ago. Goddamn you, Sweeney. Jack folded the note and stuffed it into his pocket, then turned to the training schedules.

He needed Duane. Duane would have to know about the changes since he had helped work up the original schedules. He would also have to notify the affected pilots. Jack checked his watch. He hated to pull Duane out of the rack at this time of night, but the work had to be done. Jack straightened the desk top and left, carefully locking the door behind him.

He found Higgins' stateroom on the deck below and went in without knocking. Duane's roommate, a lieutenant who flew with the torpedo squadron, looked up from the lower bunk where he was reading a letter under a small bunk light. Duane's bunk was empty.

"Sorry to bother you," said Jack.

"It's all right," said the lieutenant. "I wasn't asleep."

"I'm looking for Mister Higgins."

"He's not here."

Brilliant, thought Jack, I figured he was in the bottom drawer. "Any idea where he is?"

"I heard he was getting into a big poker game somewhere below. I haven't seen him for a couple of hours."

"Thanks," said Jack, and left. That tears it, he thought. When you need the guy, you can't find him. He was undoubtedly somewhere in the bowels of the ship, out of sight and out of touch with the rest of humanity. Jack could look all night and not find him. He sighed and dug in his pocket for a cigarette. The pack was empty. Beyond anger now, Jack trudged back up the ladders. Without thinking, he headed topside. It took him five minutes to reach the deck edge elevator. Fred Trusteau was there.

"Well," said Jack, speaking to a dark form whose face he couldn't see. "You're getting to be a regular up here."

"I like the price of admission," said Fred. God, but it was good to have the skipper alone here in the dark.

"The lowest in town." Jack looked up and scanned the heavens. He pointed. "That's the planet Jupiter."

"Really?" said Fred, craning his neck to see where the Skipper was pointing. "How can you tell?"

"Magical powers," said Jack, "and a course in celestial navigation."

"That must have been pretty interesting."

"It was boring as hell."

The conversation spiraled down to nothing. Fred looked toward the Skipper but could barely see him.

Finally Jack spoke. "You did well today."

"That's what everyone says."

"Well?"

"Everyone can't be wrong. But it was nothing special, really."

"I get the feeling that you're not overjoyed about being in the limelight."

Fred was stopped for a second, and his hand went automatically to his pocket for a cigarette. He remembered about smoking in the open and returned the pack. "It isn't that, sir. It just seems that all these guys think about is girls and how they're going to win the war single-handedly. They're nice guys, really. I mean I like them as people and all. But you have to get away from them once in a while."

"It's pretty tough to get away by yourself on a ship," said Jack, "especially a carrier." He laughed. "Look at us. We both come up here to be alone and we keep running into each other. Before you know it, the whole squadron'll be up here with us."

"God, I hope not," said Fred.

"Me, too." Again, nothing. "How's the Diary coming along?"

"It's no problem. Half an hour a day, at the most."

"You're the only man I know who ever volunteered to write the War Diary."

"Does that make me someone special?"

"I don't know. Maybe the others just never got up the nerve to ask." Somehow, he thought, I can't picture that.

"Pardon me, sir, but somehow I just can't picture that."

He reads my thoughts, thought Jack.

They stood in silence, no longer awkward.

"Well," said Jack finally, "I've got work to do."

"I should be turning in, but it's kind of hard to sleep with twelve horny pilots shooting the breeze in your room," said Fred. Then they turned together and crossed the expanse of the elevator.

"You flying tomorrow morning?"

"First CAP."

"Okay," said Jack, as they stepped over the chain and entered the hangar, "tell you what I'm going to do." He put his arm around Fred's shoulders and pulled him closer. "I'll do a lights-out on the whole squadron."

"That'd be nice, Skipper, but—"

"Don't worry. You go in first. I'll come through in five minutes and you'll have your stateroom back."

"You're something else, Skipper," said Fred as they descended into the warm bosom of the ship.

Jack went around to all the pilots' staterooms and ordered them all to bed, breaking up the raucous games of sex and manhood that only men at war can play. He felt better when he was finished, and stayed up most of the rest of the night to finish the training schedules.

15

"Goddamn, but you wouldn't catch me flying one of those crates." Brogan leaned against the edge of the flight deck and watched as a heavy Helldiver turned ponderously into its final approach and lumbered toward the carrier. Fred leaned against the flight deck as well, to the right of Brogan, and watched the dancer-like motions of the LSO who stood several feet to his right on the very corner of the wooden deck.

"They say the tail hook doesn't hold up after a dozen or so landings," said Fred, talking loudly to overcome the rush of the wind.

"That makes every landing a thrilling adventure," said Brogan. All around them clustered the flight deck crew in their colored jerseys, waiting for the aircraft to land so they could ply their trade. The Helldiver roared into the groove, cut his engine, and sank toward the deck. The deck crew ducked as one, as the bomber struck the deck, leaving Brogan and Fred the only ones still standing.

"Why do you suppose they do that?" asked Fred, as the Helldiver caught an arresting cable and plowed to a shuddering halt.

"Beats the shit out of me," said Brogan. He turned to talk to one of the enlisted men, but they all scrambled out of the catwalk, loped across the expanse of flight deck, and dove under the tail of the Helldiver to release the hook. Brogan laughed.

"They look like termites," he said. The two men watched for several more minutes as the plane pushers took over, and the tail hook team came back to the catwalk. Brogan caught one of them by the arm and pulled him aside. Fred turned to look and saw that he was a young boy, all of maybe seventeen years.

"Hey, sailor," asked Brogan, "how come you guys don't watch the planes come in?"

"We just want to keep our haids," said the sailor, speaking with a Midwest twang that brought to mind a place hundreds of miles away from the nearest ocean. "Don't wanta end up like Randy Gillous did."

"What the hell happened to Randy Gillous?" asked Brogan.

"One of these here wires busted right outta the hole when one of you aviators came in, and I tell you, sir, it went switching round this here deck just like a great big bullwhip, and it hit Randy and broke every one of his ribs and one of his arms and almost took out his eye, too, only they won't know about that until he comes to."

"I guess that explains it," said Fred. He saw that the next Helldiver was beginning its final approach.

The sailor left Brogan to rejoin the tail hook team. All watched apprehensively as the plane came in.

"You going to duck?" asked Fred.

"And make the crewmen think we're chicken?" Brogan eyed the incoming plane and thought for a second. "Few broken ribs isn't too much to pay for being off flight duty for a few weeks."

"Speak for yourself," said Fred, and he ducked. The Helldiver roared in, the giant propeller windmilling, the pilot waggling his wings to correct his flight path. As he hit the deck and caught a wire, there was a sound above the clamor of the engine of rending metal and popping rivets, and the slender, dangling tail hook was torn out of the tail of the plane. Small, heavy chunks of metal scattered and bounded down the flight deck. The bomber raced along, weaving and skidding as the pilot tried to brake to a stop. He zoomed past the island, through desperately scattering flight deck personnel, bumped over the flattened and useless crash barrier, and plowed into the tail of the Helldiver that had just landed. The two aircraft careened around like toys. The right landing gear of the first plane collapsed, and the engine of the second ground to a smoking halt. The pilot and crewman of the second bomber scrambled from the wreck and dove for the safety of the catwalk.

"Jesus H. Christ," said Brogan.

"A thrilling adventure," said Fred. Alarm horns were

sounding now, and fire-fighting teams converged on the wrecks, dragging hoses and long, metal nozzles. White foam began to smother the two smoldering aircraft.

"Remind me to check out my tail hook the next time we fly," said Brogan.

"You bet," said Fred.

The two planes were covered with foam now. The plane pushers arrived and began to poke around cautiously between them. A blue-shirted mechanic clambered into the cockpit of the second Helldiver and exited just as quickly. The tail hook team formed a wide-spaced line across the flight deck and started gathering up the remains of the defective tail hook.

Brogan heaved an audible sigh. "Doesn't look like they're going to burn."

"Let's get out of here," said Fred. "I've seen enough for one day."

"And the nearest bar is a thousand miles thataway."

The two pilots climbed down the ladder into the hangar deck and twisted their way through the tangle of wings and tails, wheels and fuselages. On their way down the ladders to officer's country, they passed a pair of grease-covered engine room sailors and caught part of their conversation.

"Some ships have it," said one of the sailors, "and some don't."

"All this tub has," said the other, "is the fleet's share of hard fucking luck."

"Hard fucking luck?" queried Fred, when the two had disappeared above them.

"That doesn't mean a bad time with the girls," said Brogan.

"What exactly does it mean?"

"It means, my son, that the next time you get all soaped up in the shower, they cut off the water for twenty-four hours."

They reached the third deck and turned toward Brogan's stateroom. When they arrived there, they found it full of argumentative pilots.

"What the hell's a high-water casualty, anyway?" asked a young pilot from the bomber squadron.

"That's when the crapper overflows."

"You don't know shit, Charley."

"Hey, Brogan, you been on one of these boats before. What the hell's a high-water casualty?"

"It's the opposite of a low-water casualty." Brogan forced his way to the bunks opposite the door, with casual disregard for those he stepped on in the process.

"Hell, he doesn't know."

"Who's got one?" Brogan reached the bunks, grabbed an ensign by the leg and pulled him off the upper bunk, making room for himself and Fred.

"We do. Who else?"

"Who says we got a high-water casualty?" Brogan hauled Fred up beside him.

"Some engine room flunky just came by."

"Looked like he was looking for his mama."

"'Oh, dear, we have a high-water casualty.'"

Laughter filled the room.

"Will someone please tell me what a high-water casualty is?" asked Fred.

"You know what a turbine is?" said Brogan. The compartment fell into silence to hear him. "That's one of the engines. And they heat the water in the boiler and turn it into steam and shoot it into the turbine blades, and that's what turns the propeller shaft. Well, a high-water casualty is when they get too much water in the boiler and some of it goes with the steam into the turbine and tears the guts out of the turbine blades. Makes the engineers shit in their pants." Some of the pilots laughed.

"Does that mean we've lost one of the main engines?" asked Fred.

Brogan waited for silence before continuing. "That depends on how soon they catch it and shut down the boiler. If they get it before any damage is done, all they have to do is wait a couple of hours to get the boiler back on line. If they don't catch it in time, some engineering officer gets promoted to fireman recruit and the ship gets a yard period."

"Whooee doggies," said a torpedo pilot, "I could go in for a yard period stateside."

"Not a chance. If the ship has to go in for a yard period, they'll leave us in Pearl and use us for replacement pilots." Fred nearly stopped breathing as the unpleasant prospect of going back to Deal's Deadly Dealers surfaced in his mind—and the thought of losing the Skipper.

"Wouldn't bother me," said the torpedo pilot. "I've been on better ships before."

"Seems like every time you turn around, something's getting screwed over on this ship."

"You think things are bad now, wait till the day after tomorrow. We're going to launch a full deck load before sunup."

"Who says?"

"It's in the Op Plan. Called a battle problem."

Fred leaned back into the bunk, listening to the bickering pilots, and wondering what it would be like in a squadron without the skipper. The afternoon wore on; just before the evening meal, word went around that the high-water casualty had been caught in time and there was no damage to the main engines. Fred breathed a very private sigh of relief.

1 August 1943: F4U Corsair piloted by Lt. C. T. Schuster lost power on takeoff and crashed into the sea off the port bow. Lt. Schuster was uninjured and escaped from the craft in time to be picked up by destroyer U.S.S. *Hardy*. Time of the crash was 0900 hours. Mr. Schuster was returned by highline at 1600 hours.

2 August 1943: At 0530 hours Ordnanceman 3rd Class Antony D'Aquilo walked under the propeller of aircraft number 20-F-12 as engine was in the process of being started by Chief Mechanic Rickles and was killed instantly by decapitation. Petty Officer D'Aquilo had not been wearing red goggles prior to entering the unlighted hangar deck. Chief Rickles has been reprimanded for not adhering to established safety principles for starting aircraft engines.

3 August 1943: Air Group Twenty today participated in Operation Scavenger, a full-scale battle problem involving a predawn rendezvous, an attack on a simulated enemy task force, and a return to the ship. Original launch time of 0500 hours was delayed for fifteen minutes due to inclement weather. The strike force consisted of twenty (20) Hellcats of this squadron led by Lt. Comdr. Hardigan, twelve (12) SBD Dauntlesses of VB-20, and eighteen (18) TBF Avengers of VT-20.

Strike Force launch was interrupted by inclement weather after approximately one-half of the participating aircraft were launched but was resumed after twenty minutes had passed. This interruption caused a delay in rendezvous, and a number of aircraft became lost in weather and darkness. Approximately one-half of participating aircraft located the target and carried out simulated attacks. As the return route was followed, it was discovered by members of this squadron that ship course and speed had been given incorrectly prior to launch. After unsuccessfully searching for the task force, most aircraft had to resort to the use of YE homing gear. All aircraft were aboard by 1300 hours. There were no losses. Flight deck crew and air group performance in this exercise have been rated unsatisfactory by the force commander.

"Gentlemen, I think you know the reason why I've called all of you together. I am the captain of this ship and I alone am responsible for its safe and effective operation. You, as department heads and squadron commanders, are responsible to me for the compliance of your units with orders and safety regulations. I don't think I need to remind you that this training cruise will be over in a few weeks at the latest, and that this ship then will become involved in combat operations somewhere to the west of here. This worries me for one reason.

"I have here a piece of paper found on a bulletin board in the deck division's living spaces. I don't mean to imply, First Lieutenant, that your men are in any way responsible for the posting of this paper, but I think that it is indicative of the prevailing attitude aboard these days. I won't read it to you, even though the wording and construction is quite well done; the gist of this announcement is that the War Department will be issuing a campaign ribbon for members of the crew who survive this training cruise. Under different circumstances this little production might be considered humorous.

"Gentlemen, scuttlebutt has it—and I do hear the scuttlebutt even though I am the captain—scuttlebutt has it that the *Ironsides* has become a hard-luck ship. Now I don't know if any of you have ever been on a hard-luck ship before. It's even doubtful that such an animal exists. But there is one thing I want to make perfectly clear. This is my ship and while I am in command, my ship will not be a hard-luck ship. I will remind you of several important facts. One: Seventy percent of the officers aboard the *Ironsides* are reserves who have been away from sea duty for anywhere from one to ten years. Two: Sixty percent of our ensigns were civilians six months ago. Three: Seventy percent of our enlisted nonrateds have never even been to sea before. In case all this doesn't suggest something to you, gentlemen, I will explain it to you. What I am trying to say is that what we have here is an accident-producing situation like I've never seen before, and the root cause of it is inexperience. Inexperience can be remedied, gentlemen, by time, but a bad attitude is much more difficult to fight.

"Not all of our people have this bad attitude. I will call to your attention that instead of throwing up their hands and bowing to fate, some of our inexperienced crew members and

officers have been instrumental in heading off what could have
developed into major catastrophes. The high-water casualty last
week was discovered by a nonrated fireman by the name of
O'Dell. A plane pusher named Rumbago discovered the
five-hundred-pound bomb with the defective detonator and
jettisoned it without waiting for orders. Our own Ensign
Trusteau discovered the error in the ship's posit data while his
squadron was two hundred miles away in the middle of the
ocean and recomputed the ship's actual position to enable the
fighters to come back without the use of homing gear. These
men, gentlemen, can teach us all a lesson. That lesson is that we
have here the makings of a topnotch crew and air group; and all
they need is the motivation to perform in a responsible fashion.
That motivation is your job, gentlemen. Now get out there and
do it."

"Would you say the captain is pissed?" asked Boom
Bloomington as they left the wardroom and headed up the
darkened passageways for their staterooms.

"Quite possibly, yes," Jack replied.

They passed a water cooler and both stopped for a drink.
Woody Heywood found them there seconds later. "Well, fellow
skippers, the air group commander will see us in his stateroom in
fifteen minutes. Three guesses as to what he wants to discuss."

"The state of the art," said Boom. They began walking slowly
toward officer's country.

"Why don't you suggest to the air group commander that
he take over the flight testing of the Helldivers?" said Jack.

"Are you kidding? Since the crackup last week he hasn't even
mentioned the new birds. He wouldn't fly one for a million
dollars."

"Are you suggesting, sir, that CAG is a coward?" said
Woody.

"I was merely trying to prove the existence of a bad attitude
in the air group commander."

"I don't like your attitude, Mister. I want a written report on
how to improve your attitude in five minutes. You're restricted
to the ship until that report is in my hands."

"I can't do that, sir, my attitude is too bad."

"Attitudes," said Jack. "If I hear that word one more time, I'll
resign my commission and join the Merchant Marine."

"You and me both," said Boom. They walked in silence to
Boom's stateroom. "Can I interest you gentlemen in an

after-dinner drink?" Boom began spinning the dial on his desk safe.

"Why not?" said Woody. "I could use the courage for the next hour."

Boom opened the safe and took out a stack of paper cups and a bottle of Scotch. He handed the cups around and poured. He was just putting the bottle away when there was a knock on the door. Fred Trusteau opened it and entered. He was carrying the War Diary.

"There you are, sir," he said. He held out the Diary. "You asked to see the Diary today."

"Well, well, well," said Woody, "it's the squadron navigator, come to save us all from the wrath of the Almighty."

"You're the toast of the air group, Ensign," said Boom. "Would you care to join us in some liquid courage?" Fred looked around, obviously feeling out of place. His eyes settled on Jack.

"It's all right," said Jack. "Go ahead, Boom." He took the War Diary from Fred and laid it on the desk. "I'll look at this later. We've got a meeting with the air group commander in a few minutes."

Fred accepted the cup from Boom Bloomington and a shot of Scotch, held it nervously for a few seconds, raised it to the *Ironsides* salute offered by Woody, and downed it in a single gulp. "That was good," he said, "thank you."

"You're most welcome, Ensign. Keep up the good work."

"Well," said Fred. He turned to go. "Good luck with the air group commander." He nodded to Jack, went through the door, and closed it behind him.

"Nice kid," said Woody.

"Yeah," said Jack, gazing at a spot on the far bulkhead. "He's a good man." Yes, he was thinking. He is a good man, and I like him more than any of the other men in the squadron.

"Shall we go, gentlemen?" said Boom. He swept the door open to indicate the way.

"Sure," said Jack. "Might as well get it over with."

"What do you say, gents, another shot of courage?" The three squadron commanders let themselves into Boom Bloomington's stateroom and closed the door behind them.

Woody and Jack sat down silently on the edge of the bottom bunk. Woody held out his hand and said, "It might help stop the shaking."

Boom began to open the safe.

"I don't believe that man," said Jack. "He can't really mean the things he says."

"Don't worry about it, Jack. He's just a commander bucking for admiral. He honestly believes that if he shouts loud and long enough, they'll give him a carrier or a staff in Washington."

"I can't help it," said Jack. "I've never had a skipper like this one before."

"Makes you wonder how he'll do in combat." Boom passed the cups around again and quickly poured the Scotch, replaced the bottle in the safe, and locked it up.

"Prick made us miss the movie again," said Woody, checking his watch.

"The only sensible thing he did was to cancel the flight ops with the Corsairs and Helldivers."

"All I can say," said Woody, "is if he cancels my liberty when we get back to Pearl, I'm going to have a little talk with Admiral Berkey."

"I'll drink to that," said Boom, and the three tipped their cups. Jack stared into space, his brow furrowed. "You ought to get some sleep, Jack," said Boom. "I don't think you look too good."

"Hell," said Jack, "I'm all right." He finished his Scotch and crumpled the cup into his palm. The air group commander bothered him somewhat, but Fred Trusteau kept slipping into his mind and he couldn't quite shake it. The young man was like an oasis of sanity in a desert of punishing responsibility. This was a world he had looked forward to returning to, only to find out that it wasn't the same anymore. The things Fred Trusteau said made sense: the things he did made him easy to work with. Why didn't someone else volunteer to write the War Diary? Why did it happen to be he who had discovered the navigation snafu? Why couldn't a few more of his pilots be that observant?

"Mooning over your chances with Eleanor Hawkins?" asked Wood.

Jack snapped back to the present. "Eleanor Hawkins?" His voice was very serious. "The only chances with her end up in a wedding. I'm not ready for that right yet."

"That's what I say," said Boom. "When you add up what it costs to have a wife, not to mention the kids, you could save enough for a different lay every night for the rest of your life."

As he said it, Jack realized that it had been over a year since he had been to bed with a woman. Why did I think of that? he thought. How can that be important?

"I don't know about you guys," said Boom, "but I'm going to

get a little shuteye." He gathered up the three empty paper cups and dropped them into the wastebasket.

"Not a bad idea," said Woody, stretching.

Jack stood and headed for the door. "I'll see you guys in the morning," he said. But he had no intention of going to bed; his body was tired, but his mind was far too active to sleep.

After leaving Boom's stateroom, Jack went up three decks to the hangar deck and checked out the deck edge elevator. No one was there, so he climbed another level to the flight deck and began to tramp the length of the ship, leaning into the wind as he went forward and letting it push him along on the trip aft. Jack walked for over an hour, about two miles, meeting and nodding to Admiral Berkey and the force commander, but not stopping to talk because he was absorbed in his own thoughts: There was Eleanor Hawkins and the fact that he had slept alone since Midway; there was Fred Trusteau and the War Diary; and then there was the uncomfortable way the Navy had changed since he was just a do-as-I'm-told division leader on the *Hornet*. When he was exhausted and the flight deck was empty, he looked at the rising moon and decided that when they got into combat, CAG would be too busy with his own job to harass him unduly. Things will be better then, he decided, and went to bed.

16

Duane Higgins pulled his Hellcat into a wide, leisurely circle and watched the panorama of naval conflict spread out below him. In the mock engagement, the strike aircraft of the *Ironsides* main battery were closing in on a circling jeep carrier and her three escorts. The Avengers had split into three groups and were attacking from both sides and ahead. The bombers were coming down on all four ships. High overhead, Duane and the more experienced pilots had pulled away to allow the greener fighter pilots to engage the Wildcat CAP in a tumbling, sliding free-for-all. All concerned seemed to be enjoying it. It was, Duane decided, quite a good battle problem. Compared to their first attempt at a coordinated strike, this one was developing into a model of well-oiled perfection.

"Take the can on the right, Jake, we'll get the flat   "

"Rocket Two Seven to Rocket Leader."

"—pull out too high—"

"—lead angle's all wrong, Two Four   "

"—on your tail, Jimbo—"

The pilots' voices were a scrambled mishmash saying nothing of importance and depriving home base of an accurate picture of what was happening over the target. They'll get their asses chewed for this breakdown, Duane thought. But what the hell. Battle problems were flown for this reason, to let everyone see how badly things could get screwed up when fifty-odd aircraft tried to fly through the same square mile of air space. If they thought this was difficult, they should see it when the ships belong to the Japanese and are throwing up enough flak to walk on, and the Zeros are competing for the same square mile. He remembered how a similar scene had been enacted over the *Hornet* at Santa Cruz: The attacking planes had rising suns on their wings and the bombs were real, and they were falling on the ship he had to land on when his fuel ran low. He and Jack had circled nervously outside the range of the flak, watching *Hornet* disgorge a huge pall of black smoke, and then he had shot down the damaged Zero who had the guts to attack with a smoking engine. During these moments, his future had seemed chancy, very chancy indeed. Yet here he was today.

"All Banger aircraft rendezvous." It was the skipper slipping a message into a moment of relative quiet. Duane waved at Bracker, who was flying the loose wing position on him, then patted his head in the "follow me" signal. The two fighters crossed over the circling ships and headed south, looking for the main body of the squadron. Below them a flight of Avengers struggled for altitude, one by itself hovering high over the rest, circling and obviously observing. Duane knew it was the air group commander, damn his soul—a petty, disagreeable man with an undisguised dislike for any pilot who flew a Hellcat. Then he caught sight of the gnatlike, black specks of circling aircraft. He increased power to catch up. Now the short trip back to the carrier, and once again the permanent poker game could be picked up where it had been left off in its trail of broken straights and endless pots.

The poker game had begun about a day after the *Constitution* sailed from Pearl and hadn't stopped since, except for the frequent general quarters alarms and other shipboard developments that required most of the participants to leave temporarily. The players changed constantly—even Duane Higgins had to eat and sleep occasionally—but on the whole it was limited to about a dozen top-ranking chief petty officers and lieutenants, and a single lieutenant commander. Duane had recognized one of the chiefs as an enlisted cook, another as the head steward. Most of the rest were from the aircraft maintenance departments, although a wrinkled boatswainsmate was also a regular. The officers were drawn in equal numbers from the air group and the force commander's staff, except for the lieutenant commander. Conveniently enough, he worked in the disbursing office and could help out when a big winner needed to change a stack of bills into larger denominations.

None of the officers held a direct supervisory role over any of the chiefs, so the mixture of officers and enlisted men had never struck Duane as unusual. The common denominator was simply professional competence: An ensign, even if he had lots of money, would never have fit in. The location of the game, of course, varied greatly for the sake of security, although it was fast becoming universally known and achieving an almost legendary quality.

Duane recognized the circling, disorganized gaggle up ahead as Hellcats. As he and Bracker approached, it was easy to spot the Skipper and his wingman Trusteau. They were the only pair flying with any sense of direction. He tried to count the number of fighters there, but the milling about prevented it, so he settled back and waited for the skipper to head for home so they could join up. It was a simple matter. So long as they circled, forming into a squadron echelon was relatively difficult. As soon as the leading division, the skipper's, was complete and they set course for the carrier, the rest of the divisions could fall into place as necessary.

Duane relaxed but tried to stay alert. Situations like this, he knew from experience, were potentially dangerous. A sort of poststrike letdown would be gripping the newer pilots, making them careless, forgetful. Duane checked his instruments and tried to keep out of the way. His fuel indicator showed a little more than half a load remaining, plenty for the trip back. They had spent an interminable length of time over the target as the bombers set up their attacks and went in. Had it been the real thing, the attack would have been made so that the pullout would be on the course back to the carrier. There would be damaged planes that couldn't take the time to get into perfect formations, and there would be downed pilots who would be easier to find by rescue craft if they were somewhere along the return route.... I'm starting to think like a squadron commander, thought Higgins, or heaven help me, a group skipper.

The swamped radio circuit was beginning to clear now, as the excitement of the attack receded and the missing pilots found the rendezvous point. The skipper finally decided that everyone was present, and he and Trusteau straightened out and settled onto the course that would take them to Point Option, the location of the carrier. Immediately, the other divisions began to fall into place. Duane increased throttle and climbed slightly so that he and Bracker could catch up. He spotted their place in line and headed for it.

"Leader to One Three. That was pretty fancy flying back

there." It was the skipper talking to Fred Trusteau.

"Thanks, Skipper. Just doing what comes naturally."

Duane felt a twinge of animosity for Trusteau. He had flown wing on Jack Hardigan for a lot longer than the ensign, and in situations of danger the younger man couldn't possibly comprehend. He hoped Trusteau appreciated the privilege of flying wing on a veteran like the skipper. Then he realized he was yearning for the good old days of the Wildcats and the *Hornet*, when he and Jack had shared a stateroom and hit the beach together in Pearl and San Diego, Auckland and Noumea.

"Banger Leader to One Seven. Any stragglers you know about, One Seven?"

"One Seven. Hard to tell Skipper, but I didn't hear anyone in trouble."

"Roger, One Seven. Division leaders report any latecomers."

There was silence on the circuit for perhaps a minute, then Duane spoke. "See there, Banger Leader? Nary a casualty. We got this strike business down pat."

"Roger, One Seven. Keep up the good work."

Duane smiled to himself and instinctively patted the fat bulge under his flight suit, a roll of bills amounting to almost a thousand-dollars. He had trimmed eight hundred of it from the chiefs in a single evening of play; that was the night he couldn't go wrong and every hand was a winner. He hoped this cruise would wind up sometime soon now, because he was anxious to get back to Pearl and deposit the money in the bank. Courtesy dictated that he stay in the game and give the losers another crack at their money, but if he had anything to say about it, he was going to bring most of it back to Pearl with him, and put it into the savings account which already had over two thousand dollars in it. He knew it would surprise most people if they knew he had saved so much dough. He had always carried on like a carefree, big-spending bachelor. But he had learned long ago that images could be carefully and adequately constructed.

He wasn't quite sure what to do with the money. His upbringing in a houseful of brothers and sisters in financially tough times made him want to save every penny. The urgency of the war, the danger of being killed, and the raise-hell attitudes of the men he ran with made him want to blow it all on a good time. But upbringing won out and some got saved, although the fire in the cockpit he had had while on CAP had reminded him that his life was temporary and could end on very short notice.

Below them, the Pacific Ocean was its most beautiful white-flecked royal blue, occasionally spotted by the shadows of

clouds drifting above like cotton puffs through the bright
sunshine. Duane glanced around and saw that the squadron was
pulling into place quite nicely. They weren't the flawless,
all-or-nothing men who had held the line from Pearl Harbor to
Guadalcanal, but they were damn good, he thought. Good
enough to carry this war on to a successful if distant conclusion.
Duane fought back the feeling that he was just a small,
insignificant part of a much bigger process, then reluctantly gave
in to it. It was true. The war was picking up now. Dozens of new
ships crowded Pearl. Hundreds of new pilots with new aircraft
were forming into competent air groups to man those ships.
Soon, he was absolutely positive, the *Constitution* would join
those new carriers and battlewagons and sail for the enemy
somewhere in the reaches of the vast Pacific. Where will I be a
year from now? he wondered.

"Banger Leader to One Three. Any navigation snafus this
time?"

"Everything looks all right to me, Banger Leader." It was
Trusteau.

"Let's take 'em home then."

"Roger, Banger Leader."

Duane snorted to himself, annoyed that the skipper could be
so chummy with a boot ensign. Trusteau was a hotshot,
never-wrong-always-right sort of guy. He wasn't exactly the
John Wayne of the skies, but he always managed to be in the
right place at the right time and volunteered for things and got
close to the skipper in a way that was just this side of
brown-nosing.

Duane was aware that he didn't really like Fred Trusteau, but
he couldn't put his finger on the exact reason why. After all, the
Skipper had to have a wingman, and if it couldn't be Duane
Higgins, it might as well be Trusteau. Still, there was something
there that ruffled the surface of Duane's otherwise calm
temperament. He put it down to the war, and tried to forget
about it.

The flight back to *Ironsides* was uneventful, even boring. The
recovery was flawless, but the quiet feelings of accomplishment
that should have followed the completion of a near-perfect
battle problem were lost in the symphony of rumors that swept
the ship that afternoon. Scuttlebutt said that for sure the task
group was heading for Pearl, and that a combat cruise was
forthcoming. The fact that the Pacific was such a big place and
most of it was still in Japanese hands provided for a stimulating

diversity of speculation, but still it made Duane secretly glad. He had now only to last in the poker game for several more days at the most and thus would retain most of his winnings. Also, he was tired of training. Like warriors through the ages, Duane felt that his training should not be wasted. The war should be prosecuted with dispatch, if only to allow him to go home when it was over and find something to do with his savings.

"Ah," said Fred Trusteau, stepping into the squadron office, "there you are, Skipper." Jack stopped writing and looked up.

"Come in," he said, genuine warmth in his voice.

"I'm not disturbing you or anything, am I, sir?"

"Just writing a letter home. What's on your mind?"

"The War Diary. I was wondering if you had finished looking it over so I could get today's entry in." Fred closed the door to the small office and sat in the only other chair, a folding steel-tube type in front of the desk. Jack put the cap on his fountain pen and reached under the desk. He came up with the Diary.

"Finished up a little while ago. It's excellent." He handed it across to Fred. "I want to compliment you on the effort you've put into it."

"Thank you," said Fred. He stood up. "Guess I'll get to it."

"Why don't you stay awhile?" asked Jack. He leaned back and stretched. "There's no big hurry on today's entry, is there?" Fred dropped back into the folding chair and lay the Diary across his lap.

"Not a bit," he said. A tiny chill ran through him. The skipper wanted to pass the time with him.

"I suppose by now you've heard the news," said Jack.

"Yes, sir, I sure have. How long do you think we'll be in Pearl?"

"I'm willing to bet it won't be very long. They've cut short the training cruise, and I know they don't like to keep a lot of ships sitting around Pearl for months doing nothing. I'd say we sail in two, maybe three weeks from the day we get there."

"I guess this is it, then," said Fred. "I sure hope we're ready."

"We're as ready as we'll ever be." Jack thought for a moment. "Being ready, I think, is more a matter of proper attitude at this point in the game." CAG would love to hear me say that, he thought. But what does CAG know about proper attitudes? "We've got the equipment. The training. It'll all come together when we need it."

"I hope you're right, sir," said Fred. Why do we have to talk about the war? he was thinking. We'll find out how we'll do when the time comes.

"I know I'm right," said Jack, seriously. "I've been there." He pushed his chair all the way back against the bulkhead and propped his feet up on the desk. "What's your hometown?" he asked.

The question caught Fred by surprise. "I was brought up in San Jose," he said, after a pause.

"You sound like you're not sure."

"As a matter of fact, I'm not. I was adopted when I was six and went to live in San Jose. I was there the rest of my life. Until now."

"I didn't know. Your real parents, they passed away?"

Fred shrugged. "I don't know that, either. My adopted mother never wanted to talk about it. I can't even tell you where I was born. It could have been anywhere, I guess."

"I didn't mean to pry," said Jack, catching Fred's eye for a moment.

"It doesn't bother me to talk about it. It's just something you learn to live with."

"What'd your father do?" asked Jack.

Before Fred could answer, they were interrupted by the ship's address system booming into the small compartment: "The evening movie is now being shown in the wardroom."

"You want to go?" he asked.

"I've seen it," said Fred. "*Sergeant York*. Once was enough."

"I've got better things to do, too. But you were talking about your father."

"He runs a hardware store in San Jose. Wants me to take over someday."

"You were going to college, weren't you?"

He's read my jacket, thought Fred. "I was going to start at San Francisco State, but the war came along."

"You made the right choice, coming into the Navy."

"I always admired the flyboys. Landing on a carrier seemed like a fantastic thing to do. Now I'm not so sure."

The skipper laughed. He was enjoying talking to Fred. He was easy to talk with.

"Now you know my life story," Fred said. "It isn't what you'd call exciting."

"Then I won't bore you with mine."

"I'm sure it wouldn't be boring," said Fred quickly.

Jack put his hands behind his neck and looked at the overhead. "My father's a banker in Portland, Maine. My older brother is married and working at my father's bank. My older sister is married and having babies in Leeds, Ohio. And my younger brother is with the Seventh Army in Sicily."

Fred was counting up on his fingers. "Four children. A large family."

"Five," said Jack. "One died as a baby."

"To someone who grew up in a family of three, it's still quite a number."

"My mother used to whale the stuffings out of me with a birch rod. It was a right typical upbringing, I would say."

"I wonder what our mothers would have thought if they'd known that their sons would be flying airplanes around in the middle of the Pacific Ocean in 1943."

"Disappointed, no doubt. I'm sure both of them would have preferred a doctor or a lawyer."

"Or even a banker," said Fred.

"The crew's movie is now being shown on the hangar deck," said the loudspeaker.

"*Foreign Correspondent*," said Fred. "I've seen that one, too." On an impulse he pulled out a pack of cigarettes and offered one to Jack. He shook one out for himself and searched for a match. He had none.

"Wait a sec," said Jack. He opened the drawer of the desk, rummaged briefly, and came up with a chrome Zippo lighter. He lighted his cigarette, then handed the lighter to Fred. "Keep it," he said. "I've got another one just like it."

"Thank you," Fred managed to say. He looked at the lighter with a mixture of awe and wonder, thrilled that the skipper would give him something personal. On one side was the enameled insignia of an aircraft carrier and the words, "U.S.S. Hornet, CV-8." On the other side were the initials, J.E.H. Fred thought for a moment that he should return it, that something this personal probably meant a great deal to the Skipper. But it meant even more to him. He polished the initialed surface on his shirt front.

"What does the 'E' stand for?" he asked.

"Guess."

"Edward?" Jack shook his head. "Ernest?" Another shake. "Emilio?"

"Jack laughed. "Do I look Italian? It stands for Errol. As in Flynn."

"Errol," said Fred. "That's a good name." As he said it he realized that he hadn't lighted his cigarette. He did so, then tucked the lighter into his shirt pocket, and buttoned the flap.

"You'd think with a name like that, I'd be a little more dashing. Have a pencil-thin mustache, smoke cheroots."

"*Thirty Seconds Over Tokyo*," said Fred, "starring Clark Gable and Errol Hardigan."

"Not bad. Has a ring to it. Maybe after the war. . . ." Jack considered the overhead for several seconds, then suddenly dropped his feet to the floor and scooted his chair up to the desk. "If I don't finish this letter soon," he said, "I never will. There's a mail plane leaving in the morning, you know."

"Yes, sir," said Fred. "I've already got a couple of letters finished." He moved to the door, reluctant to leave. Jack was already writing, head bent over his desk, fountain pen scratching away. "Thanks for the lighter, Skipper, and have a nice evening." Fred opened the door.

"Sure," said Jack. He didn't look up. "See you in the morning."

Fred closed the door quietly and was gone. Jack looked now at the shadow on the deck under the bottom of the door. The soles of Fred Trusteau's shoes stood there for almost a minute before moving away.

He looked back at the letter to his mother and continued writing.

. . . Incidentally, I've been thinking that you'll probably see a lot more of me when all this is over. What I mean is that the Navy has been good to me up until now, but maybe it isn't completely right for me after all. It's changed a lot since 1935.

I was just talking to a young man named Fred Trusteau who grew up in San Jose, California. That's about as far from Portland, Maine, as you can get and still be in the USA. He was in college when the war came and left it all to join up. More than once now I've been glad he did. Last week on a training exercise he discovered an error in our navigational data and quite possibly saved a number of lives by preventing us from being lost. Unfortunately he isn't completely typical of the kind of man I have working for me—I could use about ten more of him. That's just another way the Navy's changed.

Write soon and keep me up to date on what Robert is

doing. He never writes, probably he's too taken up by those Sicilian women. I miss you all.

Love, Jack

When he left the skipper, Fred wasn't sure where he wanted to go; he just knew he had to be alone. He had thought before going into the office that if he got to know the skipper better; if he talked to him more that maybe, just maybe the feelings would go away and be replaced by something simpler, like friendship. But it wasn't working that way.

He loved the skipper. He would do anything for him without a second thought. But the skipper would hate him if he knew what he was thinking. Fred could never be to Jack Hardigan what Jack Hardigan was to Fred. It just couldn't happen. Fred touched the lighter through the pocket and wondered for the thousandth time how this painful, dangerous situation would work out.

17

---

12 August 1943: Made preparations for entering Pearl Harbor. All aircraft of this squadron and the air group will be brought aboard prior to arrival at Pearl Harbor, scheduled for tomorrow morning at approximately 1000 hours. They will remain aboard for the duration of the stay in port, an unspecified length of time.

At 1800 hours this date, aircraft flown by Lt. (j.g.) Heckman and Ensign Peckerly participated in an attack on a suspected enemy submarine discovered ten miles southwest of the task force. Other engaged aircraft included on SBD bomber of VB-20. Results of the attack are unknown.

Fred knocked loudly and clearly three times just below the brass plate which read "Admiral T. H. Berkey, U.S.N." From inside a muffled voice bade him enter. He opened the door and stepped through, surprised at the spaciousness of the suite. Admiral Berkey was packing folded shirts into a battered valise which lay open on a vinyl-covered couch that stretched the length of one side of the compartment.

"Admiral Berkey, sir," Fred said. He swung the door shut and waited while the Admiral pushed some shirts into the valise and turned to see who had entered.

"Ensign Frederick Trusteau," the Admiral said, turning back and continuing the packing. "Good to see you again. What's on your mind?"

"I just wanted to see you again before we anchored, sir." Fred looked through the uncovered porthole on the outside bulkhead. The green mass of land was passing by the side of ship. "I wanted to say it's been a pleasure sailing with you this cruise and I hope we do it again sometime."

"Well, son," said the admiral, stuffing one last item into the valise and slamming it closed. "I think that's right thoughtful of you. Seeing as how you're the only one who's seen fit to say good-by, come on in and sit down." He shoved the suitcase aside and indicated the couch. Fred sat down and the admiral sat beside him, putting an arm up behind Fred on the back of the couch.

"Yes, sir, that was very nice of you to come up here. Tell me what you think of this training cruise, now that it's over."

"I think it was very instructive, but I wish we could have looked better."

"I'll tell you, son, you pilots looked as good as any I've worked with, so don't you let that bother you." The admiral ran a hand over the stubble on his chin, and Fred noticed that the worried look was still in his eyes.

"What's really going to matter is how we all look in this next operation."

"The next operation," said Fred. "Everyone has his own ideas, but the truth is, no one knows anything about it."

"Well, Fred," said the admiral, looking across the room but leaning close to Fred's ear. "Can you keep a secret?"

"Yes, sir, I can."

"When we left for this training cruise, I bet you didn't even have time to say good-by to your girl friend, now did you?"

Fred smiled. "No, sir, I didn't."

"Well, I'll give you a little head start this time. You better get all the kissing and loving out of your system in about a week, 'cause after that I can't promise we won't be leaving on very short notice."

"A week, sir?" I can't believe, Fred thought, that he's actually given me the sailing date.

"And as for where we'll be going, I'm afraid I can't tell you that, but I can tell you something else."

"What would that be, sir?"

"Well, son, it seems we've got all these new ships and airplanes, and we don't really know the best way to use them. I mean, we used to operate each carrier in a task group of its own, and that was fine back when all we had was two or three. Now, Fred, now we've got so many flattops that if we did that, we'd plumb run out of destroyers and cruisers after task group number six or seven. We've got to find a way to put two or three, maybe even four carriers in each group and not have them get in each other's way when we operate. Do you follow me so far?"

"Yes, sir," said Fred seriously.

"So what we're going to do, Fred, is pick out some nice fat Jap target—not too big a target but not a small one, either—and we're going to sail out there and blast it to hell and back, and then come on home, and meanwhile we'll be fiddling around with ship formations and group strikes and all that. Should be a right interesting cruise, all things considered."

"Then, sir, the basic mission of this operation will be training."

"You're right on the ball, there, son." The admiral dropped his arm and squeezed Fred's shoulder tightly with one hand. "You know, Fred, we've got to hurry up and get this war over. I don't want to croak of old age before it's over." He laughed.

"I don't think there's much chance of that, sir," said Fred.

"I wouldn't bet on that, Fred." The admiral stood up and walked to the porthole. He looked out and said, "I guess I better be getting up to the bridge. Be setting the special sea detail in a few minutes." He turned and offered his hand to Fred and they shook.

"Thanks again, sir, and good luck."

"Good luck to you, son. You're the one who's going to need it."

Fred smiled at the friendly, worried old man. Then he went topside and watched the Hawaiian Islands—the gems of the Pacific—pass by.

Duane picked up his two hole cards and cupped them carefully in his hands. Holding them up to his face, he took in the bottom card, the Jack of hearts, then slowly slid the top card until an edge of it was visible. It was the Queen of hearts. He quickly closed the cards and slipped them under his first up card, the eight of hearts, which lay on the playing surface. His mind was racing, but his eyes and face told nothing. He had the makings of a flush at least, and a million-to-one shot on a Queen-high straight flush. He glanced around the table at the other four players and saw that they were all pushing in their one-dollar ante. He selected a bill from the top of his pile and dropped it into the pot, then pulled another and placed it there, too.

"Up a buck," he said.

The game was being played in a compartment, which someone had referred to as a workshop, several decks below the water-line. If it was a workshop, it had no tools, no workbench, and was shaped very oddly. The table was a piece of sheet aluminum balanced precariously on a bale of rags. The players sat on an assortment of small crates and stacks of life jackets. Improvisation had kept the game alive this long.

Duane watched each of the four players meet the raise. In particular, he watched the grizzled boatswainsmate chief with a "Mother" tattoo on his forearm. He was a shrewd and dangerous player. He seldom bluffed but was superb when he did. Another card slid to a stop in front of Duane. It was the eight of spades.

"Eights have it," said the dealer, and Duane pushed out three more dollars. The chief on his left suddenly flipped his cards face down, picked up his bankroll, and left the compartment without a word. The other players met the raise.

It's going to be a good hand, thought Duane. Another card arrived: the three of hearts. Duane felt like shouting for joy. One more heart, baby, he thought, one more heart. The chief next to Boats folded, and the three remaining players paid for the next card and a three-dollar raise by the lieutenant commander on Duane's right. He had a pair of Kings. Boats had a Jack, a seven, and a four. The sixth card was dealt. Duane got the five of diamonds, the chief another seven.

The lieutenant commander looked at his hole cards again and folded. "Too rich for me," he said.

"Raise ten," said Duane, thinking that it was bad poker to bet a potential but this was most likely the last hand. Anchoring was an hour away, and already he could smell land. Besides, he wanted like hell to beat the chief.

"You're on," said the chief. The money rustled into the growing pot. The last cards came out face down, and Duane bent the edge of his just enough to see it. It was the seven of hearts. The chief looked quickly at his, then ignored it.

"Ten," said Duane, counting out the bills. There were at least fifty dollars in the pot now.

"Good," said the chief, "and add about a hundred to that." The older man pulled a sheaf of bills from out of his shirt and dropped two fifties. Duane breathed in heavily and blew the air out. He didn't want to go that high. He wanted the money for his savings account. He was still ahead by about six hundred, and he wanted badly to keep it. He checked the chief's cards again, trying to figure the best he could have. A full house was likely, with all his up cards different. A flush in clubs was possible also. Outside the compartment, a loudspeaker growled to life.

"Now go to your stations all the special sea and anchor detail."

"Too bad this has to be the last hand," said the chief.

For no particular reason Duane brought the six hundred dollars from his hip pocket and put a hundred of it on the pot. The chief flipped his cards and Duane nearly choked.

"Queen-high flush," said the chief, "in clubs." He reached for the pot.

"Queen-high flush," said Duane, turning his hole cards over.

"Queen, Jack, seven," said the chief.

"Queen, Jack, eight," said Duane. He covered the stack of money and pulled it to his side of the table. The chief stood up heavily, pocketing a small pile of ones and fives in front of him.

"You play a good game," he said. "We'll have to get together again sometime."

"Count on it," said Duane. He divided the wad of money up among three of his pockets and left. When he reached the hangar deck, he blinked in the bright sunshine, then gaped at the unfamiliar sight of land slowly passing by on the starboard side. He went aft to the starboard gallery deck. Trusteau was there.

"Well, well, well," Duane said, "it sure looks good, don't it?"

"I was beginning to forget what it looks like."

"Shoot," said Higgins, "we only been gone two or three weeks."

"It was a long time for me," said Fred.

"Well, you ain't seen nothing yet," said Duane. He didn't feel like talking to Trusteau, so he started to walk away. Before he was out of hearing, though, he heard the ensign say, as if to himself: "No, I don't suppose I have."

Duane left him standing there alone and went in search of another vantage point from which to view their entry into port.

Jack Hardigan sat at the squadron office desk and considered the sudden proliferation of leave requests that the early end to the training cruise had brought on. Pulling out a line calendar for the past year—a diagram of when each member of the squadron had taken leave—he compared the requests and came up with four who had not gone in the past six months. All four wanted two weeks of leave, although he couldn't imagine what they could do for that length of time in the Hawaiian Islands. If he went, he would run out of things to do in about two days. He decided to grant them one week each—two to begin immediately and the other two in four days. On all four he wrote tersely: "Approved. Leave your address. Check in every two days. J.E.H." The rest of the requests he denied.

In the passageway he heard the tramping of feet—a team of seamen engaged in some routine activity necessary to bring the huge ship into port. The loudspeaker outside his door called for the setting of a lessened condition of watertight integrity and specified the uniform for entering port. Already the smell of the islands—that pleasant mixture of earth and vegetation so noticeable after a period at sea—was sweeping slowly through the ship. But to Jack, it wasn't an engaging aroma. It meant that they were back in port, and they were there for one reason only.

Jack was aware of the implications of the air group staying aboard. Normally, they would have been flown off to Ford Island so that the pilots could get in additional flight time. If they were kept aboard, it meant that they would be in port a very short time—perhaps two or three days—or that space on Ford Island was limited, or a combination of the two. Limited space on Ford Island could only mean an unprecedented number of carriers and air groups present in Pearl Harbor. This he could only surmise to mean impending action.

There was a noise in the passageway vaguely reminiscent of a drill instructor on parade. The door was snatched open and Commander Jennings threw the door open. Instead of coming into the office, he kept one hand on the doorknob and one foot in the corridor. Jack looked up in surprise.

"No one in this squadron goes on leave. No one. Is that clear?"

"Yes, sir."

"I will hold a general inspection of all your men in one hour. On the hangar deck. Dress khakis. Is that clear?"

"Yes, sir."

"No one goes ashore without my permission. Is that clear?"

"Aye, aye, sir. Will there be anything else?"

"See me in my quarters after the inspection." The door was slammed violently and CAG was gone.

Jack inhaled slowly and completely, held it for a moment, then allowed himself to deflate slowly. This exercise usually helped when Jennings tossed thunderbolts in his direction. He repeated the exercise, not really feeling any better. It was beginning to look as if he were destined to fight on two fronts: the Japanese when the time was appropriate, and the Air Group Commander when the time was not.

He tore up the leave requests and threw them into the wastebasket, then went looking for Duane Higgins.

Part II-A

Interim:

Pearl

18

"You just stick with me, Trusty," said Brogan. "I'll show you a good time."

Fred sighed and sipped on a scotch and water, heavy on the water. Despite the late hour and the fact that this was the fourth Honolulu bar they'd visited—each one more dingy than the last—Brogan still hadn't shown him a good time.

Schuster emerged from a door marked "Gents" near the end of the dimly lighted room and came back to the bar. "Nothing better than a good beer piss," he said, pulling on a nearly empty bottle.

Fred turned away and looked around the bar. He couldn't remember the name of it. The three pilots were the only customers.

"Another round, barkeep," said Brogan, sliding his empty glass across the bar and almost off the other side. He was clearly drunk, but not nearly as drunk as he'd been that night a month ago when he had come upon Fred sitting on the bench; he probably had no recollection of that conversation at all.

The bartender put down a dirty white towel and started to fill the order. He's the only one who looks at home in this dump, thought Fred, feeling very tired and regretting the lack of stools at the bar. The bartender brought drinks to him and Brogan and turned back for another bottle of beer. The saloon-style doors at the other end of the room swung open to admit a prostitute who looked like she'd just finished with a hard-to-satisfy customer. She stopped at the end of the bar next to the door, hefted up a heavy purse, and rummaged in it for a cigarette.

"Hiya, Trix," said the bartender. He drew her half a glass of beer and carried it down the bar.

"Thanks, James," she said. The fatigue in her voice matched her appearance. She tamped the end of the cigarette on the bar, and cautiously eyed the three pilots. The cigarette went to her lips but no one moved to light it.

"Well, James," she said, "I guess there aren't any gentlemen in the house this evening." Her hand went back to the purse and came out with a book of matches. She was about to scratch one, but Brogan beat her to it. His lighter popped a flame into the air near her face. She was slightly startled but steadied herself quickly, grabbed Brogan's hand, and pulled it up to meet the end of the cigarette. She took a puff and exhaled the smoke out of the corner of her mouth.

"Looks like there might be a few gentlemen left after all," she said.

"Would the little lady be so kind as to allow me to buy her a drink?" asked Brogan.

"Watch this," said Schuster in Fred's ear. "The master at work."

"Suppose so," said the woman to Brogan. She watched him out of the corner of her eye, holding her cigarette near her face. It dribbled a stream of smoke that disappeared into a gray layer of unmoving air just above them.

Brogan held up two fingers. "Another round, James," he said. He turned back to her and moved in close. "And what's a nice girl like you doing out so late without an escort?"

The girl rolled her eyes to look at Brogan. "I just got off work. You know. The war effort and all that."

"That's very patriotic."

"Thanks."

The drinks arrived and she lifed her glass in a toast. "Here's to the war, buddy." They clinked glasses and drank; she was still eyeing him, sizing him up.

"Now that you're off work," said Brogan, "perhaps you would like an escort home. The streets are full of undesirable characters—like soldiers."

"Watch it, buddy," said the prostitute. "My boy friend's in the Army."

"Poor choice of words. What I meant was Marines."

"Never met a Marine I didn't like. I'll tell you, buddy, the only men I ever worry about are sailors. They float around out there in them boats until a lady just isn't safe when she's alone with one. Know what I mean?"

"Harmless fun," said Brogan. "They're just kids trying to forget the miseries of war."

"Sure," she said, "and I'm the Queen of Sheba." While she talked, she flicked ashes to the floor between them, and now she dropped the cigarette, too, and ground it out with her foot.

"You still haven't answered my question, ma'am," said Brogan.

"You mean about escorting me home." She pulled a compact from her purse and checked her face.

"Yes, ma'am," said Brogan.

(Fred almost started laughing. It was truly strange to hear Brogan say, "Yes, ma'am.")

"Well," she said, putting the compact away. "There's always cab fare to consider."

"Have no fear, ma'am. I will cover all expenses. How much do you expect it to come to?"

"Twenty bucks, buddy, paid in advance."

"Goodness," said Brogan. He pulled a wallet from his pocket and considered the contents; then he held it open so she could see inside it, too. "Six, seven, eight, nine. All I've got is ten dollars, ma'am. Do you think that would be enough?"

"No," she said, with utter finality.

Brogan looked at Fred and Schuster and shrugged. Schuster leaned close to Fred again and whispered, "He'll never get the price down. It's a seller's market."

"Perhaps I could borrow a few dollars from my friends over there. What do you say, Trusty?"

Fred shrugged and nodded. He knew Brogan had a roll of bills ten times that amount in another pocket.

"Take it or leave it," said the woman, not unpleasantly. She took a sip of beer.

"Shall I call a cab?" asked Brogan

"Don't bother. I live across the street."

"You're cute," said Brogan. He slid one hand up her arm and over her shoulder and touched her on the chin. She flashed a fake smile at him and picked up her purse.

"See you later, James," she called, as she left.

Brogan hurried after her, stopping at the swinging door to motion to Fred and Schuster. "Come on," he said, "hurry up. We don't want to lose her."

Fred put down his drink and picked up his cap to follow. He

wasn't sure what he was getting into, but it was better than standing there paying for drinks he didn't want. Schuster followed.

Out in the street, they saw the girl enter a house across from the bar. She left the door open and a dim light peeked out. Brogan took Fred by the arm and hustled him across the street and up the short flight of stone steps to the door. "Come on, Trusty. I told you I was going to show you a good time."

Fred pulled to a stop. "What do you mean? There's only one girl. She's yours." Fred looked through the open door and saw a corridor with several doors, one of which was open.

"Come on," said Brogan, "you can have her first. I want to see how you last for seventeen minutes."

"You're kidding."

"Hell, no, Trusty. You'll like it. Come on."

The girl stuck her head out of the open door and yelled down the hallway: "Hurry it up, buddy. I won't wait all night."

"She's not my type," said Fred. "I like, you know, younger women. Maybe next time."

"You're sure?"

"Absolutely. Go ahead. She's waiting."

Brogan glanced down the hall and squeezed his crotch with one hand. "I'd sure hate to let it go to waste," he said. Grasping Fred's neck with his free hand, he added: "You're all right," and headed down the hall. He had his coat off before he reached the door to the girl's room.

Almost sighing with relief, Fred turned around and climbed down the steps. Schuster was waiting for him and they headed back toward the bar.

"He's kind of wild," said Schuster.

"Yeah," said Fred. He didn't feel completely at ease with Schuster. The man talked little and never said anything of importance. When they reached the door to the little bar, it shut in their faces, and a sign that said "closed" appeared in the window.

"I was thinking about heading back to the ship anyway," said Schuster.

"Okay," said Fred. "But I think one of us should wait for Brogan. He won't be very long." Schuster followed Fred across the street, and Fred lowered himself gratefully to the steps of the apartment house. He took out a cigarette.

"I'll keep you company. Don't feel like walking back alone anyway," Schuster said, sitting next to Fred. He took out a

cigarette also and accepted a light from Fred. Fred was careful
not to let Schuster see the initials. He wasn't sure what Schuster
would think, but he didn't want anyone to know. It was a part of
the Skipper that belonged to him, and he wasn't about to share it
with anyone.

The dark city hovered around them. There were no cars on
the street; no people strolled past them. Out of boredom Fred
had to talk to Schuster, and out of boredom Schuster had to talk
to Fred. They waited for an hour, speaking only in short
sentences and grunts. When Brogan came out, sloppily dressed
but happy, he had an almost-full pint bottle of bourbon with
him.

Without consulting either of the other two men, Fred led
Brogan away from the bars, toward downtown, where they
caught a bus to the naval station, where they caught another bus
to the fleet landing, where they caught a liberty boat to the
Constitution. And had a very unpleasant adventure.

"I'm an old cowhand," sang Brogan, not very musically,
"from the Rio Grande."

Over a dozen sailors in various stages of drunkenness sat in
the liberty boat with them. They all were wearing dirty white
uniforms and held their hats in their hands or pushed far back
onto their heads. The boat moved past the darkened hulks of
ships at anchor as if it were a commuter bus, the coxswain
calling out the names of ships he was approaching to see if he
had any passengers for it. Fred was thinking that it was a very
logical arrangement, this harbor-wide liberty boat system; it was
much better than every ship running its own boats and cluttering
up the harbor.

"Just bury me...on the lone prairie." Brogan was getting
less and less musical. He'd absorbed a prodigious amount of
liquor that evening, finishing off the pint of bourbon only
minutes earlier and splashing the empty bottle into the dark
waters of Pearl Harbor. Fred was surprised Brogan could talk,
or sing, at all. Schuster sat on the other side of Brogan and
appeared to be nodding off.

"That prick," said Brogan. "That motherfuckin' prick. Can
you imagine that asshole giving us a dress inspection before
letting the guys go?"

"You don't mean the skipper?" said Fred.

"Shit," said Brogan. "Skipper's an all-right guy. Wasn't him
that pulled that shit on us. It was that prick of an air group

commander." He spoke loudly, and several of the sailors forward of them turned around to see who the drunken pilot was.

Brogan burst into song again.

"Out. On the tumblin' tumbleweed." Brogan was one of those painfully strong men whose bodies keep going when their minds are totally gone. Fred almost felt sorry for him.

"*Constitution*," said the coxswain. "Anyone for the *Constitution*?"

The ship towered over them, and an accommodation ladder with a lower platform came alongside the liberty boat. Fred stood up. "That's us," he said. He reached down and tried to pull Brogan to his feet, succeeding only when Schuster lent a hand. Together the two men got Brogan onto the platform. The liberty boat throbbed away into the night.

"Happy sailing," said Brogan, and he tried to wave at the disappearing launch.

"We gotta clean you up," said Fred. He glanced up the awesome length of the accommodation ladder and saw an officer in dress whites standing at the top. Fred pushed Brogan upright, buttoned his uniform coat, and straightened his cap. The necktie was looped around his neck, untied. Fred wasn't sure how to tie a necktie when he was drunk and the tie was on someone else. In any case, they had stood at the bottom of the ladder long enough. "Come on," he said, and the three of them started up the ladder.

It was a long, harrowing trip. The steps were slippery and spaced close together; a single low handrail separated them from a fall which would have been nearly a hundred feet when they neared the top. With Brogan unable to find the steps and the ladder only wide enough for two, they barely managed to reach the quarter-deck at all.

Fred would remember best the Officer of the Deck's jaw. It was big and square, much like the jaws of comic book heroes. Since the man stood over six feet tall, Fred was at eye level with that strong jaw. It was impossible to ignore.

"You are out of uniform," said the OOD, who was a full lieutenant. His voice was not pleasant.

"Permission to come aboard," gurgled Brogan. He was seeing nothing, feeling less.

"He's had a pretty rough time," said Fred, saluting as best he could with Brogan hanging all over him. "We'd like to get him below."

"If I'd wanted to speak to you, Mister," said the OOD, "I

would have addressed you. I was talking to you." He looked into Brogan's face with glinting eyes.

"Permission to come aboard," answered Brogan.

"You will not come aboard the *Constitution* until you are in proper uniform."

"Hey," said Schuster, who was also a full lieutenant. He came up beside Brogan and helped to steady him. "We don't need a hard time," he said. "We just want to get him below where he belongs."

The OOD snapped his fingers and two Marines in dress uniform appeared magically behind him. They were wearing side arms and nightsticks. "The quarter-deck of this ship will not be degraded by the presence of drunks," he said.

"You gotta be kidding," said Schuster.

"Identify yourself," said the OOD. His voice was becoming harder and harder.

"Shit," said Brogan. He broke away from Fred's grasp and began to walk across the quarter-deck.

"Restrain that man," said the OOD, and the two Marines blocked Brogan's way. "These three officers are on report for improper conduct. Now tell me who you are."

"Motherfucker," said Brogan. He struggled away from the two Marines and fell on the OOD.

The scuffle lasted for a grand total of about five seconds, ending just as Brogan took a swing at the OOD and hit Fred instead. Then suddenly all three were up against the bulkhead, with Brogan being held up by the two Marines and a burly petty officer, all with drawn nightsticks. Fred felt something wet on his upper lip. His nose was bleeding profusely.

"They're with the fighter squadron," Fred heard someone say; then he heard the OOD send a messenger to find the squadron commander. He was so enraged that he knew he would try his best to break the OOD's nose if he ever caught him alone. Or his ridiculous comic book jaw.

Within ten minutes the skipper had arrived on the quarterdeck. Then Fred wished he were somewhere else—or dead. He had never felt so ashamed.

The skipper talked for a few minutes with the OOD. It was obvious that he had been in bed when the messenger found him; he was not wearing a tie and his hair was still slightly tousled from sleep. Then, leaving the OOD, the skipper came over to the three pilots and looked them over. He stopped in front of Fred first. "You all right?" he asked. His voice revealed nothing.

"Yes, sir," said Fred. "Just a little nosebleed."

Jack glanced briefly at the other two pilots. Brogan was quiet now, standing on his own. Jack turned to go. "You three are restricted to your staterooms until tomorrow morning. Be at the squadron office at 0700." And he left.

Fred looked once at the OOD, who was standing stiffly at the head of the ladder, long glass under his arm, white-gloved hands clasped behind his back. "You son of a bitch," Fred said quietly. Then the three pilots wove their way through the planes in the hangar deck, the ladders and pipes and labyrinthine passageways, to officer's country and their staterooms.

I wonder why he saved me for last, thought Fred. He was leaning against the bulkhead outside of the squadron office, suffering from a brutal hangover. He and Schuster had waited while the skipper talked to Brogan; then Brogan had walked out of the office without a word, and Schuster had gone in. Fred didn't feel as if he had done anything wrong, but he was still apprehensive about facing the skipper. He figured he must have looked pretty bad the night before, held at bay by the Marines and bleeding like a stuck pig. He was wondering how to get blood out of dress khakis when Schuster came out. "Could have been worse," he muttered under his breath. Then Fred entered and closed the door behind him.

"Sit down, Fred," said the skipper. He was sitting at the desk, writing on a tablet in front of him. As usual, he was using his fat fountain pen. When Fred sat down, he remembered how the skipper had given him the lighter that other time. He waited politely for the other man to speak.

"I'm not even going to ask you for your version of what happened," Jack said without looking up. He stopped writing and capped the pen. Fred wanted to speak but couldn't make his thoughts coherent. So he remained silent.

"What I find surprising is how you managed to get hooked up with those other two. If I were your father, I would tell you that they have an unwholesome influence on people like yourself."

For some reason, the reference to "father" sent a surprising, uncontrollable shiver down Fred's spine.

"But since I can't dictate what you do with your spare time, I won't lecture you on who you should keep company with. I will tell you that, despite the fact Lieutenant Brogan is a fine pilot and good officer, he doesn't at all times display the best of judgment, and he gets himself into trouble." Fred looked right into Jack's eyes while he spoke. He didn't want to show how badly he felt. The skipper continued: "I don't think you had anything to do with that scuffle last night, despite what Lieutenant Overstreet says. I have the feeling Mister Overstreet overreacted." Fred let the faintest touch of a smile cross his face. "However, regulations require that punishment be administered to all concerned. Mister Brogan, Mister Schuster, and yourself are all restricted to the ship for a period of one week, beginning today."

Fred broke his gaze and looked down at the deck. The restriction wasn't that much of a shock; he could find numerous ways in which to amuse himself aboard ship. And the skipper spent a great deal of time there, too, so it might not be so bad at all.

"Do you have anything to say about all this?"

Fred looked up. "I'm just sorry if I made the squadron look bad, sir."

The skipper returned his stare for several seconds without blinking, then smiled ruefully. "Don't worry about what the squadron looks like. In the eyes of some people aboard this ship, you were only meeting their expectations."

Fred smiled back, then stood to go. "Will there be anything else, Skipper?"

"No, I think that'll be all."

"Thank you, sir."

When Fred was gone, Jack uncapped his fountain pen and continued writing. He was working on an official reprimand for the men involved, which would be typed up by Sweeney and entered into their jackets. That bastard Overstreet had seen to that by going to the air group commander and the ship's executive officer as soon as he got off watch. Both had ordered Jack to see them before six o'clock that morning. The only real man among them had been the executive officer, who wanted everyone to forget about it after a short restriction. But Jennings had seen in the incident another chance to harass the fighter squadron and insisted that notes of reprimand go into their jackets. Jack finished the rough draft of the small note, then copied it carefully two more times, inserting one name on each. When he was finished, he clipped them together with a note of instruction and dropped them into his "Out" basket. Then he sat and thought, wondering why he had told Brogan and Schuster about the reprimand but not Fred. It was a strange oversight.

Before Sweeney came to pick up the morning's work, Jack

took the three reprimands out of the basket, removed the one for
Fred Trusteau, and dropped the other two back. He folded it in
half and inserted it in his folder marked "Hold." There would be
time later, he decided, to judge Ensign Trusteau. Plenty of time.

19

Jacks. It had to be one of the Jacks.

Fred Trusteau was alone in his stateroom, lying on his back in the upper bunk and shuffling through a deck of playing cards. He extracted all the Kings and all the Jacks and laid them out on his chest, where he could see them. It had to be a Jack, but Jacks didn't carry swords the way Kings did. Well, almost all the Kings did, anyway. The King of diamonds had a battle-axe behind his head but held out an empty hand as if he were saying, "Hi there, neighbor." For his purposes, though, maybe he could modify one of the Jacks to hold a sword, unmistakably an instrument of war. Now which Jack would it be?

A club could be construed as an instrument of war, but the Jack of clubs was all wrong. It had a rather feminine face. For the same reason, the Jack of diamonds was also out. Very well, it would be a one-eyed Jack. They had something else going for them, too: a pencil-thin mustache, like Errol Flynn. The Jack of spades was fine but was looking to the right. The only one left was the Jack of hearts, who was perfect, except for the fact that he was holding onto a ridiculous, limp-looking leaf. But the leaf could be changed to a sword and the suit might be interpreted as one of mercy, but it could also mean guts. And the guy sure had a mean look about him. Besides, by the time Fred was finished, the suit wouldn't show, and unless someone decided to take out a deck of cards the suit of hearts would remain a hidden statement on kindness in war. So be it.

Fred gathered up all the cards except his chosen one and replaced them in the pack, then checked his watch. It was almost eleven, and he hadn't even shaved yet. Such was a Sunday morning on a carrier anchored in Pearl Harbor. Holiday routine was in force and one-third of the crew was ashore. That, of course, included most of the pilots, since they could do nothing to help get the ship underway. Flight ops were out of the question with the ship at anchor and the planes aboard.

Fred stretched long and hard and rolled out of bed, dropping the five feet to the deck with practiced ease. Opening one of the three steel lockers that were shared by the six pilots in the stateroom he pulled out a shirt and a pair of trousers. He put on the trousers, buckled his belt, and stepped into his shoes; then he stood in front of the small metal sink. He studied himself briefly in the tiny mirror over the sink and was none too pleased with his appearance. Then he opened the medicine chest for his shaving goods.

Stupid slobs, he thought. All his razor blades were gone except for the one in his razor, the toothpaste tube was squeezed empty and left uncapped, and Brylcreem from a mangled tube covered everything. That was the last time he'd suggest they pool their supplies. While he searched the cabinet for the Burma Shave, the door to the stateroom opened and Jacobs entered.

"Hi, Trusty," Jacobs said, walking across the compartment and sitting on the edge of a freshly made bunk.

"Hi, Dave," said Fred, looking at Jacobs in the mirror. He wasn't all that fond of Jacobs. He was a nice kid, but he was very young. And he did such dumb things. More than dumb, thought Fred. I do dumb things; he does stupid things. He found the can of shaving lather and began to soap his face.

"Whatcha doing?" asked Jacobs.

"Shaving," said Fred. He put the plug into the drain and began to fill the sink. The tap made a noise like a split air hose, and water splattered down the front of Fred's trousers.

"You always got something funny to say," said Jacobs, laughing a little.

"What are you doing aboard this morning?" asked Fred. He cupped his hand around the tap's mouth and directed the water into the sink.

"Nothing much," said Jacobs. He leaned back into the bunk and watched Fred shave.

"I hear there's a big party at the O Club on base with all the girls provided. How come you're not there?"

"Yeah, I know. I was going to go, but I changed my mind."

"Even with girls there?" Fred trimmed a sideburn (lowered to where the skipper had his) and dragged the dull blade across his cheek. It was so worn that it hurt. He unscrewed the head of the razor, turned the blade over, and tried again. It was not much of an improvement.

"My girl was going to be there. She's probably there now," said Jacobs.

"You asked her to come, and then you decided not to?"

"Yeah."

"You stood her up?"

"It's all right. There's lots of other guys there...."

Fred thought about the skipper, who was at that party right now, maybe meeting Jacobs's girl and dancing and buying her a drink. It was not a pleasant thought, and Fred forced his mind back to Jacobs. "Why did you do that?"

"I just didn't want to see her again."

"Why?"

"Well—" Jacobs fidgeted on the bunk. "She's really a nice girl and we were, I mean I was seeing her for about a month now, she's with the USO downtown, and I couldn't get her to, uh, you know, to..."

"Go to bed with you." Fred reached his chin, where the whiskers were the toughest, and decided that it was time to take some action. He opened the chest, found one of his roommate's razors, and switched the blades. There was a noticeable improvement.

"Yeah, that. Well, you know, I sort of told her that, uh, that, uh..."

"Dave." With his face still rimmed with lather, Fred set his razor down on the edge of the sink and turned to face the other pilot. "Dave. Did you tell her that you would marry her if she went to bed with you?" Jacobs almost started squirming. Fred didn't really care what Dave Jacobs told his girl friend. Their affairs didn't interest him in the least. But he did like to see Jacobs squirm.

"Well, I didn't really come right out and tell her that; I mean she sort of jumped to conclusions...."

"Dave." Fred turned back to the mirror to shave his upper lip. This was the real test of a razor blade, and Fred ignored Dave Jacobs while he found another pilot's razor and switched blades again. "Dave," he said finally, "that was a goddamn rotten thing to do."

"Well, hell," said Jacobs defensively, "it wasn't my fault."

"It was still a rotten thing to do."

"You know how it is. I mean, you get sort of crazy, you'll say anything. . . ."

"Yeah," Fred lied, "I know." He finished shaving, rinsed the razor, and pulled the plug. When he tried to clean out the sink, he got more water down the front of his trousers. "Besides," he said suddenly, "you couldn't get married anyway."

"Why?"

"You have to get permission from the skipper. That's why."

"Really?" said Jacobs, the wonder of discovery in his voice. "Is that right?"

"Would I lie to you, Dave?" Fred dried his face and began to brush his teeth.

"Hey," said Dave, suddenly changing the subject, "did you really slug that prick lieutenant on the quarter-deck the other night? That was sure a—"

"No," said Fred loudly. "I didn't slug anyone."

"Was it one of the jarheads that gave you the broken nose?"

"No. I fell against the life line." He hadn't talked to Brogan since that night. He felt a twinge of guilt. "You haven't seen Brogan around, have you?"

"He's in his rack. Been there almost full time since the Skipper confined you guys. That was sure a rough thing to do."

Fred wiped the toothpaste from his chin and some shaving lather from one ear. "That's all right," he said. "We can take it."

"Geez," said Jacobs. "You guys are something else." He got up from the bunk and left the stateroom. Fred combed his oily hair, put on his shirt, and went to find Brogan.

The party at the Officer's Club had been going full steam at an early hour. It had begun at eleven with something called a Sunday brunch, a sort of breakfast-luncheon, accompanied by lots of free booze. To Jack, it was just another excuse to begin drinking early in the day. He helped himself to goodly portions of food, mixed a weak screwdriver, and retired to a table on the edge of the dance floor—dancing before noon, he couldn't believe it—to watch the rest of the pilots enjoying themselves.

The girls had been there first. They had set up chairs, put out aluminum trays of steaming food, poured orange juice, and never stopped smiling. He wasn't sure just who was responsible for the party; it was CAG perhaps, with one of the other air groups, in which case the fighter pilots were lucky to be invited at all. Jack ate slowly and drank sparingly. He wasn't surprised when Higgins approached with a loaded plate and what looked like a glass of straight bourbon or scotch. He sat down beside

Jack and pulled a chair around to prop his feet up on.

"Food's not bad at all," he said.

Jack thought for a moment, then nodded in agreement.

"But some of those girls. Whoever rounded them up ought to be taken out and shot." A four-piece combo arrived now and began setting up on the small bandstand. A pair of sailors in working whites set up a microphone with a long, trailing cord. The other pilots were clustering around the buffet table or the bar and making conversation with the girls. They were probably from the USO. Who else would volunteer to host such an affair?

"Everyone says we're headed back to the 'Canal in the next few weeks," said Higgins.

"I wouldn't know," said Jack. He finished his food and leaned back with his screwdriver. And I don't really care, he thought.

"But what I hear," said Higgins, around a mouthful of toast and eggs, "if you can believe the news reports, is that they've finally wrapped it up on the 'Canal and are moving up towards Rabaul. What are those islands called, Shortlands?"

"Probably the Russells. They're closer to Guadalcanal."

"Vella Lavella. Kolombangara."

"New Georgia."

"Kolombangara. Who the hell thought up a name like that?" Duane stopped talking and watched a pair of girls slowly cross the dance floor to sit at a table near his and Jack's table. The way they walked suggested that they were tired, that they wanted to sit quietly by themselves for a little while. Duane appraised them for several moments, then turned to Jack. "What do you think? Take a chance?"

Jack didn't feel like picking up any girls. Quite honestly, all he wanted to do was head back to the ship and try to catch up on the paperwork while it was quiet and no one would bother him. But he wouldn't think of offending the Air Group Commander, whom he had just seen come through the door with a tall blonde woman.

"Would you look at that," said Higgins. "Where do you suppose he digs them up?" The tall blonde looked around hesitantly, then let Commander Jennings lead her toward the tables. She was, by any standards, a looker. Jack twisted around and looked at the two girls who had sat near them. Neither could be called beautiful, but one of them had on a sleeveless summer dress with thin straps that showed some of her breasts and a lot of her back.

"On second thought," said Jack, jutting his thumb over his

shoulder, "if you make the introductions, I'll take the brunette with the low top."

"Now you're talking," said Higgins. He picked up his drink and headed for the girls' table. Jack watched Jennings and the tall blonde—bleached, he was sure—take a table and begin eating. No one, thought Jack, particularly the honorable air group commander, will outdo Jack Hardigan.

Fred found Brogan where Jacobs said he would be: in the rack. He was facing the bulkhead and was only partly covered up. Schuster was there, too, sitting in a chair balanced perilously on two legs, reading a magazine. Neither was speaking. Schuster looked up when Fred entered.

"Hi, Trusty, how's it going?"

"Is he asleep?" asked Fred, pointing to Brogan.

"Naw," said Schuster, flipping a page, tearing it. Brogan turned over, and the single sheet that had covered the lower half of his body was pulled away. Fred saw with a mild shock that Brogan was naked. He leaned against a locker and tried not to look below Brogan's shoulders, but something about the man's hairy body sent a sharp little bolt of energy through him and made him feel tense.

"What do you want, Trusty?" Brogan asked.

"Just wanted to see how you were doing these days."

"I'm doing fine. Just fine." But his tone of voice belied his assertion.

"You recovered from the other night? You sound like you're still hung over."

"Ha," said Brogan. "Ain't never had a fucking hangover." He scratched himself in a personal spot, but Fred didn't look away from him.

"Well, what the hell're you just laying around for?" Fred asked. "The guys say you haven't been out of the rack in two days."

"I'm trying to lose weight," said Brogan. He propped himself up on one elbow. "Hey, Schute, you ugly son of a bitch, why don't you get the hell out of here. Getting so a man can't get any goddamn privacy."

Schuster tossed the magazine to the deck in a fluttering heap. "Why don't you take a flying fuck?" he said, standing up.

"I tried it once," said Brogan, "but the broad thought the stick was the dick and we nearly crashed."

Schuster laughed and ambled out of the compartment. Fred and the naked pilot were alone.

"Come over here," said Brogan. He motioned at Fred to

come up to his bunk, and when he got there, grabbed him by the back of the neck and pulled him up close. "Look," he said, "I haven't apologized to a man more than three times in my entire life, and that's the Lord's truth. But I figure I got it coming this time since I got you screwed up with me and that asshole Schute. So listen close, Trusty, 'cause I won't say it again. I'm sorry I got you into this fuckup with me. Okay?" He turned Fred loose but Fred didn't move.

"It wasn't your fault," Fred said. "It was that prick lieutenant who had it in for us."

Brogan searched Fred's face, reached out, and playfully clipped the end of his nose. "I didn't break your schnozz, did I?"

Fred felt his nose carefully. "It still works." Then, surprised: "You remember that?"

"Hell, I wasn't drunk. Two more minutes and I'd have had that jerk of an oh-oh-dee and all four of them gyrenes punched out for good."

"There were only two," said Fred.

"No shit?" Brogan looked at Fred closely again. "You're sure I didn't hurt you?"

"Don't worry about it," said Fred.

Brogan thought for a moment, not looking at him. "You're all right," he said, finally.

"You need a shave," said Fred, "and how long's it been since you brushed your teeth?"

"You think my breath's bad," said Brogan, "you should have smelled that whore's pussy. Like last week's dead fish. Whooee," he said, and rolled onto his back. "That was something fucking else."

Fred stepped back so he could see all of Brogan at the same time. The man was fascinating. "Look," he said, "you get out of the rack and get yourself put together, and I'll let you teach me the finer points of a real man's game."

"Acey-deucy?"

"No, dum-dum, old maid."

"You're on, pal." Brogan rolled out of the bunk and rummaged around in a lower drawer. Fred decided he liked Brogan better with his clothes on. "If I teach you one-quarter of what I know about the game, you'll be a rich man inside a week."

"Ready room?" asked Fred.

Brogan sat on the bunk and put on a pair of socks. "No, dum-dum, the captain's sea cabin." Brogan laughed.

It wasn't until Fred had left the stateroom and was walking alone in the passageway that he realized he had a hard-on.

❉   ❉   ❉

Taking an early liberty boat back to the *Ironsides* had been a good idea. There was no one else on it from the *Constitution*, so no one would know, at least for now, that Jack had abandoned a promising date with a good-looking girl before the sun even set. She had seemed pleased, or maybe just content, when Jack suggested they break it off early in the day; she was a nurse at the Naval Hospital working the day shift six days a week, and she said she could use the rest. Before getting into the cab he had paid for, she had written down her address on a paper napkin and given it to him, but he knew now that he probably would never see or speak to her again.

The harbor sparkled under the late afternoon sun. The gray ships that lined the quays or clustered in anchored groups looked more asleep than alive, but Jack knew that wartime manning procedures required every ship to keep at least half the crew aboard even the smallest vessel. He didn't really think the Japanese would try another sneak attack, but it was sound policy not to take any chances. Halfway back to the ship, he spotted the emerging remains of the *Oklahoma* and asked the coxswain if he could move in a little closer. The sailor obligingly swung in until they were less than fifty yards away.

"You know, sir," he said, "they say there's a couple of hundred men still inside her."

"I don't doubt it," said Jack. He was fascinated by the salvage project, with the cables and the oil boom and the winches on Ford Island, and the great rotting carcass of the stricken ship. It appeared to be upright now, but a closer look showed parts of the main deck still under water. Small, oily waves broke around twisted stanchions and lapped against the forward-most main turret. No one was working on the ugly wreck at this time, and from the harbor side it looked completely abandoned. As they passed down the ship's port side, Jack was surprised to see a small American flag flying from the sternpost. He wondered who had the unlucky duty of holding reveille and taps on the old ship. Until now, the thought that she might still be in commission had never occurred to him.

"They're going to refloat her and give her another crack at the Japs, from what I hear," said the coxswain.

"Is that right?" Jack thought that rather preposterous. If the ship had sunk as fast as they said she had—fast enough to trap hundreds of hapless men blow decks—then she undoubtedly had massive hull damage below the waterline. With all the new ships coming out now, especially the new battlewagons that made her look puny by comparison, why would the Navy spend the time and the money to patch her up? The sunken ship passed astern of them and Jack could now see the *Arizona*.

"But you know, sir, there's one that's never going to sea again," the coxswain said.

The *Arizona* had sunk on an even keel, but workers had cut away most of the wreckage above the water line. The waves now washed crazily through the middle of the upper turret's gun barrels.

"How'd she sink?" asked Jack.

"Jap bomb went right down her stack. Split her open like a sardine can. Someone said they found the ship's bell over in a canefield near Diamond Head."

Jack chuckled at how the sailor glibly passed along ridiculous information. Who cared where they found the *Arizona*'s bell? The men caught inside when she blew up sure didn't give a jolly goddamn.

"What ship are you headed for, sir?" asked the coxswain.

"*Constitution*," said Jack. He lit a cigarette.

"Pardon me, sir, but is it true what they say about the *Constitution*?"

"What do they say about her?"

"That she's a hard-luck ship."

"That's no one's business except the men who have to sail her," Jack said sharply; then he realized what he'd said was as good as saying, "Yup, she's a hard-lucker all right." The coxswain seemed to understand and didn't offer any more conversation, but as they reached the accommodation ladder for the *Constitution*, Jack turned and said: "If you want to see a hard-luck ship, steer back over to the *Arizona*. She's got the worst luck in the whole fleet." He started up the ladder.

"I'm sorry, sir," said the sailor. He changed gears quickly and the liberty boat rumbled away.

Jack climbed the ladder thinking, this isn't a hard-luck ship. It's just a hard-luck crew, and mine's the hardest.

20

"Pardon me, Skipper," said Fred. He opened the door to the skipper's stateroom and entered. Jack Hardigan had one foot up on the seat of a chair, buffing his shoe with a white rag. He looked up. "Come on in. What's on your mind?"

Fred closed the door but stood close by it. He was carrying a single, unmarked manila folder. "Have you heard the news yet, sir?"

"What news?"

"Some staff officer just came aboard with sealed orders and they canceled all liberty. Word has it we sail the day after tomorrow, in the morning."

"I guess it's about time," said Jack, tossing the rag into an open drawer. He closed the drawer with his foot, then pushed the chair back under the desk. Yes, it was about time, he thought. It had been a long time coming; finally it was here. "I guess I better get ready for a briefing with the air group commander."

"Yes, sir," said Fred. He looked at the folder hesitantly, as if debating whether to go on.

"Was there anything else?" Jack had to go to the chief's quarters to talk with Chief Carmichael about inoperable aircraft, and he didn't want to be late.

"Well, Skipper," said Fred, "I've been sitting around the last couple of days"—Jack smiled at the admission—"and I got to thinking that the squadron doesn't have an insignia. I was just wondering if anyone had made plans to work on one."

No one had ever mentioned a squadron insignia, but if they were going into combat maybe they should have one. "No," Jack said, "we've never had the opportunity. Why?"

Fred opened the manila folder and took out a piece of paper. Jack caught a glimpse of a brightly colored drawing, "I made up a drawing, just some doodling." Fred turned the piece of paper around and handed it to Jack. "I thought it might start some ideas with you or the guys."

"You think we should suggest improvements?" Jack asked, looking closely at the drawing and seeing quickly that it would be difficult to improve. The insignia was a shield, not unlike those found on coats-of-arms, divided diagonally by a single gold bar. The upper left half consisted of a four-color drawing of a face card—a Jack—brandishing a short sword. Across the top of the space, above the Jack, was the single script word: "Jack's." The lower half of the shield had the naval officer's insignia of shield, eagle, and crossed, fouled anchors. The piece was blue, yellow, and red, with black trim and a silver eagle. With little hesitation and no comparison, Jack decided it was the best squadron insignia he had ever seen. And it had his name in it.

"What made you pick the Jack of hearts?" he asked. He was amused at the surprise that showed on Fred's face.

"The mustache, I think," Fred managed to say.

"Did anyone help you on this?"

"No, sir," said Fred, still standing uneasily by the door.

"You've got a flair for it," Jack said. He couldn't take his eyes off the picture, kept discovering details not apparent from the first glance. He was trying to imagine how it would look on the nose of an aircraft just forward of the windscreen and above the wing root.

"What do you think of it?" asked Fred.

"I think we've got ourselves a squadron insignia."

"Oh, it's not that good, Skipper."

"No, it isn't," said Jack. "It's better." He took the manila folder from Fred's hands, opened it, and placed the picture inside, taking one last look before closing the folder. "It just so happens that I'm heading down to talk with Chief Carmichael right now. We'll see if he can handle the paintwork."

"But shouldn't we see if the rest of the guys like it?" asked Fred.

"Fred, have you ever tried to design anything by committee?" Jack smiled ruefully. "Can't be done. Besides," he rested one hand on the doorknob, "it's my squadron and I have final say. Case closed." He started to leave, but Fred stopped him.

"In that case, would you mind not letting on that I drew it up? I mean I don't think I deserve..."

"Sure, Fred, no problem. It'll be our secret—just between the two of us."

"Thank you, sir," said Fred, but the skipper was already gone.

Chief Carmichael obviously had mixed feelings about the new insignia. After they'd spoken, Jack went up to the squadron office and allowed himself a private chuckle. The proper amount of bullying and mild insinuation had got the job done. The drawing was a fine piece of military art and the chief knew it. But it was also a formidable challenge to the mechanics, who would begin transferring it to the individual aircraft to be finished in time for the first day of action. Jack figured professional pride would get the job accomplished. And since that was something in desperate need of reinforcement, Fred's insignia was a minor godsend.

Jack leaned back in his chair and contemplated a series of black-and-white drawings on the opposite bulkhead silhouettes of Japanese aircraft for identification training. He wondered if the enemy had new planes now, too. Most of their pilots must be new, like his were. Would they be as good as, or better than, his own? The enemy no doubt had taken some of their experienced veterans and had placed them in command of new squadrons, as Jack had been. How would they measure up?

Death. That was what it all came down to, and Jack wondered for the hundredth time how he'd ever become involved in this business. At the bottom line of a civilian enterprise was a figure representing monetary gain or loss; his bottom line was the number of men he lost or brought back. His own body, his own life, could be a part of that statistic. Jack sighed. The war was no longer the adventure it had started out being. Now it was merely depressing. Even the fear was almost gone.

He sat forward and opened the top drawer of the desk. There *was* something he could do that wasn't depressing. It was a small thing, perhaps, but it was positive, and it needed doing. He took out his "Hold" file, removed the rough copy of the reprimand for Fred Trusteau, tore it into little pieces, and dropped them into the wastebasket. He felt better immediately.

The sound-powered phone on the bulkhead by the desk

yelped in its peculiar way, and Jack picked it up. It was CAG. He was seeing all the squadron skippers in his quarters right now. Would Jack kindly consent to join them? Jack said he'd be there in three minutes and hung up. In a moment, he was locking the office door behind him and pushing through the crowded passageway. He saw his pilots gathered in front of a bulletin board, admiring a hastily rendered reproduction of the new insignia. Chief Carmichael was wasting no time. The pilots parted to let Jack through.

"Is that our insignia, Skipper?"

"It isn't the torpedo squadron's," Jack replied.

"That's pretty good. Who drew it up?"

"That's a secret. I promised not to tell."

"How many Nips you gonna nail this time, Skipper?"

"I'll leave a few for you guys."

"You think we're ready, Skipper?"

"Just bring on the Jap planes. We'll show 'em."

We'll show them, indeed.

As it became increasingly obvious that the bitter struggle for the Solomon Islands was not necessarily the shortest route to the ultimate encirclement of the Japanese homeland, so also did it become increasingly clear that the lethal power of the mobile carrier forces could not and should not be tied down to the conduct of an essentially land-oriented campaign, as the Solomons–New Guinea route led by General MacArthur would surely become.

Although it is a fact not generallly known, the training raids on enemy-held islands did not end with the raid on Wake on October, 1943, but became a precedent for the breaking in of new air groups on their way to the front area combat zones. Truly, aircraft and pilots were lost on operations that did not materially affect the outcome of the war, but the experience gained by these air groups during the raids allowed many an aviator to survive the grim aerial campaigns that marked the final year and a half of conflict.

(J.E. Hardigan, Commander, USN (ret.),
*A Setting of Many Suns: The Destruction
of the Imperial Navy* [The Naval Institute
Press, 1962], p. 201.)

Part III

Combat One:

Marcus

21

Fred Trusteau carried the War Diary under one arm and forced his way through the crowded passageways leading to the squadron office. He'd just come from the ready room, which was full of bickering pilots speculating over the upcoming mission, philosophizing about their chances of coming through it, and trying like hell to guess where it was they were going. They had been at sea for two days and still no word. Fred didn't find this unusual or unexpected. He knew they wouldn't tell the pilots, or anyone else for that matter, what the target was until they were at least halfway there. This was done in case a ship or aircraft had to return to Pearl Harbor because of breakdown. If that occurred, there might be a chance of word leaking out before the strike had actually begun. He had tried to explain it to Jacobs but was not successful. And the anxiety was beginning to affect him, too.

When he reached the office, he found his way blocked by a second-class mechanic named Peters, who was sitting in a chair facing the closed door of the office and deftly wielding a palette and a long thin paintbrush. Fred came up close behind him, bent down to examine his work. He was surprised to find a nearly completed rendition of the squadron insignia, Jack of hearts and all. "Mind if I go in?" he asked.

"Just a sec. Just a sec." Peters spoke without breaking his squinting concentration on the insignia.

"That looks real nice," said Fred, switching the Diary impatiently from one hand to another.

"Yeah, sure it does," said Peters. He dabbed at the palette and continued his work, still without looking at Fred. "You would say that. You don't have to paint the damn thing."

"Will you be very much longer?" asked Fred.

"Just a few seconds more. Just a few seconds more."

Fred bent down again and looked closer. It was really quite attractive. Peters was adding black highlights to the wings and feathers of the silver eagle. Sometime after he had produced the original drawing, the coat-of-arms shield had been broadened, and the single word had been changed from script to an Old English style and placed in the dividing bar between the Jack of hearts and Navy insignia. It was looking nice, very nice indeed.

"They look good on the planes, too," said Fred.

"They'd better. I was up forty-eight hours straight to get the goddamn things done. Whoever designed this nightmare ought to have one tattooed on his butt." Peters finished with the eagle, switched to another brush, and began to touch up the Jack's colorful uniform.

"Maybe he already does," said Fred.

"You think so?" asked Peters. He stopped painting and looked up at Fred. "Oh," he said, "I didn't know it was you, sir."

"I have to get in," said Fred distinctly. He put his hand on the doorknob to emphasize the point.

"Okay, okay," said Peters. He scooted his chair back. "Just be careful and don't touch it."

Fred opened the door, went through, and closed it behind him. On the other side of the door was a large sign reading, DO NOT OPEN THIS DOOR. He chuckled. Sweeney, the yeoman, was hunched over the typewriter, pecking away at the keys.

"What's the good word, Sweeney?" Fred asked, laying the Diary down on the edge of the desk.

"Nothing," said Sweeney. "There aren't any good words anymore."

"Sorry I asked," said Fred. Now he almost hated to ask Sweeney what he had to ask him.

"That's all right, sir," said the yeoman, punching savagely at the typewriter. "It isn't your fault."

"How do you know it isn't?" said Fred. Sweeney looked up suspiciously, and Fred said quickly, "I need a little help."

"What kind of help?"

"I need CAP rosters for the last couple of days."

"What for?"

"The War Diary," said Fred. He leaned over the typewriter to look at what the yeoman was typing and saw the words, "Ammunition Expenditure Report." Squadron leader business.

"Don't you know where to find them yet, sir?" asked Sweeney, managing to sound mortally offended.

"If I did, would I ask you?" Fred glanced down at the papers Sweeney was copying and caught a glimpse of something red several sheets down. "Every time I need them I find you've moved them somewhere else." He came around the desk where he could read better and fished with one finger for the red-marked sheet.

"Don't mess things up," said Sweeney. He pushed his chair back, opened the filing cabinet behind him, took out a single folder (without looking), slammed the drawer explosively, and tossed the folder to the empty side of the desk. He started typing again, but Fred stopped him.

"Where'd you get this?" Fred asked. He was holding a single page of blue-mimeographed type. Across the top of the page was rubber-stamped, in blood-red: "Top Secret."

"Get what?" Sweeney strained to look, half-standing, half-sitting.

"You're not supposed to have this." Fred read through the first sentences, realizing immediately what he had. Under the "Top Secret" was a little block of words: "Operation FASTFOOT, CINCPAC INST 020844-1342Z." In the upper right hand corner was another rubber-stamped block which read: "PAGE___OF___ COPY___OF___ CUST___" The first two blanks were inked in with the numbers "15," the third with "9," the fourth with "11." Beside the "CUST" blank were the initials "JEH" and the date "24 Aug 43." Fred now knew he held the fifteenth and last page of the ninth of eleven copies of a Top Secret instruction which the skipper had signed for only yesterday.

"What is it? What is it?" whined Sweeney.

"Where did you get this?" asked Fred again. "It was in these papers here."

"I got it off the skipper's desk, in his stateroom."

"Did he give them to you himself?"

"He was there when I took them, getting ready for the briefing."

"*The* briefing?"

"He's in it now. With the other two skippers and CAG and

some big shots from the *Yorktown*." Sweeney was sitting back in his chair, looking somewhat frightened. "You mean it's something important?"

Fred ignored the question and continued reading. The body of the material on the page began with paragraph 34-(c), and had the heading, "Wireless Procedures: Target Area (cont.)." The paragraph described transmission times for the submarines operating in the area. Beneath paragraph 34-(c) was paragraph 34-(d) with the title "Call Signs," and there followed a list of call signs. He found VF-20's, *Banger*, under that of the bomber squadron, *Red Rocket*. There were at least twenty more, but he didn't stop to count them.

What interested him most was the final paragraph, entitled, "Cancellation." He read it carefully.

"35-(a) Cancellation. This instruction is canceled in its entirety 2 Sep 43 2400Z. All pages of all copies in custody of Air Group Commanders and below will be visually accounted for following command level briefing 25 Aug 43 by briefing officers involved." Fred gave a low, ominous whistle. That was the briefing the Skipper was at right now. Somehow the last page of the op plan he had signed for had come unattached and found its way to the squadron office in Sweeney's work. When the briefing was finished, or maybe when it was begun, the Skipper's copy would be collected and inspected. If they found a page missing, all hell would break loose. Fred thought fast. "Get me an envelope," he said. "A big one."

"Did I do something wrong?" Sweeney asked.

"Not yet," said Fred. He tore a piece of paper from a pad and scribbled a hasty note. He snatched the envelope that Sweeney had produced from a drawer in the desk and stuffed the page and note in it.

"Where'd you say the briefing was?"

"In flag country, somewhere. The admiral's quarters, I think."

Fred was already at the door. "Don't say a thing about this," he said, "and someday you'll make first class." Fred jerked open the door, forgetting that Peters was still outside. He rushed past him, nearly bowling him over. The outstretched paintbrush left a little red smear on Fred's cloth belt, but he didn't notice it.

He found flag country in the island with remarkable ease, and found the briefing compartment just as easily—it was the door with the armed Marine standing rigidly outside. The Marine, colorful in his full-dress uniform, sprang to attention as Fred stopped in front of him.

"I'm looking for Lieutenant Commander Hardigan," said Fred, almost prancing with anxiety.

"I'm sorry, sir, but you are not cleared to go in there." The Marine stared at a spot on the far bulkhead as if Fred wasn't even there.

"I have an important message for him," said Fred. "*Really* important."

"My instructions were to let no one pass," said the Marine. Fred noticed that he wore a corporal's chevrons and that he had the look of a man who followed orders, come hell or high water. He tried another tack.

"Can you give this to him?" he asked. He held out the sealed envelope.

"I..." said the Marine. This was obviously not in his instructions. "I, uh..."

"Sure you can," said Fred. "Just step in and hand it to Lieutenant Commander Hardigan."

"I don't..."

"He's the tall man with black hair? Good-looking, sideburns?"

"I know which one..."

"Good. Just hand it to him. See? It has his name on it." Fred shoved the envelope into the marine's hands, stepped back quickly.

"Well," said the Marine.

"Come on," Fred cajoled. "It'll only take a second."

The Marine took a deep breath, released it; then, as if his mind were made up completely and there were no longer any questions, he resolutely opened the door, stepped inside, and closed it behind him.

Fred ran the back of his hand across his brow and thought, I sure hope it was in time.

"We've given a lot of thought to composite strike composition," said the lieutenant commander from CINCPAC Operations, "just as we've given a lot of thought to the hows and whys of operating four carriers in a single group, as we have here now. We don't really care how you represent this info on composite strikes to your own men, but the real reason is simply this: We wish to establish patterns and procedures in this strike that can be developed into guidelines that we can follow in later strikes, and what it boils down to is that we don't want to ever lose a lot of aircraft from any single squadron. Therefore, the bombers for each strike will be drawn from all three engaged air groups, as will the fighters. *Independence*, as specified earlier, will provide force CAP and ASW searches and not participate in any of the strikes."

Jack sat and listened and was chilled by the casual manner the briefing officer used when referring to aircraft losses. It was as though the aircraft flew themselves, unaided by human hands; it was as though men were not involved at all. The briefing officer was a paper-shuffling war technician—cold, impersonal, calculating. He didn't have to fly the planes out to the enemy-held island of Marcus.

"Approach will be made during the night of the thirtieth to the north of the island. We will then turn and launch from the northwest and be over the target by dawn. Flight time for strike aircraft should be forty-five or fifty minutes. I know the targets we've assigned are sort of general, but we feel as if we've covered all the possibilities."

Jack moved uncomfortably in his seat. He was glad the briefing was nearing its end. He was having serious misgivings about the entire affair. Marcus Island was isolated for sure, isolated deep in enemy-controlled waters. Midway Island was fifteen hundred miles to the east, Tokyo barely a thousand to the northwest. Strong enemy bases existed less than four hundred miles away in the Bonins and Marianas. This briefing told them what they had to do, but not why. The lieutenant commander had spent the greater part of the lecture explaining cruising formations for the four carriers, rotation of ASW searches, and expected weather conditions between Pearl and the target. The only picture Jack had seen of Marcus Island was vintage 1942, February to be exact, taken when Admiral Halsey hit the atoll with the single carrier *Enterprise*. Jack had seen that photograph months and months before.

"You still don't have any information as to fighter wings based there?" asked Woody Heywood. He had asked the same question before but hadn't received a satisfactory answer. Jack could see that he felt the same way he did about the operation—that they were risking four new, inexperienced carriers with their air groups on an underplanned foray far into enemy territory for one day of strikes against an island with no strategic value whatever.

"We don't know for sure. We do know that they've expended hundreds of aircraft and crews in the Solomons during the last nine months, so the isolated island garrisons may be entirely stripped."

"Or they may have strong wings."

"That's why we're sending the fighters in first."

"You lucky dog, you," said Boom Bloomington to Jack, then withstood a withering glare from Buster Jennings for his lapse of discipline at such a serious moment.

Jack flipped through his copy of the attack instruction. It typified the entire affair: It was a grand total of fifteen pages, saying less about the true nature of the strike than the briefing officer had. He'd seen longer instructions for off-loading ammunition in peacetime.

He reached the back pages of the plan. With a stomach-turning wrench, he realized that the last page was missing. He went back through it quickly page by page, remembering how he had signed every one in the presence of the briefing officer. Every one had been there then. Trying to appear calm, he checked through all his papers and his notes. He even looked surreptitiously under the table.

"Okay, gentlemen," said the lieutenant commander, "Bill here will take your copies of the instruction. Please be sure to destroy any notes you've taken after your own briefings. I guess that's it. . . ."

A grimly efficient-looking lieutenant with a crew cut and black-rimmed glasses, came to the table and took up Buster Jennings's copy. He checked its number against a list he carried on a clipboard, then flipped quickly through the pages from front to rear, checking them all. Jack felt doomed. The lieutenant finished with CAG's copy and took Woody Heywood's. Jack stacked all his notes together with the copy of the instruction and stood, prepared to look surprised when the lieutenant found the page missing.

There was a noise at the door and a Marine came in. "Lieutenant Commander Hardigan?" Jack looked up, surprised. "This is for you, sir," He handed Jack a single sealed envelope with "Lt. Comdr. Hardigan—Impt." written in ink on the outside. Jack thanked the man. Meanwhile, the lieutenant finished with Woody's copy and moved mechanically to Boom's. Jack opened the envelope, turning so that Buster Jennings, who was now talking with the briefing officer, wouldn't see. His heart leaped when he saw the page of the instruction. There was a note with it. "Skipper—Sweeney had this with him in the squadron office. Do you need it? Fred T."

What timing, thought Jack. He crumpled the note into his pants pocket and slipped the errant page to the back of the instruction. No one took any notice.

"If I may, sir?" said the crew-cut lieutenant. He took the little booklet from Jack's hands and began his check.

"You know, Lieutenant," said Jack, "you ought to get something better than staples to bind these things. That back page is coming off there."

The lieutenant squinted through his glasses at Jack. "I'll pass your suggestion along," he said.

"Milk run," said Boom loudly. "It'll be a pushover. They won't know what hit them." ·

"Just be careful not to get yourself expended," said Heywood.

"Yeah," said Jack, "that's worse than getting shot down." How could he thank Trusteau? A seventy-two hour pass? A promotion to j.g.?

"What did that Marine want, Hardigan?" CAG asked. They were leaving together, passing the Marine himself. ·

"Nothing," Jack said.

"Must have been something."

"One of my men was working on a plane report. He thought it might be important for the briefing, so he had the guard deliver it."

"You tell your man not to interrupt a closed briefing again," said Jennings officiously.

"You bet," said Jack. They passed a drinking fountain and Jack stopped to get a drink, letting CAG walk on ahead and disappear. "You bet," he said again, and went in search of Fred.

"I owe you one," said Jack to Fred as they paced the flight deck. The sun was sinking into the sea—a gaudy display of tropical splendor they'd learned to take for granted by now.

"It was nothing. Really," said Fred.

"It was everything. It saved me from a very embarrassing moment. That goddamn Sweeney. You have to watch him every second."

"I told him not to say anything about it. I don't think he will."

As they plowed through the wind toward the bow, they passed a single fighter spotted for launch on the single starboard catapult.

"I don't suppose I can count on you not to have read that page," Jack said.

"That was the first thing I did," said Fred. "I couldn't resist."

"Then I suppose you know where we're going."

"No, sir. That part wasn't in it. All I remember is the code name: Fastfoot."

"Even that's more than you should know. Until tomorrow, anyway."

They walked on in silence, reaching the very end of the flight deck, which curved smoothly, suddenly, into nothingness. Under the overhang below them was a forty-millimeter mount, sailors hunching there to escape the wind. Jack and Fred turned mechanically and began to walk back again.

"Marcus Island," said Jack. "Ever heard of it?"

"Marcus? Never."

"Minami Tori Shima. That's the Japanese name for it."

"That's where we're going?"

"Don't tell a soul."

"No, sir. I won't. I promise."

"But there's something I don't understand." Jack stopped and gazed out at the horizon. The rapidly failing light showed the boxy shapes of two more carriers, as well as battleships, cruisers, destroyers. "All this power, these carriers, these planes—and all we're going to do is raid the place. Marcus isn't even very big." Jack turned and started walking. "I mean, if we wanted to take the island, you know, land the Marines and all that, it might make some sense."

"Admiral Berkey called it a training strike."

"Admiral Berkey? When did you talk to Admiral Berkey?"

"Back before we pulled into Pearl. He even told me when we were going to sail, more or less."

Jack chuckled aloud. "You're amazing," he said.

"No," said Fred, "really it makes sense. We've got four carriers in this force alone. That's more than we've ever had in one place at the same time. And there's two or three more back in Pearl that aren't ready yet. No one seems to know how it's going to work having all these flattops in the same force. So we try them out on something small."

"You sound like a staff officer."

"And who knows? Maybe the Japs'll think we really want to take the place and send in a couple of thousand troops and a bunch of planes they could use somewhere else."

"I'll write a letter to Admiral Nimitz recommending you for flag aide."

"Would you do that?" He sounded genuinely surprised.

"You want me to?" asked Jack, enjoying Fred's naiveté.

"No, sir. Really, I like it here."

"You do, huh?"

"More than anything," Fred said intensely.

They walked on in silence for almost a minute, coming abreast of the island. Jack had been almost embarrassed by the way Fred had said, "More than anything." He angled off toward the island and belowdecks with Fred dutifully following.

"What's the movie tonight?" Jack asked.

"*The Public Enemy*. James Cagney. Good picture."

"Want to take it in?"

"Yes, sir. Sure."

"I'm treating. I'll even buy you a cup of coffee." They reached the hatchway just as a seaman arrived to close it down for the night.

"That's very generous, Skipper."

In the dark confines of the island, Jack stopped suddenly. He touched Fred on the shoulder. "Seriously," he said. "I owe you one."

Fred looked at Jack as well as he could in the darkness and shook his head. "Sure, Skipper," he said. "Whatever you say."

"Well, I say," said Jack, laughing, roughing up Fred's neck, "they don't call you Trusty for nothing." And the two men headed down and aft to the wardroom, had some coffee, and watched *The Public Enemy*, with James Cagney.

22

A red-goggled Fred Trusteau sat in the cockpit of his Hellcat and tried not to be nervous. The cavernous interior of the hangar deck stretched ahead of him almost, it seemed, into infinity. A forest of folded wingtips and unmoving propellers obstructed his view of everything except the two fighters in front of him. Their engines and his, too, produced a maelstrom of wind and noise and vibration that made thinking a difficult project.

Four Hellcats were warming up in the hangar deck this morning, the day of their first combat mission as VF-20. Four others were warming up on the flight deck above Fred. It was Fred and the skipper. Fitzsimmons and Hughes who together formed the first division of the squadron and one-half of the fighter force that *Ironsides* was due to launch for Marcus in a few minutes.

Fred shuddered slightly as he recalled how, minutes earlier, after a thorough briefing in the ready room, the eight pilots had trooped to the flight deck expecting to find their aircraft ready and waiting, only to discover that their Hellcats were still on the hangar deck because of some confusing oversight that he still didn't understand. While the minutes ticked away toward the time when they had to launch in order to be over the target at the break of dawn, deck officers and pilots, plane pushers and crew chiefs, staff officers and air officers, shouted, cursed, exchanged angry phone calls, got enraged, became confused, gave contradictory orders, lost their tempers—until now, when it was decided that the first four fighters could warm up on the hangar deck and could be sent aloft with their engines running in time for the launch.

When it came right down to it, thought Fred, they had no choice. Men's lives would depend on their timely arrival over Marcus. Recriminations would flow freely when the strike was over. Perhaps careers would suffer. So the four Hellcats warmed up on the hangar deck.

The lights above him blinked once. Fred glanced over his gauges, satisfied that everything was all right. A young mechanic appeared at the side of his cockpit, tugged at the straps, checked the buckles that held Fred in place, touched Fred's legs, shoulders, and arms like a nervous mother hurrying her son off to his first day in school. The mechanic gave a thumbs-up to someone to the side of the aircraft and hung on to the edge of the cockpit. The lights went off completely now, and Fred stripped off the goggles and handed them to the mechanic. The young man gripped Fred's shoulder in a friendly squeeze and was gone.

The Hellcat suddenly shuddered and began to move backward. Fred knew by that that they had already moved the Skipper's plane, directly behind him, to the elevator, and sent him aloft. There was a slight bump. The plane stopped moving. Fred looked up. There in the huge square hole of the elevator, he could see the brilliant, white tropical stars. The square grew larger and larger, the air fresher and cooler. Suddenly he was on the flight deck. Jack's fighter, marked by a single blue light beneath its tail, hurtled off the deck.

Shadowy shapes moved around Fred, and a single red wand popped into existence in the hands of some invisible deck officer. Taxi her forward, said the wand. Fred released his brakes and increased his throttle, rolled the Hellcat forward. Hold it there, said the wand. Fred stood on the upper portion of the rudder pedals and felt the plane hunker to a stop. Run her up, said the wand.

Fred stood on the brakes with all the strength he possessed and increased the throttle smoothly all the way to the stop, feeling the cyclonic power of the engine lift the tail into the air. Then he leaned all the way to the left and found the hooded deck lights that told him where the deck was, and where it wasn't. In that brief interval, before the wand snapped downward and he released his brakes, he had time only to think that despite the chaos of the launch, he was ready for whatever would come ready because the only man among them who had kept his temper and remained calm through it all would be flying there in front of him.

Go, said the wand, and Fred flew away into the night.

Jack checked over his left shoulder and saw Fred's Hellcat blotting out the stars, hanging off his left wing like a great amorphous shadow. He liked having Fred out there—just as if he were an old, tested friend rather than the untried rookie he was. But despite Fred's youth, despite his inexperience, he flew with a confidence in his aircraft and his abilities that was just this side of jauntiness. It was pleasing to watch, and Jack knew he was dependable, too.

Looking over his right shoulder, Jack could see the other two elements of the first division, Fitzsimmons and Hughes. But the other division taking part in the first wave was not visible against the black sky and ocean. Those fifteen harrowing minutes prior to the launch came back to Jack and he smiled. Something like that was bound to happen on the first combat mission. It always did. But they had been flexible enough to make it work, and the first division was winging its way to Marcus. Even if the rest of the sweep was not right behind him, even if they had been delayed slightly, they would still reach the target at about the same time. Then all of them would be cutting through the skies over the target at eighteen thousand feet, protecting the six Avengers that would come in low to lay incendiaries on the airstrips as illumination for the bombers from the other two carriers. Jack wondered if they had radar, and if they would have time to get fighters to their altitude. Something tickled Jack's side. His flight suit was soaked with sweat. Just like old times.

He swept his eyes over his instruments, saw nothing amiss, and focused briefly on the panel clock. Five minutes until the target. He had complete faith in the navigation of the task force. He knew if they said the island would be under at such and such a time, it would be. He stretched and rubbernecked and noticed the beginnings of dawn—the lightening around the edges of the great bowl of sky that always preceded the sunrise.

Something on the surface of the ocean caught his attention. He stared hard. The white brush marks of waves breaking on a coral atoll. It was an enemy atoll, an outpost of Japanese filled with deadly aircraft, accurate guns, and burrowing troops of the kind that had sniped at him and Duane Higgins as they huddled in foxholes on the miserable island of Guadalcanal.

Daylight comes so quickly out here, he thought. Already the

stars were magically disappearing, and the sky was turning a deep royal blue. He looked back and saw that all eight of his Hellcats were indeed there. With that reassurance he led them into their first combat experience as Fighting Twenty.

The black mass of the island of Marcus was below them. There were no enemy fighters. On land, the first of many bombs burst like flowers blooming in the clinging darkness, throwing out brilliant streamers from fiery red centers.

They made a complete circle of the island in the growing light, looking for enemy aircraft, but found none. The small group of Avengers came around again and dropped their remaining bombs on buildings and vehicles, airstrips and towers. Several raging fires were easily visible now. A heavy cloak of black smoke began to rise and drift with the light tropical breeze.

Jack went to his throat mike. "This is Banger Leader. Looks like we caught them on the ground, fellas. Let's take it on down." His own voice in his ears sounded amazingly calm and composed, and he hoped it sounded that way to his pilots. He waggled his wings once, then peeled to the right, and headed down. Fred and the second section followed in smooth coordination.

Jack watched the island grow in size and detail as he dove. From this viewpoint it looked smaller than the pictures and the maps at the briefing. Jack could take in its entire length in a single glance. Acres of vegetation had been cleared away for airstrips. Clusters of buildings squatted at the ends of the runways; a few of them now were engulfed in sweeping flames and clouds of boiling black smoke.

He searched for the Avengers, but they were nowhere to be seen. And then he found their target: a row of twin-engined aircraft, still vague in the early morning light. He adjusted his course to sweep in over them, holding his altitude to two hundred feet, remembering all too clearly how he had lost the wingman at Buka by strafing too low and getting caught in the explosion of an enemy bomb. It was better if the enemy planes were armed and gassed; then they would burn easier, and fewer passes would have to be made. Jack lined up the aircraft in his sights and checked once more for Fred. The targets filled his gunsight. He squeezed the trigger.

The pass was over in seconds and the enemy planes—they were Bettys he was sure—had indeed been armed and gassed. Jack touched his rudder pedals lightly to sweep his concentration of fifty-caliber slugs and tracers back and forth through the neat row of planes. Before they could clear the area the planes began to burn and explode. One in particular went up with a violence that caused him to duck involuntarily and pull to the right. Then it was over, and they were over the black water, which was turning dark blue. And Jack glanced over to check on Fred. But Fred wasn't there.

To Fred, the skipper seemed especially precise, confident this morning. When he went down, he did so without hesitation. And when he reached his altitude, it was as though his aircraft moved on solid, unseen rails holding it in place. Fred found himself flying the same way, as he watched morning come to the island of Marcus, which he had first heard of three days ago. It looked much the same as some of the islands in the Hawaiian chain. Those were the only real, live Pacific islands Fred had ever seen. The only difference lay in the fact that this one was inhabited by the Japanese—nefarious beings who shot at pilots in parachutes and themselves died in droves in banzai charges.

When Fred followed the Skipper down, and they began their first pass over the row of dark, twin-engined aircraft (so that's a Betty, he'd thought), he had tried to spot some Japanese. They were totally invisible, of course. There was not even any antiaircraft fire yet—at least none that he could see. As far as you could tell, this was just another training mission, with dud bombs and color-coded tracers that would tell who had shot the best when it was all over. At least it seemed that way, until the first Betty went up like a volcano and caught Fred's Hellcat in its blast.

Fred opened fire a split second after the skipper did, and he watched his tracers tear into the ground around the nose of that first Betty, throwing up chunks of material and firing showers of colorful sparks into the air. Then they were over the rest of the Bettys, and some were already starting to burn. Then a big orange-red blossom of fire and smoke enveloped his plane and hurled him upward. Before he could emerge from the other side of the black cloud, something hit his plane from beneath with a solid "thunk"; instinctively, Fred had pulled the stick to the left to escape the rest of the explosion. He knew almost instantly, though, that something was terribly wrong with his big blue fighter.

The first thing he noticed was the vibration. He'd had enough hours in the Hellcat to know its every bump and shudder, and this one he felt now was all wrong. He fought back a feeling of overwhelming fear and looked around for the rest of the division. How the hell could they disappear so fast? He continued turning to the left, feeling out the new vibration, until he was out over the water. Then he checked his instruments and found his oil pressure dropping slowly, his cylinder head temperature climbing perceptibly. He had no idea what was wrong, and throttled back to save the engine. As his air-speed dropped through 180 knots, the entire aircraft shook and shuddered like a frail building in a windstorm. He immediately gave the engine more throttle. The shudder passed.

"Oh, Jesus," Fred said out loud. Here he was, in a shaking, dying plane a mile off the beach of an enemy-held island, all by himself, with the carrier an impossible two hundred miles away.

His first thought was of the radio. "Banger One Three to Banger Leader. I am—" He stopped, realizing that he could be telling the enemy, too—that he was a lone cripple. Just then, the engine gave a heart-stopping gasp and backfired and began running rough. Fred pulled out his plotting board, found the course back to point option, and vowed to put as much distance between himself and Marcus Island as his faltering engine would allow.

Oh, Skipper, he said to himself, what did I do to deserve this break?

"Banger Leader to all Banger elements. Did anyone see him go down?"

Jack didn't need to say who it was he was talking about. The other six pilots could see the gaping hole in the formation where Fred should have been, as they formed up to head back to the *Constitution*. Jack, Fitzsimmons, and Hughes had circled the island once, while the second division strafed again, burning all the visible aircraft on the field below. But Fred hadn't shown up. He had simply vanished, so quickly that no one had seen him go.

Jack had fought back the sickening feeling rising in his throat, and they had continued their attack; they were diving on the antiaircraft guns that were now spotting the air with dirty brown explosions and showing their positions with little spits of flame in the green jungle below. When the next wave of *Essex* and *Yorktown* bombers glided in with heavy bombs, the fighters broke off the attack and formed up on the course back to the task force.

"Don't worry, Skipper," said Fitzsimmons. "He'll probably be waiting for us back at the ranch."

"Cross your fingers," said Jack.

They flew the rest of the long trip without speaking. Once, they spotted a flight of Avengers on their way to Marcus, high above them, but neither group of planes took any formal notice of the other. Several minutes before they spotted the outer destroyers of the task force, Jack thought he saw something on the surface of the water, and he went down to look. It was nothing—an illusion, a trick caused by light refraction, or a broaching fish, or Jack's imagination. When they reached the ship, they landed without fanfare and turned their aircraft over to the hustling plane pushers.

On his way down to the ready room, Jack went through the hangar deck and looked at all the Hellcats there. Fred's wasn't among them. When he reached the ready room, he went straight to the debriefing officer to ask if he had any word on Fred, even though he knew what the answer would be. "No word yet," said the officer. "But he's still got half an hour of fuel, so he could show up at any time."

"Sure," said Jack. He dropped into his reclining seat and closed his eyes. And thought: The rest of the squadron mustn't see me like this. Men die in war. It's happened before; it'll happen again. Only why did it have to be Fred? "Okay," he said aloud. He stood up, dropping his plotting board, headgear and lifejacket into the chair. "Let's get this debriefing over with. We've got another strike in two hours."

The pilots chattered away as if they were impervious to what had happened. The returning men were pressed for information on the progress and difficulty of the strike. But Jack knew they were watching him, knew they looked to him for how they should feel about losing a member of the squadron in battle. They must see that life goes on, he thought. But why did it have to be Fred?

His part of the debriefing was short. It was, after all, a simple strike without airborne opposition. Jack showed the intelligence officer where they'd strafed the Bettys, corrected the map as to the position of a radio tower, and tried to point out where the antiaircraft batteries were that they had attacked.

When he was through he felt no better. He went topside to watch the launch of *Constitution*'s second strike of eight Hellcats under Duane Higgins and twelve SBDs under Boom Bloomington. The frenetic activity on the flight deck did nothing to cheer him up, so he headed up into the island to the flag plot compartment where the progress of the strike was being monitored by the air officer and his staff. No one there had received any word from other ships as to the whereabouts of missing pilots, so he went back down to the ready room and the rest of his charged-up pilots.

Jack reached the ready room at the same time as two stewards carrying a huge platter of sandwiches and several jugs of coffee. But he didn't feel like eating. In three minutes all the food was gone, but he didn't notice.

He tried to force his mind away from the increasingly apparent fact that Fred was not coming back. He talked with the other pilots about their parts in the mission. He tried to tell himself that it was amusing how their stories got exaggerated; soon the whole Japanese air force and most of the Imperial Army began appearing on the little island of Marcus and was single-handedly destroyed. But he kept coming back to the fact that nothing this day and many days afterward would be amusing—the only man he had ever really cared about, he knew now, was missing, and probably dead.

Around noon, the teletype in the forward part of the ready room came to life and began clattering out information on the second strike. The bombers had just destroyed what looked like an ammo dump. One of them was down on the reef. Then the teletype said that a four-plane section of the *Independence* CAP had destroyed a four-engine Japanese search plane north of the force, which started the pilots talking about retaliation from Japanese subs and fleet units, which of course was only speculation and would never materialize. Finally the teletype printed one last story and fell silent. It said that Ensign Trusteau was alive and well on the *Essex*. His shot-up plane was being patched together again. And Jack almost started crying, which his pilots interpreted as meaning that the old man really cared about his pilots.

The *Constitution*'s final wave against Marcus went off as scheduled, at 1330 hours, with Jack Hardigan leading the same two divisions (with Ensign Jacobs flying wing on him) and escorting six SBDs and six Avengers. By this time, the little island was so battered that the airstrips were the only visible sign of human habitation. The aircraft didn't spend more than five minutes over the target. When they got back to the carrier, the task force was already headed back to Pearl, and the strike on Marcus passed into history.

23

Step on a crack and break your mother's back. For no particular reason, the childhood ditty popped into Fred's mind as he and the skipper trudged up and down the vast expanse of wood planks known as the flight deck. The cracks were rows of tie down cleats, recessed into strips of steel slightly lower than deck level. There were no aircraft topside this evening, perhaps in expectation of heavy weather. There were lots of other people, though, enjoying the aircraft carrier's peculiar advantage over other warships when it came to recreational room. Some ran. But Fred felt that it was the continuous hissing of the wind and the privacy it afforded that brought everyone up here as the sun sank and night lowered around them.

"I don't mind telling you," said the skipper, "that we thought for a while yesterday we had really lost you." He kept his hands in his pockets and his head down, but his voice carried clearly.

"I thought you had, too, Skipper, for a while there," said Fred. He was thinking how great it was to be back among friends, especially the skipper. The *Essex* had been the first carrier he had come to. He hadn't even looked for *Ironsides*. The two carriers were identical in their major points of construction, but the ready room, the wardroom, the people, were uncomfortably different. It was like being a kid transferred to a new school.

"I guess it just goes to show you how fast things can happen when you're over a target. One second things are all right, and the next..." The skipper didn't complete the sentence.

"On the way back I kept thinking how big this ocean is," Fred said, "and how they'd never find me. But old number thirteen just kept on running." He remembered the sweat, and the pounding heart that wouldn't quiet, as the minutes stretched into an hour, and still the hot, rough engine ran and backfired, coughed and shook, losing oil steadily. And the great waiting Pacific passed unhurriedly below him as he checked his parachute pack, first-aid kit, raft, pistol. He knew that he was making himself ready to put down in the middle of an enemy ocean but also knew that no one is ever ready for a slow death.

"Makes you feel better when you know how well they build these birds."

"Maybe I'll write them a letter when I get the chance," Fred replied.

"Do that. I'm sure they'd be glad to get it."

"I wouldn't think they get many complaints."

Jack smiled to himself as he realized the similarity of Fred's remark to the old, well-known joke about what to do when your parachute doesn't work.

"Admiral Berkey was over there," said Fred.

"Where?"

"On the *Essex*. They didn't have any spare staterooms so he got me set up with one of his staff officers."

Jack felt a stab of jealousy. Ensigns don't hobnob with admirals and they sure as hell don't—sleep with them either. Jack realized with a jolt what he'd been thinking. "That was generous of him," he said.

"He's a good person," said Fred.

An officer in shorts and T-shirt jogged past them. Fred remembered the previous night—a sleepless affair since the lieutenant commander in the rack below talked to his wife in his sleep. In the morning, he'd move around the stateroom with a very noticeable erection.

They walked with the wind at their backs, in a spot of silence that stretched into a minute, then two. Fred was inwardly reveling at this private moment with the Skipper; he was still intoxicated with the thrill of being alive to enjoy it. They were abreast of the island and virtually alone when the Skipper suddenly stopped. Fred stopped and turned to look at him. He couldn't see his face, but he felt that something was wrong.

"Are you all right, Skipper?" Fred asked involuntarily.

The words almost didn't penetrate Jack's consciousness. He was deep in a mental turmoil triggered by the ridiculous picture of Fred Trusteau sleeping with Admiral Berkey. It had been replaced in Jack's mind with the next logical step: Fred Trusteau should have been here, sleeping with Jack Hardigan. The thought that it would be a nice, pleasant thing to do was disturbing. Immediately, he tried to reject the idea. When Fred spoke, Jack found that he was standing still in the middle of the flight deck looking at the man he wanted to—sleep with. He started walking again, struggling to control his thoughts.

"I just thought of something," he said, after a moment. Fred had fallen into step beside him. They walked on in silence again.

"Must have been pretty important," said Fred, wondering what it had been.

"No," said Jack. "No, it was very unimportant." He turned abruptly and headed for the hatch in the island that Fred had entered on his first day aboard, now so many weeks ago.

Fred went after him like a perplexed little dog following his master.

They reached the rounded entrance; Jack entered first, without ceremony and without waiting for Fred to close the heavy steel door and catch up with him.

Fred caught up with him on the hangar deck. "I guess I'll be turning in, sir," said Fred.

"That's fine," said Jack. "I'll see you in the morning."

"Yes, sir," said Fred. "Good night."

The skipper's back vanished into the darkness. Fred waited for several minutes to make sure Jack had gone ahead before he started for his stateroom. He was vaguely upset; he wondered if he had said or done something to disturb the skipper. It bothered him for several hours that night before he was able to fall asleep.

TO: LT COMDR J HARDIGAN USN USS CONSTITUTION FPO SF
FROM: M HARDIGAN PORTLAND MAINE
DAD NEAR DEATH STOP MOM BAD OFF STOP PLEASE COME IF ABLE STOP

        MONTY

6 September 1943: Air Group Twenty debarked this date U.S.S. *Constitution* for Naval Air Station, Ford Island, Oahu, arriving 1300 hours without incident. Upon arrival, Lt. Comdr. Jack Hardigan, USN, Commanding Officer VF-20, was detached for emergency leave to commence immediately. Lieutenant Duane Higgins, Executive Officer, has assumed command responsibilities until further notice.

Part III-A

Interim:

Leave

24

Duane Higgins pulled hard on his scotch and soda and pondered his restless pilots gathered at the bar. His pilots. It felt good to be thinking of them that way, even though in reality they belonged to Jack Hardigan, or the Navy, or nobody. Regardless, he could divide them nicely into two mutually exclusive groups, just as they themselves were quite unconsciously—though accurately—doing right now. It was Saturday night at the Officer's Club of the Ford Island Naval Air Station. It was a natural for pilots because line officers frequented the club on the naval station across the harbor.

The first group was the hell-raisers. Brogan seemed to be the natural leader of this group. It was characterized by heavy drinking, easy brawling, and probably an abundance of venereal disease. Their idea of a good time was not complete until someone got arrested or rolled, which for them were sources of exciting, postliberty sea stories. They were big talkers, sure enough, but they usually backed up their boasts with plenty of action.

The other group was composed of big talkers, too, but it was easy to see that the similarity ended there. When a hell-raiser begged one of this group to hit this or that whorehouse, whose specialty was the oriental basket job, he would bow out with the excuse that he had a date with a very nice girl who had her own car and apartment. They would be going to dinner and a movie;

then they would go back to her apartment—for who knows what? They were usually in bed—alone—before midnight, after an evening movie with a couple of the guys, or maybe a few drinks at the O Club. Duane had seen several of them a couple of months back, coming out of a museum of Hawaiian history in downtown Honolulu when it closed at nine o'clock. Some of this second group were married and very, very sober. But then some of the hell-raisers were married, too. Membership in either group was determined by other, more subtle, distinctions.

Duane was in a quandary this Saturday night. His pilots were dividing themselves up and leaving in groups of three and four, laughing and singing, until their voices faded out of hearing in the cool tropical twilight. The problem was his temporary status as skipper. He was traditionally a hell-raiser, but out of respect for Jack Hardigan and a left-handed logic which said that skippers don't do the things hell-raisers do, he found himself marooned and alone with the meek and sober. It was, thank God, not a permanent situation. And, yes, he did know this nice girl who drove her own car and had her own apartment and for whom he had a grudging respect because she hadn't gone to bed with him yet. Maybe I'll give her a call, he thought, and see if she's free tonight. A last group of VF-20 pilots left the bar. Duane finished off his scotch and soda—his usual was straight scotch; the soda was a concession—and turned to go. In the entrance to the bar he ran into Fred Trusteau.

Fred's appearance forced Duane to reevaluate his two-group theory. He instantly concluded that this ensign didn't fit well into either group. There had been something about him the past several days that made a man uncomfortable to be around him. Duane had been unable exactly to put his finger on what it was.

"Trusty," said Higgins, as they stopped together just inside the door of the bar. Duane had made an effort since the skipper left to learn everyone's first name or nickname and to use it whenever possible, even if he hated to be personal. This was such a moment.

"Mister Higgins," said Fred, without enthusiasm. "Buy you a drink?"

Maybe that was it: Trusteau lacked his usual enthusiasm. But that was too simple. To be more precise, he carried gloom like a dark cloud over his head wherever he went.

"Pleasure," said Duane. The nice girl could wait, he decided, until he found out what was bugging the skipper's wingman.

"Scotch," said Fred to the barkeep.

"Scotch and soda," ordered Duane. A moment of silence

descended on the two men. "Well," said Duane, leaning an elbow on the bar and facing Fred, "hitting the beach tonight?"

Fred shifted his weight and lighted a cigarette. "No, don't think so." His drink arrived and he took an immediate slug, wincing slightly at the bite of the liquor.

Duane thought, I've seen more cheerful faces at a funeral. "How come?"

Duane's drink arrived, and he held it up in a short toast which Fred reluctantly returned.

"I don't know," Fred replied. "Just don't feel like doing much tonight."

"Flying too hard these days?"

"No." Fred looked down to avoid the executive officer's eyes.

"You're not going to waste one of our few precious Saturday nights, I hope?"

"Waste?" said Fred.

"Tell you what," said Higgins. He tapped Fred's arm lightly. "Let's you and me hit the beach tonight, you know, take in a few places, maybe meet a couple of young ladies..."

"Not tonight," said Fred. He finished his Scotch and signaled for another. He was thinking that Duane Higgins had never been so friendly before and wondering if he was after something. "I don't feel that hot. I think I'll hit the sack early."

"Maybe you ought to talk with the Flight Surgeon Monday morning."

"It isn't that bad, really." He's pushing me, thought Fred. Why?

"Well, look. I want my pilots in top form all the time. If you don't feel well then you ought to see the Doc. Right?"

Fred sat down his drink and faced Duane squarely. "Look, Mister Higgins, I'm not sick. I just don't feel up to hitting the beach tonight, with you or anyone else. Maybe I'm just a little let down after the mission and all, and to tell the truth I just want to be alone for a while, and Saturday night is as good a time for that as I can think of. So don't worry about me, and if you've got something lined up for tonight, go ahead and enjoy it." He tried to soften his voice a bit. "I'll be just fine." A second of silence, and then he added: "Really."

Duane knew he had just been told to get lost, in as polite a fashion as an ensign could tell a lieutenant. And he also knew that something was stewing there inside Fred's mind, something he wanted to know about. But the doors to that mind would not open for him. It didn't anger him especially—he had never been comfortable when people tried to unburden themselves to him—but who wanted a wingman with deep, dark, depressing secrets? What if the skipper didn't make it back before they sailed, and he had to take the squadron into combat? Maybe Trusteau was a psycho case about to go off the deep end, off his nut. He picked up his drink slowly. "Okay, okay. Don't get all hot about it."

"I'm not."

"I was just trying to be friendly. You know, cheer you up."

"Thanks, but I don't need cheering up."

"Okay." Duane finished his drink and slapped the top of the bar. "Well," he said, drawing himself up and straightening his shirt. "Think I'll carry on with the evening's plans."

"Have a good time, Mister Higgins."

"That I will, Ensign, that I will."

Higgins left the bar without a backward look, and Fred was alone. At last. He sighed and pushed his drink to the side, unfinished. It didn't feel good to get drunk; it only made him feel worse. He was so lonely he could hardly stand it. And there was no one to whom he could talk, pour out his feelings. He wasn't even sure that would help. It certainly wouldn't change those last three days of the Marcus cruise, when the skipper had been short to the point of rudeness with him. And now he was gone entirely, not due back for another week. Fred couldn't live with him, and he couldn't live without him. He left the bar then with no definite plans in mind, nowhere to go, nothing to do—and utterly sick to death with everything.

The September countryside around Portland was beautifully foreign to Jack. The evenings were beginning to chill now, although autumn was still a month away, and some of the trees had begun to change. It was so different from the grays and blues of Pacific waters, so different from his life in the Navy that Jack felt grossly out of place. His childhood in these same fields seemed impossibly remote, another life entirely. And a great piece of that other life had just recently been taken away from him.

He had, of course, been too late to see his father alive. Monty had sent the telegram on the afternoon of the heart attack, and even then Randall Hardigan had hovered near death. When Jack had reached San Francisco, he had managed a telephone call and learned his father had died. They postponed the services for three days until he could plane, train, and bus across three thousand miles of wartime America. The casket had to be closed because the body just wouldn't keep that long.

Jack had cried some, but death was hardly something new to him now. And men weren't supposed to cry, anyway. He tried to think of the good times he and his father must have had when he was little. But he couldn't remember any. He ended up helping console his mother, who was completely grief stricken.

He had been away from the ship for exactly a week when he took the family car and drove into the countryside, on the pretense of seeing an old friend in Waterboro. In reality, he wanted to be alone. He had never been very good at "thinking things out," because things had never needed thinking out—before now. His life had clicked smoothly along on hidden paths, like a train in the dark. The rough spots were infrequent. But now he had grown away from his family—mother, father, brother, sister—and the close family ties with the community of Portland, its churches, shops, streets, and schools. Eight years of flying for the Navy had taken him everywhere but back home. Until a week ago, he had been half a world away in a place where you could take a leisurely swim in a warm ocean on Christmas day, if you were so inclined.

He asked himself what had gone wrong.

The little country road he drove on was straight out of a Currier and Ives print—or perhaps a Norman Rockwell cover for the *Saturday Evening Post*. He rolled over a little stone bridge, stopped by the side of the road, and got out to look at the stream. Even though he had seen it before, many years ago, it seemed quite picturesque to him. He walked out on the bridge, leaned on the retaining wall in mid-stream, and looked down at the water. And thought of Fred Trusteau.

That evening on the flight deck was almost two weeks behind him now, but somehow the effects of its revelations lingered. He had avoided Trusteau in the intervening days, until they reached Pearl, where the telegram waited. In all that time he had not faced his thoughts; instead, he had kept busy with the everpresent paperwork, and daily flying. He had even spent time on CAP to give some of the other men a rest. All of his instincts had told him that it was the wrong time and the wrong place for anything—of that nature. For that matter, the time and the place for anything of that nature didn't *exist*, in peace or in war. He asked himself if he would have had those feelings if the war had not come along, and concluded that he couldn't have. After all, the pressures of combat, the basically unfriendly surroundings, new men in new situations that were always changing—all this had naturally made him grow overly fond of someone as friendly and helpful as Fred. Embarrassment welled up in him as he wondered what Fred would think if he knew—

Below him a trout patrolled the shallow water like a tiny submarine and gobbled up a thrashing insect on the surace of the water. His eyes followed the fish as it swam upstream with effortless ease and grace, keeping in the shadows of the drooping trees that hung over the water and dangled their leaves in its currents. Jack breathed deeply and tried to relax. He wanted to feel that something good would come out of this emergency leave, even if it had been initiated by death. The time away from the squadron was bound to be good for his overwrought emotions. When he got back he would discover that the feelings he had had about Fred Trusteau had been totally false, brought on by stress and overwork and harassment from CAG. When he got back—and he found himself wanting to go back—things would be better. His mind would be clear. He could get down to what was important: surviving the war so he could come home to his family and his birthplace and lead a normal life. He straightened and slapped his hand on the top of the short stone wall.

"Well, now, got it all figgered out?"

Jack whirled at the sound of the voice. An elderly gentleman was leaning against the retaining wall on the other side of the narrow bridge. Jack had no idea how long he had been there.

"Didn't mean to startle you, son, but you looked so wrapped up I just didn't have the heart to interrupt." The old man was dressed like a farmer in worn blue overalls, plaid shirt, big black shoes.

"Good afternoon," said Jack. The man crossed and stood beside him, leaning on the retaining wall.

"Howdy," he said. "You from the navy station in Portsmouth?"

"No, sir," said Jack. "Home on leave."

"Like I said, I didn't want to interrupt your thinking. Man needs time to himself once in a while to sort of jiggle things around in his mind and decide what to do. What was it you were pondering on?"

"It was personal," said Jack, turning to leave, slightly peeved at the man's intrusion.

"Well, far be it for me to butt in on a man's personal life. You know, I got a son in the Navy myself."

The two men fell into step together and headed for Jack's car, a hundred yards distant.

"Where is he stationed?" asked Jack.

"Some place called Jacksonville, in Florida. A training outfit. Suits the hell out of me, if you know what I mean. I want him back when this war's over, even if he does bring some strange girl from down south with him." Jack said nothing. They reached the big blue Chrysler. "You know, son," the man went on, "I think this war can do a lot of good for a lot of folks. Take my son, now. He's just like a heap of other youngsters who're gonna bring back some new bride from wherever it was they was serving. And that's a good thing because these little towns like Waterboro and Quincy really need the new blood, if you know what I mean. Back in '39 and '40, they was all talking about leaving and heading for the big cities to try and make a bundle of money. Then this war comes along, and they all go off to the Navy or the Army, and when it's all over they've seen the world. Home all of a sudden looks mighty good to them. Especially if they have a new wife to support. And all these little towns like Waterboro and Quincy will be doing better than ever, if you know what I mean." They were standing by the driver's door; Jack wished the man would quit talking so he could be on his way. "That wouldn't be your problem, now would it, son?"

"What's that?" asked Jack.

"You wouldn't be wondering whether or not to get hitched up to an out-of-state girl, now would you?"

This man's world is so well ordered, thought Jack. He's got it all figured out. He knows just where everything is and where it's going to end up when the war is over. And no one will convince him otherwise.

"No, sir, that isn't my problem." Jack opened the car's big door. "Could I give you a lift into town?"

"No, thank you, son," said the man, "the good Lord gave me two feet, and they been serving me well for over fifty years. But thanks kindly for the offer."

"You're welcome," said Jack. He climbed into his car and closed the door. He glimpsed the man in his rearview mirror. Then he drove down the Norman Rockwell country road, telling himself that everything was all right and that when he got back to the ship on the other side of the world things would be better.

Part IV

Combat One:

Wake

25

The barber shop was incongrously like the one Fred had gone to in San Jose every two weeks for most of his life. There were three chairs and big mirrors and stacks of tattered magazines. The rows of little shelves over the sinks were filled with the same after-shave lotions, hairdressings, talcum powders. But for the occasional swooping feeling one had when the ship heeled over or took a heavy swell, the spacious shop could have been in landlocked Idaho or Nebraska, on some small main street where cars were parked in front and people stuck their heads through the door to say hello.

The big chair was comfortable, but the sheet the barber spread over Fred cut out more of the already meager supply of air and made him warm and sweaty. As the taciturn barber, who was a third class petty officer, clipped away slowly and carefully, Fred thumbed through a magazine which he only now discovered to be the same issue of the *National Geographic* that had been in the ready room back at the air station on Oahu. The pages were coming out of the binding. There was a picture of navy fliers in their ready room prior to the landings in North Africa, and someone had made them appear to be reciting a dirty limerick which began, "A clever young girl from Duluth," by writing in the words with a ball-point pen. There wasn't enough room on the page to complete the poem, however, and Fred had just turned the page to see if it was completed elsewhere when there was a commotion in the corridor outside. Two men came in. It was Jack and Duane Higgins.

The commanding officer of VF-20 entered first, taking off his hat. For a second he didn't notice that the man in the end chair was his wingman. Duane came in behind him, and he did notice. Fred and Duane exchanged a long look. The barber stopped his work and impatiently stepped aside to clean his clippers as Fred turned his head and said loudly, "Welcome back, Skipper." Jack stood quite still for a moment, caught in the act of tucking his garrison cap under his belt. He looked hard at the other pilot. "Thank you, Ensign," he said.

The barber resumed his work, and Fred had to look back down at his magazine. He could think of nothing else to say.

There was only one other barber in the shop, a grim-faced Filipino steward. He had one customer, and two more officers were sitting and waiting in the only two chairs; now one of them stood and offered his chair to his senior, Lieutenant Commander Hardigan. Jack waved him back, though, and swung up into an unused barber chair. Fred watched it all through the corner of his eye, electrified by Jack's presence. He tried to calm his nerves, slow his pounding heart, but was not successful.

"Any word yet on where we're going?" Jack asked Higgins.

"Not officially," said Duane, "but it has to be somewhere important. Six flattops," he said. "We got six carriers with us this time."

"I know," said Jack. "I saw them on the way in. Any casualties since I left?"

"The airplanes are in good shape. Schuster had a blowout when he landed this morning but it's all right now."

"Anybody hurt?"

"Nah. Hughes came down with appendicitis about a week ago. Doesn't look like he'll be ready for the strike if it's within a week or ten days." Higgins leaned against the bulkhead near the door and looked around as he talked. He had noticed immediately the unspoken tension that sprang up the instant Fred had seen him and Jack. He could draw no conclusions yet, but he did notice that the Skipper's wingman couldn't sit still now. His foot was twitching and his fingers drummed nervously on his magazine. "And we got a new LSO, too. Guy named Asper."

"Experienced?" (The skipper was ignoring Fred purposely, with effort.)

"Nothing operational. Seems pretty good, though."

"What happened to Harden?"

"Fell into the gallery deck and broke his ankle." Higgins laughed. "Clumsy fool."

"Has the first briefing been scheduled yet?" Jack concentrated on his executive officer, anxious to get back into the swing of command, eager to know what had happened since he had left. The presence of Trusteau in the same room caused him a momentary twinge, but on the long flight out to the task group he had prepared himself for this meeting by telling himself repeatedly that Fred was just another pilot—a valuably trained, highly motivated pilot, yes, but in the end, just another man with whom Jack could be friendly and perhaps close. It could go no farther. After all, Fred could be gone tomorrow, like so many others who had crossed Jack's path.

"Tomorrow morning at nine, in the wardroom," Duane was saying.

"The wardroom?"

"Yeah. The whole air group's invited this time."

"That's good."

The two barbers finished with their customers at the same time, both sweeping off the sheets with practiced flair and shaking the clippings to the deck. Fred climbed down first and started for the door, but he couldn't avoid confronting the Skipper, who was heading for the chair Fred had just vacated. As they passed, Fred had to stop and move aside for the Skipper. Both were careful not to touch. In that short interlude, their eyes inevitably met and Fred said, simply, "Sir," and nodded. Then he left as quickly as he could, relieved to see Jack again but anguished at being virtually ignored by him.

Duane watched the ensign leave and made a mental note to the effect that, yes, there was something odd between the Skipper and Fred. He moved over to lean against another bulkhead so he could talk to Jack. One of the other officers took the second chair; now both barbers were working again. "One of the crew chiefs missed movement," Duane said to Jack.

"Which one?"

"Pullet. They'll probably give him a special."

"That's too bad. He was a good man." (Just another pilot, Jack thought. Remember. Just another pilot.)

"Come on," said Brogan sharply, "get your mind on the game." The backgammon board occupied the little desk in the cubicle used for combat debriefing, in the forward section of the ready room. Brogan had just thrown the final roll of the dice and moved his last two men home. Fred still had four markers on the

board, two of them in the first table. "Some player you are," said
Brogan, "after all I taught you." He gathered up the dice and
swiftly moved the men on the board back to the starting
positions. "Let's try it again. Come on."

Fred sat half in and half out of the debriefing cubicle. He was
perplexed. Tomorrow was the first day of two days of strikes on
the Japanese-held island of Wake. Tomorrow they were going
into combat for the second time. And all Brogan could think
about was how well he was teaching Fred to play acey-deucy.
The ready room was crammed with men in flight gear and in
regular uniform. A dozen conversations filled the compartment;
the noise level ruled out careful meditation.

"Not another one?" sighed Fred.

"Come on," said Brogan. "It'll take your mind off things."

"My mind isn't on 'things.'" Fred picked up the dice cup,
shook it once, twice, then sat it back down on the table. He
didn't feel like playing another game.

"Aw, shit," said Brogan, leaning back in his chair and
pushing the board aside.

Fred could say nothing. In a curious sort of way, there wasn't
very much on his mind; the threat of combat held no fear right
now. His thoughts, meager as they were, he thought wryly,
swam through a sea of numbness and sank into nothing. He
looked and saw his hand still holding the dice cup; he tried to
move it and found he couldn't. It just sat there as though welded
to the table, immobilized. There was something hiding just
below the conscious level of his mind; he knew it was unpleasant
but for the moment it had been forgotten. What could it be?

He had felt this way since the day of the first briefing. All the
pilots had gathered in the wardroom right after breakfast; the
dishes had been cleared away save for coffee cups and ashtrays,
the serving doors to the galley closed up, the stewards
conspicuously absent. The male spirit of camaraderie in the face
of impending danger was very much in evidence. Then the
briefing officer and one of his aides had dramatically swept the
cover off the great easel in front of them, and the pilots had
leaned forward to see the map. It showed a single little atoll
called Wake. The feeling that they were part of something great
had gripped everyone, it seemed, but Fred. He had just felt
numb; probably he would have felt the same had the map shown
the island of Honshu.

Wake was something they could get their teeth into, the
briefing officer had said; it was something the Japs had taken
from us at the start of the war. As the vital statistics of the enemy

base were reeled off (fighter strength, radars in operation, search patterns flown through the area, airfields, installations, guns, and on and on) Fred couldn't help wondering if one day the map actually *would* show Honshu. And then he wondered if he would still be alive to see that day. And would anyone really care if he wasn't?

"Look," Brogan was saying, "you gonna play or not?" Then Fred heard his own voice saying, "No." Simply "No," with no explanations. Explanations were too hard to find right now. He let his mind slip further down, down toward the unpleasant something that lay submerged there.

"Listen up," someone was saying. That voice. That was it. "Quiet," it said, controlled and strong, deep and resonant. It was the skipper's voice. Lieutenant Commander Jack E. Hardigan. "E" for Errol, as in Flynn, only without the pencil-thin mustache. It was going on, and he, Fred Trusteau, the skipper's wingman and holder of the seventeen-minute record, had already missed part of the speech.

". . . submarine. It's official now. They just sent word. There will be a lifeguarding sub." Other voices, indistinct and babbling, broke in, but the skipper's voice swept them aside. "Hold it down." A space of relative quiet. "The sub will be stationed to the southeast of Wake at a distance of about eight miles. That's southeast, in the direction of the arrowhead. If you're going down, follow the arrowhead of the island and get as far from the reef as you can. Stick together. Like glue. If you see someone else going in, mark the position on your map and get word back to home base. They can get word to the sub and he can be picked up. Okay?"

Fred found himself turning now, turning to get a look at the skipper standing in the front of the ready room, surrounded by rapt faces.

"We'll go over all this in detail tomorrow morning at prelaunch. I'll answer all your questions then. Till then, I want to see all you flyboys in the rack getting some sleep time. You'll need it. Now get to it."

He was a good man, the skipper was, thought Fred. Such a good man. He cares for his men like they were his own. . . .

"Look, fella," said Brogan. His voice had a cutting edge to it, and he reached over the table and grabbed Fred by the front of the shirt, pulling him over the playing board, close to his face. "I don't know where you're at right now, Trusty, and I don't give a shit. If you're worried about the next couple of days, you better drop it. I ain't shitting you, Trusty. You drop it. Nothing's gonna happen to you 'cause you fly wing on the old man and nothing happens to him. Ain't nothing gonna happen to me 'cause I haven't beaten every one of the suckers in this air group at acey-deucy, and by jolly Jesus I intend to before I buy it. Now wake up and play it, fella."

He released Fred's shirt and Fred sank back into his seat. He became aware again of the roar and rumble of voices in the ready room, and he knew no one had heard what was just said. He picked up the dice cup. "You're wrong," he said.

He saw Brogan open his mouth to speak but heard instead another voice. It was loud and insistent. "Come on, guys. We got everybody here now. It'll only take a second."

Fred put down the dice cup and looked.

"Jesus H. Christ," said Brogan. He pushed back his chair and stood. "Come on, Trusty," he said, all traces of toughness gone now from his voice. "Let's do it for the suckers and get back to the game." He pulled Fred up by the arm and they went to stand up against the wall with the other pilots.

"Where's the skipper?" someone asked.

"You guys in front, down on one knee. That's good."

"Push it together. Push it together."

"Let the skipper in. There you go. Okay, Trusty, here you go. Hold it up." Fred found himself, not unwillingly but hardly aware of what he was doing, standing against the status board in the front of the ready room, holding a painted wooden plaque—next to Jack Hardigan. An arm reached around him and grasped his shoulder, pulled him close.

"That's good, guys. Turn the plaque more this way, Trusty." Fred looked down at the squadron insignia—the suitless Jack of hearts brandishing a sword, and the skipper's name emblazoned on it. He glanced at the skipper, realizing that it was his arm that held him. He looked away. A flashbulb popped and brilliant colors danced in front of his eyes.

"Don't move guys. Just one more."

Again the flash, then the crowd of men pushed and broke apart and the arm left his shoulders. Without looking around him, Fred made his way back to the debriefing cubicle, laying the insignia on the table next to the backgammon board. He picked up the dice cup.

"Now you're talking, fella," said Brogan, sitting down and eagerly pulling up close to the board.

"Sure," said Fred. Everything was perfectly clear to him now, as if it had all been illuminated by the exploding flashbulbs. To die tomorrow might be a good thing—a way out. He wanted to say something dramatic, like they did in the movies. Something like, "I just have a feeling about this one, Smitty," or, "One of us isn't going to make it back tomorrow," But he knew Brogan would think him very foolish, so all he said was, "Roll them dice." And he rolled them.

26

Jack glanced over his shoulder, in the direction of his ten fighters; beyond them, light on the horizon and the fading stars told him dawn had arrived. Looking back to the southwest, in the direction of flight, he searched hard for a sign of the target but saw nothing more than ocean and sky. He settled his mind once more into the routine of waiting for the action he knew would come.

The premission briefings meant so little now, Jack thought. The entire air group had gathered in the wardroom to hear a lieutenant commander point to a map of Wake Island and say: "Here is your target. Destroy it." That was fine, Jack thought. A force of six carriers could certainly do a great deal of damage to a small island like Wake. But what then?

He remembered the stirring, shaky-knees speech that an admiral named Spruance had given prior to their epic mission at Midway: "You, gentlemen, are quite possibly all that stand between victory and defeat for the forces of our country..." And another, read over the address system by the captain of the *Enterprise:* "On August seventh, this force will recapture Tulagi and Guadalcanal Islands which are now in the hands of the enemy." Apparently this mission to Wake was to be another Marcus Island operation—a raid and nothing more. It angered and confused Jack to think that in the coming clash (and he knew there would be opposition) aircraft and pilots might be lost just so that the brass back in Hawaii would have a better idea as to how many carriers could operate in a single task group. The entire affair sat wrong with Jack, even though he knew it was wrong to question orders, even to himself. A vindictive air group commander did not make things any better.

Jennings had chewed him out again the night before, catching him as he was taking off his pants, turning down his bunk. CAG could make him look so ridiculous, he thought, and for such a little reason. This time it was haircuts. Jack had spotted Brogan leaving the wardroom a few hours earlier, and he obviously needed a haircut. Jack intended to mention it to him. Why did CAG have to bring it up then—the night before a strike launch—when Jack needed the sleep, the time to himself? The only reason Jack could fathom was hatred: The man hated him, probably wished him dead. What else could it be?

They had gone together then, through the darkened passageways of the carrier to Brogan's stateroom to find him and inform him that he needed a haircut. And Jack had looked stupid again because he couldn't find Brogan's stateroom in the maze of passageways and compartments in the forward part of the ship. And when they finally did find it, Brogan of course wasn't there and no one knew where he was. So CAG raised his voice in the corridor and informed Jack in front of pilots of his own and other squadrons of just exactly what he was to do about the situation. Jack found it enormously embarrassing. Just the thought of the air group commander stalking through the ship looking for pilots with long hair was harrowing.

Takeoff had not gone well, either. A rain squall swept in just as they began the launch, and the first aircraft, a Hellcat flown by Bigelow, had gone off the deck at an angle and exploded on contact with the water. Although he couldn't be sure, the awful display of burning gasoline flaring quickly in the dark and passing rapidly astern virtually assured Jack that Bigelow was dead. He could only assume that one of the destroyers in the rear would make a search. He had been the third plane in the air and so had no idea how the rest of the strike had fared. Looking back now, he could make out the aircraft of Trusteau, Fitzsimmons, and Patrick—bulky shadows weaving and bumping around in the dark. He could see no others. For all he knew, they could be alone, heading for certain death at the hands of scores of savage Zeros.

The sky was turning a lighter shade of blue now, revealing piles of puffy clouds clinging close to the surface of the ocean—probably they wouldn't be able to see the target until they were directly over it. Jack checked his instruments and his heading, satisfied that they would be there soon. It was almost comforting to be so close; the sooner they arrived, the sooner they could leave. But why did so many things have to clutter up his mind at a time like this?

Fred Trusteau hung off his right wing like an ever-present specter, reminding him of feelings he was unable to control. Just this morning, only minutes before launch, he had stepped into a head to relieve himself—a faithful prestrike ritual—and was confronted by a Dumb Dilbert training poster hanging over the urinal. The poster showed the fatuous trainee hopelessly lost over an empty ocean with a setting sun, pondering his navigation notes—"Was that 320 or 230?"—while his cartoon plane wept great tears. Jack immediately thought of Fred and the error he had discovered on the training cruise battle problem. Fred had probably saved a number of lives when he did that. That good, warm feeling had welled up and then been pushed back down, with great effort. Now Jack had a vague feeling that something was wrong. He looked out at Trusteau's number thirteen and the indistinguishable figure that sat in its cockpit. It would go away, he was sure, in time. Everything would be all right.

Far ahead of them now, in the rapidly brightening sky, Jack caught a movement in the air. Tiny specks flared like burning matches and began a long slide toward the ocean, leaving barely visible streaks of delicate smoke in the sky. He knew at once that another squadron had arrived before them and that the surprise had been lost. He checked his radio. It was on the correct frequency. He pressed his throat mike. "Bogeys, twelve o'clock low," he said, "close it up."

He looked over his right shoulder, surprised at how light the sky had become, and saw quickly that all of his fighters were indeed there. They were strung out for at least a mile, badly out of formation. Even as he looked, though, they began to close it up. Trusteau's Hellcat moved inward and locked itself below and to the right of his wing. The helmeted, goggled figure in the cockpit looked up at him and waved slightly. Jack turned back and scanned the sky, the clouds, the ocean below. A movement below caught his eye and he quickly identified the white brush marks of surf on coral reefs. They had arrived.

Ahead of them, the smoke trails drifted in the winds. The planes from the other squadron had disappeared into the clouds below. Jack scanned quickly from left to right, low to high, seeing no aircraft. Below the formation, a triangular atoll appeared sporadically through the clouds. This was Wake. There was a small fire burning on the main island. Jack began a turn to the right to keep his flight over the target, and the other fighters dutifully followed.

"Tallyho. Three o'clock low."

Jack recognized the voice of Lieutenant Bradley. He turned immediately and saw the rear division of four Hellcats begin a steep right turn and head in unison toward the clouds below. He touched his mike button. "Banger Two Three stay high. I'm heading down to take a look."

"Roger one," came the reply. Brogan's voice. The man who needed a haircut. Jack pushed the stick to the right and forward, saw Trusteau and the other two aircraft follow, and felt his speed build. The first four Hellcats were tiny crosses against the cloudy backdrop as they pulled down and away.

"There," came Bradley's voice, "to the right. Three of 'em. Take the one on the right, Jimbo." The voice had an intense, concentrated sound to it, a quality the radio could not mask. As Jack watched, two of the blue Hellcats peeled off to the right and vanished into the clouds.

"Watch it, Hermy. Stick in there."

"Holy Christ, look at that bastard burn."

Wispy shreds of ragged white began to whip past Jack's cockpit; then the great mass of cumulus leaped up and engulfed his plane. He glanced for his wingman, saw only cloud. He flew for long seconds in the unreal, cotton-candy world of zero visibility; then suddenly they were in the clear again, bursting into bright sunshine, blue water sparkling a mile below them. Far ahead and below, a moving tangle of toylike airplanes twisted and turned. As he watched, one of them flamed brightly and fell like a stone toward the water.

"I can't cover you, Brad."

"Hey, Rube, come on down." Bradley again. "There's more here than we can handle."

Jack watched the approaching dogfight, concerned with covering his rear. He was about to call for Brogan, but Trusteau's voice interrupted. "Bandits, two o'clock high."

Jack searched quickly, found three dark green, square-winged fighters plunging from the clouds, heading for the same fight he was. "Let's take them, guys," he said. "Two Three come on down. We need you."

He corrected his course to the right to close the three enemy fighters—they were Hamps, he thought, clipped-wing Zeros—

checking as he did so that his three wingmates were still with him. Trusteau clung there like a shadow, imitating his every move with tight precision. That was good, very good. Jack adjusted his goggles. His face was slippery with sweat. It was time to ply his chosen trade.

The dogfight off Wake was short but appallingly violent. To Fred it bore no resemblance to the stories of gallant, skillful fighter pilots jockeying for position and saluting the fallen vanquished. It was much more a question of who shot first and had someone upstairs to cover his tail. When he spotted the three Hamps diving toward Bradley's division, he knew he would have a chance to score a kill. All the ugly thoughts of dying were gone; now he had a job to do, something he had been trained for. It was tremendously exciting to be doing it.

The three Hamps appeared not to notice the Hellcats closing on them from their own left and above, but Fred could see that they were rapidly walking up on the lower Hellcats led by Bradley. They flew in a small backwards V, as though it were standard practice for a wing leader to have two wingmen, unlike Fred's service, where it was one for one. The lead Hamp had a wide orange band around his fuselage, forward of the tail. Fred caught a movement out of the corner of his eye and turned to see Patrick and Fitzsimmons pulling away, moving to the right to trap the enemy fighters between them and Fred and the skipper. That was good. They had them now. A few more seconds...

The lead Hamp was firing; little flashes of light were jumping from his wing edges and smoke was trailing behind. The Hellcats in his sights began turning and diving frantically. And now the skipper was firing, too, although Fred felt sure they were still out of range. He looked through his gunsight, and yes, they were still far away, too small to fill the sight ring. The skipper's tracers leaped across his field of vision, and suddenly the Hamps were turning, too, away from them, to the right. One of the wingmates was slow to turn and fell out of formation. The Hellcats ate up the distance and caught them on the water, when they could dive no more.

The first to die was the straggler who had fallen out of formation. Patrick and Fitzsimmons jumped him as he turned hard to the right, and the shells cut a swath through the water, then chopped the Hamp almost in two, knocking off a wing and sending the wreckage spinning crazily into the sea. The lead Hamp with the orange band continued straight, keeping temporarily out of range. But the remaining wingman turned as if panic-stricken, to the left. That allowed Fred and the skipper to catch him. Fred could see immediately what was happening. He opened the distance between him and Jack by swinging wide to the right.

It was a wise move. The Hamp, still turning to the left, saw the skipper and frantically went to the right. He entered Fred's gunsight, and Fred squeezed the trigger, not really thinking he could make any hits. The shells tore into the water in front of the Hamp and he weaved back to the left, like a doomed sparrow, right into the skipper's guns. The deadly concentration of gunfire hammered the little fighter into the sea. It struck the top of a wave like a skipped stone and bounced, scattering debris into the air, caught a wingtip in the water and cartwheeled in, throwing a geyser of spray into the air higher than Fred was flying. Fred dodged the geyser, looking for the third and last Hamp. He was rewarded by the sight of a burning, falling plane and two Hellcats circling above him.

"Whooee doggies." It was Brogan. "The cavalry has arrived."

Fred found the skipper climbing and circling, and latched himself onto his right wing. Brogan and his wingman disappeared below. Fred began to breathe easier and thought: So this is what it's all about. He noticed an odd smell, a chilly sensation. His flight suit was absolutely drenched with sweat.

"All Banger aircraft rendezvous," said Jack through his throat mike. He and Trusteau had climbed back to their original altitude well above the cloud cover over Wake. None of the other Hellcats of his squadron were in sight yet, but he knew they would show up soon. The rendezvous point and altitude had been chosen well in advance. He hoped passionately that all ten would make it back. He had seen aircraft going in, but only from a distance. Some of them might have been his. One, at least, he didn't have to worry about: Trusteau had clung to his wing with professional tenacity all the way through the short tangle that had ended in the death of the three Hamps.

It was easier than he had anticipated. Even the enemy wing leader with the orange band had shown a fatal ignorance when he tried to escape by diving. And his two wingmen were obviously quite new, untrained. They hadn't been nearly as good as his own wingman—and, goddamn, had he been *good*. He had executed the simple trap maneuver as if they had practiced it specifically for this mission. Jack vowed to himself that when they got back he would corner Fred and compliment him on his flying. . . .

"That was terrific shooting there, Brad."

"Jimbo got two of the bastards. You should've seen it."

"You all right, Fritzi? I lost you in that last turn."

The voices of his scattered pilots reached Jack's earphones and he waited for a quiet moment. "All Banger aircraft rendezvous." It irritated him to lose control over the squadron like this, but it appeared as if they had done the job they were supposed to do. No enemy planes were in sight. Jack checked his instruments, his fuel, decided they had maybe fifteen minutes of time remaining over the target. A mile or so away a pair of Hellcats climbed through the clouds and headed in their direction. Another one appeared by itself behind them. In ten minutes they could be headed back for the ship.

"Banger Leader, this is Turkey Trot, over." The transmission surprised Jack somewhat as it was the first time home base had communicated with him since the launch nearly two hours ago.

"Turkey Trot, this is Banger Leader. Go ahead."

"Banger Leader, we have a buddy down off the arrow head. Can you lend a hand?"

Jack looked around at his arriving pilots. Seven or eight had shown up. He knew they would have to postpone the rendezvous for a few minutes. The first pair of Hellcats were quite close now, and he recognized Brogan and Jacobs.

"That's a Roger, Turkey Trot. On my way."

"Very well, Banger. Give 'em hell."

"Two Three, this is Banger Leader." Jack waggled his wings.

"That you, Skipper?" Brogan circled in, joined up in a loose division formation.

"Follow me down, Two Three."

"Roger Doger," said Brogan.

Jack pushed his stick forward and the four fighters cut through the clouds.

The main island of Wake was churning with activity. Gnatlike aircraft swooped and circled; black spots of antiaircraft explosions dirtied the sky. Dense, billowing clouds of black smoke poured up from burning buildings and wrecked planes. Jack oriented himself, headed for the southeast corner of the island. As they drew close, what was happening there became apparent.

An Avenger was down several hundred yards from the beach, the tail assembly and one wing sticking crazily out of the water. Two survivors in tiny rafts were rowing away from the wreck, followed at a distance by a small, very Japanese boat. Shells splashed in the sea; an occasional airburst splattered handfuls of shrapnel around them. Jack searched the beach and the foliage near the crash site and saw a puff of smoke and flame from a concealed gun. Seconds later a shell exploded in the air over the rafts. Jack took a deep breath. He hated attacking gun installations like this. But the poor guys down there needed the help. If they could get out of range of the beach, they might even be picked up.

"Stand by for a target," Jack said.

"Ready when you are," said Brogan.

The four fighters began a wide, sweeping turn out to sea. As they came around, Jack saw two Hellcats make a run on the Japanese boat; the splashes caused by their fifty-calibers washed over the small craft and nearly obscured it.

"Take the beach," said Jack, "the first line of bushes there. Trusty and I will take the big gun."

"Roger Doger," said Brogan, and the two Hellcats pulled up loosely abreast of Jack and Fred. Ahead of them the two fighters which had strafed the boat circled out to sea; the boat was stopped. As they drew closer, Jack noticed small waves breaking over the sides. The little deck house was charred and blasted. Pulling his attention back to the beach, he lined up the area of undergrowth where he had spotted the muzzle blast of the gun. They were close. The breakers on the beach, then the line of undergrowth swept under them, and Jack opened fire.

The tracers disappeared into and were absorbed by the green, bushy trees. He had thought the island was covered with jungle, but from up close it was apparent that the foliage was not nearly so thick. Bare, sandy places showed through quite clearly, and Jack saw a dark pit nearly covered with sandbags and netting. The gun barrel protruded over the top edge of the sandbags. A clump of branches and leaves was fastened to the snout. The bullets from his guns churned the sand into a haze, tossed up bits of greenery and chunks of wood, sparkled like fireflies on the metal of the gun.

Then they were over it, crossing the surf and tearing back over the blue ocean. Jack pulled up slightly and began a turn to the left. Glancing back, he caught sight of the three Hellcats that had made the run with him, still in line abreast. Brogan and Jacobs were slightly ahead.

"You see who that was?" asked Brogan.

"What do you mean?"

"That Turkey down on the reef. Plane number double-oh. It's the head honcho."

Jack felt a strange feeling deep down in his body. "Sure it's not from another group?"

"Sure as shooting, Banger Leader. It's him all right."

The four fighters completed a great circle and headed back toward the island. The gun they had attacked fired again, and the shell exploded out over the water. CAG or not, they still needed help. It was something they had to do.

"Go around one more time," Jack said. "Break off into singles and go in one at a time. Get that gun. Trusty, you follow me." They went around again, tighter this time, Jack feeling driven to get the job done. He knew without checking they could afford to spend only a few more minutes in the area before they had to head for home. This run would have to do the job. Jack watched Jacobs break off first and begin his run. Seconds later Brogan followed him. Then it was Jack's turn; as he lined up the target once more, the first Hellcat was already shooting and pulling up.

They were crossing the island from the lagoon side this time and would sweep over the gun first, then the surf, and finally the Avenger. As he centered the gun in his sights, he noticed Brogan's fighter swerve to the right sharply, gunsmoke trailing from the wings. Something was wrong.

"Holy Christ." It was Brogan. "There's another—"

A black puff of smoke burst under the right wing of the blue aircraft, then another burst just ahead of it. Before Jack could look away, the Hellcat flipped over on its back and dove into the beach with a sickening explosion of orange flame and smoke. Another gun. Jack watched the first target hurrying toward him and knew there wasn't time to switch. He squeezed the trigger and thought, If there's another, maybe it'll get me, too. It's too late to do anything about it.

Something jarred the Hellcat, pushing it up and to the left. Then he was over the surf. The Avenger passed below him. He looked back at the death site of Brogan. Then noticed vaguely that the end of his right wing was shredded and broken, but he was shocked and numbed by seeing Brogan going in; thinking was difficult. Almost automatically, he began a right turn that would allow Trusteau to catch up and also give him a better view of the beach. Below, the two tiny figures in the rafts were moving further out to sea, almost out of range of the gun. Their frantically flailing shapes might have been funny, but Jack could not laugh. Something bright, something wrong, fluttered through the edge of his vision. It was Trusteau. His aircraft was on fire.

The first explosion filled the cockpit with smoke and rattled Fred's instruments the way heavy turbulence did. Before they could settle, there was another explosion, jarring the stick from his grip and heaving him against the straps. He suddenly realized that he couldn't see very well; the smoke was too thick. Without thinking he reached up, unlatched the canopy, and slid it halfway open. The wind whipped the smoke away and he could see again. What he saw was that he was already past the island and heading out to sea. He tried to remember where he had seen the skipper's plane last. He was beginning a right turn when the last explosion came.

The sound of it was a dull *whump*. It buffeted the Hellcat up and down and sent more smoke pouring into the cockpit from somewhere under his feet. When it was over, he straightened out and trimmed the aircraft, feeling carefully for any unusual responses in the controls. Everything seemed all right at first, but then Fred looked up and around, and then down, and saw the flames. They were coming from beneath his right wing and trailing out of his line of vision to the rear. Various things flashed through his mind: the skipper, the ship, the sub. He knew he would have to ditch—and do it quickly. Already the controls felt sluggish. He was momentarily glad he had trimmed the aircraft seconds before and was already so low to the water. He had time to look around him once, but he saw nothing, not even the island, before his sinking plane touched the crest of a wave. He fought to keep control, to keep the nose up, but was only partly successful. Before he was ready, the Hellcat hit again. This time it plunged to a stop and was deluged by sea water. Smoke and steam hissed up through the cockpit as Fred unlatched his straps. He left the parachute behind, grabbed the seat cushion, and stepped from the cockpit to the wingroot.

The nose of the Hellcat was low in the water. The wings were beginning to go under as Fred walked to the end of one of them and stepped into the sea. It was quite warm at first, so he relaxed a little and pulled the ring on his Mae West. Reassuringly it fluffed into a bulky plastic vest, and he bobbed up like a cork. Then he found the controls on the seat cushion and inflated the life raft. It, too, blew itself up with a gratifying rush of compressed air. He struggled into it.

He looked around. Number thirteen was gone; not even a cloud of smoke remained to mark its passing.

The sound of distant engines caused Fred to look up. Two fighters circled high above him. As he watched, one peeled off and came closer, lowering flaps to slow down. It drifted directly overhead. It was the skipper. Fred raised his hand and waved. The Hellcat passed and began climbing. Soon it was out of sight.

Fred felt moisture on his face and wonderingly removed his glove to wipe it away. It came from his eyes. He was crying.

Jack raised his flaps and increased throttle to take him and Jacobs up and away from the crash site. Seeing Fred climb from the sinking plane had been momentary but small comfort. He was still a hundred miles from the carrier. Jack signaled Jacobs to join up on him, and the two fighters circled in toward the beach where Brogan's wreck burned and CAG paddled furiously toward the open sea. Jack's mind was churning. He felt lightheaded, almost nauseous. He wanted to kill something.

Ignoring his temporary wingman, Jack wheeled and headed for the beach where CAG's Avenger still protruded from the waves. He spotted the two rafts and their occupants below him, and he passed over them at a scant hundred feet in altitude. The beach loomed in front of him, but the danger from the hidden enemy could not touch him. Halfway between the rafts and the beach he turned again without decreasing speed; it was a great up-and-over course reversal that pushed him against the straps first one way, then the other. He leveled out, found the rafts, swept down low, and centered them in his gunsight.

I could kill you now, you bastard, he thought. I could splatter your lousy guts for a hundred yards. His trigger finger hovered over the button. But he was moving too fast and his mind could not let him kill an innocent man, as the crewman down there with CAG surely was. He hurtled over the waving, shouting figures, recognizing both. He was relieved and ashamed that he could think of killing them. But you've cost me two good pilots, he thought, and one was very important to me.

If you make it back and he doesn't, I won't forget it. By God, you bastard, I won't forget it.

27

"Strip down to your skivvy shorts, Ensign."

The doctor had his back to Fred and had not even turned around when he came in. He appeared to be writing in a personnel jacket, but Fred couldn't be sure.

He began taking off his clothes—his crusty flight suit and soiled underwear. He laid it all on the end of the examination table. The compartment was small and crowded; there was a desk, a table, filing cabinets, and equipment lockers suspended from the overhead. A bright fluorescent lighted the space with a harsh, greenish glare. A little shakily, Fred took off his socks and placed them on top of his other clothes. He was still weak from the sleepless night spent aboard the submarine and the jarring, rough handling by the destroyer and breeches buoy. His ankle was swollen and very, very painful.

"You ditched, did you?" asked the doctor, still not looking at Fred.

"Yes, sir," said Fred. He pulled himself up and sat on the edge of the examination table. He was so fatigued that he felt he would never get to sleep.

"What happened?" The doctor finished writing and slapped the personnel jacket closed. Stepping up to Fred, he pulled a small flashlight from a top pocket of his white lab coat and began to peer into one of Fred's eyes.

"I caught fire. I crashed. Ditched. The sub picked me up." He shut his eyes as a sudden, vivid picture of Brogan's Hellcat smashing into the beach flooded his consciousness.

"Open your eyes," the doctor ordered. There was a knock on the door and someone entered. The doctor glanced up briefly, then looked back at Fred's eyes. He finished and put the flashlight back into his pocket. "Lay down," he said.

Fred pulled his feet up onto the table and scooted down into a prone position. He looked up and saw who had entered. It was the skipper, standing opposite the table, leaning against the desk, his arms crossed in front of him. He said nothing.

The doctor gathered up Fred's clothes and tossed them into a chair. He ignored Jack as though he were a piece of furniture and continued to work on Fred.

"Did this happen in the crash?" The doctor probed a large, bluish bruise on the outside of Fred's left thigh.

"I don't know. I guess so."

"And this?" He picked up Fred's swollen ankle, squeezed it, rotated it, so that Fred sucked in his breath and clawed the table cover with pain.

"Climbing up the cargo net from the sub to the can. It was dark. I couldn't see very well." The doctor laid the ankle down.

"Tell me if anything hurts." Starting with the feet and working up, the doctor bent or rotated each of Fred's joints. Aside from the ankle, none of them hurt. As the doctor worked, Fred watched the skipper out of the corner of his eye. It was strange, lying there almost naked in front of the skipper. He thought he caught a glimpse of his face, imagined he saw the brow furrowed in deep thought (or perhaps consternation), but couldn't really be sure. He couldn't bring himself to look right at him.

"Tell me if anything hurts." Now the doctor began to probe Fred's abdomen and ribs with stiff fingers, pulled down his shorts to feel his testicles. Fred closed his eyes. A cold stethoscope came down on his chest, hesitated, moved to another spot, hesitated, moved again. "Breathe deeply." Fred did so. "Roll over on your side." Fred did, and the stethoscope moved between his shoulder blades. "Okay." The doctor seemed satisfied. He turned to the desk, began writing in the personnel jacket. "You can get dressed now." Fred sat up slowly and swung his legs down.

"Excuse me," the doctor said to Jack, who moved so he could open a large drawer in the desk. He pulled out a bottle of liquor and a stack of paper cups, poured a cupful for Fred, and handed it to him. "Drink this, then get some rest." He put the bottle away. Fred took a short sip of the liquor, a poor quality brandy, and shuddered.

"Drink up," said the doctor. Turning to Jack, he said, "He's grounded for a week. No flying, no calisthenics, light duty only as necessary." Finished now, the doctor picked up the personnel jacket, placed the pen in his pocket beside the flashlight, and left the compartment. The door closed.

Jack and Fred were alone.

Fred spoke first. "Brogan...?"

Jack looked into Fred's eyes. His own eyes softened. He shook his head, looked away.

Fred lifted the cup of brandy, drained it, and swallowed heavily. He set the empty cup beside him on the examination table and lowered himself carefully to the deck. "I guess I'll turn in," he said. He moved toward the chair where his clothes were, hobbling slightly.

"Can you make it?" asked Jack. He stood immobile at the desk.

"Yes, sir," said Fred. He picked up his socks and sat down on top of his other things to pull them on. "I'll be all right. I'm just tired."

"Okay," said Jack. He breathed deeply—it was almost a sigh—and turned to go. "You're sure you don't need any help?"

"Yes, sir." Fred pulled a sock over the sprained ankle and tried to ignore the pain shooting up his leg.

"Okay." Jack opened the door and left.

Fred stopped dressing for a moment, feeling the brandy begin its work on his empty stomach. Things were just as they had been before. Brogan was gone. He wasn't sure how he felt about that. He didn't know how he was supposed to feel about anything now. He was just very tired.

He finished dressing, resolutely straightened his uniform, even laced and tied his boots. Then he painfully limped the length of the ship and one deck up to his stateroom, took his clothes off again, and passed out in his bunk.

6 October 1943: En route Pearl Harbor Naval Station. VF-20 has been officially credited with the destruction of seven enemy aircraft following two days of strikes on the island of Wake. Operational Missions on this the second, and last, day of strikes, were limited to high cover and ground attack roles, no enemy aerial activity being in evidence. Three strikes totaling twenty-six sorties were flown. No aircraft were lost, although aircraft number forty-one flown by Lt. (j.g.) Heckman has been classified as scrap after receiving severe engine and fuselage damage from enemy gunfire. Squadron effective strength on this date totals thirty pilots and thirty-one aircraft, including one pilot, Ensign Trusteau, temporarily grounded due to minor injuries suffered during ditching procedures on 5 October.

7 October 1943: VF-20 today flew sixteen sorties, all routine Combat Air Patrol with no unusual activity or losses. Inclement weather conditions forced cancellation of all flight operations after 1400 hours. At 1300 hours squadron members attended a short memorial service for those pilots and crewmen lost during the preceding days of action. VF-20 pilots officially listed as killed in action are Ensign David Bigelow and Lieutenant Hanson T. Brogan. Their loss is keenly felt by members of the squadron. . . .

Duane Higgins stretched luxuriously and settled into his chair near the rear of the ready room, where he could watch the other pilots. They were unusually animated today, he thought, probably due to the bad weather, which was allowing them an unexpected day off from flying. Despite their two times in action, they were still an inexperienced lot. Duane thought about the first eighteen months of war, when the few carriers had operated for the most part independently, which had meant continuous CAP duty for the fighter squadrons embarked. Now, in a six-carrier force, CAP duty could be rotated from ship to ship, giving the other air groups a chance to catch up on much-needed rest and training. At Midway, he and Jack had flown one CAP on the morning of June fourth, then participated in the big strike which sank the three enemy carriers and lasted a marathon six hours of continuous flying. They had landed in the afternoon, flew the dusk CAP, slept like inanimate objects, and then did essentially the same thing the next day. Although he never bragged about it, Duane knew it was generally conceded that there was more experience between him and the Skipper than in the rest of the squadron put together. That made Duane feel good.

There was a commotion in the forward part of the compartment as three pilots came in. All were in nonflying uniform. Duane opened his eyes only enough to see who they were. Lieutenants Bradley and Schuster were leading one of the new men, Ensign Patrick, and talking earnestly about souvenirs. Duane listened in for a few seconds and knew immediately what they were up to.

"Wait till you see this, Patrick," said Bradley.

"You won't believe it," said Schuster.

"What is it?" asked Patrick.

The three pilots reached the far corner of the room from Duane and rummaged in a pile of flight gear. Bradley came up with a leather flight helmet and put his hand inside. "You ought to send this to your girl friend back home," he said. "Then she'll get an idea of what we're up against out here."

"Yeah," said Schuster. "Quite a man filled this baby."

"What is it?" asked Patrick, leaning closer, eyes wide with wonder. Bradley was slowly pulling an enormous rubber condom from the helmet.

"Look," said Schuster, "I got one of our own so you can compare the sizes." He pulled another, smaller condom from his pocket and held it up beside the big one. The difference was striking. The big rubber was fourteen inches long and as big around as the business end of a baseball bat.

"Geez," said Patrick. "Look at the size of that thing." He touched it gingerly but Bradley quickly pushed it back into the helmet, looking around furtively and tucking the headpiece under his arm to hide it.

"Don't want anyone else to know we got one of these."

"Yeah," said Schuster. "They're pretty rare, you know."

"How'd you get it?"

"Intelligence Officer who owed me a favor took it off the body of a Jap pilot they pulled from the drink the other day. One of the Emperor's hand-picked boys."

"That's how they pick the pilots for the Emperor's squadron," said Schuster. "They gotta be good, you know, really top aces. And they gotta be really *big* men."

"Not more than a dozen or so like this in the whole world," said Bradley.

"Really?" Patrick was buying the story. Duane grinned to himself at the half-truth they were plying him with. The rubber *had* come off the body of a Japanese pilot, but all Japanese Army pilots carried them. Two or three each, in fact. They used the rubbers to protect survival equipment from saltwater, in the event of ditching. He guessed they would ask Patrick for at least twenty bucks for it. And Patrick would probably pay it.

"Thirty bucks," said Bradley, "and it's yours. That's pretty cheap, you know, but you're a member of the squadron and all. We try to take care of our own."

"That's kind of high," said Patrick uncertainly.

"Yeah, but where else are you going to find one of these?"

Duane closed his eyes again, thinking that maybe they were taking the kid for a ride, but what the hell. It was taking the kid's mind off the death of Bigelow, who had come aboard the same time he had. The two had been good friends. In this business, maybe it was better...

Duane opened his eyes. Something nagged at the back of his mind. Without moving his head he surveyed the compartment full of men and found who he was looking for. Trusteau was sitting at the debriefing table, working away with pen and paper.

The War Diary. Trusteau was writing something in the Diary, copying from what was probably a first draft of a long entry. As Duane watched, Trusteau stopped writing, put the pencil down, folded his hands in front of him, and stared at the bulkhead opposite. His face was as blank as the bulkhead. Duane looked across the ready room and found the skipper.

Jack was sitting in one of the front row chairs, leafing through a stack of papers. His brow was furrowed in thought, even though he was flipping through the papers far too fast to be absorbing any of the information on them. Duane looked back at Trusteau.

Trusteau had stopped looking at the bulkhead. He was looking at the skipper. Not a casual glance. An unmoving, unblinking stare. Jack had to notice.

Duane's eyes moved again, and yes, the skipper was looking back at Trusteau. All around them, the men of the squadron talked, got up, sat down, did the things men at ease do with each other. But the skipper and his wingman were off somewhere else, somewhere very private. They held the stare for at least half a minute. To Duane all the life in the room seemed to recede into the distance; all the sounds became muted. Then it ended, suddenly. Trusteau turned back to his book and his writing. The skipper, as if coming to some important decision, straightened the papers on his knees, stood, and strode from the room.

It's none of my business, thought Higgins. He closed his eyes.

"Okay. Twenty-four bucks." Bradley and Schuster closed the deal with Patrick, and the condom changed hands. It was all right, even if Patrick eventually found out what the rubber was really for. Bradley and Schuster would play innocent, saying that that was what the Intelligence people had told them, and Patrick would still have a hell of a souvenir to show the people back home. Some of the people, anyway.

Higgins opened his eyes. Trusteau was gone; the little desk was empty.

It's none of my business, he thought. But I've got to find out.

Part IV-A

Interim:

Decisions

28

"Hi." Eleanor Hawkins sidled up behind Duane Higgins and playfully pinched the back of his neck. Duane, surprised, set his drink on the bar in front of him too quickly and spilled some. He turned on his bar stool.

"Well, hello." His first feeling was mild annoyance. A first date shouldn't be that intimately casual. Besides, Duane didn't like to be surprised. But then, as she swung up onto the stool beside him in her full, swishing skirt, without waiting for him to stand or assist, he was moved by her breezy smile.

"So how are the flying navy men these days?" Eleanor crossed her legs and leaned on the bar with one elbow, letting her skirt fall where it may—just over her knee. Her low-heeled shoe touched the cuff of Duane's pants leg.

"Better than ever," said Duane. He signaled the bartender. "You look gorgeous."

"The Royal Hawaiian," said Eleanor. "Isn't this a bit fancy for an afternoon cocktail?"

"Only the best, for the prettiest girl in town."

"You mean the *only* girl in town. There aren't many of us left around here these days." The bartender stopped in front of her. "Gin and tonic," she told him, and turned back to Duane. "I was surprised when you called," she said.

"Why, if I may ask?"

"Oh, I don't know . . . I guess, I don't really know you that well."

"But you came."

"Yes, so I did."

"And I'm glad you did."

They stopped talking for a second and looked into each other's eyes. The bartender set a tall, frosted glass in front of her. She picked it up, took a sip, set it down.

"Well," she said.

"Well," said Duane, not looking away. "I still think you're gorgeous."

"You can't fool me," she said. "I was married to a Navy man. After you've been out on the bounding main for a few weeks, anything in skirts would look gorgeous." She said it with a touch of playfulness in her voice, and accentuated it with a raised eyebrow, a hint of a mischievous grin.

"Not true. Anything in skirts would be merely beautiful. You're gorgeous."

"Say it often enough and I might start believing you." She took another sip, then asked suddenly, "How's Jack?"

"He didn't come back with us," said Duane, draining his glass and letting the ice cubes rattle to the bottom.

"What?" Eleanor's voice raised an octave in pitch and carried across the wide, darkened bar. A couple in a booth on the far side and several officers at the bar turned and looked.

"Oh," said Duane. "Bad choice of words. Sorry."

"You mean he *did* make it back."

"He flew off the day before we came in. Right now he's out with another carrier shooting landings with a bunch of Marines and those new Corsairs." Eleanor visibly relaxed. "He'll be back in a week or so."

"You scared me for a moment."

"I'm sorry. You like him a lot, don't you?" Duane watched her closely. This was one of the things he wanted to find out, and the subject had come up sooner than he had hoped.

She thought for a moment, looking into her drink and touching the top ice cube with her index finger. "Yes," she said at last, looking decisively at Duane. "He's a very good friend. A close, dear friend."

Her tone and her choice of words, her emphasis on those words, told Duane a great deal about Jack Hardigan. He decided to press on. "He's a good friend of mine, too. You might say he's my best friend."

"You've known him for a long time?"

"Long enough." Duane held up his empty glass to catch the bartender's attention.

"And how long would that be?"

"Long enough to know he wouldn't mind if I asked you to have dinner with me tonight."

There. He had done it. Now she knew that he wanted to know her better, that he wanted to be a bit more intimate.

Eleanor twirled her glass slowly in the puddle of cold water that had formed under it. "I think you're right. He wouldn't mind if you asked me to dinner."

"Okay. Here goes: Can I buy you dinner tonight?"

"I don't think Jack would mind if I accepted either," she said slowly.

"Then you will?"

Again, she thought for a second, looking at Duane quizzically, as if trying to find some hidden motive, some reason other than the obvious fact that she was an available, attractive woman, and he a man.

"Yes," she said. "I'd be pleased to accept."

Duane reached over and touched her on the hand. They linked fingers.

"Thanks," he said. "We'll have a good time."

Eleanor smiled. "I'm sure we will."

The barkeep set Duane's drink in front of him. He picked it up. "Drink to it?" he asked.

Eleanor picked up her gin and tonic. "Here's to us," she said, and they clinked glasses and sipped together. Duane watched her eyes, then followed the curve of her face and neck down to her lovely breasts. Jack, Jack, he was thinking, how could you ever let something like this get away?

The carrier's name was the *Belleau Wood* and like nearly all of the carriers then in the fleet she was brand-spanking-new. Something about the cramped, pitching flight deck made Jack Hardigan very uneasy; it seemed incredibly small compared to the *Constitution*. The tiny, button-like island was further forward on this ship than on the ship he was used to, and there was no deck edge elevator.

He had flown over in his Hellcat and come aboard the day before *Ironsides* had docked in Pearl Harbor. That afternoon the entire squadron of Avengers had flown off, taking him as a passenger and dropping him off at Ewa Field on Oahu. There he had given a one-hour, supposedly refresher lecture to a squadron of marine pilots; then they had all flown back to the *Wood* in Corsairs. That evening he had learned that three-quarters of the Marines had never landed on a carrier before and that the ship derived its name from an auspicious marine engagement of the Great War in France. This seemed to please some of the marine pilots. To Jack it only reinforced the belief that the only auspicious marine engagements were those in which most of the participants died.

Jack could think of many days in his life that were better than the days he spent on the *Belleau Wood*. Comforted by the fact that he would only have to spend three, or at most four, days there, he was nonetheless irritated to discover that the regular air group commander had assigned both him and the marine squadron commander to the same stateroom. From their first meeting ashore only hours before, the marine C.O. had been snootily amazed that a navy pilot could tell *his* men anything at all about flying, especially someone with such little time in Corsairs. Jack realized that the C.O. was good when he saw him in the air; but somehow the man had missed or avoided combat duty from the first days of the war and had no kills to his credit. He had made only two or three carrier landings in his life, and that had been years before, in a Buffalo, an obsolete fighter that had been pitted in combat against the Zero with sad results.

The commander, on the other hand, turned out to be a man Jack had flown with in the days before the war, and Jack was sure they would hit it off. But it was not to be. *Belleau Wood*'s CAG was a nervous, harassed man, sure that he was going to be stuck permanently with the marine fighter squadron. Thus, on the second day of the cruise, he put Jack in front of the Marines in the absent Avengers' ready room, where he lectured the bored group on shipboard routine and carrier air doctrine. Jack was not pleased. He wondered more than once how he had been selected for this duty. He was infinitely glad that it was temporary.

The Corsairs were as unpredictable and dangerous as ever. On the third day of operations, one of the new young pilots missed the last wire, bounded high in the air, and came down on the other side of the crash barrier. A dozen parked planes— Corsairs and Hellcats equally mixed—cushioned his fall. Even though there was no fire, Jack's aircraft, with its colorful insignia, had its right elevator surface knicked off by the windmilling propeller of the errant Corsair. When the pilot climbed out he was laughing like an idiot. And in the staterooms that evening, Jack could hear them all laughing and joking about the incident still. It made him long for the friendly, sensible crew of the *Constitution*.

On the fourth day of operations, Jack nearly lost his temper. In the morning he was in the midst of a lecture on Combat Air Patrol and radar direction when he realized that a small group in the rear of the ready room weren't listening to him. They were, in fact, giggling and whispering among themselves like schoolchildren. Jack stopped talking and pointed to one of the young pilots, who was still stifling a laugh. "You," Jack said.

"Me?" he said.

"Stand up, Mister."

The pilot sat up straight in his seat and glanced around the room to find the Marine C.O. He made no move to stand.

"I said stand up," Jack said. There was no mirth in his voice.

"Now wait just a minute." It was the marine C.O. half-rising from his seat near the front of the room.

Jack turned on him. "Stay out of this, Major." He turned back to the pilot. "Get off your butt."

The pilot, a first lieutenant, squared his jaw and stood. He was a good head taller than Hardigan. The room was suddenly very silent. "Yes, *sir,*" the pilot said. His face was red.

Jack let him stand in silence for a good part of a minute. When he spoke, his voice was icy calm and clear. "You may think you're the hottest thing in the air since the Red Baron, but I don't give a damn what you think. When you're in my classroom, you will afford me the courtesy you are required to show every senior officer, and that means keeping your trap shut until I require you to speak. Is that clear?" Inside Jack was boiling. It was as if all the frustrations of the last three days had come to a head and this man standing in front of him was personally responsible for all of them.

"Yes, *sir,*" said the first lieutenant.

"You may sit down." Jack turned back to the blackboard and continued his lecture; he could almost feel the thick animosity that rose from the seated pilots, but there were no more interruptions. He finished the lecture and asked for questions. Not surprisingly there were none. He dusted the chalk from his hands.

"Well, Lieutenant Commander Hardigan." It was the Major. "That was a fine lecture. I'm sure we'll all benefit greatly from it." The room was silent. No one had moved.

"Thank you," said Jack.

"But it seems we've spent too much time lately on these little procedures and not enough time on flying. If you feel like you're man enough for it, I think maybe my boys and myself could teach you a thing or two about real flying. All in the spirit of learning, of course." The seated pilots stirred and nudged each other with their elbows, smiling.

Jack looked back at the Major. He could no more refuse this challenge than he could swim back to Hawaii. "This afternoon all right?" he asked.

"Fine with me," said the Major.

"Bring a wingman." Jack picked up his notes, stacked them neatly. "And no water injection."

"I won't need it," said the Major.

Jack pushed past him and left the ready room. Behind him he could hear the laughs and hoots of the assembled marine pilots. It worried him. Nothing good could come of it. But he would do it. Jack made his way down to the hangar deck, found his Hellcat. The elevator surface had been replaced and the entire aircraft waxed and polished. That much pleased him. But there was something else he could do. He went in search of a crew chief.

"This meeting of the Saturday afternoon strategy conference will now come to order." The speaker was somewhere in the press of bodies around the end of the bar at the Officer's Club on Ford Island. Fred leaned on the bar, sipping a Scotch on the rocks. The twenty or so listless pilots there in the muted luxury of the lounge had been singularly quiet. They were bored.

"Come on, fellas," said Duggin. He had been the one who called the meeting to order. "What're we gonna do tonight?"

"Hey," said Peckerly, "remember that time Fritzi brought that girl back to the BOQ? And she could tie a knot in a cherry stem?"

Oh, no, thought Fred, it's back to the Trusty thing.

"Yeah," said Heckman. "Trusty beat her by a minute and a half."

"I don't get it," said Patrick. "What are you guys talking about?"

"You had to be there," said Duggin. "It was something else."

Now they're going to ask me, thought Fred.

"Then Bracker gave the girl to Trusty 'cause Fritzi was wiped out."

"And it took him seventeen minutes. Remember that?"

Fred pushed away from the bar and looked at the assembled group. He was trying unsuccessfully to remember the details of that night. The only man he remembered being there had been Brogan, when he had leaned out the door and said, "You're all right." Brogan could no longer attend the Saturday afternoon strategy conferences.

"Come on, Trusty, do it for us again." Fred closed his eyes and tried to think.

Frank Hammerstein patted him on the back and said, "Come on, Fred, do it for the guys."

"I don't have a cherry," Fred stalled. I won't do it, he was thinking. I just won't do it.

"Someone get him a cherry." Glasses were probed, and someone with a whiskey sour gave a triumphant yell. The little round fruit was passed through the crowd to Fred, arriving smashed and mangled. Fred held it by the stem for a second. Silence fell. A single red drop of juice, like blood, fell from the cherry and spotted the polished toe of Fred's shoe.

"I can't do it," he said. He tossed the cherry on the bar.

"Why not?"

"Come on, Trusty."

"I can't do it. I promised the skipper the next time I did it he could see. He isn't here so I can't do it." That was good. And almost correct.

"You can give the skipper a private showing." There was laughter.

Fred held up his hands for silence. He had thought of something. And Brogan would approve. "There *is* something I will do." He paused for effect.

"Yeah?"

"Well?"

"I will. Personally. Beat every man in this squadron at acey-deucy before we sail again."

The pilots turned away, mumbling.

"Wait a minute." Fred pulled a small roll of bills from his pocket. "We'll make it interesting."

Interest quickly returned.

"Every time I lose, I'll pay the winner five bucks." He peeled off a five spot and held it aloft. "Every time I win, the loser pays me three bucks. I'll take each man and play until I beat him. What do you say?"

More murmuring. "What if someone doesn't want to play?"

"Then that counts as a win for me, only the loser doesn't have to pay." No one came forward. "What's the matter?" asked Fred. "Look at the odds I'm giving you."

That was enough prodding. There was a taker. "You're on, hotshot." It was Schuster. "Anyone got a board?"

Fred picked up his drink and took a sip. Okay, Brogan, you

gotta help me pull this off. You didn't get the chance to finish it, but then you never put it on a paying basis. Now we will. Because a man has to accomplish something before he dies.

The bartender provided a board, markers, and dice cups, and the entire Saturday afternoon strategy conference moved to a vacant booth in the rear of the club. The first official acey-deucy championship of Fighting Twenty began in earnest.

Jack was the last to land that afternoon—right after the marine major. The major was waiting for him as he shut down his engine, and stalked over to stand by the wing root of Jack's plane, to catch him as he climbed down. Jack could see that the Major was livid with rage even before he could make out his face clearly; the way he walked bespoke it eloquently. Jack tarried in his cockpit and let the major stew for two or three minutes. Then he casually hoisted himself up and stepped onto the wing root. He dropped down in front of the major.

"Well, Major," he said.

"You could have spared me that."

Both men had to raise their voices to be heard over the rush of flight deck wind.

"I told you to bring a wingman, not half your squadron."

Jack remembered how seven or eight Corsairs had appeared on the scene, and how their scrutiny had affected the Major's abilities to the point where it had been rather humiliating. The man had simply tried too hard.

"Is this your aircraft?" the major said.

"Nope. It belongs to Uncle Sam."

"You know what I mean."

"Yes. This is the aircraft I generally fly." Maybe I shouldn't have gone "tacka-tacka-tacka" so much, thought Jack, every time I cornered him. Or maybe the triple victory roll was a little too much.

The major pointed up, but did not look at, five small Japanese flags which had only hours before been painted under the edge of the cockpit. "Are those yours?" he demanded.

Jack became very serious. "Yes," he said. "I got every one."

The major thrust his face up close to Jack. "Why didn't you tell me?"

"You didn't ask."

"Hardigan." An index finger stabbed upward and hovered under Jack's nose. "How dare you. How dare you humiliate me in front of my pilots. These boys are going into combat soon. They look to me. They look to me for leadership. Confidence.

Inspiration. If they don't have confidence some of them may die. How dare you—"

"Major," broke in Jack. He reached out and put a hand on the other man's shoulder, turned him around, and began to walk toward the island. "Major, some of your boys are going to die no matter what you do, even if they think you're God's Son returning."

A pair of the marine pilots who were standing near the island saw them approaching and disappeared into a hatchway.

"Hardigan—"

"Did you lose any in training yet?"

"No."

"I did my damndest, but I lost one, anyway. And two more last week over Wake." Jack thought of his squadron of Brogan and Bigelow, of CAG and Fred Trusteau—and suddenly wanted very much to be with them. Just the thought of seeing Fred again caused a lonely, empty ache to spring up surprisingly deep down inside of him.

The major stopped walking and pulled his shoulder away from Jack's hand. "Don't tell me how to run my squadron, Hardigan."

Jack looked at him, feeling the wind tousle his hair and flap the legs of his flight suit. He wanted to leave so badly he could almost taste it.

"I'm sorry about your men. But don't tell me how to run my squadron." The major pushed past Jack and disappeared into the island.

Jack sighed to himself. Now things were really going to be bad.

But it was something he didn't have to endure very much longer. Before he could reach his stateroom (hoping that the major wouldn't be there), a messenger from the bridge found him and informed him that the captain sent his respects and wanted him there right away. Jack thanked the seaman and left immediately, stopping only long enough to pick up a garrison cap.

When he arrived on the bridge, he found the captain of the ship, CAG, and the major, who elaborately ignored him. When the four men were together, the captain told them that the *Belleau Wood* was headed for Pearl and Hardigan was forthwith detached, with the Marines, and would fly off the ship in less than an hour.

Jack hurried back to the stateroom. He and the major packed in icy formality. Three hours later Jack landed at Ford

Island, parked his Hellcat among the familiar aircraft of Air Group Twenty, and caught the first boat to the *Ironsides*.

It was a late Saturday afternoon. After he had changed out of flight gear and into working khakis, he learned from the duty section that CAG had returned from the hospital and that the rest of the squadron was encamped in the O Club, where a marathon contest was in progress. Not wishing to talk to Jennings, Jack went back to his stateroom, changed into tropical whites, and headed for the Officer's Club.

"That was a very nice dinner," said Eleanor. She leaned on the big, rounded front fender of her car and looked out to sea.

"I didn't cook it," said Duane Higgins, "or pick the place to go." He stood beside her, not touching her, marveling at the unreal beauty of swaying palms, rising moon, and soft island breezes. He understood now how men and women fell in love so easily under these skies, on these beaches.

"A good dinner is a lot more than just food," said Eleanor. She brushed back a strand of hair in a way that made Duane long for the chance to hold her, stroke her neck and arms, entwine his legs in hers.

"I think you're paying me a compliment," he said. Her perfume wafted enticingly about him. He was thinking that she was the most perfect woman he had ever known.

"You are an officer and a gentleman," she said, not seriously, but it made Duane think of the original reason for asking her out.

The dinner had been most enjoyable, true. But he couldn't get Eleanor to talk about Jack, or, at least, about Jack and her. The way she spoke of him—when she did—indicated that they were good friends. What he could not get her to reveal, no matter how carefully he camouflaged the question, was whether they were romantically involved. But here we are now, he thought, alone on a deserted beach, with a blanket in the back seat. If she goes for me, he reasoned, then she isn't Jack's any longer. He put a hand behind her, on the hood of the car.

"It's nice here," he said.

"You mean right here, right now? Or Hawaii in general?"

"Both. I mean, it's so . . . I mean I bet it looked just like this a hundred years ago."

"Oh, aside from a few pillboxes, a roll or two of barbed wire," she said—and it seemed strange to Duane to hear her use such words—"I imagine it did."

Duane pulled back his arm and took her by the hand. "Let's

go for a walk," he said and started to pull her from the car.

But she resisted, gently. "No," she said softly, "not tonight."

"Okay," he said, genuinely disappointed. He leaned back against the car, but continued to hold her hand.

"Don't sound so dejected," she said. "There'll be other nights."

Although he couldn't see for sure, he felt her smile as she said it. He leaned over and kissed her on the cheek. "You're fantastic," he said.

"So I've been told." She broke loose from his hand, and for a second Duane thought she was going to get back into the car. Instead she put her arms around him and kissed him full, long, on the mouth. Then she turned her head, and he felt her draw in her breath and sigh deeply, as if in relief.

"I needed that," she said.

"Yes," was all Duane could say.

She pulled away. "I know it's not really late, but I think I should be getting back."

"Okay."

"I'll drive." She let him walk her around the car and open the door for her; she started the engine while he climbed in the other side.

"You don't trust my driving?" Duane asked.

"Truthfully, no."

"I fly the hottest fighter plane in the world and you don't think I can drive a car?"

"Truthfully, no."

Duane laughed out loud. Inside he was thinking that Jack, if he still wanted Eleanor Hawkins, would have a fight on his hands. But his instincts told him that there would be no contest for the hand of this wonderful woman. And that was not as it should be. It was perplexing.

Eleanor drove Duane to the gates of the naval station, and Duane caught a boat to Ford Island. There he chanced to stop at the Officer's Club and found Jack and Fred engaged in a hotly contested game of acey-deucy.

Fred leaned back into the thick leather cushions of the booth and watched as Jacobs took out three dollars and tossed them across the table. Seconds earlier Fred bore off his own last man, while Jacobs still had two on the fence and one in the starting quarter. Still, that particular game had been closer than some. Of the twenty-two games he had played since early afternoon, seven or eight had been utter routs, embarrassing runaway victories. Twenty members of the squadron had played him. All went down in defeat and handed over their three dollars. Two—Schuster and Bracker—had won their first games and received five dollars, but went on to lose their second. It was magical. It was amazing. And Brogan had been right: One-quarter of his knowledge had made Fred a rich man—fifty dollars richer to be exact. He thought briefly, not sadly, of buying a wreath for Brogan and casting it into the sea the next time they went out, but decided that even Brogan would consider that an outrageous waste of hard-earned cash.

"What's going on here?" The big voice boomed out of the darkness and caught Fred by surprise. He knew who it was even before several voices called out his name. Why did the Skipper have to show up right in the middle of one of those ridiculous escapades Fred got himself involved in? He tried to shrink back into the leather cushions, but it was no use. Jack pushed his way through the crowd of pilots until he stood in front of the playing table.

"Hi, Skipper," said Fred. "Welcome back."

"It's good to be back," said Jack. He looked around at the circle of faces and down at the backgammon board. "How much did you trim off these poor guys?"

Fred pulled his hand out from behind him, where he had hidden it as soon as he heard the skipper coming. There was a great wad of cash in it. "It's really less than it looks like, Skipper," he said.

"How much?"

"Fifty dollars even." Fred could not lie, or even stretch the truth with the skipper.

"Not bad for an afternoon's work. You buying the drinks?"

Fred grinned. "For you, Skipper, yes. But not for these other suckers." Fred climbed out amidst boos and hisses, and the whole crowd descended on the bar.

It felt good, so good to have the Skipper talking to him like that. He bought a drink for Jack and one for himself. "Sir," he said, holding up his glass in a little toast, and their glasses touched before drinking. For just a second their eyes met, and Fred could see no guardedness, no dislike there. It was like old times—old times only several months before.

"Hey, Trusty," said Jacobs. "What about the skipper? You haven't beat him yet."

"The skipper doesn't count," said Fred.

"You said everyone," chimed in another voice.

"What about it, Trusty?"

"The skipper doesn't count," he said again.

"What do you mean, I don't count?" asked Jack. "You think I don't know how to play the game?"

"Oh, no, sir. It isn't that."

"Well, what is it?"

Fred hesitated.

"Well?"

"I don't want to have to beat you, too." Fred looked away. That *was* how he felt. He knew he could beat the skipper, and he didn't want to.

"We'll just see about that." Jack grabbed Fred's arm and pulled him toward the booth and the acey-deucy game. "I'll give you one chance to back out," said Jack, and a few of the pilots laughed. "I mean I've played a few games of acey-deucy in my time," he continued.

Fred offered him a dice cup. "Thank you, sir," he said, "but I'll take my chances."

They piddled for first roll. Fred won, and the game was never even from that point on. Fred rolled doubles time and again, acey-deucy several times, and moved his blockades steadily around the board. It was over in ten minutes. Jack looked perplexed.

"You've got a lot of company," said Schuster, standing right behind him.

"That'll be three dollars, Skipper," said Fred. He accepted the money with polite thanks and stuffed it into a pocket. "I guess that about does it," he said, looking around. "Any more takers?"

"He did it," said Jacobs.

"Did what?" It was Higgins. The crowd parted, and the executive officer came to the table.

"Hello, Mister Higgins," said Jack.

"Skipper," said Duane. "I didn't know you were in yet."

"Pulled in about an hour ago."

"Trusty's the acey-deucy champ of the whole squadron," said Jacobs.

"You don't have to play him," said Schuster, "but it'll count as a win for him."

"Three will get you five," said Jack, getting up from his seat across from Fred. "And you might as well get your money out before you sit down."

Duane looked down at Trusteau, who shrugged noncommittally. It irritated him to see the ensign sitting there like a champ, a victor over him when they hadn't even played. He sat down.

"Don't count your money yet, hotshot," he said.

And the final game began. But Fred finished off Duane easier than he had Jack Hardigan, and the first official acey-deucy championship of Fighting Twenty came to an end, with Frederick Trusteau the undisputed champ. That night, on the boat back to the *Constitution,* Duane noticed that Jack and Trusteau sat together in the stern of the liberty boat, talking about a marine major and his bunch of paper-tiger pilots.

And up until the announced sailing date for the Tarawa offensive a week and a half later, a confused Higgins could see that whatever tension had existed between the skipper and his wingman before was certainly gone now.

26 October 1943: Commander Buster Jennings, USN, Commanding Officer AG-20, arrived aboard today after two weeks in the base hospital for treatment of exposure and minor wounds suffered when he ditched off Wake Island on the fifth of this month. Lieutenant Commander J. E. Hardigan, Commanding Officer VF-20, is back aboard after temporary duty on board U.S.S. *Belleau Wood.*

10 November 1943: Task Group 50.2 sortied from Pearl Harbor this day, including carriers *Constitution, Enterprise, Belleau Wood,* and *Monterey.* To this date, the target area has not been announced.

The islands of Micronesia are insignificant in matters of world population and economy. For the purposes of war, however, they became vitally strategic points. The lives of thousands of American and Japanese military men was not too high a price to pay for their seizure or defense.

The central Pacific campaign began in November, 1943, with the capture of several islands in the Gilberts chain, an action American planners were certain would provoke a strong naval reaction from the enemy. But it was not to be. The dead end struggle in the upper Solomons, resulting ultimately in the encirclement and reduction of the Japanese stronghold at Rabaul, had proved so costly to the Japanese that they finally committed their last trained carrier air groups to its defense. These air groups were virtually destroyed by the meat grinder attrition there. And thus it was that when the prows of hundreds of American warships swung around and pointed to an atoll named Tarawa, the decisive engagement of fleets that both sides sought so eagerly was postponed to an uncertain date in the future.

(J.E. Hardigan, Commander, USN (ret), *A Setting of Many Suns: The Destruction of the Imperial Navy* [The Naval Institute Press, 1962], p. 141.)

Part V

Combat Two:

Tarawa

29

"Okay, gentlemen, if we could settle down here and give me your attention, we'll get this road on the show. Wait till you see what we got for you guys today. Lotsa big things happening and some bigger things in the making. Before we're through here, all you guys are gonna be aces and heroes and that's no joke. Okay. What I have here is a map of the islands of Micronesia. Colorful places where the girls don't wear no shirts and the breezes keep the grass skirts from hiding too much. Up here we got the Marshalls and down here the Gilberts. Now you gotta have a doctorate degree in linguistics to pronounce the names of some of these islands, but I'm gonna give it the old college try, anyway."

Jack Hardigan leaned back in his chair and glanced at his pilots, sitting seriously around the great green table in the wardroom. The whole air group was there this evening, along with the captain and the ship's XO, while the briefing officer, a full commander, began the first briefing on the upcoming operation. He had a giant map fastened to the bulkhead behind him and carried a pointer of the kind favored by briefing officers: It was a good three feet long, tapered like an arrow, with a small metal cap on the business end. Jack was mildly amused by the man's sense of humor. Apparently the operation was not going to be all that difficult.

"On twenty November—that's six days off for you fighter

jockeys—the jarheads are gonna land on and take from the Japs the islands of Betio and Butaritari in the atolls of Tarawa and Makin respectively. That's Makin," he prounounced it muck-in, "and it rhymes with man's favorite sport, if you know what I mean. Here they are right here. Now what part, you may ask, are we going to play in the grand scheme of things? Well, that's what I'm here to let you know, and as soon as I get my notes together and all you guys light up one more cigarette and get yourself another cup of coffee, I'll tell you."

The commander shuffled through a stack of papers at the end of the table. From where he sat, Jack could see the red, rubber-stamped words "Top Secret" adorning most of the pages. He remembered the Marcus strike and the lost page. It made him want to smile. He looked around. A number of his pilots had indeed used the break to take out another cigarette and light up; Fred sat opposite him and Jack caught a glimpse of the Hornet Zippo lighter he had given him. It flashed briefly in the light, then disappeared quickly into Fred's shirt pocket. It seemed like years ago when they had sat together in the squadron office and he had given the lighter to Fred in a spur-of-the-moment gesture of friendship. He was glad now that he had.

"Everyone lit up? Good. I want to tell you boys that this time we got not only the first string on the field, but we got the second string and the third string and the water boys and the coaches. We got the whole team on the field this time. As I'm sure you've seen, here in this group we got the *Big E*, the *Ironsides* here, the *Monty,* and the *Wood,* and we are headed right—here." (He pointed to a patch of ocean midway between Makin and Tarawa.) "What you don't see is another group of three more flattops and other heavies north of us and they are headed here." (He indicated the Marshall Islands and circled the pointer to take them all in.) "Their job is to attack the Jap airfields on Mili and Jaluit and Maloelap and keep the Nips from sending in reinforcements to help out on Makin and Tarawa. Our job will be to make the first strikes on both of the target islands and then just hang back and wait for the Emperor's fleet to show itself, at which time we will promptly give it its one-half of the ocean: the bottom half."

He waited a second for the nervous, polite laughter to subside, then pressed on.

"But we are not alone. No, sir. Because coming up from the New Hebrides from the south we got, count them, not one, but two more task groups with a total of five carriers and assorted heavies to help out—if we leave them anything to shoot at. Now the jarheads are coming from two places: The northern force came right behind us from Pearl, and is headed for Makin. The southern force came out of the New Hebrides and is headed for Tarawa. We expect it'll take 'em one—maybe two days—to close the real estate deals and turn the deeds over to Uncle Sam, and they've got jeep carriers for close air cover, too. What we'd like to see is the Imperial Navy, so we can teach them a thing or two about flying. Okay." He stopped talking and scanned the pilots. "Any questions?"

Jack had plenty of questions, not the least of which was where the Navy had dug up twelve fast carriers. That fact alone was astounding. The old days are gone for good, he thought. The Navy's here to stay.

"Opposition: Here's what we expect to find when we get there. The Jap doesn't know we're coming, so the first planes we're gonna run into will be Army. Bettys and Nells most likely. The fighters will be Zekes and Hamps and maybe Tojos. They'll be flying from the fields here in the Marshalls and from both Makin and Tarawa. So you fighter boys will have your work cut out for you. As for you bomber jockeys, there's good news for you guys, too. Intelligence says there's lots of shipping around the islands—merchants and escorts most likely—but you never know what else will turn up. And we have to plaster those islands like they've never been hit before. When we're through, all the gyrenes'll have to do is walk ashore and count the dead Japs, and that's no joke. Now, some miscellaneous info before we break up into groups and go into the details.

"We are badly in need of destroyers, so there'll be some mighty lengthy ASW patrols for you bomber pilots. We want to get there without being seen, and in the process put any Jap sub that crosses our path on the bottom where it belongs. When we get within five hundred miles of the target area, we will institute a reinforced CAP, so don't you flying aces think you're getting off easy. More on this later. Unfortunately, we will not cross zero degrees latitude so you polywogs will have it easy this cruise. But you wait. We'll get you before long."

"How about that guy?" asked Boom Bloomington. He was stretched out on Jack's bunk with his feet on the blanket at the foot and his hands behind his head.

"You mean the commander who did the prebriefing?" Woody Heywood sat on the bed near Boom's feet and leafed through a much-handled magazine.

"Yeah," said Boom. "A real comic."

"He can afford to be," said Jack, sitting at the little fold-down desk. "He doesn't have to drop the bombs."

"He makes it sound like a goddamn practice exercise," said Boom. "Like those fleet problems they used to have back before the war. 'Now you guys are the blue fleet and those guys are the orange fleet,'" he sing-songed.

"'And your aircraft carrier just got sunk by that battleship that snuck up behind you and shot the hell out of you with its big guns.'"

"There's only one thing I don't understand," said Jack.

"What's that?" asked Woody.

"Twelve carriers. How did they come up with twelve carriers?"

"General Motors builds them, just like Oldsmobiles."

"Last March they brought in that old British carrier because all we had available was the *Enterprise*. Remember that?"

"I was too busy trying to teach these lads how not to crash," said Boom.

"Now we've got twelve of our own."

"Maybe so," said Boom, "but I wouldn't put any money on us being home for Christmas."

"Me, neither," said Woody. He dropped the magazine to the deck with a plop. "Jesus Christ," he said. "They can put twelve carriers to sea in the space of six months, but they can't get a newer magazine than December '42 out to the boys in blue."

"Aluminum drives," said Jack.

"Aluminum drives?"

"When I was stateside, they were having an aluminum drive. They take a big truck around the neighborhood and ask everyone to bring out their pots and pans."

"That explains it," said Boom.

"What?" asked Woody.

"Where they got the twelve carriers." Boom pounded his fist against the bulkhead. "Somebody's Aunt Maude gave her all for this ship."

Jack laughed. "My right gear strut was probably a bumper on a Chevrolet."

"I knew there was a reason why they didn't put partitions between the stools in the head."

"Yeah," said Boom. "You can only do so much with spare pots and pans."

"As it is," said Woody, "there's a community pissoff in the head every morning."

"The air group that pisses together," said Jack, "stays together."

All three laughed a little, then fell silent.

Boom turned over and raised himself on one elbow. "You know," he said seriously, "we're heading into a goddamn hornet's nest of Jap airfields. We'll be in range for days at a time. And not just one or two little strips. More like seven or eight."

"Like the man said," Jack said, "we got our work cut out for us."

"What do you think our chances are?" asked Woody.

"Of what?" asked Jack.

"Oh, say of coming through alive."

"I don't have the slightest idea. I try not to think about it."

"I don't think I like this war business anymore." Boom rolled onto his back.

"I never did," said Jack.

"Say," said Woody. "Have you guys noticed any difference in the old man lately?"

"Jennings?" asked Jack.

"Yeah," said Boom, rolling over again and propping himself on one elbow. "Yeah, I noticed it."

"I haven't even talked to him since he got back from the hospital," said Jack.

"Exactly," said Woody. "He hasn't had anyone on the carpet since they fished him out of the drink."

"Actually," said Boom, "I think I made an excellent temporary air group commander."

"No, really," said Woody. "I think he's mellowed."

"Mellowed," said Jack. "No. I don't believe it."

"You'll see," said Woody. "Mark my word."

"I want to know something else," said Boom. "Word has it that your own Ensign Trusteau is a child prodigy at acey-deucy. What do you know about that, Fighter Leader Hardigan?"

Jack shrugged. "The squadron champ. That's all."

"Ah, yes. But he made a few bucks doing it. Think he could use a manager? Say 10 percent of the gross, and I'll arrange the matches?"

"Sorry," said Jack. "He's all mine."

"He sounds like a real go-getter," said Woody.

"Pretty good at bridge, too," said Jack.

"And navigating."

"And a few other things that officers and gentlemen do not discuss in polite conversation." Boom laughed. "An all-around man, that's what he is. He's what the Navy's coming to."

"Sure," said Jack. "The new Navy."

"You know," said Woody. "The one with twelve carriers."

"Twelve carriers," said Jack, "the new Navy."

"Aw, write a book on it."

"I think I will," said Jack. "I think I will."

"So this is the so-called acey-deucy champ of the *Ironsides*."

Fred was hanging up his Mae West and flight helmet on a hook on the side bulkhead of the ready room. He glanced over his shoulder at the big man in the officer's uniform. He was very tired.

"What's the matter, kid," said the man heartily, and he clapped a hand on Fred's shoulder, tried to turn him around. Fred resisted until he finished hanging his things, then allowed himself to be turned. He studied the man through aching, bloodshot eyes, and only then realized that the officer was a full commander, with the little gold leaf clusters of rank on either collar.

"I'm sorry, sir," he said. "I didn't see—"

"You brought me all the way down here to talk to an ensign?" The Commander talked over his shoulder to another pilot, whom Fred recognized in the dim red light as Schuster. "Hell," said the commander, "I ain't had an ensign for dinner in ages."

"Do I know you?" asked Fred, trying not to sound impolite. He had just come off the last CAP of the evening, landing just as it was getting dark. He had been awake since three that morning and wanted nothing more right now than to fall unconscious into his bunk.

"Hell," said the commander. "Do I *know* him? Schute, you scroungy son of a bitch."

"That's the one," said Schuster. "Shellacked every one in the squadron, and nearly everyone else in the air group."

"Well, well, well," said the commander, turning back to Fred and looking him up and down. "A hotshot shavetail. The things they drag out of OCS these days."

Fred tried to feel offended but was too tired. "If you'll excuse me, sir," he said. "I have to turn in." He tried to pass the burly roadblock, but it had other ideas.

"Hold on just a damn minute there, son," he said. "Don't get all hot and bothered." The commander turned and winked broadly at Schuster. "I was just funnin' you."

"Sure," said Fred.

"I hear you play a pretty mean game of acey-deucy."

"I . . . win sometimes." Please, Fred was thinking. Not tonight. Please.

"He *wins* sometimes." The commander found this uproariously funny.

"Do you play, sir?"

Again the booming laughter. "Do I play? Hell, son, I invented the fucking game."

"That's nice," said Fred. "It's a great game." He tried again to leave.

"Hell, son, ain't you even going to ask me if I want to play a game or two?"

"No, sir, I don't think I will. I mean, not tonight."

"Hell, Schute, this here ain't no champ. Look son, if you don't play me a game tonight, you won't be the champ no more."

"Couldn't we do this another time, sir? I've got to fly early tomorrow and I really think—"

"No, we can't. Tomorrow I got to fly back to the *Yorktown* and dig up some more crazy islands to bomb. Tonight, son."

Fred looked around and saw no courteous way to escape. Maybe one game wouldn't take too long. "One game, sir. Then I have to turn in."

"That's more like it. Come on up to my cabin. You, too, Schute, you ugly bastard, and let's have a go at it."

Fred followed the man up to flag country and one of the spare staterooms intended for use of embarked admirals' staffs. There he took a seat at a little table bolted snugly to the deck. The commander took out a game board and placed it over a haphazard pile of papers on the table. The top one was a closed manila folder with the words "Galvanic—Top Secret" on it.

Fred played the best his tired mind would allow. Fifteen minutes later he had another victory under his belt. The commander was disturbed and showed it.

"That was the most chickenshit way of playing I've ever seen," he bellowed.

"Well, if that's all, sir," said Fred, starting to rise.

"Like hell it is. You sit your ass down there and play it again, or I'll get you transferred to a honey barge in the Aleutians."

Although he wasn't particularly worried about the man's threat, Fred was now somewhat more awake. He decided to humor the man. They played another game. Fred won again.

The commander glowered across the board with such a vengeful look that Fred was afraid to get up. The silence hung thickly for a moment; then the older man spoke. "Son," he said, "who taught you how to play this game?"

"Brogan, sir. Lieutenant Brogan."

"Didn't I tell you," said Schuster.

"Shut up, Schute. Let the man tell me himself."

"You knew Brogan?" asked Fred.

"Taught him every fucking thing he knew about the game. Picked it up real quick and then never let me win another game. I must've lost a thousand goddamn bucks to that mangy, good-for-nothing—"

"Hey," said Fred, looking up and catching the commander's eye. "Don't say that. He was a..." Fred looked down at the deck between his feet and tried to think of one word to describe Brogan, could only come up with "...a good man."

The commander looked surprised at Fred's outburst. His face softened. "Don't listen to me, son. Sometimes I say things kind of funny."

"I guess I'd better go," said Fred.

"Yeah. You'll need the sleep." The commander saw Fred to the door, but followed him into the black shadows. Red pools of light marked the passageway.

"Good night, sir," said Fred, and he started to leave.

The commander stopped him. "Don't go yet," he said. When Fred faced him again, he said. "It's a mean damn game."

"What?" said Fred, maybe a little too sharply. "Acey-deucy?"

"That," said the commander, "and all this." He indicated the carrier with an eloquent roll of his eyes. Fred felt something tugging, hurting, inside his chest.

"He called it a man's game."

"He was never wrong." The commander took Fred by the arm and pulled him up close, so close that Fred could smell the tobacco on his breath as he spoke. "Did you see when..." he began. "When he..." He couldn't finish. Fred nodded. "I miss that good-for-nothing, little—" and he stopped again. Fred thought he could see his eyes glistening.

"I do, too," he said.

"You're all right," said the commander. Fred could almost hear Brogan saying the same words. "You take care of yourself up there, son."

Almost gently, Fred said, "I don't intend to leave until I beat every sucker on this ship."

And the commander reached out and clumsily patted Fred on the side of the face, his hand stopping for an immeasurably brief time to let his thumb brush the cheek. "You do that," he said.

Fred left him then, not happily, looking back once. He saw the big man push a wadded handkerchief into his hip pocket, then reenter the stateroom. And when Fred had undressed and climbed into his bunk, he realized just before falling asleep that at least one other person in the world mourned for Brogan.

30

It was horrible yet spectacular; it was at once gruesome and fascinating. Duane Higgins circled at five thousand feet with the three Hellcats of his division and four more from another, and watched the invasion of Betio Island in the atoll named Tarawa. The eight fighters had been there for an hour. They had made a single strafing run on an island named Bairiki at the request of a nameless air controller. Now they waited for another assignment and watched the spectacle below them.

Tarawa lay on the surface of the ocean like a dazzling string of beads on a bed of coral. Betio Island lay at the southwest corner of the squarish arrangement of islands. All the other islands were almost mythically beautiful with swaying palms and bright sandy beaches bordering a deep blue lagoon. Betio was an unreal panorama from the depths of hell.

When the trade winds shifted and parted the smoke to reveal the tortured little island, Duane thought that the surface of the moon was probably more hospitable. Every square foot of land was blasted and cratered. Shattered palm trees stood bedraggled and headless, occasionally blown into the air to topple, in seeming slow-motion, to the ground. Huge rolling clouds of greasy black smoke rose from a dozen locations, drifting across the lagoon, sometimes obscuring the clumps of small boats that churned in frantic circles there, forming into lines abreast and heading for the beach. Shells splashed amidst them.

On the ocean side of the atoll a fleet of transports and warships covered miles and miles of water. Duane counted more than a dozen transports. Three bulky, bristling vessels that he assumed were battleships prowled up and down the length of the island, loosing massive broadsides of flame and smoke every so often, which would terminate on the island in towering, earth-shaking explosions.

The reef stretched several hundred yards out from the beach. The water was a lighter shade of green there, and the approaching landing craft inevitably stopped at its edge, lowered prows and disgorged groups of men, who struggled through the knee-deep surf to the beach. When they strafed the island of Bairiki, Duane led his aircraft down and along that same beach toward which the Marines were struggling. From that altitude, he could see what had been invisible from higher up: All along the reef and up to the beach were scores—no, hundreds—of bodies, dark, huddled masses of them, face down in the water or piled in groups along the beach. Even as he crossed overhead, a line of twenty or so Marines, slogging through the water, heads down, was cut down like tenpins and dropped in a neat line. They didn't get up. It was unbelievable.

As they waited for another assignment, Duane couldn't help but remember the briefing officer's remark that the Marines would walk ashore and count the dead Japs. And this was the second day of the assault. They were supposed to have completed the "occupation" by this evening. It was sickening. Duane knew he would never forget those piles of bodies, those suddenly-dead Marines dropping in the water.

"Scarlet One to Banger Flight, over." It was the air controller.

Duane went to his throat mike. "This is Banger Leader, over."

"Are you on station, Banger Leader?"

"That's affirmative, Scarlet One, eight VF orbiting the lagoon at this time."

"Roger, Banger Leader. Stand by for target." Duane signaled his wingman, Bracker, then glanced over his shoulder at the other section of Hellcats. Both waggled their wings expectantly, pulled in closer to the leading aircraft.

"Banger Leader, your target: Beached freighter west of long pier, that is freighter beached on reef two five zero yards from beach and west   that is west   of long pier. Six VB will precede your flight with bombs, attack time approximately ten, one zero, minutes. Landing craft are clearing the area at this time.

Make your approach from west to east, that is west to east.
Report when you are attacking. Acknowledge please, over."

Duane looked and found the pier, and then the freighter. It
was indeed aground, keeled over on its side, with water lapping
across the main deck. It looked deserted, but since they were
using valuable bombs on it, there had to be Japanese causing
trouble there. "Target acknowledged, Scarlet One. Beached
freighter by itself west of long pier on the lagoon side."

He noticed now that the waves of landing craft, like legions of
disciplined water bugs, were giving the ship a wide berth. "We
will attack after flight of six VB in about ten minutes." Duane
listened for a return acknowledgment from the controller, but he
had already started talking to a unit called Ginger Baby, asking
it to scout the southern beach and look for friendly troops.
Duane looked around for the bombers, certain they would be
Dauntlesses. Six of the *Ironsides* dive bombers had been there
earlier, but they had been called on to targets on the island
almost immediately and, their bombs expended, had headed
back for the roost.

"Scarlet One, this is Sparrow Flight. We are commencing
bombing run at this time."

"Roger, Sparrow Leader. Hit 'em with gusto."

Duane looked again. The first of six dive bombers began its
run on the freighter. Duane signaled his seven fighters and they
circled around to the west, to be in position to attack when the
bombers were through. Presently, they arrived off the western
end of Betio, over the transports, and watched the first of six
bombs explode near the freighter. The second went off, then a
third. They were all misses and threw huge columns of water
harmlessly into the air. Four and five detonated. They, too, were
misses.

Duane peeled off and began his run. He went to his throat
mike.

"Scarlet One, this is Banger Leader. We are beginning our
attack at this time."

The sixth and last bomb exploded near the freighter. It was
no more effective than the previous five.

"Roger, Banger Leader. Can you observe results of Sparrow
Flight's attack?"

"Affirmative, Scarlet. Sorry. They missed."

"Very well, Banger. Give 'em hell."

"You got it, Scarlet." Duane watched the island grow in size
and detail as he gathered speed. "Banger Flight, this is Banger
Leader. Keep speed down to one eight zero, fellas, and let's do

a better job than the buzzard boys." His altitude fell sharply and Duane leveled off over the reef. He was closer this time, closer to the death and destruction that littered the island. There were more bodies in the shallows by now—many more—but Duane kept his eyes on the target looming in his gunsight. He squeezed the trigger.

His bullets cut a swath through the water and fell on the wreck. Keeping his nose down and deftly using his rudder, Duane hosed a stream of missiles over all the portions of the ship above water. They sparkled on the steel plating and ricocheted wildly about. His speed was low and he kept the target under fire for a few strangely prolonged seconds, then the target passed below him, and he pulled back on the stick to go back up. Sweeping out over the lagoon, Duane passed over a landing craft filled with wounded Marines. Corpsmen bent over the prone figures. His low-flying Hellcat attracted no attention whatsoever.

Looking back, he watched the second division execute their firing runs. The concentrations of fifty-caliber gunfire tore up small pieces of decking and tossed the debris high into the air. A tiny fire sprang up near the bow, but the target was far from being destroyed.

He began climbing to their orbiting station and called the controller again. "Scarlet, this is Banger Leader, over."

"Go ahead, Banger Leader."

"We have completed our runs. I didn't see anybody aboard that tub. You want us to go around again?" The controller didn't answer at once, and the scattered Hellcats began to pull back into their cruising formation.

"That's a negative on your last, Banger Flight," said the controller finally. "We're going to let the big boys handle this one."

Somewhat rankled at the implication that they couldn't handle the job, Duane checked his fuel and figured they could spend maybe ten more minutes over the target. Since the "big boys"—whoever they were—thought they could do a better job, maybe the ten minutes could be spent more profitably heading back to the ship. He had a berth in the poker game waiting for him, anyway.

"Scarlet One, this is Banger Leader, over."

"Go ahead, Banger."

"We're getting kind of low on go juice. Request permission to return to base." Scarlet One was slow to answer again, and the eight Hellcats made a great circuit of the lagoon. Duane was about to ask again when he got his reply.

"Banger Leader, this is Scarlet One. Permission granted on your last, and happy landings."

"We'll try, Scarlet. Banger Leader out."

"Y'all come back now, y'hear?"

Duane decided not to answer that one, and on their last pass over the little lagoon, he was able to see who the "big boys" were. The battleships—two of them—were firing over the island and demolishing the wreck. The big guns blasted out (although he couldn't hear them over the roar of his engine), rippling the sea around their own hulls in great concentric circles. Seconds later came the salvo—six or eight shells at a time—a forest of splashes that was first over, then directly on target. For a few seconds the freighter was totally obscured by the explosions. Then the explosions stopped abruptly. When the last geyser had subsided, the freighter was gone.

Duane turned back to his flying, impressed with the power of the heavy ship-borne artillery. It dawned on him that he had just witnessed a good example of the controversy that raged in the upper command levels between the carrier officers and the Gun Club: The old battlewagons still packed quite a punch, and sometimes the aviators dropped the ball. He shrugged to himself, completely confident nonetheless that his job was not endangered.

"Okay, fellas, close it up. We don't have all day." Duane, checking back on the seven other Hellcats, was not surprised to find them tagging along behind him in a loose, ragged formation. He knew they were tired, overworked. They had been in continuous action for six days, flying twice the normal number of hours per day, enduring the pressures of flying over enemy islands. They were bound to lose some of their fighting edge. But that probably didn't matter. Since their first day in the area, the *Ironsides* fighters had not encountered a single airborne enemy aircraft. It was as if the Japanese had completely written off the Gilbert Islands, leaving the trapped soldiers on Betio and Makin to fend for themselves.

The eight Hellcats droned along at six thousand feet, leaving the atoll of Tarawa behind them. Halfway back to the task group, they passed another flight of Hellcats and Dauntlesses headed in the opposite direction, toward the beautiful little ring of islands that the Navy and Marines were so horribly disfiguring. Duane wondered how much longer they would be here, in this obscure little corner of the world he had never heard of ten days before. If they stayed in the area much longer, they could broadcast their exact position in the clear every morning. The entire Japanese empire knew where they were, anyway. Duane pulled out his plotting board and checked their position. They would be spotting the outer ships of the screen soon.

"Okay, fellas, IFF on. We don't want them taking pot shots at us." He knew there was little danger of that. The gun crews aboard the ships were probably as tired and bored with the operation as the pilots were. But procedures were established to be followed, and Duane was not one to flaunt procedure. He told his charges to close it up so they at least looked sharp as they flew over the task group; then he looked down and found the first destroyer of the screen. As the tired pilots cleaned up their formation, the first carrier hove into view, followed shortly by two more. Duane contacted the FDO and was told to wait for a few minutes while the *Constitution* launched another strike and four fighters for CAP. The eight Hellcats circled high above the carrier as the tiny, cruciform airplanes below rolled down the deck and soared gracefully into the air. He switched over to the CAP control circuit.

"Rooster, this is Banger Zero Two. Airborne." It was the Skipper, taking a turn on CAP.

"Roger, Banger Zero Two. Report when on station."

"Affirmative."

"Rooster Base, this is Banger One Four. I am airborne." And that was Trusteau.

"Roger, One Four. Report when on station."

"Wilco, Rooster Base."

"Ever seen a better day for flying, Trusty?" The Skipper again.

"Possibly, but I can't remember when."

"You still got all your wheels?"

"Last time I checked they were there."

"I hear that when all the tires are gone, they're going to give us pontoons and let us land on the water."

"Sure beats not landing at all."

"Roger to that, Trusty."

Duane flipped back to the strike control circuit and wondered if he and Jack had sounded like that when they flew together all the time. Now it seemed they were never doing the same thing at the same time. The skipper would take one flight, the exec would take the next, and never the twain would meet.

The little exchange about wheels concerned a recent tendency for the tires to blow on landing, a perilous experience if

ever there was one. The skipper and Trusteau had chatted about
it as if they were old buddies from before the war. That,
combined with the fact that Jack just didn't pay very much
attention to him anymore, disturbed Duane. Why did people
have to change like that?

"We have a clear deck at this time, Banger Leader. Bring the
chickens on home."

"You got it, Rooster Base. Let's put 'em down, guys."

Duane banked to the left, slipping easily into the pattern he
knew so well. The landing was made almost without incident;
seven times the landing signals officer slashed his paddles in the
cut sign and seven times a Hellcat sank to the deck, caught a
wire, plunged to a halt. The eighth one, however, was different.
Ensign Peckerly made a good approach, took the cut, caught the
wire, and had a blowout in his right main gear tire. The Hellcat
swerved to the right, nosed up sharply, stood for a second on its
nose, then slowly, uncertainly, tipped over, and crunched to the
deck upside down. Its wheels stuck straight up as if it were some
great, dead insect. Duane Higgins stayed on deck long enough to
determine that Peckerly was all right—he was hanging upside
down in his crushed cockpit while dozens of mechanics and
plane pushers struggled to free him—then headed below to his
waiting berth in the great floating poker game.

31

23 November 1943: VF-20 today flew a total of forty-two missions including sixteen sorties as air support off the island of Betio and the remainder as combat air patrol. Effective squadron strength is down to twenty-seven aircraft after numbers five and twenty-three experienced blowouts upon landing. The tire situation is considered critical as it is believed that spares cannot be received prior to 30 November.

Aircraft piloted by Lieutenant Bradley and Ensign Duggin at 1110 hours participated in an attack on a probable enemy submarine approximately twenty miles west of the task group. Results of the attack are not known.

Aircraft piloted by Lt. (j.g.) Hammerstein and Ensign Patrick attacked and shot down an enemy search plane of the Dave variety with a single float, believed to be flying from a base in the northern Marshalls. The attack occurred at 1330 hours. The aircraft was destroyed in a single pass by Mister Hammerstein within sight of the task group.

Reports indicate that resistance on Betio is nearing an end, although all carrier groups are expected to remain in the area for at least three more days.

Jack Hardigan flew his Hellcat mechanically, barely thinking about it and worried about his men. Below him, the last of the day's CAP, except for himself and Fred Trusteau, were being taken aboard *Ironsides*. It was the twenty-sixth of November, six days since the landings on Betio, and the air group had been in continuous action since two days before that. Waking time eventually began to merge into a single unending grind of launching, patrolling, vectoring, escorting, strafing, landing, launching again. His men were ragged and tired and he knew it; he was in the same condition himself.

It was late afternoon. The sun dipped close to the horizon and shone red on the low-lying, scattered clouds. The ships below slashed the sea with parallel wakes. Jack looked over his shoulder, knowing without seeing him that Fred was there as before—consistent, uncomplaining, utterly reliable. Fred was tired, too; he looked it when they were aboard ship. But in the air he was better than ever.

The entire squadron had been as sharp as nails going into this operation. The training he had put them through since Wake had brought them to a peak of proficient readiness. Eight days of this, however, had worn them into a sloppy, mistake-prone gaggle.

And the planes. That was another story. The situation with the tires was astonishing. Now they had four inoperable Hellcats; tires were blowing on all the planes with sobering regularity. Ensign Rogers had gone over the side two days before when his left tire went on landing. Only a miracle had saved him from certain death: The fighter had hung up precariously in the port catwalk, its wheels snagged by the life line, the right wing propped up against a forty-millimeter gun mount. As soon as Rogers had scrambled to safety, the life line snapped and the Hellcat slid into the sea, crashing into the side of the ship on its way down. The experience made Rogers into a swaggering, hardened veteran overnight, but Jack knew now that all the men were getting somewhat edgy about landing.

At least there was one thing Jack didn't have to worry about. It had come about several days after the original briefing. It still made him wonder. On that particular evening, Commander Jennings had called him to his stateroom and made small talk until it was time for the movie. Jack guessed that he was trying to find the nerve to thank him for his protection in the water off Wake. Jennings had just said he was sure sorry about Lieutenant Brogan and sure glad about Ensign Trusteau when the address system announced the wardroom movie. He had suggested they see it together. Jack accepted, convinced that Woody Heywood had been right: CAG had mellowed. But actions spoke louder than words. The petty harassment simply stopped, leaving Jack with the energy and time he needed to keep his pilots alert and his planes in the air.

"Banger One, this is Rooster Base."

"Go ahead, Rooster Base." Jack looked around. They had better be taking them aboard pretty soon. There were maybe ten minutes of daylight remaining.

"Banger One, what is your fuel situation?"

"Fuel is no problem, Rooster. Daylight is. Suggest you bring us aboard asap."

"We have a foul deck at this time, Banger. Fifteen minutes should clear it."

Fifteen minutes would be cutting it very close. Darkness fell out here like a door slamming. Jack wondered what had caused the fouled deck, but decided he didn't really want to know until he had to. He looked over at Fred. The ensign's oxygen mask was dangling and his face was ruddy with reflected sunlight.

"Everything all right over there, Trusty wingman?"

Fred gave a smiling thumbs-up. "Peachy keen, Fearless Leader."

"Fifteen more minutes won't make a diff, will it?"

"We can sleep an extra fifteen minutes tomorrow morning." Jack laughed to himself, not afraid to exchange a little small talk over the empty circuit. They circled leisurely, keeping the ships of the group in sight below, not wanting to be far away when they were called in. In about ten minutes they were notified.

"Banger One, we have a clear deck at this time and can bring you aboard."

"That's what we want to hear, Rooster. Let's go home, Trusty."

The two Hellcats descended in a sharp bank, reversing course directly into the rapidly setting sun. They were on the downwind leg, crossing the outer destroyers of the screen, when another call came.

The director's voice was strained, hurried.

"Banger One, climb to angels five. Stand by for vector."

"Roger, Rooster." Jack increased his throttle, checked his instruments, glanced back at Fred. Fred shrugged exaggeratedly; then he pulled up close under Jack's wing. The two fighters clawed upward in the failing light.

"Banger One, we have an unidentified bogey bearing zero niner zero, true range ten miles. Do you have sufficient light for interception?"

"We will intercept," said Jack. He pulled around in a tight turn to the left, still climbing. He wasn't sure just how they would intercept a bogey in the dark, but they would try. The ship must be protected at all costs. He would worry about landing later.

"Vector zero niner two, range ten miles and closing, altitude angels three, buster." It was close. Ninety degrees true was due east, into the darkest part of the sky. Behind them, the sun's rim sank below the horizon. The first stars appeared overhead. Jack tightened his straps, pulled his goggles over his eyes. Throttles to the wall, the two Hellcats rushed into the blackening sky, leaving the ships behind.

Fred heard the vector report and knew then that they would have to land after dark. But the skipper would never refuse an interception if there were even a slim chance of making it. Night operations had never been pushed on the new pilots, although the older squadron members talked of flying at night before the war. Would they turn on the lights and risk giving away the position of the ship to enemy snoopers and subs? They wouldn't just leave two pilots up there in the dark to fly until they ran out of fuel.... Or would they? Fred pushed those thoughts from his mind and concentrated on the mission at hand. He was mildly excited, although he didn't expect anything to come of the vector. After all, if they couldn't find the bogey, the bogey probably couldn't find the task group. It sounded simple.

Checking his instruments, Fred figured he had enough fuel for maybe a half-hour of fast flying. The engine was running smoothly, all indicators in the green. The skipper was plainly visible in the gathering dusk, but ahead and below lay only darkness. He touched his throat mike.

"See anything, Banger One?" he asked.

"Nothing yet. But hang in there. We may see some action yet."

"Righto, Leader." The words did nothing to cheer Fred. He didn't want a fight in the dark and a night landing. He remembered the words of Brogan. "Nothing will happen to you 'cause you fly wing on the old man and nothing ever happens to him." He hoped Brogan was right.

The engine droned away. It got darker. Directly in front of him the constellation Orion hovered over the horizon, only the brightest stars in it showing. They were five minutes away from the original vector report now, and nothing had appeared. It was a dud—a false radar image most likely. Fred relaxed. Then something moved in the corner of his eye.

It was an aircraft. Black. Low to the water, almost invisible in the darkness. Fred banked to the right to get a better look, assured himself that it wasn't an illusion, and went into a steep right-hand turn to follow. His hand tried to reach the throat mike but the heavy g forces plastered it to the side of the cockpit until he leveled out. He found the mike and talked. "Tallyho. Bandits in sight."

The western sky was before him now. There was still a trace of light. The plane had disappeared into the gloom, flying toward the task group. He was sure it was a plane, even though he had seen it for only a second. It had to be here.

Fred pushed the stick over and went down, knowing that if he went lower than the unidentified plane, it would show up, outlined against the lighter sky. He searched until his eyes ached from the strain and concentration. He heard the skipper calling him. He was about to answer when suddenly there it was, right in front of him, silhouetted against the gray sky.

Single engine, low wing. A Kate. A torpedo bomber. Fred checked his guns and found them unarmed, flicked the switches that charged them. The electric sight ring sprang to life. It was so bright it momentarily blinded him, but he found the dimmer knob and turned it all the way down. The Kate was still in front of him.

His heart pounded in his ears. He was approaching the enemy bomber from its right side. He was level with it and slightly to the rear. He eased the throttle all the way to the stop and watched the target fill the sight ring. He flew the Hellcat now as if it were a part of himself, an extension of his body. The stick and trigger were molded to his right hand, the rudder pedals extensions of his feet. He thought: Bank slightly to the right and come in behind him. The Hellcat did just that. The target filled the outer ring. Fred squeezed the trigger.

The tracers blazed through the night sky. He hardly noticed the vibration of the guns. Fred edged the fighter's nose down and to the left and watched the tracers appear to pass ahead of the target. A piece of debris detached itself from the Kate and tumbled back over his head. Now the Kate's right wing sank downward, the left went up, and the bomber began to slide toward the water. Fred was about to follow when something else caught his attention.

A small bright flame had sprung to life in the darkness in front of him. But it wasn't the first bomber. It was a second.

Suddenly the first Kate burst into ragged flame, rolled over on its back, and headed down. Unbelievingly, Fred continued toward the little flame and there   yes   there was not one, but two more Kate torpedo bombers. Fred's Hellcat devoured the distance to the two bombers.

He was still trying to comprehend how his gunfire had reached out and accidentally hit a second target when something sounded in his ears. It was the skipper's voice, distant and far away. But Fred couldn't answer. He was far too busy.

The little flame had grown, and Fred saw that it was coming from the right wing of one of the Kates. The target filled his sight ring. They're making no effort to escape, he thought. Why? His finger depressed the trigger button. Again the tracers arched out through the night, splitting the darkness like Fourth of July fireworks, but far more deadly. They found the enemy bomber. Fred was almost directly behind the doomed plane, holding the trigger down. A puff of orange flame. The Kate slanted to the right like the other one had, and Fred followed it, still firing.

The Kate's right wing dipped low now, and something very strange happened. It touched something. The water. They were at zero altitude and Fred had not even known. He pulled back on the stick violently as the enemy plane went in, the right wing digging in, the left coming over, cartwheeling, exploding into a cloud of bright flames that briefly reached out for Fred's Hellcat but were quickly left behind.

Another enemy plane still was loose in front of him. Fred kicked left rudder and pushed the stick over to take him back to where he had last seen the Kate. He found it with no trouble.

It couldn't have been more than fifty feet from the white-flecked surface of the ocean. As with the first two, Fred approached from the right side aft, level. The sky was completely dark now, but there was no need for light. The third and final victim lay before him. Mechanically, swiftly, Fred closed until he could see the plane clearly. It turned to the left. Fred followed; his speed was obviously much higher because he continued to gain even after the turn. The Kate turned back to the right, closer to the guns that would tear it to pieces. Fred concentrated. He did not even see when the enemy fired back.

His first indication that the Kate was returning fire was an incredible whanging crash that threw his head back into the rest and nearly tore the stick from his hand. Then he saw them: dim, round tracers that seemed to float motionless in front of him until he flew under them. Then they soared overhead, snatched quickly out of sight. Regaining control, Fred felt and heard a horrible rush of cold air, like a hundred singing voices, surging around his face. His goggles were up, so he pulled them down in a single logical movement, and he could see again. The sight ring still glowed; the trigger was still beneath his index finger. And suddenly Fred was mad. Every Japanese bullet that was fired at him seemed to find his plane, and if they were going to get him, by God he would take a few of them with him. He centered the target in the sight ring and prepared to fire.

A huge black object bounded out of the night and passed below them. Ships. They were over the task group. Fred jinxed quickly to the right to avoid a destroyer, then back to the left, closed to pointblank range, and gunned the enemy Kate from the sky.

An irrational urge to see what was happening drove Duane Higgins out of the claustrophobic confines of Ready Room One and made him hurry through the hangar deck to the aft starboard gallery deck. Once there, he pushed his way through the silent ammunition carriers and gun crews until he could stand at the edge of the deck, lean on the life line, and stare out to sea. But there was nothing to see or hear, only the hissing of water far below and the dark shapes of escorting ships. A phone talker murmured something aloud, but Duane couldn't make out what he said. Suddenly the forty-millimeter gun mount next to him whined and buzzed and rotated until its twin barrels were leveled out to sea.

Duane strained to detect something, anything. He knew only that the skipper and Trusteau were still up and had been vectored onto an approaching bogey that had since disappeared from the screens. The ship was buttoned up for general quarters and he knew he shouldn't be here, away from his station in the ready room. But they wouldn't launch more fighters after dark.

Suddenly a bright orange light popped into being, arched downward, and flared quickly into a raging, faraway fire. Someone, something had gone in. Eager voices murmured about the crashing plane. The darkness was almost complete now. Duane despaired of seeing more. He was about to turn and leave when another flaming aircraft became visible, and then another, further out. It was chilling. Someone out there was having a field day. The second flamer sailed into the sea several miles away, bounced crazily, and crashed again. A quiet cheer went up from the sailors in the gallery deck. Duane gripped the life line until his hands hurt. Suddenly another blossom of flame exploded in the darkness out to sea, closer than the last, and immediately went out. Four flamers. Duane stared in disbelief, eager for more. He got it.

"There," someone said, "I got him. Holy Jesus."

"Stand by, stand by," said a calm voice. The gun mount whined and the barrels elevated, following something that Duane couldn't see. Then he heard it, faint at first, then gathering volume. He knew it was an aircraft. No, not one. Two. A dark shape screamed out of the darkness. While it was still two hundred yards away it began to burn: Yellow streamers of fire shot out into the blackness. Behind came a Hellcat, guns chattering, engine howling at full power. The two planes snarled overhead, and the men around Duane instinctively ducked. As the first plane passed over them, barely clearing the flight deck, it exploded with a roar and a flash that lighted up the gallery deck like daylight. Then it disappeared from sight on the far side of the ship.

Duane stood and gawked, flabbergasted. To have been this close to the violence of a downed enemy plane left him breathless. He knew that the Hellcat, now yammering away into the darkness, had to have been the skipper. Only the skipper could have flown like that, followed the enemy plane right into the guns of the task force, to bring it down in plain view of the entire ship. It was thrilling, fantastic. Awed, Duane stood there and watched for more action, but there was none.

The ships of the force plowed on as though nothing had happened. A sliver of moon was just rising over the eastern horizon. The gun crew shuffled and stamped in the dark, eager, expectant, unknowing. The tension mounted for five minutes. Then Duane realized that they were still up there in the dark, and would be trying to land. He could learn nothing from down here.

Leaving the gun deck, he made his way through the hangar to the island, and then went up through the hatches and ladders to Primary Flight Control. When he entered Pri-Fly, he saw men huddled anxiously over radar repeaters and radio gear; then he heard the calm, almost playful voices of the two who were in deep trouble.

"Banger Leader, assume a heading of two seven zero."

"Roger, Rooster. How's that?"

"Perfect. One Four, assume a heading of zero niner zero."

"Roger, Rooster Base. I am coming to zero niner zero at this time."

"Very good. Banger Leader, One Four, our scopes are clear at this time except for you two. However, we do recommend that you keep IFF operating until you're aboard."

"Good idea, Rooster."

"Thank you, Banger Leader. Thought of it myself. May we also suggest that you rendezvous outside of the group and come in together. All ships have been warned of your situation."

"Sounds fine to me, Rooster. Trusty, where'd you go back there?"

"Here and there, Skipper. I just wish I knew where I was right now."

"Banger Leader, you bear zero one zero from our position at this time. One Four, we have you three miles from Banger Leader on an approximate heading of two seven zero. How is your fuel situation, gentlemen?"

"As well as can be expected, Rooster. How about you, Trusty?"

"Enough for a pass or two, if it's within the next ten minutes."

Duane Higgins eased his way into the press of bodies and found a place against the bulkhead where no one would notice him. Ten minutes' of fuel. He remembered an earlier flight with Trusteau when he had been worried about half-an-hour's fuel. It was so long, so long ago.

The two pilots continued talking, with the FDO occasionally interrupting to ask about position and fuel and altitude. After several minutes, at the FDO's insistence, Trusteau blinked his landing lights and the two fighters joined up. They had just assumed a new heading which would bring them to the *Constitution* when Trusteau cursed and said that all his panel lights had just gone out; he couldn't see any of his instruments. Then Jack Hardigan said he had been counting on Fred to lead them in because his canopy was smeared with enemy oil. Duane listened to the two men calmly discussing their chances of reaching safety and realized that he was sweating like a pig. And praying for the skipper to make it down.

It was fully dark—the depths of night—when Fred found the Skipper. They had been coached into each other's vicinity by the FDO on board *Ironsides*, making the final linkup when Fred blinked his landing lights. Above the two groping fighters the Milky Way blazed gloriously and the constellations of the southern and northern hemispheres mingled almost indistinguishably with millions of dimmer stars. But the stars gave very little light and the moon was barely past the new stage. Fred forgot about the three kills he had just earned and concentrated on the fact that the coming landing would be perilous in the extreme. Surprisingly, the fact that the skipper was with him did little to lessen his fear.

They had joined up into their standard formation and turned to what the FDO said was the downwind leg when Fred noticed the smell of burning wire. It was very faint, and it came and went with the eddies of air coming in through the hole in the upper panel. But it was there and couldn't be ignored. When they passed over the outer escorts of the task group, the panel lights, normally a dim green, blinked twice and went out.

"Oh, hell," he said. "I got another problem, Skipper." He hoped his voice didn't convey the panic welling up in him.

"What is it?" asked the Skipper.

"Panel lights just went out. Must be a short somewhere. I can smell it."

"Have you tried the dimmer rheostat?"

"That's affirmative, Skipper. No go."

"Well, that's all right. Just keep close to me. I was kind of hoping you'd take me down, though. Seems I've got oil all over the screen."

"You got one, Skipper?"

"Shucks. 'Tweren't nothing."

"Gentlemen, suggest we discuss box scores when you're back at the roost. One Four, suggest you try the flashlight on your life jacket for illumination. Let us know if it works." Keeping an eye on the dark shadow that was Jack's Hellcat, Fred groped for the little one-cell light. He found it with his left hand and unpinned it.

"That, incidentally, was suggested by Mister Higgins, who is here with us now."

"And the XO said, 'Let there be light,'" said Jack.

"And there was..." Fred worked at the switch, clumsy with his left hand, flicked it on. "...light." His heart seemed to fill his throat. His fuel gauges were both on empty. "Suggest we speed things up a little, Rooster Base," he said. "I'm on fumes now."

"Very well, One Four. Continue on present course, gents. Cruiser on our port bow will show single red truck light. Rooster Base will show single white truck light during approach and hooded landing lights for touchdown. We'd appreciate one approach each, so make it a good one."

"You got it," said Jack.

"Roger," said Fred. One approach was probably all he had time for. "I'll make the first one," he volunteered. There was a moment's silence on the circuit, during which the red truck light of the cruiser flared and they passed over it.

"That's a negative, One Four. Banger Leader will make the first pass. Please acknowledge."

There was another moment of silence. The truck light of *Constitution* appeared to the left of Fred's field of vision, and the dark bulk of the carrier and its white wake were suddenly visible. Fred understood what they were doing. Hardigan was the more experienced, and more valuable, flyer. He was less likely to crash on the approach and foul the deck. Fred imagined he heard a sigh from the skipper.

"That's affirmative." The older man's voice sounded flat and dry.

"Roger," said Fred. The two Hellcats turned across the wake but Fred kept going, crossing it as the skipper dipped away and disappeared into the gloom.

The next five minutes were the longest of Fred Trusteau's life. He made the single orbit of *Constitution* with wheels and flaps up to lessen drag and the fuel mixture leaned to the maximum. The tiny, dim survival light burned away steadily, showing a set of fuel gauges whose needles had stopped moving downward and sat below the "E" for empty.

Again the red light of the cruiser guided him on the final leg, again the single light of the carrier beckoned him, and he brought it in on the first pass. The row of landing lights seemed all too short and the dark deck appeared to leap up at him before he was ready. As he sat in the fighter waiting for the hook crew to release him and the deck officer to direct him forward, his engine sputtered and died, and he was still sitting in the cockpit, strapped in, when Jack pulled himself up to his side to help him out.

The muted voices of deck officer, helmsman and lee helmsman, messengers, staff officers murmured in the dark, on the bridge. Jack and Fred stood for a moment on the port wing and let their eyes adjust to the dark. But even after several minutes all they could see was the dark forms of people; faces were impossible to make out.

"Come on," said Jack. He pulled at Fred's arm and Fred followed. "Can someone tell me where the captain is?" he asked loudly. Silence fell and Fred could feel, rather than see, that many eyes were on them.

"Silence on the bridge," said a voice, sternly. A dark form hurried over to them. "Who are you and what are you doing here?"

"We were asked here by the captain," said Jack. "If you could just point him out for us. . . ."

"What are your names?" Fred thought he could make out the shape of binoculars hanging around the man's neck and figured that he was the officer of the deck. He had heard before that they were pretty strict about who entered the bridge. Consequently, he had never been there before. It was even more forbidding at night, and he was glad the Skipper was with him.

"Lieutenant Commander Jack Hardigan. Ensign Trusteau. The captain asked to see us when we got down."

"*You* were just up there?" asked the officer. "*You* got those Jap planes?"

"That was us," said Jack. "Now please, we don't want to keep him waiting."

"On the starboard wing," said the OOD. His tone of voice had changed considerably. "Follow me." He led them past the great brass wheel that gleamed dully in the dark, past two talkers with bulky headsets.

"Captain, you asked to see the two pilots," the OOD said to a shadowy mass that leaned against the steel retaining wall marking the edge of the bridge. Fred thought for a moment that the captain was impossibly tall, then discovered that he was sitting on a pedestal chair that raised his head a foot over theirs.

"Oh, yes," said the captain. "Mister Hardigan. Mister Trusteau." The OOD had vanished in the gloom and they were alone with the captain, in the stifling, windy darkness. "Come on over a little closer so I can see you." Fred grabbed Jack's arm and they moved closer. Fred kicked his toe painfully against some unseen projection on the deck.

"Yes, sir," said Jack.

"Are you there, too, Ensign?"

"Right here, Captain."

"Well, now that I've got the two of you here together, I just want to say that I've seen some flying in my time, but I've never seen anything like what I saw a little while ago."

"Thank you, sir," said Jack.

Fred said nothing until Jack elbowed him lightly in the ribs.

"Yes, sir," he said, "thank you."

"Well, tell me about it," said the captain. He had turned in his chair to face the pilots, but his face was still unreadable.

"I guess there isn't much to say," Jack said. "We weren't together when I found the three Kates. I think they were Kates. It was sort of dark. I got two of them. I'm sorry, but one got away."

"One got away," said the captain. "What about the rest?"

"What rest, sir?"

"Mister Hardigan, I and about fifty other people up here saw five planes go into the drink."

"Oh," said Fred. "I guess that was me. I only saw one at first and I went after him. That's when I lost the skipper."

"I only got two," said Jack, wonderingly.

"I got three," said Fred. "The second one almost pulled me in with him. The third had a tail gunner. Put a slug through the canopy. That may have been what caused the short that killed my panel lights."

"Three?" said Jack. "You got three Kates up there just now?"

"They were all together. I think I got two on my first burst. I still can't believe—"

"Mine were in a sort of slanted echelon formation..."

"Left to right, one on the left in the lead."

"Exactly."

"And they were dropping altitude pretty fast, toward the ships. Only I didn't know that until that second one went in—"

"Captain." The OOD had returned. "Coming to one eight three in one minute."

"Very well," said the captain. "Kentworth." Another man materialzed out of the gloom at the captain's elbow. Fred jumped.

"Yes, sir," he said.

"Mister Kentworth, I am recommending both Mister Hardigan and Mister Trusteau for air medals. Draw up the necessary paperwork, would you please?"

"Really, Captain," said Jack. "I don't think..."

"Mister Hardigan, Mister Trusteau, see me in my cabin tomorrow when you get a chance. The morning would be a good time. Can't talk worth a damn in the dark like this."

"Yes, sir," said Jack. "Is that all, sir?"

"Trusty," said the captain. "Is that what they call you?"

"Yes, sir."

"An appropriate title. I'm glad you're on our side, killer." The captain laughed.

Fred and Jack groped their way off the dark bridge and down the red-lighted passageways and ladders until they were on the hangar deck. There Jack stopped. "You got three kills in one mission," he said, still amazed.

"You got two."

"Why didn't you tell me?"

"I guess we were just too busy trying to get back down." Jack laughed. "I think this is one for the record books."

"It sure rates an entry in the War Diary," said Fred.

"I should say it does." Jack grabbed Fred by the shoulder, roughed him up playfully. "Got a cigarette?" he asked.

"Sure," said Fred, "if they're not all soaked with sweat." He shook a cigarette out of the flattened pack. Jack struck a flame with his lighter, lighting Fred's first. Fred cupped his hands around the skipper's as the flame flared in his eyes.

"Hey," said Jack. He closed the lighter, extinguishing it. Taking Fred by the shoulders he pushed him into the passageway they had just left, which was lighted by a single feeble light. Jack held Fred up against the bulkhead under the light and looked anxiously into his face. "You're bleeding."

Fred touched his face. "Me? Really?"

"You're bleeding," said Jack again, and he touched Fred's face with his fingers. They came away wet with blood. "We've been wandering around in the dark all this time and you're bleeding."

"I didn't know," said Fred. "The canopy glass..."

"Come on," said Jack, "we're going to sickbay." He led Fred, almost like an anxious parent leading a child, down and around to sickbay. And the enormity of the whole night began to dawn on Fred as he realized that he had indeed gained three kills and probably an air medal and that Jack Hardigan, really, deep down, cared for him. It made him feel very, very good.

32

5 *December 1943:* U.S.S. *Constitution,* as part of TG 50.3, assisted in strikes on the Japanese-held atolls of Kwajalein and Wotje. This squadron provided force CAP during the morning hours, flying a total of sixteen sorties totaling sixty-four hours of flight time. No interceptions were made. Launching at 1330 hours for strike on Wotje were eight aircraft of this squadron led by Executive Officer Higgins escorting sixteen aircraft from VB and VT squadrons. No aerial opposition was encountered, but Mister Higgins and Lt. (j.g.) Bracker assisted in the destruction of at least one grounded amphibian aircraft found at the target sight. All aircraft returned by 1600 without loss.

6 *December 1943:* En route Pearl Harbor naval station. Operating with standard CAP for first time since 17 November. Squadron available strength totals thirty aircraft following receipt of numerous spare tires during underway replenishment this A.M. Squadron Leader Lt. Comdr. Hardigan attended memorial services for pilots of other two squadrons lost in action since 18 November.

Late dispatch from Personnel indicates the following ensigns have been promoted effective 1 December to lieutenant (j.g.): Hughes, Levi, Jacobs, Rogers, and Trusteau.

Duane eased himself into the cushioned seat of a small-wheeled tractor that was parked on the starboard side of the hangar deck and idly watched a volleyball game between members of VF-20 and the torpedo squadron. Much to his irritation, CAG had instituted an intersquadron competition in basketball, volleyball, and weightlifting, and indicated that every pilot would take part, without exception. To make it worse, hardly anyone could see how juvenile all this was; they threw themselves into the games with unbounded enthusiasm. It reminded him of when he'd been a teenager in parochial school, where the sisters made everyone wear the same sweater and pants and play the same little games. Duane had known there were much better things to do with the girls on the recess field. But he didn't grumble out loud. He seemed to be a minority of one.

The volleyball game was being played forward of elevator number one, which had been lowered slightly to provide fresh air and light. Eight fighter pilots, including the skipper and Killer Trusteau, were battling it out with their counterparts from the torpedo squadron. Everyone was serving, setting, and spiking with a fervor that was almost embarrassing. Most of the fighter pilots were in athletic shorts and T-shirts, but Jack Hardigan had merely removed his shirt and put on a pair of sneakers. Sweat had plastered his T-shirt to his chest and stained the waistband of his trousers.

As Duane watched, the fighter pilots (they called their team the Aces) scored a hard-won point by a clever deception: A rear man set the ball high; both the skipper and Trusteau in the front line jumped as if to spike in a different direction, and Trusteau slammed it into an unexpected corner of the opposing court. The team cheered as one, snatched up the returned ball and served. The game went on.

It was galling to Higgins to see Trusteau do so well in everything he tried. He realized that it wasn't healthy to be envious of another pilot, but the acclaim that had been heaped on the new j.g. since that night was sickening. The Captain's casual remark about being glad that Trusteau the Killer was on our side had spread through the ship with predictable, though still remarkable, speed. And now wherever he went, crewmen and officers whom he hadn't known until now would nod seriously to Trusteau and say, "Hi, Killer." To make matters worse, the force OTC, a vice admiral from the *Enterprise,* had flown over the next day and met with the skipper and Trusteau in the captain's cabin. They had been in there the better part of an hour, prompting fantastic rumors about their careers. True, it had been a neat bit of flying and shooting, but Trusteau himself admitted that he had been blessed with a great deal of luck when he made his first turn and found himself in perfect attack position. Duane had convinced himself that almost anyone could have done the same thing if they had been fortunate enough to have the last CAP of the day.

The Aces scored again and cheered like high-school kids at a football game. A rear man had set to tall Frank Hammerstein on the end of the front row and instead of spiking it himself, Hammerstein had tipped the ball the length of the net to Killer Trusteau who dunked it in for the point. The torpedo pilots were being routed. Jack called the team into a huddle; they conferred earnestly, standing with arms over shoulders and heads close together, for secrecy. When they broke, the Skipper clapped Trusteau on the back in a chummy gesture. They looked for all the world like fraternity brothers or sand-lot athletes happily proving their prowess over a neighborhood gang.

They spent a lot of time together now, the Skipper and Trusteau. Higgins had kept an eye on them for quite a while now. They were indeed very close. Just last night at the crew's movie on the hangar deck they sat in the front row, on the very end. Duane had sat behind them and noticed that as soon as the movie was underway, Jack leaned over against Trusteau, and they watched the whole movie (a Basil Rathbone–Nigel Bruce affair with Sherlock Holmes pursuing a runaway matchbook containing secret information) with their shoulders touching.

There was plenty of room; they weren't crowded together. The hangar deck was so big that on the other side of the screen, a half-dozen mechanics and a crew chief were lowering a spare Dauntless from the overhead. It made Duane wonder.

The sunlight streamed through the huge square hole in the flight deck and crept up to where Duane sat in the little tractor. It felt warm and good to sit there in the cool breeze and have a little sunshine soak into his body. Duane closed his eyes and thought about Pearl, and Eleanor Hawkins. They had been so busy the past few weeks that he hadn't thought of her more than two or three times. His mental picture of her voluptuous body, her unspoken promise of "other nights," made him smile. He closed his eyes.

"How come you're not playing, Mister Higgins?" Without looking, Duane knew Carmichael's voice, a crew chief for the fighter squadron. He opened an eye to be polite. Carmichael was an old-timer, a cynical, bored man with a crew cut and the usual tattoos.

"They don't need me, Chief," said Duane, to the accompaniment of another round of cheering from the Aces.

"I see what you mean," he said. The chief came closer and propped a big boondocker up on the fender of the tractor.

"So what's going on that's important, Chief?"

"Nothing much. Just thought you might like to know there's a game making up."

"Isn't there always?"

"You being one of the regulars, I just thought you might like to know."

"Does that mean I'm invited?"

"You didn't suffer none last game."

Duane smiled. "Nope," he said.

The chief squinted into the sun and said, "About eight o'clock, I imagine, if you were to drop by the chief's quarters, we might be able to show you a good time."

"Where's it going to be this time, the chain locker?"

"You just leave that to us, Mister Higgins. We got it all figured out."

"Think I might spill my guts and tell the master-at-arms?"

"Hell, he's invited, too. Can't play a hand worth a shit." The chief snorted. "You ought to join the college boys over there, Mister Higgins. Looks like they're having themselves one hell of a time."

"Nah. Too much like work."

"You know our new hero with the big balls was luckier than a home port whore?"

"You mean Trusteau?"

"Two red cunt hairs to the left and that Jap shell would have taken off both his ears at the same time."

"Some of us were just born lucky."

"Right," said Carmichael. He turned to go. "Tonight. Chief's quarters."

"Sure."

"And bring your bankroll." The chief sauntered off.

Duane closed his eyes. The game would help pass the time until Pearl and Eleanor. The game itself was always something to look forward to, and sometimes even profitable. And it was always entertaining to find out at the last minute which oddball, obscure little compartment the chiefs had chosen as the game site. Last week it was in something they called "rag stowage," a tiny, cramped little room on deck five, forward of the torpedo magazine. It had never occurred to Duane that there was a separate compartment solely for the stowage of rags. Live and learn, he had thought at the time.

On the volleyball court, the last point was scored by the Aces and the game broke up; the losers stayed behind to take down the net and stow the ball. The fighter pilots began to pick up shirts, wallets, cigarette packs, and to head below. Hardigan and Trusteau came over to Duane and sat down heavily on the tractor fender. They were panting and perspiring, exhilarated by the win.

"Good game, Fred."

"You did all right yourself, Skipper."

"I take it you guys won," said Duane.

"Easily," said Jack. "You should have joined us."

"Some other time."

"You have to play one of the sports, Duane."

"I will. I will. Just give me time to decide." Duane, he thought. He called me Duane.

"Better decide quick. It's only a few days to Pearl."

"Yeah. I know."

Jack stretched a sleeve of his T-shirt and wiped the sweat from his eyes. "I don't know about you," he said, "but I think I need a shower."

"That sounds like a good idea," said Trusteau. He heaved himself to his feet.

"Don't stay out in the sun too long, Duane. Might get burned." Jack laughed as he got up. The two sweaty wingmen walked away.

Duane sat up and opened his eyes to watch them go. He called me Duane, he thought. In front of Trusteau he called me Duane. Just before they disappeared into a door in the island, Jack grabbed Fred's neck in a rough, playful gesture, and they both laughed loudly, openly.

Duane sat in the sun for a few minutes more but had to leave when the hangar crew came to raise the elevator back to closed position. Then he went down to his bunk and lay down to think.

Fresh, clean, and dapper, Jack Hardigan sat at the desk in the squadron office. He was reading through the memo from CAG one more time. It was neither unpleasant nor demanding. It simply informed him that the entire air group would spend three days and two nights of rest and recreation at the Moana Hotel in Waikiki. Two men would be in a room, and there would be no curfew or bed checks. The squadron would like that.

Jack leaned back and thought hard for several minutes. Death came so frequently these days that he had no fear of it. He didn't even fear his own death very much. But it was disconcerting to think that he might die without ever discovering the truth about the strange, complicated feelings he had for Trusteau. He accepted them now as a part of life, just as he accepted the fact that CAG no longer hated him. Both sets of feelings were new and curiously appealing. He sat forward suddenly and drafted a note to be pinned to the bulletin board outside the ready room.

"Fighting Twenty will spend 24, 25, and 26 December 1943 on stand down at the Moana Hotel, for rest and recreation. Two-man rooms will be provided and will be assigned on the basis of the section leader and wingman per room. Specific room numbers will be posted when available."

Jack signed the notice, appended the date. Christmas would be as good a time as any to find out what he had to know.

Part V-A

Interim:

The Affair

33

The awards ceremony was long and complicated. Had Fred Trusteau not been among the recipients he would have been horribly bored. As it was, he was merely uncomfortable. The ceremony was held on the flight deck of the *Enterprise,* at pierside in Pearl Harbor. Carrier flight decks seemed to be perculiarly well suited for the sort of function that needs space: There was room for not one but two marching bands, one Navy and one Marine; the speakers' platform held at least fifty chairs for dignitaries and, of course, the recipients themselves; spectators occupied about a hundred chairs on either side of the platform; formed-up detachments of ship and squadron personnel stood across from the platform.

The sun was hot. A stiff breeze pressed continually against the side of Fred's face and made the job of the Marine color guard distractingly difficult. Fred looked up and down the brigade of white-uniformed officers and men until he found the *Constitution* detachment. The officer in front, complete with ceremonial saber, was Duane Higgins. He wondered if every ship in the harbor was represented or just the ships or units of the men receiving awards. Then he decided he didn't care. All he wanted right now was for the ceremony to end so they could get on with the party at the Officer's Club. Although it was being called a wetting-down party for the new j.g.'s, it had turned into a sort of congratulations party for the skipper and him, the only members of the air group to be decorated.

The ceremony had begun with everyone rising to their feet ("attention," they called it) for the arrival of none other than Admiral Nimitz himself. Then the people on the platform and the spectators were allowed to sit down in their folding chairs. There were two speakers: The first was a civilian from the Defense Department, the second an admiral who talked too long. Before he finished, there was a slight commotion in one of the formations and a hapless sailor had passed out on his feet.

Then everyone stood again and the colors were marched up and down the line. Then the Marine band marched up and down the line. Then the Navy band did the same thing. There were no surprises; the briefing and rehearsals had been thorough. After the music and the marching, the citations were read and the medals given out.

Eight men were decorated this morning. When Fred had first discovered that it wasn't just him and the skipper getting awards, he had been mildly disappointed. Now he was glad there were others to take the attention away from him.

Instead of starting with the minor heroes and working up to the most glorious, the most important citations were read first and the appropriate medals were pinned on. As each man heard his citation read, he stepped out of line, walked ("smartly," as the captain had said at the briefing) to front and center, saluted, shook hands with Admiral Nimitz and had the little decoration (of gold or silver or bronze with a brightly colored ribbon) pinned to a vacant spot over his heart. After that minor trial, the recipient walked "smartly" to the other side of the platform and stepped into line next to the color guard. Fred and the skipper were the last in line.

Among the first to be decorated were men who had performed specifically heroic acts: a navy corpsman who had carried wounded Marines out of danger; a boat coxswain who had piloted his burning, sinking landing craft through incredible peril to its assigned landing spot, carried five wounded Marines into his unloaded, still-sinking boat and made it back to his mother ship before the boat finally went under; a gunnery officer on a battleship who had saved a number of lives when his mount exploded. There were also several officers whose deeds had been more general: a planning staff captain who continually inspired the men under him to greater levels of efficiency and output; a submarine skipper who carried out all his assigned tasks in an inspiring manner; a commander in charge of a photograph interpretation outfit whose predictions of enemy strength had been extremely accurate. Then they came to the skipper. Fred listened to the citation with interest, to see if they got it right. It was accurate, though it sounded melodramatically unreal, and Fred couldn't help thinking that citations and medals had been the furthest thing from his mind that dangerous, dark night in the skies over the task group. When Jack left Fred's side to receive his medal, Fred drew himself up a little straighter, feeling immensely priviliged to be so close to such a man.

Then they read *his* citation. It was identical to Jack's. As it was read he felt the eyes of hundreds of people settle on him. His starched white dress uniform felt tight and constricting. Sweat puddled in the small of his back. His nose itched. Finally the reading was finished. He felt horribly clumsy as he traversed the short distance to Admiral Nimitz—perhaps trying too hard to walk "smartly." For a second he worried that he might knock his hat off when he saluted or forget to shake hands with the admiral or trip and fall in front of all those people, instantly bringing shame on himself and the skipper. But the admiral's hands were competent and practiced as they pinned the medal to Fred's blouse, and his handshake was firm and friendly. Then Fred looked into a pair of startling, steel-blue eyes, as Admiral Nimitz said softly, "Thank you"; and Fred thought, He really means it, he really is thankful to me for doing what I did. And he squeezed the admiral's hand again before stepping back and saluting a second time. Then he was in line next to Jack, and the band was playing "Anchors Aweigh"—which sent an uncontrollable shiver down his spine and brought tears to his eyes.

When it was over and the neat lines of men were dissolving into a snowy white mass, Jack turned to Fred and clapped him on the shoulder. "Well, Trusty," he said, "how does it feel to be a hero?"

"Terrible," Fred replied, pulling at the high-necked collar that threatened to choke off his breath. The new medal dangled strangely on his chest. The shoulder boards were brand-new and had one more stripe than he was used to wearing. In contrast, Jack Hardigan looked impossibly comfortable in his dress white uniform; his trousers were unwrinkled from an hour of sitting, his shoes were a pure, dazzling white. He had two other medals beside the new one.

"Let's take a look around," said Jack cheerfully. "It's been a while since I've seen the Big E."

"You've been aboard before?"

"A couple of times." They picked their way through the crowd, heading for the island.

"It looks different," said Fred.

"It is different. A few years older."

"There aren't any guns."

"Not as many, but they're there." They reached a rounded hatch left open for the ceremony, and entered the island. The differences in construction below decks were greater than topside. In minutes Fred was completely lost. But Jack seemed to know where he was going, so Fred dutifully followed.

"Where are we heading, Skipper?" Fred asked.

"Squadron office. There's someone aboard I want you to meet."

Fred was now beginning to pick up on some of the similarities of the *Enterprise* to the *Constitution*. Some of the passageways could have been on either ship—there were the same steel bulkheads cluttered with pipes, insulation, electrical conduit, and firefighting equipment, the same everpresent smell of hot oil that pervades every ship. The *Enterprise* was, he noticed, remarkably clean and shipshape; but then, with Admiral Nimitz aboard, they'd probably spent the last forty-eight hours frantically swabbing and polishing.

They reached a right-angle turn and stopped. Jack looked around perplexedly. "Maybe we're on the wrong level," he said.

"We're lost," said Fred, somewhat amused.

"No, we're not. They've just changed things around a bit." Jack struck off in another direction, looking carefully at compartment identification plates. Presently they came to a normal-looking door with the words "Fighting Six" painted on it. Jack opened the door without knocking and entered.

"Jack Hardigan!"

"Mat Braden!"

A man in working khakis stood up behind a desk and came forward to shake hands with Jack. "How've you been keeping yourself?" he said warmly.

"Fine, Mat, fine. I want you to meet one of my pilots." Jack put his arm around Fred's shoulders and pulled him forward. "Fred Trusteau, Mat Braden."

"Pleased to meet you," said Fred as they shook hands. Mat Braden was a full commander.

"Mat was my boss on the old *Hornet*," said Jack.

"Yeah," said Mat. "Those were the days, weren't they?" He

sat on the edge of the desk. "That was some bit of flying you did out there."

"You heard about it?"

"Word gets around," said Braden. "Congratulations."

"Thanks," said Jack. "But Trusty here did most of the work." He still held Fred's shoulder, and now he squeezed it.

"So you got three Japs at one time. At night."

"I was lucky," said Fred.

"They don't give air medals to lucky pilots," Braden said.

Fred felt himself blush and looked away.

"What's that on your finger?" asked Jack, nodding toward Braden's left hand. A thin gold band adorned the ring finger.

"That, Jack, is called a wedding band."

"Finally hooked you."

"Yeah. She's a real honey."

"In the States?"

"Philadelphia."

"Never thought I'd see the day."

"Me, neither. But it kind of works on you, if you know what I mean. You'll throw in the towel one of these days."

"Nah."

"You wait and see. Some nice little gal will get her hooks in you and the next thing you know it'll be wedding bells and crossed sabers." Braden laughed. "What about yourself?" he asked Fred.

Fred had to pry his mind away from the incongruous, unsettling picture of the skipper and a woman coming through an arch of crossed sabers. "I beg your pardon," he said.

"You married?"

"No, sir."

"Any plans?"

"Sure," said Fred, and Jack raised his eyebrows in surprise. "I plan to avoid it as long as possible."

Braden laughed at that, but Jack didn't. He looked thoughtful. "Say, Mat," he said, "we're having a little party over at the Club. Why don't you drop by and we'll chew the fat for a while."

"I'm awful busy, Jack. I'll have to pass on this one." There was a sharp knock on the door; then Duane Higgins opened it and poked his head in.

"Anybody here?" he asked. He spotted Fred and frowned. "Trusty, what are you doing..." Opening the door further, he saw Jack and Mat Braden.

"Come on in, Higgins," said Braden. "Always room for one more." Duane edged himself into the crowded little room. He closed the door behind him and shook hands with Braden.

"Long time no see," said Higgins.

"Did you know Duane's my XO?" asked Jack.

"You two guys are still together," said Braden. "It's good to see you again," he said to Duane.

"Yeah, Jack and I have really been around," said Duane. He worked his way between Jack and Fred. "But they keep sending us back to the same air group."

"There's nothing wrong with that," said Mat.

"Remember Punchy Drake?" asked Duane. "Whatever happened to him?"

"I don't know," said Mat. "Last time I heard from him he was in the Atlantic on one of those jeep carriers."

"And Herb Edelman," said Jack. "What's he doing these days?"

"You didn't hear? They lost him up the Slot in January, I think. New Georgia, somewhere along in there."

"Say," said Duane. "You're married."

"You bet," said Braden. "Here, I got a picture of her." He pulled out a wallet and began to pass around some snapshots of a nice-looking woman in a tight sweater.

Fred wasn't interested. Then the three old friends began talking again about marriage and women, and he decided that it was time he left. He waited for a chance to interrupt politely, then excused himself. When he closed the door behind him, they were laughing uproariously over some comical mishap they had all shared on Guadalcanal.

Without trying to find his own way, he collared the first sailor to come by and received explicit instructions to the quarter-deck. In fifteen minutes he was at the O–Club, Scotch and soda in hand, waiting for the skipper.

The party was a rousing success. Duane had tried to persuade Mat Braden to come, and he'd finally said that he would try to get away, but he never showed up. Jack was actually a bit more comfortable not having him there. He had had several conversations with old friends who had turned out to be married and it always made him uneasy. Inevitably, they would say just what Braden had said: It's only a matter of time, kid, before you decide that's what *you* really want—even if deep down it wasn't. How could he (or anyone else) know what Jack wanted, when he himself wasn't sure?

Duane didn't stay for the entire affair. At about six in the evening, just as things were beginning to warm up, he made a quick phone call from the booth outside the club and left just as quickly. It probably wouldn't be considered a serious social breach, even though it was as much the commanding officer's party as it was the new j.g.'s. By the time Duane left, the party had enough momentum to continue quite well without him.

More surprisingly, a totally unexpected guest showed up in the form of Buster Jennings. With him was one of his really smashing girls, and nearly everyone was suitably impressed. He drank a toast to the new j.g.'s, and then a toast to the two decorated men, and then one to his girl friend, and then one to the Navy, and then one to the United States of America, and then one to Eleanor Roosevelt. All in all, he was being a good sport about staying and having a few with the boys. As Woody Heywood had said, he was indeed a changed man. If getting shot down did that for a man, Jack was suitably glad it had happened to Jennings.

The last liberty boat to the *Constitution* wasn't crowded. Counting himself, there were three men from Jack's squadron on board as it chugged away from the fleet landing past old Battleship Row toward the East Loch where the carriers were anchored. Ensign Duggin (who had drunk himself into a stupor because he hadn't been among the promoted) and Fred were with Jack. As the afternoon waned and night came on, the party had dwindled to a few die-hard drinkers who had no thought for the morrow, a nonflying day. Jack had got the distinct impression that Fred wanted everyone to leave so they could be alone, but it hadn't worked out. Duggin had stuck it out to the very last, morose and self-pitying in his drunkenness. So Fred started drinking coffee hours before it was over, and Jack had nursed each of his own drinks for at least an hour. But both had consumed a fair quantity of booze, and they were beginning to feel it.

The dark harbor around them was thronged with quiet ships, more than Jack had ever seen there at one time before. A partly obscured half-moon provided light with which he could see Fred's face as they faced each other. Duggin was stretched out across three of the benchlike seats and was definitely not conscious. The night air was humid, almost chilly.

"I think I'm already developing a hangover," said Fred.

"You always were ahead of everyone else," said Jack.

"Praise the Lord we aren't flying tomorrow."

"You can say that again."

"Praise the Lord..."

The coxswain, who was standing and steering behind Jack, chuckled out loud. "That must have been some party, sir," he said.

Jack turned and regarded him blearily. "You may think, sailor, that being an officer is all fun and games. But the truth is, it isn't. Now take this party, for instance."

"Please," said Fred. "Take the party."

The coxswain laughed.

"They ought to give us hazardous duty pay for wetting-down parties." Jack turned back around and settled his head in his hands.

"That's all right," said the coxswain. "I may not be able to go to the Officer's Club, but I don't have to fly off in those airplanes and look for Japs."

"It all evens out in the end," said Fred.

Another boat rumbled past them in the dark.

"Yes, sir, it does." The friendly coxswain fell silent, obviously well acquainted with the foibles of drunken officers. The little boat chugged on through the smooth waters of the harbor for several minutes. No one spoke.

Then Jack looked around and pointed. "She's not there anymore."

"Who's not where?" asked Fred.

"The *Oklahoma*," he said. "She's not there."

"They put her into dry dock," said the coxswain. He pointed over his right shoulder. "Back there. They moved her yesterday."

"That's a battleship, right?" asked Fred.

Jack sighed. "We'll make a navy man out of you yet, Fred Trusteau."

"They found some more of her crew today," said the coxswain.

"Where were they?" asked Fred. He didn't seem to understand.

"They were dead," said the coxswain.

"Oh."

"They say they're going to fix her up and send her out again. But I don't know. I wouldn't want to be on a ship where all those men got killed."

"Me, neither," said Jack. But he was thinking that the sailor had missed his point entirely, which was that the Navy had changed. He had seen the new battleships and the new carriers and knew that the old *Oklahoma* was hardly a vital part of the fleet. Death ship or not, she simply wasn't needed any longer.

"Oh, hell," said Jack.

"What?" asked Fred.

"I was going to ask you to do the cherry-stem trick for me tonight. I forgot to ask."

"That's all right. I'll give you a private showing. First chance I get."

"I'm going to hold you to that."

The shattered *Arizona* passed slowly down their port side, but Jack had had enough of sunken ships and dead sailors. Fred Trusteau seemed uninterested in the wreck. "How's the Diary coming?" Jack asked.

"Fine. But..."

"But what?"

"Some of the entries are getting kind of long. You know, we get into these big operations and a lot of action and it takes a lot of time to get everything down right."

The admission caught Jack by surprise. He had no idea Fred was having trouble with the extra work. "Why didn't you ask for some help?"

"I didn't mean I needed help, Skipper."

"I'll get someone to help out on it," said Jack. "In fact, I'll get someone else to take over the whole thing." He leaned forward and shook Fred lightly by the shoulder. "You've done your share. I understand."

Fred smiled obligingly. "Okay," he said. He noticed the bulk of an aircraft carrier looming on their port side. "Home sweet home," he said.

"*Constitution*," said the coxswain, pulling the boat up smartly to the accommodation platform. Fred and Jack stepped out. "Good night, sir," the coxswain said.

"Same to you," said Fred.

"You see any Japs out there tonight," said Jack, "you come and get us. We'll take care of them for you."

"You got it, sir." The liberty boat hovered close for a second as the coxswain changed gears, then moved away quickly.

Jack stood on the platform and straightened his uniform. Fred nudged him and said, "Guess what?"

"What?"

"We forgot Duggin."

Jack looked for the liberty boat, but it was gone. He stood still for several seconds, then shrugged. "He's in good hands."

They started up the ladder.

"Guess what else?"

"What else?"

"Look who's on deck."

Jack stopped climbing and stared hard. It was Lieutenant Overstreet, the man with the comic book jaw. "Have no fear. I outrank the bastard." They continued climbing. "Besides. We're not out of uniform." He laughed, knowing it was true in word only. Their dress white trousers and blouses had long ago ceased to be presentable. The party had not been a delicate affair. But as they trudged up the steps, Fred checked his collar to make sure it was hooked and his shoulder boards to make sure they were on straight. His medal was still shiny. He was ready.

"Permission to come aboard," said Jack, throwing as sharp a salute as Fred had ever seen. Without waiting for a reply, both pilots wove across the quarter-deck, passing the little podium-desk that was the deck officer's station.

Overstreet watched them impassively. "I see the squadron commander had a good time tonight," he said.

Jack stopped in front of him and the two exchanged cursory up and down inspections. "You bet your sweet ass we did," Jack said evenly. "You ought to try it yourself sometime."

"I do try to get away occasionally." Overstreet glanced at Fred. "But I choose my company carefully. And never overdo it." He smiled with wan superiority.

"I'll remember that," said Jack. "Next time I throw a tea party, you'll be at the top of the list."

"Will the commander require assistance in finding his stateroom?"

"Thanks for the offer, Lieutenant, but I wouldn't want to take you away from your duty on the quarter-deck. Think of all the drunks that might come aboard while you're gone." The petty officer behind Overstreet snickered aloud, and the OOD silenced him with a single, cold glance.

"Good night to you, sir," Overstreet said.

"Same to you," said Jack. "Come on, Fred." He threw an arm around Fred's shoulders and they marched unsteadily off. When they were ten paces from the quarter-deck, Fred began a refrain that Brogan had sung before: "I'm an old cowhand from the Rio Grande . . ." Jack picked it up and increased the volume, and they bellowed out an entire verse, their voices echoing and rolling through the great empty hangar.

Fred carefully removed the medal and laid it next to his wallet on the tiny desk. Then he stripped off the white uniform and dropped it to the deck in a heap. Two of the four bunks had sleeping figures in them. Climbing up to his own, he thought, It's only a matter of time before he'll come to me. When the time is right, he'll come. His euphoria was finally overcome by alcohol and fatigue, and he fell quickly to sleep.

Jack removed his medals and put them away in a little steel case he kept for them. Locking the case in his safe, he turned down his bunk and sat on the edge. As he was taking off his shoes, he thought, So far I've done nothing wrong. But we've got two nights, two nights together at the Moana coming up. And no one else need ever know. He hung his rumpled uniform on a hanger, placed the shoes neatly on the floor of the metal closet, and went to bed.

34

"Hiya, Sweets." Duane climbed into the car on the passenger side, leaned across the seat, and gave Eleanor a peck on the cheek.

"My, but aren't we cheerful today," she said. She started the engine and pulled away from the main gate.

"I've got every right to be."

"Well, I don't. I waited an hour. That hulk ~~with~~ the gun wouldn't even let me park in the shade inside the gate."

"I'm sorry. It took longer to get away than I thought."

It had taken longer because Jack Hardigan wouldn't let him leave until he had completed the next week's training schedules, a task he could have done on Sunday afternoon. But his irritation slipped away when he looked at Eleanor. It would be a nice evening.

"I'm letting you off easy this time," she said. "I brought a picnic lunch." She wore a colorful print dress. A simple white elastic band held her hair back.

"Potato salad and fried chicken?"

"No, silly. Breadfruit and raw fish."

"Always the perfect hostess."

"And I've got the perfect place picked out. A little waterfall and a hidden lake. Off the beaten track."

"Sweets, any place you take me would be an island paradise."

"You've been at sea too long. You're starting to sound like John Wayne."

"All fighter pilots sound like John Wayne." Duane sat as close to Eleanor as safety allowed. But it was awkward with her driving; he couldn't even get an arm around her shoulders. They drove in silence for several minutes, passing a slow-moving column of Marines and artillery.

Eleanor spoke first. "I haven't heard from Jack lately."

"He's been pretty busy. Working us day and night. He got a decoration, you know."

"No, I didn't know."

"Splashed a couple of Jap torpedo bombers. At night. Pretty dangerous work."

"No. He didn't tell me. I would like to have been at the ceremony."

"You didn't miss anything. It was pretty boring."

"Well," she said. And then she was quiet, as though she could think of nothing else to say. They were on a small, two-lane road now, dense foliage on either side. They passed an olive-drab jeep with two uniformed riders, going in the opposite direction. She pulled up suddenly in front of a long wooden sawhorse blocking the entrance to a side road. A sign on the barricade said the road was closed to civilian traffic.

"Oh, darn," she said. "It looks like the Army appropriated our waterfall."

"Is there somewhere else we can go?" asked Duane.

"On a moment's notice, the best I can do is my place." She was already turning the car around. They headed back in the opposite direction.

"I don't want to take you out of your way or anything."

"It's only a little further, and we'll be more comfortable, anyway." She reached over and touched his hand lightly. Then he took her hand up in his. "My, what strong hands you have," she said.

"The better to hold you with, my darling."

Eleanor laughed. "Come on," she said. "You've got a better line than that."

Duane pretended to think. "Okay," he said. "How about, the better to squeeze you with, my darling."

"You're on the right track. Being squeezed implies a little more affection than being held. But I don't know . . ."

"Well, then, the better to *caress* you with, my darling." Duane reached out and touched her cheek with the backs of his fingers, then thought at once that he might have been too forward.

"Now you're talking, Sailor," she said, patting his knee and leaving her hand there until he picked it up and placed it firmly on the wheel.

"You just keep your mind on the driving, Sweets. Leave the caressing to me." He was surprised with her boldness, and slightly flustered by her physicality. He wasn't sure if he liked that or not. They continued driving for half an hour, far into the interior reaches of Oahu. Duane had been to the place before, months earlier. It was very quiet and very secluded.

"I hope you brought your bathing suit," Eleanor said as she parked the car in the long gravel driveway.

"Nope," said Duane. "But that's never stopped me from going swimming before."

"Well," she said with mock huffiness, "I am properly scandalized." Duane opened the front door for them and helped her carry the picnic hamper into the kitchen. They set it on a table in a breakfast nook that had a window looking out onto a lushly vegetated hillside. The afternoon sun was already throwing long shadows across the fields and trees. As she turned away from the table. Duane caught her in his arms and kissed her quickly on the mouth. She pulled away.

"Drinks," she said, "why don't you fix us a drink?" She pointed through the door to the bar Duane and Jack had leaned against together at the party so many months ago.

"Good idea," he said. Eleanor began setting out the meal, so that when Duane came back with two tall glasses of bourbon on ice, he found chicken sandwiches, potato salad, a pineapple pie. He set the drinks down on the table and wrapped his arms around her from behind.

"That looks fantastic." He nibbled at her neck. "You'll make some man a great wife."

"I sure hope so," she said. Again she pulled away. "You sailors are all alike. One thing on your mind all the time."

"Almost all of us, anyway," said Duane.

"Go put some music on. We're going to do this up right." Duane took his drink and obediently went back through the kitchen door.

Presently Eleanor could hear the sound of Hawaiian music. When Duane came back into the nook she was sitting, nibbling at a sandwich. He sat down beside her.

"You women are all alike," he said. "You never have the same thing on your mind."

She laughed. "Never attempt a seduction on an empty stomach," she said.

Duane shrugged and picked up a sandwich. He was thinking

that seduction was a fancy word for it, but yes, that was what he wanted. The sandwich, after months of navy food, was almost exotically good.

When they finished eating the sun had disappeared, leaving a cool, glowing twilight. Kicking off their shoes and taking their drinks, they walked out the back door together and onto a wooden deck surrounding a small swimming pool. Duane rolled up his pants legs, Eleanor hitched up her skirt, and they sat on the edge with their feet in the cool water.

"'Tragic Tarawa,'" said Eleanor. "'Bloody Betio.' That's what all the newspapers were saying. Was it all that bad?"

"I don't know," said Duane. "I haven't read any newspapers lately." He was much more interested in her long bare legs, and the inside of her thigh, just above her knee.

"But you were there. You must have seen something."

"I flew over the island a few times. There was fighting. You couldn't see much." He leaned close to her and kissed her bare shoulder. She had a faint, erotic smell about her.

"And what did Jack do that was brave enough for a decoration?"

"Nothing much." Duane straightened up. "Why?"

"I like Jack a lot. But he doesn't keep in touch very well."

"He's busy," said Duane. "Running a squadron takes all his time." He thought, Maybe that explains it. Maybe.

"Did you know Stan?" she asked.

"Your husband? No. Jack mentioned him, but I never met him."

Eleanor leaned way back and splashed her feet in the water. "Oh, he was big and strong." Her voice was light, not at all sad. "I miss that man more than anything in the world." Duane didn't know what to say, so he said nothing. "I need a man like that in my life," she said, sitting forward and linking her arm in his. "It's one of those things you get used to, and then when it goes away you suddenly realize how much you depended on it." She stopped paddling her feet and was still. "I guess you don't know what I'm talking about, do you?"

"I . . ." said Duane, thinking hard for a comeback, "never thought about it."

"No," she said. "I don't suppose you have. But you're not the only one."

"Jack," said Duane. "He doesn't think about it either, I guess."

"Yes, you could say that." She leaned her head on his shoulder. Duane lifted her chin with the fingers of one hand and

kissed her on the lips. This time she responded. Her mouth
opened and their tongues touched briefly. They drew apart.

"My goodness," she said quickly. "It's dark. I almost forgot
about the blackout. I better turn off some lights." She stood,
pulling her skirt down to hide those beautiful, exciting legs.
Duane reached for her calf as she skipped away but missed it in
the dark. "Come on in and help me," she called. Duane got up
from the pool's edge and followed her wet footprints into the
house.

The music was still playing in the living room. He looked
around at the tasteful wealth of furnishings. He realized that if
they were to marry, she could probably support him in style,
instead of the other way around. He was not used to thinking
that way. Also, the fact that she might spring the question on
him, that she was obviously a woman looking for a "strong"
man, was somehow unsettling to him. He went to the bar,
poured himself another two fingers of bourbon, and added an
ice cube.

"There," said Eleanor, coming back into the living room.
"All finished." She was wearing a housecoat of Oriental design
now. "I hope you don't mind my getting out of that awful dress,"
she said.

"No," said Duane. "Not really."

"You shouldn't drink so much," she said, joining him at the
bar. "It dulls your senses." She plucked the glass from his hand
and set it on the bar, drawing up so close to him that their thighs
touched. She placed both her hands on his sides, just above his
hips, and pulled herself close till she could rest her chin on his
shoulder. Her smell was enticing, but Duane just stood there.
She sensed his reluctance almost immediately and stepped back
lightly.

"What's the matter?" she asked.

Duane smiled perplexedly. "Eleanor..." he said.

She looked deeply into his eyes, seeing confusion there.
"Oh," she said, "I understand." She left him and walked quickly
across the carpet to the sofa where she sat demurely at one end,
crossing her legs at the knees, and folding her hands in her lap.
"Whose seduction is this..." She said it playfully, not
sarcastically.

"I've never met anyone like you," said Duane. He picked up
his glass of bourbon, drained it with a single gulp, and turned to
the sofa. Unusual or not, she was a damned good-looking
woman, and he wouldn't disappoint her the way Jack had. He
sat down beside her, placing an arm across the top of the sofa

above her shoulders. "You wouldn't want me to think you're the wrong kind of girl."

"Heavens, no," she said, leaning her head back until it rested on his arm and wriggling a hand between his back and the cushions. "I believe a girl should get to know a man better before she allows him to, shall we say, take liberties."

"I agree," said Duane, leaning over and kissing those wonderful, warm lips.

"That tells me an awful lot about you," she said.

He lowered his arm until it was around her, pulled her into an embrace, and kissed her again.

"I think we know each other pretty well now," she said.

"Does that mean we can hold hands?" he asked.

"You can hold anything you want, Sailor," she said. She ran her hands through his hair, tickled the nape of his neck. Duane kissed her lips, her cheek, her neck, toyed with the top button of her housecoat. When he had it open, he realized with a mild shock that she had nothing on under it. He opened the second button, and the third, until he could slip his hand inside and massage her warm, soft breast. She gave a delicious, arousing sigh from deep down in her throat. Duane felt the blood rising in his groin.

"I think," she said, "we'd be more comfortable in the bedroom."

"Do we know each other well enough for that?" he asked.

She shook her head to toss her hair back from her eyes and almost casually placed her right hand in his lap, feeling his erection.

"Yes," she said, "we do." She stood suddenly, took him by the hand, and led him to the bedroom.

"How long have you been at sea?" Eleanor asked.

"We were only gone about a month," he said. "Why?"

She laughed quietly. "I'm sorry," she said. "What I meant was, how long has it been since you . . . did this?"

Duane pondered this complicated question in silence, a little embarrassed.

"A month and a half," he said finally. He wanted to get up and get a cigarette, but his shirt was on a chair on the other side of the bed and he would have to walk all the way around. She would see him naked. "Why?" he asked again.

"Oh, I was just curious. You were so . . . fast."

"I'm sorry if I did anything wrong," he said defensively.

"Oh, no," she said, "don't think that." She took a deep breath and exhaled it slowly. After a moment, she said, "You would have liked Stan."

"Oh?"

"He was my first love," she said matter-of-factly. "He taught me a lot of things."

Duane was almost aching for a smoke, was still embarrassed by the things she chose to talk about, was also embarrassed by the jaunty way she had hung the housecoat on the bed post at their feet.

Eleanor went on. "We didn't have that much time together before he left, so we had to get the most out of every hour. We learned to go slower." She reached over and placed her hand on his chest, letting her fingers tickle the swirls of hair that grew there.

"What'd you do? Bring a stopwatch to bed?" He tried not to sound cynical, but knew he did, anyway.

"No," she said. "I guess it's hard to explain." Her hand went from his chest to his abdomen, pausing at the navel. She was getting close to a very personal spot, so Duane pulled her over on top of him and kissed her hard. She didn't resist as he thought she should; in fact, she stayed on top when the kiss ended.

"Sometimes if the first time wasn't just right, we'd do it again, and it was always better." She brought her knee up to his groin, worked it slowly up and down.

"You're a shameless woman," he said.

"Yes," she said, smiling. "But is there a Navy regulation that says women aren't supposed to enjoy it, too?"

"Hell, no." He loved the way her breasts flattened against his chest, the delicious way her body conformed to his. Eleanor Hawkins was definitely not like any other woman he had known, and maybe that wasn't so bad.

"There," she said with finality. "We're all ready to try again. And we'll keep doing it until we get it right."

"Yes, Sister," he said. But before he could move, she reached down and with her own hand made the all-important connection. And it was just at this moment and during the next fifteen minutes that Duane Higgins became convinced he should marry her.

35

Despite the rather abrupt cessation of the civilian tourist trade
after December 1941, Waikiki's two fine resort hotels, the Royal
Hawaiian and the Moana, had not suffered financial setbacks.
On the contrary, they enjoyed a higher level of occupancy than
ever before. Like most of the island of Oahu, they were
appropriated by the Navy and the Army for the duration of the
war and served as rest and recreation havens for submarine
officers back from long war patrols and Navy pilots returning
from combat cruises. The ballooning number of naval officers in
the islands had cut the average length of stay from over a week
during the first part of 1942 to its current three days and two
nights during the Christmas season. Thus it was on Christmas
eve 1943 that Air Group Twenty parked its aircraft in scattered
revetments on Ford Island, packed its personal gear into B-4
bags, boarded buses at the Naval Station, and transported itself
en masse to the lobby of the Moana Hotel, ready to squeeze as
much rest and recreation into that short period as was humanly
possible.

Fred Trusteau was watching two sets of luggage that
afternoon. He had found out the day before that Jack would be
tied up most of the first day of R and R in a meeting with the air
group commander and some higher-ups, and would take a cab
out to the hotel later. He had offered to take the Skipper's stuff
along with him on the bus, and Jack had accepted. Fred didn't

mind; in fact he was pleased to be able to help out.

On the trip out to the Moana, Fred's thoughts were concerned with the mysterious officers' meeting. He wasn't sure what it was about, but he felt it had something to do with what had happened the previous evening. Long after dark Fred and the Skipper had flown out over the ocean, making turns, climbs, and dives, and finally some simple formation aerobatics, and returned to Ford Island after ninety minutes. Fred felt that he was being tested and hoped he had qualified for whatever it was the Skipper was looking for. As for Jack, he had been extremely reticent about the entire matter.

Fred lugged the two heavy leather bags across the lobby (past a strangely un-Christmas-y Christmas tree), checked in, procured two room keys, then trudged up the stairs to the third floor, to their assigned room. He was anticipating sharing the same room with the skipper for two nights as much as he had anticipated anything else he had done since joining the squadron. He had no idea what the night would bring.

The room had a private bath, two double beds, a desk, a night table with lamp, and a veranda with a sweeping view of beach and ocean. He set the skipper's bag down on the bed nearest the veranda, then unpacked his own. Three sets of clean underwear, a set of tropical whites, swimsuit, toilet kit—all went into one of the desk drawers. He left the top one for the skipper.

His unpacking completed, Fred drew the drapes wide open, admitting a delicious ocean breeze and a burst of sunlight. He sat down on the edge of the skipper's bed and looked for a long minute at the water and sky, not thinking of anything in particular. It felt good for the moment to do nothing, and he let himself fall slowly back until he was on his back, hands beneath his head, feet touching the floor.

"Hey, Trusty, you still dressed?" It was Frank Hammerstein. He had opened the door without knocking and was in the room. "Come on, the guys are all going down to the beach."

Fred sat up. Frank was in his swimsuit and a pair of shower sandals; a white hotel towel was around his neck. His body and arms were almost laughably white.

"I'll be along in a little while," said Fred.

"Hey, you guys really got a room." Frank walked over to the glass doors and looked out. "Me and Patrick got a view of a bunch of palm trees. Someone said the whole top floor is full of Waves. Waves. Can you beat that?"

"Waves, huh?" Fred fell back into his prone position.

"Yeah. You going to try your luck tonight?"

Fred thought for a second, his eyes closed. "I'll just play it by ear," he said.

"Hey," called a voice from the corridor, "you guys coming?"

"Sure," Frank called back. He headed for the door. "You coming, Trusty?"

"In a little while," said Fred. He was comfortable where he was and had no desire to take off most of his clothes and expose his easily burned skin to the fierce tropical sun.

"See you later, then," said Frank.

"Close the door when you leave," said Fred, and was satisfied to hear it shut. Frank's footsteps faded away down the hall. He felt sleepy but thought it would be better to stay awake in case the skipper came back. He was trying to decide what he should do until then when he fell asleep on the skipper's bed.

He was awakened some time later by a slight commotion in the bathroom. Sitting up quickly, he noticed that it was already getting late; the sun was far over to the west and low on the horizon. It slanted through the open drapes, casting a beautiful golden glow on the far wall. Jack's bag, which had been near his head when Fred first lay down, was sitting on the desk. The skipper had arrived.

"Sorry I woke you up," said Jack, coming out of the bathroom, drying his hands on a small white towel.

"I didn't hear you come in," said Fred. He stood up and stretched. "Looks like I slept the whole afternoon."

"That's what it's for," said Jack. He tossed the towel through the bathroom door, then turned the chair that faced the desk around and lowered himself into it. He propped his feet up on the edge of the bed, put his hands behind his head. He looked completely relaxed. "Thanks for taking care of my things," he said.

"You're welcome," said Fred. He was suddenly tense, awkward. He didn't know what to say, what to talk about. "It was nothing, really."

"I still appreciate it."

Fred sat back on the bed, nearer Jack, and leaned back on his elbows. "How'd the meeting go?" he asked.

"Fine. But that comes under the heading of business, and I promised myself not even to think about it for the next two days."

"That's okay with me." Fred glanced out the glass doors. "I guess I should be getting ready for dinner." He stood up, put his hands in his pockets, looked out at the ocean. "Did you make any plans yet?"

"Unfortunately, yes. Jennings corralled me and the other two skippers into eating with him. Orders are orders."

"I understand," said Fred.

"By the way," Jack said reaching behind him and dragging his bag across the desk. "I brought a little something for you."

"For me?" Fred came over and sat on the bed near the skipper's feet.

Jack unzipped the bag and took out a bottle of liquor. "It being Christmas and all . . ." He pushed the bottle across to Fred.

"Walker Scotch. Black Label." Fred held it up in the failing light.

"I know you like Scotch."

Fred was awed. He hadn't seen a bottle of Black Label since 1941. "I do," he said. He started to take the top off. "Shall we try it?"

"Not now," said Jack, standing up. "I've got to get ready for dinner. Save it for later. Say ten-thirty tonight? Just the two of us?" He walked across the room and into the bathroom.

Fred followed him with his eyes. "Fine with me," he said.

"Good," said Jack. The light came on in the bathroom and the door swung shut. Fred sat holding the precious bottle for several long minutes, then put it down carefully on the desk. He was beginning to get a better idea of what the night would bring.

Duane Higgins sat at the Moana Lounge Bar and watched the three squadron commanders and CAG enter the restaurant, leaving their hats with the hat check boy near the door. For a man who could have had a room to himself, he thought, but chose instead to share a room with his j.g. wingman, Jack Hardigan was sure spending a lot of time with everyone else. First he had turned over the expedition to the hotel to Duane, the second in command, coming in later with CAG in a cab. Trusteau had been conspicuously absent from the festivities on the beach that afternoon, and Hammerstein had mentioned that he had probably fallen asleep on his bed. So he had to be there when the skipper checked in. He'd spent maybe twenty minutes alone with Trusteau in the room, but when he came out he was freshly showered and shaved. Did any of this mean anything?

There were ten officers in the bar for every woman. In fact, he was seeing fewer and fewer women in the area every time they came back from a cruise. But that no longer bothered him. He had Eleanor Hawkins, an affection-starved beauty of a woman with her own car and house. It was an unbeatable combination. Duane finished off his drink and ordered another. Rest and recreation was a precious time, and he meant to enjoy as little of the first and as much of the second as he could.

At six-thirty Trusteau and Hammerstein, Levi and Bagley, came through the bar on their way to the restaurant. They sat near the door and eyed a couple of Waves who came in and took a nearby table. Duane had already checked out the Waves and had been uninterested; just the thought of Eleanor Hawkins made him forget about them. Duane ordered a third drink, then stepped to a phone near the door. He dialed Eleanor's number. It rang a dozen times without an answer. Hanging up, he went back to the bar and thought, Maybe I'll try my luck with the Waves, after all.

A little after seven the CAG party came out of the restaurant and headed for the patio, a palm-frond-and-tiki-torch affair with a piano bar and a dance floor. They had a woman with them, a statuesque redhead who was not bad, not bad at all. She was obviously one of CAG's girls—he had a whole string of them, damn him, and kept close tabs on every one. But there were still the two Waves.

At seven-thirty Trusteau's group came out of the restaurant. They had the two Waves in tow. One of them was leaning on Trusteau's arm and laughing amiably. All six went through the bar to the patio. Duane cursed to himself and pulled on his drink.

Duane went back to the phone and tried Eleanor again. There was no answer. He looked around the bar, seeing a half-dozen women, each with a multiple escort of eager pilots. The odds were just too great.

He heard music coming through the door to the patio and wandered over to investigate. A stout Hawaiian woman sat at the piano bar, playing dance melodies. While he watched, the skipper's wingman and one of the Waves got up and began to dance. Duane looked away, scanned the rest of the patio. The skipper was sitting with Woody Heywood. They were talking about flying: four hands did rolls, made attacks, flew aerobatics. A couple of the new pilots who had checked in since the Tarawa operation were sitting together, drinking beer and looking very homesick. He almost felt sorry for them and decided to go over and talk. What were their names? Hill, yes. Anderson? No, Anders.

"Hi, guys," he said. Both looked up.

"Hello," said Hill.

"Mister Higgins," said Anders.

"Mind if I join you?" Duane pulled out a chair, turned it

around and straddled it. He set his drink down and lighted a cigarette. "Enjoying yourselves?"

"Sure," said Anders. "What a great place to spend Christmas."

"I've been in worse places than this for the holidays, pal," said Duane.

"Sure," said Hill.

"When are we gonna see some action?" said Anders.

"Yeah," said Hill. "All we do is sit around and practice and take vacations in the hotels."

Duane laughed. "You'll get your share of action," he said. "I guarantee it."

"How many kills do you have, Mister Higgins?" asked Hill.

"Oh, I don't know. I sort of lost track."

"Really?"

"Were you at Midway?" asked Anders.

"Sure was. Flew wing on the skipper over there." Duane pointed over his shoulder; then he saw the skipper was gone. He glanced around the patio trying to find him, but was unsuccessful.

"Are all those things they say about his wingman really true?" asked Anders.

"You mean Killer?" He looked and saw Bagley cut in on Trusteau and the Wave, and he smiled.

"Did he really get three Japs in one pass?"

"At night?"

"Not in one pass," said Higgins. "Only two in one burst. But it was dark you know, and he couldn't really have been trying for both at one time." He flicked ashes to the floor as he talked, took another drink from his bourbon. "The last one put up a fight and nearly took him out with him."

"Geez, wish that had been me. I'd have shown those Japs."

"Sure you would, Tiger," said Duane. The two kids were really kind of fun, naive though they were. If they survived the first week in a combat zone, they might develop into halfway decent pilots. Duane laughed to himself, finished off his drink, and turned to check on Trusteau and the two Waves. The two Waves were still there, one dancing with Bagley, Hammerstein and Levi. But Killer Trusteau was nowhere to be seen.

At ten o'clock Fred could wait no longer. He had left the patio bar before eight and wandered around on the beach killing time, trying to calm his racing emotions. It had done no good whatever. His stomach was tied in knots, his knees were weak and trembling. He thought about the bottle of Scotch the skipper had brought him, thinking that that might help him slow down a little. The three drinks he'd had for dinner certainly had no effect on him now. Leaving a little grove of palm trees bordering the beach, he made his way through the soft white sand, past some patrolling MPs, and up the steps to the first wing of the Moana. He went in an entrance separate from the lobby and the bar and met no one he knew. When he reached the room, Jack Hardigan was there, sitting in the dark.

"Hello, there, Killer," said Jack.

"Hi, Skipper." Fred quietly pulled the door to behind him; then he went over and sat on the edge of the bed near the chair the skipper occupied.

"Been waiting for you."

"I'm sorry."

"You're early. I'm glad."

The wind rustled the open curtains. Fred thought of his last two hours on the beach. "I ran out of things to do," he said. "Just thought I'd come on up."

Jack said, "I'm glad you did. I don't like sitting alone in the dark."

"Well, now I can keep you company," said Fred, feeling stupid.

"I was hoping you could do a lot more than that."

The easy, gentle way he said it made Fred swallow hard. Before he could think of anything to say, Jack said, "I'm about ready for that drink if you are."

Fred looked for the bottle, saw it standing where he had left it on the desk. Two short glasses stood beside it. He stepped over Jack's legs to reach the desk, broke the seal on the bottle, removed the cap, poured the two glasses a third full. Jack stood to take his, sipped at it, which surprised Fred, because he was sure the Skipper was going to offer a toast like, "Here's to us," or "Here's to better times." He took a sip, too.

"You can always tell a good Scotch," said Jack, "by how smooth it is without ice." He sat, almost casually, on the edge of the desk.

"It's very good," said Fred.

"Come over here beside me," said Jack.

Fred swallowed hard again, then moved in the half-dark to the skipper's side. Then, simply and naturally, Jack slipped his arm into the crook of Fred's elbow and left it there.

Fred felt a little of the Scotch spill onto his fingers. His heart was thudding so loud he was sure the skipper could hear it.

"You know," Jack was saying, "I really thought we'd lost you once back then."

"At Wake?"

"Before that. When you came down on the *Essex*. It was not knowing that was hard to take. And the thought of getting along without you..."

"I, I..." Fred stammered.

"You mean a lot to me," said Jack quietly. Fred felt his arm stiffen slightly as he said it.

There was a noise in the corridor. Someone crashed heavily into the wall, then loud voices broke into song. Pulling his arm away, Jack went quickly to the door and stood there, listening, while the drunks made their slow progress down the hallway. Jack turned the lock.

"No more interruptions," he said, coming back to Fred. He stopped right in front of him. "We won't get very many chances like this one to be alone, so I guess we better take advantage of it." He set his glass down on the desk, slipped his hand underneath Fred's arm and prompted him to his feet.

Awkwardly, as though he weren't quite sure how to do it, Jack embraced Fred, clasping him so tightly Fred could feel his shirt buttons press into his own chest.

"Relax now," Jack said, "it's all right." Fred realized he was still holding his glass of Black Label Scotch, turned to set it on the desk, and returned to Jack's arms.

It seemed to Fred that they stood there for a long, long time, but he lost track of the minutes as he gloried in the closeness of the big man. Jack seemed to have a dozen different scents—the Scotch, tobacco, sweat, a tantalizingly faint after-shave lotion. He felt the expansion of Jack's chest as he breathed, the roughness of his beard against his neck, and knew that this was what he had wanted all along.

At eleven-thirty, Duane Higgins came noiselessly down the hallway and stopped outside the door he knew to be Jack Hardigan's and Fred Trusteau's. He listened carefully for the sounds of anyone coming down the hall, then for any sounds coming from the room on the other side of the door. Nothing. He waited for almost a minute, listening. Then he carefully reached down and tried the doorknob. It was locked.

Duane went softly down the corridor to the head of the stairs and found a spot where he could stand and see the stairs and the entire hallway where the squadron was berthed. Then he leaned against the wall, lighted a cigarette, and waited. For most of the night, he waited.

At two o'clock, Fred woke beside the skipper, jarred out of sleep by Jack's snoring. He lay on his back and timed his breathing to that of the other man's, pleased by the sound of it. After a few minutes, fully awake, he reached over to the night table and looked at his watch; the luminous hands showed the time. He got up and looked around for his shorts, found them, put them on. Then, as quietly as he could, he gathered up the rest of his uniform and arranged it neatly over the back of the chair. He found Jack's shirt and trousers and hung them on a hanger in the closet—resisting the temptation to try on the shirt to see how a lieutenant commander's shoulder boards felt. Then he took the two glasses into the bathroom and left them on the back of the sink. He replaced the cap on the bottle of Black Label, turned down the sheets on his bed, and as quietly as he could, released the lock on the door. He thought about going to bed but wasn't really tired.

The curtains over the open glass doors ballooned into the room on a sudden gust of ocean air. Fred went to close them, then changed his mind. He stepped out onto the veranda. A thick cloud cover had moved in. It smelled like rain. Below him, the sea rolled sonorously in and out. Fred breathed deeply, feeling more alive, more exhilarated than he ever had before. It was suddenly very good to be alive, here at this particular time, in this particular place, with Jack asleep on the bed behind him. After several minutes it began to rain, and he left the veranda, pulling the door shut, closing the curtains. He climbed into the other bed and fell asleep immediately.

Duane Higgins unabashedly pounded on the skipper's door, then opened it, and went in. The drapes were drawn against the sunlight, so he dropped the packages he was carrying on the bed nearest the glass doors and threw them open with a single sweep of his arm.

"Rise and shine, men," he called cheerfully. He looked around. Both beds were occupied. Trop whites were put away or hung over the chair. But who had unlocked the door? And when?

"What happened? What's the matter?" Jack Hardigan sat up suddenly, a look of alarm on his face. Then, remembering where he was, he sank back down under the single sheet that covered him and closed his eyes. "What do you want?" he muttered.

"Merry Christmas," said Duane. He picked up the two packages and tossed one onto each bed. "Mail came last night. Nearly everybody got something."

Jack sat up and picked up the small package. He was still half-asleep. "What time is it?"

"Nine o'clock." Duane went over to Fred Trusteau's sleeping form and shook him roughly by the shoulder. "Come on, Killer. Santa Claus came last night."

Fred rolled over and looked at Duane with one eye, then closed it, and pulled the sheet over his head.

"Don't you ever sleep?" asked Jack.

"Not on R and R. I been up all night bringing cheer and happiness to the boys in blue."

"Ho, ho, ho," said Fred, from beneath his sheet.

"Come on," said Duane, "they stop serving breakfast at ten." He noticed that Jack would not get out of bed and was keeping the sheet over the lower half of his body. He had never known the skipper to sleep in the raw.

"It's from my sister in Ohio," said Jack. He began to tear the paper off the battered little package.

"Hey, hey," said Duane. He picked up the bottle of Black Label. "Fancy digs."

"The real Santa Claus came last night," said Fred. He sat up and threw the sheet back. Duane saw he was wearing shorts and it made him breathe easier for some reason. Fred picked up his package and looked at the postmark.

"A bible," said Jack, taking a small book out of a wad of tissue paper. "With a steel plate." He opened the cover and read aloud, "Trust in the Lord but give Him all the help you can." Jack laughed. "From my nieces."

"No wonder we got them by Christmas," said Fred. "They're postmarked September."

"I'll leave you two with your new toys," said Duane.

"A flying scarf," said Fred. He pulled a snowy white silk scarf from the middle of a pile of brown wrapping and tissue paper. "Just call me the Baron."

"You guys come on down," said Duane from the door. "We'll be having breakfast at 9:30 sharp."

He closed the door and they heard him pounding on the next

door down. Fred dropped the silk scarf to the bed and looked at Jack. Jack set the little bundle of paper and bible on the bed and smiled back at Fred. "Merry Christmas," he said.

"Someone should write a book," said Jack.

They were lying together in the darkened room, with only moonlight to see by. It created a ghostly gray luminescence instead of real light and made the shadows seem only more black and impenetrable.

"A book?" asked Fred. He was on his back, one hand under his head, the other under Jack's shoulder.

Jack rolled over on his side and propped his head on his hand. "A book," he said.

"What about?"

"The war. All this."

"Not us?"

"History, Killer, history. We're making history and don't even know it. All these carriers, these air groups. Someone ought to write it all down."

"I suppose," said Fred. He reached for the night table and a pack of cigarettes. There was only one left; he lighted it, dragged once, and offered it to Jack.

"We'll be heading back out pretty soon," Jack said, taking the cigarette.

"How soon?"

"CAG let it slip when we had that meeting yesterday."

"Loose lips," said Fred. "When is it?"

"Second week in January." Jack handed the cigarette back to Fred.

"I don't suppose he let slip where."

"His lips aren't that loose, or else he doesn't know. But I think we could guess if we put our heads together."

"If we put our heads together," said Fred, "I don't want it to be for the purpose of figuring out where we're going next."

"I wouldn't mind staying here for a while."

"Me, neither."

"But all good things . . ." Jack ran his fingers through the hair on Fred's chest, then suddenly bent his head to place his ear there. "I can hear your heart," he announced.

Fred reached up, with the cigarette still in his fingers, and stroked Jack's beard with his thumb. Suddenly he laughed. "That piano player," he said.

"Yeah," said Jack. "Didn't know a single Christmas song."

"How do you say 'Jingle Bells' in Hawaiian?"

"Niki naka huki luki," said Jack. He rolled over on his back, laughed loudly.

"Hum a few bars of the Hallelujah Chorus, boys, and I'll fake it." Fred shook with repressed mirth, reached over, and put the cigarette out in an ashtray on the floor.

"You're going to have a scar there."

"Where?"

"Right here." Jack touched the healing cut above Fred's right eyebrow. The ugly scabs had come off only two days before, leaving a tender pink cleft in the tight skin.

"That's okay with me," said Fred. "A little scar is better than the alternative."

Jack took a deep breath and let it out in a long sigh. "When we get back out there," he said, "you stick to me."

"All right, Skipper."

"I mean it. Stick like glue and do what I do. No more killer-type heroics."

"Whatever you say."

"I mean it." Jack was very serious.

"I will." Fred edged closer to Jack until they were touching down the length of their bodies. "I promise." He squeezed Jack's thick forearm, feeling the muscles there. "These two days sure went by fast, didn't they?"

"Too fast." Jack rolled up on his side so he could look at Fred's face. "I hope you enjoyed yourself."

"More than anything in the world. But."

"But what?"

"They're not over yet."

Jack smiled, lowered himself on top of Fred, and spoke in his ear. "I know," he said.

Fred felt the weight of the older man press him into the bed and hugged him with all his strength. He drew a long, trembling breath. "God, you feel good," he said.

And Jack whispered into his ear, "I've never felt better in my life, Fred. Never."

Part VI

Combat Two:

Kwajalein

36

"A bat team?" Fred sounded very polite, but Jack knew he was dreadfully uncomfortable sitting in the hot Sunday morning sunshine on Ford Island.

"That's what they called the first team. I see no reason to call ours anything different," Buster Jennings said.

The three men were attired in crackly-stiff tropical whites. They sat in white-painted iron chairs around an iron filigree table of a style most often found in Victorian gardens. Beside Fred, in the fourth and last chair, was a full captain from the task group operations staff. A hundred yards from the little group was a cluster of gray buildings, which included the base chapel.

"The key to their whole operation," Jennings continued, "is that first snooper. As far as we can tell, it's always a Betty. They have the fuel capacity for five or six hours on station. They find the task group in the dark or just before sundown—they might even be using a radar model—and the snooper stays out of range and shadows until the complete strike shows up. He helps them form up by dropping strings of float lights in the water. They point out the direction and course of the group. Then he goes high and does the number with the flares. That's the way they got the *Lexington* last month." Jennings paused and tried to harden his voice. "They get better at it every time they try; they circle out of range and come in low so radar can't get on in time to shoot. We don't use the flattops' guns at all because the flashes would give away their positions. Maneuvering throws off their aim, but it doesn't kill Japs."

Fred cleared his throat. "Is that why there wasn't any flak during our interception last month?" he asked.

"No," said Jennings. "The truth is, they faded at about four miles. Since we had no provision for having our own aircraft up after dark, other than IFF, it's a wonder some trigger-happy sailor didn't open up and shoot both of you down."

Jack watched Fred wrinkle his brow and sit back with crossed arms, obviously dissatisfied with the answer. Jack had been aware of the danger at the time, but he had never mentioned it to Fred. The night interception was one of two things they never talked about. (The other was the stay at the Moana a week before.)

"The bat team works like this," Jennings continued. "We launch a radar Avenger and two F6s, either just at dusk or whenever the snooper shows up. They join up and the FDO vectors them out to the snooper. The Avenger uses its radar to find the Jap in the dark, then he puts the two Hellcats on him and they splash him. The snooper's the key: With him gone, they don't have their ringmaster. They have trouble finding the group. No one drops any flares. Maybe we leave the team up, and they take out a few of the main strike and that really confuses them. It has to work." He added the last with a note of defiant finality.

"Nothing has to work," said the staff captain. "Remember what happened the first time they tried it."

"It worked," said Jennings. "They broke up the bastards. They didn't even attack."

"They were lucky and the Japs were unprepared," the captain said matter-of-factly. "Just like Mister Hardigan and Mister Trusteau on their little midnight adventure. And look what it cost."

Jack enjoyed watching Fred's reactions to the captain's opinions. He tapped a foot in impatience, cracked his knuckles loudly, raised his eyebrows in polite surprise. Obviously no one had told him about the first time a bat team was used.

"For the record," asked Fred, "could you tell me what happened?" He directed the question to no one in particular, as though he were unsure who would answer it.

CAG harrumphed and crossed his arms. "Nothing happened that shouldn't have. We lose pilots all the time."

Jack leaned toward Fred and rested his elbows on his knees. He clasped his hands in front of him. "The *Enterprise* tried it," he said. "They didn't join up right away, but the Avenger got two of the Bettys. Then when they tried to join up using landing lights, the Japs spotted them and got away. Later the skipper of VF-6—he was one of the fighters—suddenly left the formation and no one ever saw him again. They think the Avenger's turret gunner mistook him for a Japanese and killed him." He watched Fred take a sharp little breath and release it. Then he eased back into his chair.

"Butch O'Hare was worth ten Jap Bettys," said the captain. "For that matter, any one of you here is worth more than a few enemy planes when we've got a hundred five-inch and four hundred forty-millimeter barrels in every task group. What you're proposing is that we order all ships to hold their fire while a couple of blind fighter pilots try to shoot down twenty or thirty hostile torpeckers in the dark."

"We don't have to shoot all of them down," said Jennings. "Or even half of them. It's all a matter of timing, getting the snooper first." He was not giving in easily.

"You said yourself they're getting better at it. How can you be sure they won't send out two snoopers next time? If you do get one lone Nip, how do you know for sure that one was the snooper?"

"All those guns didn't save the *Lexington*," said Jennings. "Now she's in dry dock and won't make it for the next push."

"We'll have to make and distribute changes in the Op Plan," said the captain, "so that some of your flyboys can play hide-and-seek with enemy bombers while the boys on my cruisers and battlewagons sit around and pick their teeth. Why do you think they built the *Oakland*? To look pretty?"

From the brief smile that crossed Fred's face, Jack could tell he found the remark amusing. Both pilots knew the *Oakland* well. She was a hybrid cruiser built for one purpose: to shoot down attacking aircraft. A veritable forest of five-inch barrels adorned her upper levels; every other open topside space was jammed with smaller forty- and twenty-millimeter mounts. When she opened up it was awesome.

"It *can* be done. It *will* work. All we need is a chance." Jennings pounded a chubby fist on the wrought-iron table.

The staff captain merely stood. "It's too bad I don't have final say," he said. "But I'm forwarding your suggestions recommending disapproval. There's too much at stake. You'll have word before we sail. Good morning, gentlemen."

The captain turned and strode away. In the silence that ensued, Jack heard church bells ring. This reminded him that it

was Sunday, a nonflying day—and he and Fred were in here in
trop whites listening to two higher-ups debate whether or not
they would risk their lives.

"That tears it," said Jennings. "That bastard carries weight
with the ops staff."

"Should we keep up the night flying?" asked Jack.

"Sure," said CAG. "But don't let the rest of your boys slack
off."

"They're in good shape," said Jack. He was passing on Duane
Higgins's opinion since Higgins had much more chance to
observe their performance. The nightly flights and the daily
burden of paperwork were effectively cutting off his own contact
with the rest of the men. It disturbed him.

"Well," said Jennings, standing to go. "Join me in some late
breakfast?" He spoke to Jack, ignoring Fred.

Jack looked quickly at Fred and saw that amused little smile
out of the corner of his eye. "I've already eaten," Jack lied.
"Besides, I usually use this time to catch up on the paperwork."

"Suit yourself," said Jennings. He jammed his hat onto his
head in one nervous gesture and walked away in the direction of
the Officer's Club without another word.

"I'm sorry," said Jack.

"What for?" asked Fred.

"Ruining your Sunday like this." They both stood and
stretched. "After last night's flight, you probably would've been
better off staying in the rack." They fell into step, side by side,
walking in the direction of the boat landing.

"I didn't mind getting up," said Fred. "At least now I know
why we've been flying at night."

"So do I."

"You didn't know?"

"Not exactly. I had a general idea, but today's the first time
it's been spelled out."

"Will it work?"

"With the right people doing it, yes. It should."

"Is it really dangerous?"

That was something Jack had tried hard not to think about
since CAG had asked him to pick a wingman and qualify him in
night ops. Just flying off an aircraft carrier during daylight
hours, even in peacetime, was dangerous work. Doing the same
thing at night in a wartime combat zone with enemy planes in the
area and scores of itchy-fingered mount captains below, was just
this side of insanity. But so was attacking an enemy base on a
regular strike. Inevitably men died. And it could happen to him,

or to Fred—the one person he had ever really cared for.

"Yes," he said helplessly. "It is." He wanted badly to touch Fred, hold him. But he couldn't.

"So I guess we better be careful," said Fred.

"That would help." Jack smiled wryly.

They walked in silence for several minutes. The dewy grass wet their shoes and pants cuffs. An enlisted man in a smart white uniform passed and saluted. Both men absently returned it.

"Did you get any more mail from home since Christmas?" asked Jack.

"Not since the flying scarf." Fred laughed. "That was more than enough."

"I got another package from my mother. A new wallet. Very nice."

"They did really well with the mail this year."

"Took them three years to get it right."

They came to a narrow asphalt path leading down to the landing and turned onto it.

"Feel like a bridge game this afternoon?"

"Sure," said Jack. "If you get the people together."

"Okay."

They continued down the path to the liberty boat, talking about the weather, flying, the still-unannounced sailing date, the *Oklahoma* everything except themselves and each other. They were two men who were as close as two men could be, but they were still very much apart.

37

20 January 1944: U.S.S. *Constitution* sailed this day from Pearl Harbor as part of Task Group 58.1, comprised of carriers *Enterprise, Yorktown, Belleau Wood,* and *Constitution.* Air Group Twenty, including this squadron, was brought aboard ship beginning at 1300, after which standard CAP was instituted. There were no operational mishaps. Squadron strength stands at thirty-three operational aircraft and thirty-two pilots. Course of the Task Group has been determined as approximately two hundred degrees true, although the actual target area has not been announced.

This War Diary has been written for that period of time from 6 June 1943 to this entry by Lieutenant (j.g.) Frederick Trusteau, USNR. This duty will now be handled by Ensign William C. Hill, USNR.

"Did you read over all the past entries?" Fred asked Hill as they were seating themselves at a table in the ship's library. He had chosen this compartment because it was off limits at this time of day to on-duty personnel, which effectively included everybody.

"Most of them," said Hill. He was a thickly built young man with a beardless face who nevertheless managed to look grubby even after a shower. Fred doubted he could handle the chore of writing the Diary, but he was willing to help him. The skipper had wanted the new men to get more involved in squadron affairs. The fact that Hill was the junior ensign may have had some bearing on the selection as well.

"I asked you to read them all," said Fred.

"Aw," said Hill. "You read one, you've read 'em all."

"I gave you plenty of time. You had the Diary all last night. It isn't that long."

"Well, I had other things to do, too, you know."

"Like what?"

"Just things."

Fred opened the book up to the last completed page and took out his ink pen. "When someone tells you to do something, someone from the squadron, you do it. Everyone in this group is senior to you and what they say is an order. That means you jump. Okay?"

"Okay," said Hill. "Don't get all riled up."

"There has to be an entry for every day, telling basically what the squadron did. The number of operational aircraft and pilots has to be entered every other day or whenever there's a change . . ."

"I didn't do all that bad last night," said Hill. He pushed his hand into his side pocket and came up with a roll of bills.

"What do you mean?"

"There was a little game—"

"You played poker last night?"

"I told you there were things I had to do. That was one of them."

"You get caught at that and they throw the book at you."

"Mister Higgins plays."

"Put the money away." Fred uncapped the pen and shoved it in front of Hill. "Here. You're going to write the entry for yesterday, the twenty-first."

"What'll I write?"

"You could start with the date."

"Yeah." Hill concentrated briefly and wrote on the line right under the last entry "January 21, 1944."

"You didn't leave a line," said Fred, "and you wrote it wrong."

"Ah, I ain't no good at things like this."

"Can't you look at one of the entries up here and just do the same thing?"

"Yeah, I suppose." Hill crossed out the incorrect date with a thick, wet line and wrote "20 January 1944" on the line below it.

"Yesterday was the twenty-first."

"Aw, shit," said Hill, dropping the pen to the book and leaving a little splatter of ink. "I just ain't no good at this sort of thing."

"The skipper didn't pick you because he thought you were a great writer."

"Can't you tell the skipper that I can't do it worth a damn?"

"No one tells the skipper anything." Fred was getting a little heated. "Write the goddamn date." Hill crossed out the "20" and wrote "21" in the space above it. It looked awful. Fred gritted his teeth.

"Hey," said Hill. "You're the Skipper's wingman. You should know."

"Know what?"

"Me and some of the guys were talking. We think Mister Higgins is better than the skipper. What do you think?"

"Better at what."

"You know. Flying. Shooting down Jap planes."

Fred turned his chair so he could look at Hill. "What the hell difference does that make?"

"Well, Mister Higgins has more kills than the skipper so we just thought—"

"You thought wrong. The skipper has seven. Mister Higgins has four." He looked around in exasperation. "I've got three. But who gives a damn?"

"Well, we thought it was important."

"It isn't. Are you going to write that entry or not?"

"Sure," grumbled Hill. He put his head in his hands in a semblance of thinking. Fred seethed. "I bet we find out pretty soon," Hill said.

"Find out what?"

"Who's the best. I hear we're headed right for the Japs' home base."

"And where would that be?"

"I don't know. Truk, maybe even Tokyo."

"Sure," said Fred. "Tokyo."

The ship's address speaker above their heads blared, "Mister Trusteau, your presence is requested in the squadron office. Mister Trusteau, your presence is requested in the squadron office."

Fred got up from his chair, irritated at the interruption, but curious—it was probably the skipper who wanted him. He opened the War Diary to the back cover and took out a thin stack of plain white typing paper. He put the paper in front of Hill. "I have to leave for a few minutes," he said. "Take this scratch paper and write out the entries for yesterday and today. When I get back I'll read over it and let you know if it's good enough to copy into the Diary."

"What if it isn't?"

"You'll stay here until you get it right. I don't care if you have a date with Betty Grable. Now do it."

Fred stalked from the library, found the midship's passage-way, went up two decks and forward, and arrived ten minutes later in the squadron office. The skipper was there, and so was Duane Higgins.

Jack sealed the envelope carefully, laid it on top of another envelope similar to it, and put both in the top drawer of the desk in the squadron office. The single-spaced letter from his brother Monty lay by itself on the desk in front of him. He read it through again from start to finish while waiting for Higgins and Trusteau.

The letter was typed carefully, probably by Monty's secretary. It made the letter seem terribly impersonal when he thought about someone else reading it in the process of transcription. The gist of the letter was straightforward: The executor of their father's will had made public, as per prior arrangement, the details of the disposition of his estate. (The lengthy delay in the settlement had puzzled Jack.) The part about lump sums made him mad. The bulk of the estate, of course, went to their mother. A lump sum of ten thousand dollars was bestowed on his sister and her family in Leeds, Ohio. A similar amount went to brother Monty in Portland. But Jack was only awarded five thousand. Another five grand went into trust "until the day of his marriage." The first five thousand had been deposited directly into his savings account and was collecting interest; the second five sat in a safe-deposit box and collected nothing but dust. Jack wondered bitterly if it was worth five thousand dollars to get married.

There was a single knock on the door. Duane Higgins entered. "What's up, Skipper?" he asked. He seated himself in the one other chair and immediately lit a cigarette.

"Nothing much," said Jack. He folded Monty's letter in thirds, then in half, and put it in his shirt pocket. "Just wanted to go over a few things with you." He moved his chair over and back to make room behind the desk. "Move that chair around here."

Duane looked perplexed but did as he was told. He sat with his knee touching Jack's. Jack pulled open a drawer full of filing folders. "This is the squadron's file. I want to show you my system of running things."

"Sure," said Duane.

"First off I got a file on every man in the squadron. I keep notes on everyone, mainly for the writing of evaluations every six months." Jack ran his hand over the typed tabs and Duane saw his name on one of them. "The service jackets are kept in the group office and Sweeney watches them. You have to sign them out if you want to use them. Back here I have the miscellaneous files. Aircraft, Communications, Correspondence—"

"Just a sec, Skipper," interrupted Duane.

"What is it?"

"What are you showing me all this for?"

"Call it part of your training."

"Training?"

Footsteps sounded in the passageway, stopping outside the door. There was a knock and Fred Trusteau came in. Jack and Duane looked up. "Sorry I took so long, Skipper," he said. He closed the door and stood uncertainly before the desk. There was no place to sit.

"That's all right," said Jack. "I'll be with you in a few minutes." Fred leaned against the bulkhead and crossed his arms. "Now," said Jack. "Where were we?"

"Training," said Duane.

"Yeah. The book says I have to leave behind a qualified number two. Just in case."

"Okay." Higgins sounded satisfied and watched as Jack flipped through the rest of the miscellaneous files. "That's fine," he said when Jack finished with those.

"Up here we got the 'In' and 'Out' box. Sweeney brings the stuff in, mostly from CAG, and takes out anything that has to be routed to someone else. You have to make a little note and tell him what goes where, like to CAG or the personnel jackets."

"Okay." Duane was uncomfortable sitting there touching Jack, especially with Trusteau in the room.

"This is my 'Hold' file." Jack pulled it from the middle drawer from underneath the two envelopes he had put there earlier. Duane saw Fred Trusteau's name on the top envelope. "I keep things in here that are pending, or things that I'm waiting for more information on—you know, things that can't be done right now." He took a letter from the folder. "This is a request from the Bureau of Aeronautics for an evaluation on the new ammunition cannisters for the Hellcats. CAG saw it first and sent it down to me. I'm waiting for the crew chiefs to finish a report so I can send it back." Jack put the letter away in the folder and put the folder back in the drawer. Again, Duane saw the letter with Trusteau's name on it.

"I guess that about does it," said Jack. "Anything requiring action is either in the 'In' tray or the 'Hold' file. I go through both of them every day and finish up anything I can. It doesn't pay to let things get backed up."

"Sure," said Duane. "I understand." He edged his chair away from Jack until their knees were no longer touching.

"Move that chair back around," said Jack. Duane looked relieved and did as he was told, bumping into Trusteau but not apologizing. "Now," said Jack, as Duane reseated himself in front of the desk, "there's something that concerns all three of us."

Duane leaned forward. Fred stood as before, saying nothing.

"We received word from the operations staff a little while ago. We've been given the go ahead for the bat team ops." Jack watched Fred's face as he said it, but there was no reaction.

"Bat team," said Duane. "That's your night flying routine, isn't it?"

"That's correct."

"Then you're really going through with it?"

"Yes, we are."

"Sounds kind of harebrained to me."

Fred shuffled his feet, maintained his silence.

"No offense to you, Trusty," Duane continued, "but if you have to do it, Skipper, why don't you pick someone with a little more time in the air?"

"No," said Jack, a little sharply. "Fred's got excellent night vision and depth perception. We fly well together. If anyone has to do it, it's us."

"I'm sorry," said Duane quickly. "I didn't mean to imply anything."

Fred smiled, looked down at his feet.

"The point is this," said Jack. "Me and Fred and CAG will be spending a lot of time in the air after dark. Daylight training will be left to you." Duane shrugged. "There's more. The day after tomorrow is the first briefing on the upcoming operation. I know enough to tell you this: It'll be another Tarawa-type affair. We'll be making the first strikes on the target. We'll also be in range of Jap airfields the night before the first sweeps. We have to expect an attack. If there is, the bat team will be used. In that case, you will lead the first sweeps over the target, not me."

Duane's face brightened. "That's all right by me," he said.

"I don't like to see the squadron going in under anyone but me, but we don't have any choice."

"Don't you worry," said Duane. "Now you guys'll know what it's like to come in when there's nothing left to go after."

"Any questions?" asked Jack. He looked at Duane, then at Fred.

"No, sir," said Fred.

"One other thing. I'll announce this decision to the squadron when the time is right. Is that clear?"

"Sure," said Duane.

"Yes, sir," said Fred.

"Okay." Jack's voice lost its hard edge and he leaned back in his chair. "Fred, stay for a few minutes. There's something we have to go over." He nodded to Higgins. "Mister Higgins," he said in dismissal.

Duane accepted it without a word, bumping Fred again as he left, again not apologizing. Fred lowered himself into the chair.

"I'm not sure I know how I feel about all this, Skipper," he said.

"Please," said Jack. "Do me a favor. Right here, right now, call me Jack."

"Jack." Fred said it softly, studied the other man's face as he did so.

"Thank you." He opened the desk drawer and took out the envelope with Fred's name on it. "I want you to have this," he said, and he handed it across to him. Fred stood to take it, then sat back down, looking carefully at the sealed flap, the handwritten name.

"It's from you," he said.

"Yes, it is."

"Should I open it?"

"If you want, but I can tell you what's in it."

"Okay. Jack."

"It's a will. Keep the envelope sealed. If you read it, put it in a new envelope. Keep it in a safe place. Don't take it flying with you."

"Yes, sir." Fred looked down at the envelope, turning it carefully, quizzically, in his hands.

"There isn't a lot I can call my own. I left a worthless piece of land to my mother. That leaves a savings account—I put the number and current balance in the will. If anything happens to me, it's yours." Jack folded his hands in front of him on the desk, squeezed the fingers tight until a knuckle popped. "I'm sending an exact copy to the family attorney. Sweeney witnessed both copies, but I didn't let him see who was in it."

"Okay," said Fred. "I appreciate the thought, Skipper. Jack. But I don't think I'll ever have to use it."

"Look, Fred. If you don't want to go through with this bat team thing, you don't have to."

Fred opened up his shirt and slipped the will in next to his T-shirt. "The way I see it," he said, "you and I won't get sunburned anymore."

Jack smiled. "That's a good point. I'm sure it'll bring dozens of volunteers fighting for the chance to qualify at night landings."

"No doubt." Fred sat quietly for a moment, knowing he should leave but not wanting to. "Do you know where we're going, sir?"

"Yes. A place called Kwajalein."

"Roi-Namur?"

"The same." Jack pointed a finger at Fred. "Don't tell a soul, you hear?"

"Yes, sir."

"I've got enough trouble without having a general court-martial on my hands."

"At least we're not going to Tokyo."

"Tokyo?"

"Hill heard some scuttlebutt."

"How's he doing with the Diary?"

"As well as can be expected."

"He's your responsibility, Fred. You train him."

"Yes, sir." Fred stood up. "I guess I better get back to the library."

"Try to get some sack time this afternoon. You may need it."

"Okay, Jack." He reached the door.

"There's a pretty good movie on tonight," said Jack.

"*Casablanca*. Bogart's in it."

"Let's go see it together." Jack looked up and Fred smiled.

"My pleasure." Fred closed the door behind him, leaving Jack sitting at an empty desk, his hands knotted in front of him.

Hill was still sitting alone in the library when Fred came back. He was surprised to see that Hill had indeed finished the entry for the twenty-first and was halfway through the one for the present date. But it was obviously a struggle for him. Fred sat beside him, taking out the envelope from his shirt and laying it on the table.

"What's that?" asked Hill.

"None of your business." Fred read through Hill's first entry. "You spelled 'course' wrong."

"Well, how the hell do you spell it?"

Fred pointed across the small room to another table. "That book over there is a dictionary. It'll tell you how."

As Hill looked up the word, Fred smiled to himself, savoring the satisfaction of being able to call the Skipper by his first name, in private, when no one else could. He ignored Hill's whining insistence that he couldn't find a word in the dictionary that he didn't know how to spell in the first place. Fred was thinking that Jack was worried about the bat team ops and maybe even feared for his life. That was okay, he thought, because *he* knew everything would be all right. Butch O'Hare might have been lost doing it, but then he had not had Fred Trusteau, the Trusty Killer, for a wingman.

"You really think we're going to Truk?" asked Hill, looking up from the dictionary.

"No, I don't."

"Well, where are we going then?"

"Beats the shit out of me," smiled Fred.

38

Despite the fact that he would lose over fifty dollars, Duane Higgins would have another reason to regret playing in the poker game this particular evening, the night before the first strikes on Kwajalein. He entered the game after the evening meal, when most of the other pilots were retiring to their staterooms and trying to sleep. He told himself that a good night's sleep was only marginally more important than the game. It was beginning to look like he wasn't going to lead the first sweep after all, which was scheduled for 0500 hours next morning. They were well within range of enemy reconnaissance aircraft, but there had been no alarms. He had skipped up to combat and asked about contacts, and was told that a weather front was moving in and there was little chance they would be spotted or attacked that night. On his way to the game site—a line stowage compartment near the bow—he had stuck his head into the skipper's stateroom. The skipper was undressing for bed, so Duane said good night and hurried on. If things went right, he would play until maybe twelve o'clock, sleep until four, when the scheduled GQ would sound, then lay around the ready room until the afternoon strike and catch a few z's there.

Duane came to the passageway outside the line stowage space and nodded to an apparently uninterested first class petty officer who acted as the game's security agent. He let himself in through the watertight door and found four other players stacking bills in neat piles. One was shuffling a new deck of cards on an upturned reel of silky nylon line. The lieutenant commander from Disbursing was there, as was Chief Carmichael, a lieutenant from the torpedo squadron, and a chief from the Medical Department. Duane cut the deck and sat down on a great bundle of manila hemp. He lay his bankroll on the edge of the reel as the first cards began to fly.

"Goddamn flyboys," said Carmichael. The first card was down, the second up. The players automatically shelled out the ante and the high card upped the bet. The third card caused Duane and the disbursing officer to fold.

"What's the bitch, Chief?" asked Duane.

Carmichael clamped down hard on an unlighted cigar and ignored the fourth card that landed in front of him. "When the fuck are we supposed to sleep?" He dropped a couple of bills into the pot, watched the last card come, looked at it, then raked the pot to his side of the reel. "We fuckin' work all day pushing those goddamn turkeys around up there—" A new hand of five card stud began to grow. "—four fuckin' o'clock in the morning till after dark, and now they fuckin' got us working all damn night, too. When the fuck are we supposed to sleep?"

"Back off there, Chief," said Higgins. He looked casually at his two up cards, his single hole card, and folded. "I don't give the flying orders."

(He was not entirely pleased with the situation either. For the last four nights they had gone to flight quarters after the moon had set, to launch the strange combination of CAG in a radar Avenger and the Skipper and Trusteau in their Hellcats. They would stay in the air for two or three hours. After the second night, they had allowed the rest of the pilots to turn in, but the flight deck crew and numerous other involved parties had to remain on station until they came back. Sleep was lost; spare time was bitten into. People were pissed off about it.)

Having said his piece, the chief quit his complaining and concentrated on the game. Duane folded the next two hands, bet the succeeding one on a high pair, and lost to a low three of a kind. He folded the next. It was not a good night for poker.

"What about that briefing?" asked the torpedo pilot. "Wasn't that something?"

"You bet," said Duane.

Chief Carmichael muttered under his breath and chewed the cold cigar.

"I got a line of latrines as my secondary," laughed the other pilot. "We're really hitting them where it hurts the most."

Duane understood the joke. The bomber pilots in the first and second waves had been given specific targets with secondary assignments in case they had the extra bombs. The second wave of fighters were given targets on the ground as well. It was an amazing coup of tactical planning: Every protected revetment, every antiaircraft gun, every command post and troops barracks were targeted by overlapping strikes. It was obvious that extensive photographs of the atoll had been taken during their strikes in December. Nothing was being left to chance.

Duane bet heavily on a high two pair, was beat again by three of a kind. He cursed to himself and thought of Eleanor Hawkins. He was definitely going to spring the question on her when they got back to Pearl, although he hadn't told anyone else yet. When the time came, he would have to talk to Jack Hardigan about it. Regulations required that his commanding officers up to CAG's level approve of the marriage, although he couldn't imagine either of them objecting. It was just that Jack would probably be surprised. Or maybe relieved. Duane wasn't sure.

The makings of a flush in diamonds began to build on Duane's side so he decided to take a chance. He bet—and wondered for the thousandth time why Jack had so completely lost interest in women. The last time they had even talked about women was the brunch at the Naval Station Officer's Club in August, and then Jack had left his date before dark and had gone back to the ship. To the best of his knowledge, all of Jack's off-duty socializing had been with the men of the squadron, Trusteau in particular. He wondered if anyone else had noticed.

His fourth card was his fourth diamond, and he bet it. With Carmichael and the lieutenant commander still in the hand, he received and looked at his last card. It was the Jack of hearts. He held it in his hand, recognizing for the first time the squadron insignia. The goddamn Jack of hearts, holding a sword instead of a leaf. So that was where Trusteau had got it. By the process of elimination, he knew that Trusteau had done the original artwork. It had irritated him considerably to know that Jack Hardigan had accepted it without consulting him. He replaced the Jack of hearts on the reel and upped the bet.

Carmichael guffawed. "Lieutenant, you don't bluff worth a shit." He tossed in a handful of bills. "I call your ass."

Duane bit the inside of his cheek and flipped his cards face down.

As he was raking in the pot, Carmichael turned them back up and saw the Jack of hearts. "Well, bless my heart, if it isn't the fighter boys' in-sig-nee-ah. Tough luck, Mister Higgins." He laughed loudly. Duane bit his cheek until it bled.

After that humiliation, however, thing began to look up for Duane. When they switched to seven stud, he began to win. Midnight found him almost even again and looking at a full house, tens over threes, with one card still to go. Certain of a winning hand, he went down for forty dollars, only to lose to Carmichael again, with Jacks over fours. Determined to get some of it back, he stayed in the game despite the time, but only managed to lose another ten. At one o'clock he could wait no longer. He gathered up his depleted bankroll, excused himself, and hurried through the dark ship to his stateroom. He was just taking off his pants when the alarm sounded.

Fred Trusteau slept with his watch on when they were at sea. It made it easier to wake up at inopportune times (as inevitably he had to) if he could just raise his arm and see the time. Tonight, he was deep in a dream that involved the hardware store and his father and a grating voice that kept saying, "This is not a drill. This is not a drill. All hands man your battle stations." In his dream he had just inexplicably landed his Hellcat in San Jose. His father had jumped up onto the wing and said, "All hands man your battle stations." Fred raised his watch to his eyes and was awake. It was 1:05.

Jack Hardigan reached the ready room before any of his pilots. Still struggling into his flight suit and with his hair uncombed and boots untied, the first thing he did was check the teletype in the forward part of the compartment. There was a single message there: "Bat Team One report to Ready Room Two." Duane Higgins arrived next, fully dressed and wide awake. But Jack didn't have time to notice.

"When Fred gets here," he told Duane, "tell him to come on down to Ready Room Two as fast as he can." Without waiting for an answer, Jack grabbed the rest of his flight gear and left.

Ready Room Two belonged to the Torpedo Squadron. A number of the Avenger pilots and some of the enlisted crewmen were there, milling about in confusion. Jack found Buster Jennings talking on the telephone and tapped him on the shoulder to let him know he was there. Then he straightened out his Mae West, buckled on his shoulder holster and tied his shoes. Finally put together, he had some time to wonder what was going on.

"How many?" asked CAG into the phone. Jack listened in and gathered that the weather front was gone and a quarter-moon was up. A force of Japanese torpedo bombers numbering somewhere between twenty and a hundred was gathering for attacks on the fringes of the task force. Then the full meaning of the information sank through. He realized that the force was discovered. Surprise was lost. There would be a hot reception over the target in the morning. He had no stomach for thinking of how their mission in the dark would go.

Jennings had finished talking on the phone and was busily strapping a vicious-looking knife to his foreleg when Fred arrived. Without wasting time on formalities, Jennings said, "Come on, let's go," and headed for the flight deck.

The bright quarter-moon was incongruously cheerful as Fred climbed away from the deck of the *Constitution,* raised his landing gear, and made the right turn that would help him find the other two members of the team. They had practiced this link-up a number of times, relying on precise launching intervals, speeds, altitude, and courses. As he completed his second right turn, a pair of dark shapes moved across the crescent of the moon. He maneuvered to join them.

"Rooster Base, Bat One. Ready for vector."

Fred recognized Jennings's voice and glided into a loose wing formation on the bigger Avenger. Looking across his left wing, he could make out Jack's Hellcat, but it was too dark to see Jack sitting in the cockpit. He wanted to come up on the circuit and tell the skipper that everything was all right; that the hurried conference on the flight deck, huddled in the windy darkness, had been sufficient for their purposes, even though it wasn't the way they had planned it. But CAG was in charge here and needed the circuit for vector information from the radar officer on *Ironsides.* Fred remained silent.

"Bat One, we have a large gaggle of bogeys bearing two zero two, altitude maybe three thousand. Stand by for better info."

"Roger, Rooster Base. One four, move it in a little closer. That's good. Speed one eight zero, two and three. Beginning a right turn now." CAG chatted away, telling Jack and Fred what he was doing, and the Hellcats clung to his wings like two deadly hawks prowling the night sky in search of prey.

"Bat One, advise you check your IFF. We show one of you without it." Fred found the switch and checked it. It was on.

"Bat One, this is One Four. Mine's on."

"Same here, One," said Jack—and Fred could imagine the skipper's hand reaching out, touching the same switches he had.

"We all show IFF on and operating," said CAG. "Suggest you check again."

"We still show one without IFF. What do you want to do?"

"Continue the interception. We didn't come up here to chicken out." Jennings's voice had that same intense, almost manic quality to it that it had shown when he reached out and pounded the lawn table that Sunday back in Pearl.

"Come to course two six one, Bat One. Climb to angels four. You should have bogey on your scope crossing from left to right in about . . ." There was a pause and a short babel of voices in the background. ". . . two minutes. Advise on contact."

"Roger, Rooster. Making the turn now, two and three."

Fred gentled his fighter into the turn and maintained his distance. He knew CAG wanted him closer, but he was near enough to see well and that was all that mattered. The three aircraft settled into two six one and climbed steadily, reaching four thousand feet in one minute. Fred could look left out of his cockpit and see the crescent moon, half expecting a Japanese torpedo bomber to fly, witchlike, across it. Moonlight painted a glistening highway on the surface of the ocean below him, but it illuminated nothing and made the ocean seem deceptively close. He searched the darkness in front of him and to his right, seeing nothing but stars.

"Contact, Rooster Base. Just like you said. Two and three, turning right at this time. We have a contact. Coming to two five zero knots."

Fred turned and increased throttle to keep up. They made the turn smoothly, easily. The practice sessions were paying off.

"Contact turning to the left. Speed about one niner zero."

The team turned to the left, following the invisible Japanese bomber. Fred wondered if this one were the first snooper. He was slightly confused because their briefing sessions had said they would be going after a single torpedo plane, not a "gaggle" of twenty or thirty. He checked his clock. It was 1:45. They had been up for almost half an hour. A light appeared below him, a tiny white point of incandescence that winked uncertainly, as if on the ocean's swells.

"We got him, boys," said CAG, his voice edged with excitement. "A thousand yards in front of us, same course—no, he's turning again, to the right. You take this one, number three. We'll try to stay above you." Fred turned on his gun switches after dimming the gunsight all the way. Automatically, he checked his instruments, satisfied himself that everything was working well, and prepared for his interception.

"Five hundred yards," said Jennings. "He's fading. He's

below us about five hundred feet, same course. We should see him..."

"Got him," said Fred. His first indication of the enemy aircraft was an almost invisible line of thin blue light flickering steadily against the backdrop of black water and sky. Exhaust ports. Fred broke to the right and headed down, backing off on his throttle to maintain his present speed. As he closed, he first made out another set of exhaust ports, then the bulk of two engines, wide wings, and cigar-shaped fuselage. A Betty. A fast, land-based bomber carrying torpedoes for attacking the ships below. Incongruously, he remembered Jack's statement that they were making history and should be writing all this down for later use. He smiled, and centered the enemy plane in his gunsight. When the target filled the little lighted ring, he squeezed the trigger and held it down.

The armorers had filled the ammunition cannisters in the wings with a lower concentration of tracers, so Fred was not blinded by the blazing slugs. The guns rattled and shook and the tracers reached out. Fred kept the target centered, and a red flame popped into being in the interior of the speeding Japanese bomber. Fred stopped shooting and followed his victim around to the right, decreasing throttle to stay above and behind. He centered it again, fired again. The fire blazed up. As if in panic, a single gun began firing from the upper surface of the fuselage, spewing directionless tracers around the sky. Feeling deadly and invisible, Fred hung over the doomed aircraft and fired again. The flames in the Betty now lighted up the interior of the fuselage and shone through the clear gunports like lights. A tail gunner began firing, also wide of the mark.

Fred stopped firing, thinking for a horrible second that he could see the outline of a man in one of the ports, but it was only his imagination. He checked his altitude and decided to break off. The bomber torched hugely in the dark; then it rolled over as the flying surfaces lost their aerodynamic qualities and twisted toward the water below.

"Scratch one Betty." It was CAG.

Fred pulled back on the stick and increased throttle to climb. He was relieved a moment later to see the two other members of Bat Team One cross in front of him. He eased up to the wing of the Avenger and slipped into his position.

"Good shooting, Trusty." Jack's voice crackled into Fred's earphones.

"Thanks." Fred had to clutch at his throat mike to activate it;

his hands were shaking like leaves in the wind.

"We could use another vector there, Rooster Base," said CAG. "We're just starting to warm up."

The teletype chattered to life in the front of the ready room, and Duane got up wearily to see what it was. The other pilots sat in their chairs, nervous, smoking, talking infrequently.

"Lookouts report plane going in bearing zero four five relative range six miles." Duane tore off the paper and handed it to another pilot to pass around. He lowered himself to his seat, suddenly very tired. He never should have gotten involved in the game tonight. Now it looked as if he would lead the dawn sweep over Roi-Namur after all. It was almost two. Reveille would have been held at 0400, launch a little after five. Maybe he could catch a few winks here in the ready room. He leaned his head back, closed his eyes.

The address system came on with a rush of static. Startled, Duane opened his eyes and sat forward, immediately recognizing the call signs and terminology of the circuit controlling the bat team. Someone had patched the circuit into the address system leading to the ready rooms. Under other circumstances he would have been grateful; right now all it did was interfere with his sleep.

"...good shooting," said a tinny voice that could have been Jack Hardigan's. "Thanks." That had to be Trusteau. The pilots of VF-20 sat with forgotten cigarettes dropping ashes to the deck and listened to the sounds of combat in the night sky over them.

"Keep it close, gents. Coming to three zero zero. Turning now. Rooster Base, we're waiting."

"Hold your horses, Bat One. We have a big bogey forming up at ten miles. Stand by for vector."

"Ready and waiting."

"We got flares over the group at this time, Bat One, can you see—"

"Damn right we can see them, Rooster. Give us a vector. We're hot for it."

"Vector two six niner, Bat One. Try angels four."

"On our way, Rooster."

"You should show bogey on your scope in three minutes, Bat One."

"Roger Doger, Rooster. We're balls to the wall."

There was a moment of silence during which the teletype began to run. Duane heaved himself up once more to see what it had to say. As the crooked letters inched their way up the yellow paper, he made out weather data for the morning's strike—wind direction and velocity, barometric pressure, cloud formations. He left the machine clattering away and went back to his chair.

"Lookouts confirm your last kill, Bat One," said the FDO.

"That's nice, Rooster. Tell 'em to keep their eyes peeled. They'll see a lot more before we're finished."

"Bogey is circling on vector two six niner, Bat One. Seems like a whole bunch of them and more all the time."

"Think they'd mind if we join the party?"

"Why don't you ask them?"

"Number three pull it in a little. If we have more than one bandit up here, we'll have to play it by ear. Break on my signal only."

"Okay," said Trusteau. "You still there, Skipper?"

"Bigger'n life," said Jack. "Good luck, Trusty."

"Same to you, Skipper." The two fighter pilots' voices came into the ready room softly, almost playfully.

"Okay, two and three. We got the first one on our scopes—wait a sec—we got two, no, three, no, two again. They're all over the place. Take your pick. Break gentlemen, and good hunting."

CAG quit talking, and a moment of silence stretched into one, then two minutes. Duane leaned forward and sat on the edge of his seat, wishing now for some word on how it was going.

"Lookouts report a flamer going in, Bat One," said the FDO. There was more silence on the circuit. Static crackled in. A microphone was keyed and everyone listened hard for the report, but none came.

"Bat One, what is your status?" asked the FDO.

"Goddammit, I can't—" It was CAG.

"Bat One, what is your status?"

"Christ Almighty, there's too many."

"Bat One, bogey is scattering. Suggest you try to rendezvous." There was another minute of silence on the circuit.

"Skipper, you still with us?" It was Trusteau.

"Far as I can tell, Trusty."

"I think maybe we should break off."

"I think that's a pretty good idea. You know where the turkey is?"

"Beats me."

Duane sank back into his chair, curious now about how many kills, if any, they had got. Trusteau had had three going into that fight tonight. One more and he would be up with Duane. Two more and he'd be an ace before him, and Duane Higgins would find that very hard to live with.

Jack pushed his goggles up and wiped the puddles of sweat from his eyes with his hand. He looked hard all around him for signs of other aircraft, but there was only the night sky, the stars, the quarter-moon. He tried unsuccessfully to slow his breathing, quiet his pounding heart.

He had been in hazardous situations before, but never one like the melee he had just survived. They had collided with the Japanese formation at nearly three hundred knots and gone in with all guns blazing. There had been no time to talk. Suddenly the sky seemed filled with twin-engine Bettys that popped up in front of his fighter in all attitudes. At least one, he was sure, had gone in because of his shooting. At various times during the fight he had seen two or three other flamers hit the water. Before they were through, the Bettys were firing wildly at everything in the sky and scattering to the four winds. He had the vague feeling that the interception was a success, but he didn't really care. What he wanted most right now was to find Fred and make sure he was all right. He pressed his throat mike. "Number two, do you have any idea where you are?"

"Not the slightest," came the calm reply.

"I'm at angels five on zero niner zero. What about yourself?"

"The same. How about that?"

"When was the last time you saw the Bat Leader?"

"Just before the mix-up."

"Rooster base, any thoughts on the matter?"

"That's a negative, number one."

A flash on the horizon to his left caught Jack's attention, and he banked that way to get a better look. As soon as he could see better, the single flash grew into many, and a ship was outlined by dim muzzle blasts. High in the air above her, a plane burst into red flames, twisted crazily downward, and smacked into the water.

"You see that, Trusty?"

"Affirmative, Skipper. To my left, maybe one mile."

"We're close, Trusty. I just don't see you."

"I concur, Skipper."

"Number two, number three, Boozer Boy just splashed a bogey with IFF. Suggest you join up and find the roost asap."

Jack tried hard to remember who Boozer Boy was. It was obviously a ship in the screen; by the looks of the muzzle flashes, it was one of the battleships, or maybe the *Oakland*. Rooster's idea seemed eminently appropriate.

"I don't know about you, Skipper," said Fred from somewhere in the darkness, "but no one's going to get me to turn on my lights."

"Acknowledged, number three. Keep thinking like that and they'll give you a squadron like mine."

"I wouldn't take it if they did."

Despite the danger, Jack laughed. Just knowing that Fred was all right made him feel better. The knots in his stomach eased. He requested a vector to the *Constitution*, received it, and groped his way home.

He came aboard in the predawn dark at three-thirty, Fred only minutes behind him. They stood on the flight deck for half an hour watching the spotting of the dawn strike, waiting for CAG. But Commander Buster Jennings never returned.

At 0500 the dawn launch went off as scheduled. It was led by Duane Higgins.

39

Duane was tired, so very tired. He knew his flying was unbearably sloppy, but he couldn't help it. Periodically, heavy fatigue would pull his eyelids down; then he would wrench them open to discover he had wandered a few degrees off course or that he was off a hundred feet in altitude. Three times Bagley had asked him if everything was all right, the last time even offering to take over the flight. But stubborn pride—and fear—kept him going.

He was afraid, terrified, of what the skipper would say when Duane got back to *Ironsides* with five Hellcats that should have been eight. His own wingman, Hill, had spiraled in wrapped in flames, not ten seconds after the Zekes jumped them. And he had seen another parachute which he thought might have been Frank Hammerstein. But he couldn't be sure; it had all happened so fast.

One minute they were high, the way they were supposed to be, covering the bombers and four Hellcats under Schuster below. The tiny double island of Roi-Namur appeared through the clouds right on time; then the bombers and the four Hellcats under Schuster went in while Duane and his divisions circled high. Someone started talking then, saying that the airfield was alive with Nip fighters taking off, though it looked like they'd been caught with their pants down.

Without waiting for orders, Hill peeled off and headed down, intent on getting himself a kill. Groggy, indecisive, Duane pushed it over and followed him down. The other six Hellcats tagged along in confusion, jamming the circuit with questions and objections. No sooner had they passed through ten thousand feet than ten—no, a dozen—green-and-brown Zekes slashed through their formation and killed Hill—and probably Frank Hammerstein. And someone else, too, although he couldn't yet tell who it was. He hadn't checked with the others and no one volunteered the information. No one said anything. Except Bagley.

"Mister Higgins, you want me to take over the flight? You don't look well at all."

"I'm fine, goddammit. Don't ask again." He hammered his fist on the side of the canopy, slapped his face savagely to keep awake. He was so furious with himself he didn't know what to do.

The rest of the flight went the same way. Before arriving, he opened the canopy completely and let the cold air rush over him, but it didn't help much. They found the task group without difficulty, but Duane led the five fighters over the wrong carrier on the first approach. He discovered his error in time and they found the *Constitution,* steaming into the wind and ready to take them aboard. He brought it in on the first pass, ignoring a last-second wave-off from the LSO. When the Hellcat lurched to a stop near the deck edge elevator, he was filled with a nearly overwhelming sense of relief. He stepped down from the wing roots backwards, turned and ran smack into Jack Hardigan. The look on the Skipper's face told him everything was not all right.

"What happened?" asked Jack. His voice was hard.

Duane started to push past Jack, saying as he did so, "Nothing much." But Jack grabbed him by the shoulders and shoved him fiercely against the side of his Hellcat. Still holding him by the shoulders, Jack brought his face up very close, so close Duane could feel his breath as he spoke.

"I asked you what happened."

It occurred to Duane that Jack might have listened in on the tactical circuit, just the way he had listened to the morning interception. If he had, surely he would have thought something was wrong when he heard the panic-stricken babbling that had burst forth when the Zekes came down on them.

"We were jumped," he said. "They hit us good. We lost Hill."

"How could you get jumped at twenty-one thousand feet?" The noise of a second Hellcat pulling up drowned Duane's answer. Jack looked and saw it was Bagley. "Someone will tell me what happened," he said.

Jack released him, and Duane discovered that he had been standing on his toes all the while.

Jack stormed around the tail of Duane's Hellcat, leaped up on the wing root of Bagley's plane, and strode to the cockpit. When Bagley shut down his engine, Duane heard him ask the same question. "What happened?"

Bagley pulled off his helmet with an almost anguished slowness. "Hill went in. Hammerstein bailed out..." The wind on the flight deck tore at his words.

"Anyone else?"

"Anders, the new guy. They got him, too."

"How?"

"Mister Higgins took us low." Bagley began to climb from his aircraft, slowly, slowly.

Jack was already back to Duane, who was still standing by the fuselage, beside his white number twenty-three. Jack placed one balled fist against Duane's chest and pushed him up against the blue aluminum. "Schuster got back before you did," he said. "He tells me you were up all night in a poker game." There was controlled violence in Jack's voice.

"What about it?" said Duane. It was the only way he knew how to respond. He was scared. Jack kept the fist in his chest, applied pressure.

"I'll tell you what, Mister," Jack said. "You led members of my squadron into a fight you weren't supposed to find and lost three men after not sleeping, against regulation, for more than twenty-four hours. I'll tell you what I'm going to do. You see me in thirty minutes in the squadron office. I won't be alone." He gave his fist one last shove, turned away, and left.

Duane was still standing there, dazed, confused, when one of the twenty-millimeter gun mounts in the catwalk to his right suddenly fired off a short burst, with a harsh, loud report. He looked into the gun platform. It was a beehive of activity. Then two more guns further away began firing in steady, droning explosions. In a second the entire catwalk, a dozen small mounts, was blazing away. The loaders turned like mechanical dolls, retrieved ammunition, turned again. Duane stood stupidly and searched the sky, trying to spot their target.

The forty-millimeter mount on top of the island, high above his head, opened up. The concussion from its muzzle blasts, its deep drumming, struck Duane in the pit of his stomach like a bass drum in a marching band. And now he saw what they were shooting at.

A single plane wove in just above the surface of the water, dodging a destroyer aflame with gun flashes and smoke. It was still far out, but flying right for them. Exploding shells traced a dirty trail behind it, tore the water into a white froth. When it still seemed far away, the plane pulled up and dropped something that splashed in the water below it. The *Constitution* heeled as it began a turn. One of the forward five-inch mounts blasted a salvo that nearly knocked Duane down. Then, the enemy bomber, its flank exposed as it turned, seemed to disappear in a shifting web of tracers and exploding shells, caught fire, plunged into the water.

The firing stopped as suddenly as it had begun and in the deafening silence that followed, Duane could hear cheering, tiny human voices that seemed laughably puny after the voices of the guns. *Constitution* heeled again, causing Duane to stagger slightly to maintain his balance, and then he saw the torpedo.

It made a thin white wake, like a chalk line drawn on the deep blue blackboard of the sea. *Constitution* was turning toward it, to avoid its ruler straight journey. Infuriatingly slow, the huge carrier turned parallel to the torpedo, but the weapon was too close, the turning radius too big, and Duane knew that it would hit. The wake disappeared under the overhang of the flight deck. Duane waited, breathless, for long terrible seconds before it detonated against the side of the ship, near the LSO's windscreen. The cheering from the gun platform stopped.

A muffled *whump* reached Duane's ears first, and a column of water rose majestically, towering over the flight deck aft like a living thing. Then the deck seemed to disappear, just as if someone had jerked a rug from beneath his feet. He hit the deck on an elbow, just as the water from the explosion found him. And as it rained sea water, Duane felt a movement that reminded him of an earthquake in Hawaii years before. When it was over, he lifted his body painfully. Then he saw the frantically scurrying flight deck crew and the rising smoke flattening out astern of the speeding ship, and the whooping breakdown alarm told him that *Ironsides* had just finished her contribution to the assault on Kwajalein.

31 January 1944: In company with CVL *Independence,* en route Pearl Harbor naval station for repairs to damage sustained in torpedo attack 29 January. All flight operations have been suspended due to port list incurred after the hit. Squadron Commander Lt. Comdr. J.E. Hardigan has been officially credited with one kill and Lt. (j.g.) Frederick Trusteau with two kills, during the night action of 29 January. Air Group

Commander Buster Jennings has been credited with two kills during this action and failed to return.

Following first strike on Japanese aerodrome at Roi-Namur, Lt. T.J. Schuster has been credited with one sure kill and two probables. Lt. (j.g.) Heckman has been credited with one kill. Lost in action were Lt. (j.g.) F. Hammerstein, Ensign William Hill, and Ensign John Anders. Squadron Executive Officer Lt. Duane Higgins has been officially reprimanded for his actions allowing the participating divisions to be attacked without warning at low altitude leading to the loss of three pilots.

This Diary is being prepared again by Lt. (j.g.) Fred Trusteau.

Part VI

Interim:

Consideration

40

The party at the Ford Island BOQ was a pitiful simulation of the previous "strategy conferences" that had marked Fred's earlier association with Fighting Twenty. Although it was the first night ashore, a few resourceful pilots, including Fred, had managed to drop in on some of the other air stations on Oahu and draw a meager liquor ration. There was no known way to get over to the naval station across the harbor. The great anchorage was so desolately empty of warships that the liberty boats that taxied people around the harbor were not running after five in the afternoon. Fred reasoned that that was how they had managed to be bunked in the BOQ instead of staying aboard the *Constitution*. Pearl Harbor had become a backwater of the war.

"We ain't worth shit," said Duggin, sitting on the floor beside a metal wastebasket. At least twenty sweaty, smoking pilots were packed into the room of one of the new men. It was a little room with two single beds and one desk, a folding door closet and little else; the bathroom was shared by another room on the other side of the building. The hard-won liquor was in the bathtub, on ice.

"What the hell're you talking about?" asked Schuster.

"I mean, shit," said Duggin, "we ain't done nothing right since we went into action last November."

"September," said Bracker. "It was September."

"You're both screwed up. It was October. Marcus." Bradley sat on the bed next to the inevitable new men, two of them, both ensigns, both looking terribly uncertain of themselves. Fred sat in the single chair at the end of the bed and wondered what the hell kind of reception this was for a combat outfit.

"I heard someone say we'll be headed back to the States for a yard period," Jacobs said.

"Really?"

"That's horseshit," said Schuster. "We'll be out of here in a month."

"No way," said Bracker. "You see the way she's listing. Hell, she's twenty degrees over to starboard."

"The States," said Duggin, smiling stupidly. "American girls."

"They tipped her over on purpose."

"Come on."

"No shit."

"What about it, Trusty? You were over there this afternoon. Is that right?"

Fred took a sip from a glass of Scotch, diluted with water so that he wouldn't get drunk. "Yeah," he said. "That's right."

He had gone aboard with the skipper for a briefing on the single action of Bat Team One that had resulted in him becoming an ace and CAG getting killed. The list made walking belowdecks a nightmare. He was glad, doubly glad, they were staying ashore.

"That was too bad about Mister Higgins," said Levi.

"Yeah," said Jacobs. "I think the skipper was too hard on him."

"It could have happened to anyone," said Duggin.

"What the hell do you guys know?" said Schuster. "You weren't there."

"He couldn't help it if the Japs jumped him."

"The hell he couldn't."

Fred listened to the argument. Arguments—that was all they had now. They never had simple conversations anymore. He tried to think of a way to slip out without drawing too much attention. There was the chance that he and the skipper could be alone in his room for a while. But the morose, argumentative group of pilots made getting up there somewhat difficult. Fred leaned back in the chair, rested his head against the wall, and closed his eyes.

"Trusty?" A hand plucked at his sleeve. Fred opened his eyes and sat forward. It was one of the new ensigns, sitting on the end of the bed next to him. "Is that your name?"

"No. It's Fred."

"Fred. I'm Tom Jenkins." The ensign extended his hand and they shook. Jenkins was a pleasant-looking young man with short, curly hair and a smooth face. Fred leaned back again to watch the party and plan his escape.

"How come they call you Trusty?"

"Beats me."

"You have any kills yet, Trusty?"

"A few."

"Really? How many?"

Fred stood up suddenly. "You want a drink?" he asked. Without waiting for an answer he took Jenkins's glass from his hands and made his way across the crowded, smoky room to the bathroom. He refilled the glasses with bourbon; the Scotch was all gone. While he sat there, he had an idea for getting away. He carried the glasses back to his seat, sat, handed one across to Jenkins.

"Thanks," Jenkins said. "How many kills do you have, Trusty?"

"Five." Maybe Jenkins would lay off now. He would have found out on his own anyway.

"You're an *ace*," said Jenkins. And Fred thought, yes, he had killed maybe twenty Japanese, seven in each Betty and two in each Kate. "That's something else," Jenkins was saying. "You ever have to ditch?"

"Yes," said Fred. "Once." The bathroom idea would work, he was sure.

"Damn," said Jenkins, properly impressed. "I can't wait till we get back out there again."

"Why?"

"So I can get a few Jap planes. Geez, I just want to write home and tell 'em I got myself a Jap plane."

"I'm sure you'll get the chance," said Fred. He checked his watch. It was past nine. They were flying the next day, so it would be a good idea to hurry. He drained his glass and stood. "Back in a minute," he said to no one in particular. Carrying his glass, he went across the crowded room and into the bathroom. Once there, he pushed the door partly shut and urinated in the toilet, set his glass down on the edge of the bathtub, then quickly opened the door leading to the other room.

It was dark in the other room. Figuring it to be a mirror

image of the one he had just left, he walked quietly and quickly straight through to the door. On the way, he trod on an unidentified piece of clothing, realizing with a start that someone was sleeping, snoring, in the bed near the door. He tried the doorknob, found it locked, unlocked it, and went through. It clicked snugly behind him, and he was safe.

The BOQ was modern; obviously it had been built sometime during the war. It was long and rectangular, two identical stories high, and all the rooms faced the outside. Plain concrete steps led to the second-story landing. Fred knew that the Skipper's room was up there on the second floor, where the night breezes made sleeping easier. He went back around the building to the side where the squadron was berthed, up the steps, and directly to Jack's room.

He knocked softly three times, opened the door, and entered the room. It was dark there, too, but this time someone got up and came to meet him. It was Jack. He put a finger to his lips and said, "Shh"; then he jutted his thumb toward the bathroom door. There was someone in there, running water into the tub and moving about. Light shone out under the edge of the door.

Fred looked around suspiciously, but Jack embraced him strongly and whispered in his ear, "It's okay. The door's locked." He kissed Fred on the mouth, fiercely, and began slipping loose the buttons of his shirt. He led him, half-undressed, to the single bed standing forlornly in the middle of the room. Before lying down, though, Jack paused and whispered into Fred's ear again: "This is the worst thing we can do."

"Why?" asked Fred. "How could it be?"

"One of us could be gone tomorrow." Jack held him by the shoulders and looked searchingly into his eyes.

Fred stretched and peeled off his damp T-shirt, dislodging Jack's hands for a moment. He tossed the jersey into the chair. "Then let's enjoy it," he said. "We may not have another chance." He reached over and pulled Jack's T-shirt out of the top of his pants. He felt the moist, hairy skin beneath it with the palm of his hand.

Jack pulled him close, hugging him crushingly, desperately. He said nothing.

Presently, pressed for time, they finished undressing and climbed into the narrow bed.

Duane Higgins left his hot little room at a few minutes after ten. He was mildly drunk but wide awake, restless. He had called

Eleanor Hawkins and arranged a date for the next evening. Not knowing exactly what he wanted to do now, Duane wandered down the line of rooms until he came to the one with the party going on inside. He wasn't especially eager to face the other pilots, but the thought that there was free booze inside drove him to open the door and slip in. From the way the men suddenly quieted, he knew they had been talking about him.

He noticed right away that Trusteau was not there. After helping himself to the last of the bourbon, he asked Levi where Trusty Killer the Hero was. Levi said that Fred had disappeared an hour or so ago. Duane got an idea and decided to check it out.

Leaving the party, Duane made his way to the skipper's room and listened at the venetian-blinded window in the door. It was dark inside. He could distinctly hear the sound of an oscillating fan. For a second he though he heard low voices, but the fan and the sighing wind prevented his being sure. He went back down the concrete steps to the lawn below, found a spot on the grass where he could watch the Skipper's door without attracting attention, and settled to the ground with a cigarette and his last drink of the evening. He didn't have long to wait.

A single drop of sweat formed on Jack's chin and dripped onto Fred's neck. The bed was so small that they couldn't lie side by side, but Fred didn't mind. Jack's hairy, solid bulk pressing against him was far from unpleasant. A big electric fan whirred on the floor near the bed, wafting stale but cool air over them. The unseen occupant of the bathroom had long since finished his bath. Only silence came from that quarter.

"Five kills," said Jack. "It's hard to believe."

"A few more missions and I'll catch up with you." Fred joked. He wanted a smoke, but knew he shouldn't. They had to be as unobtrusive as possible.

"That'll be the day."

"Like you said, they'll give me a squadron of my own."

"Take my word for it. You don't want one." Jack shifted his weight to relieve a tingling arm.

"I've been thinking about when you said we should be writing down the history we're making."

"Yes?"

"Well, that's what I'm doing. I mean, after I started doing the Diary again I realized it. Here I am, writing down the histroy of Fighter Squadron Twenty fighting the Japs and winning glory."

"I haven't seen the glory part yet."

"It'll come. Till then you've got the background for your own book. Just copy down the War Diary and you've got it."

"My own book?"

"Why not?" said Fred, but Jack cut him off by squeezing his arm sharply and shushing him.

They lay in tense silence for a full minute. More sweat dripped from Jack to Fred. He reached up and wiped the sweat from Jack's chin. "I thought I heard something," Jack said. "Someone outside the door." He relaxed but didn't let go of Fred's arm. "I guess not."

"The other guys are talking about what you did to Mister Higgins," whispered Fred.

"What I did is none of their damn business."

"He *was* wrong, wasn't he?"

Jack thought for a moment, running his hand up and down Fred's arm. "Yes," he said finally. "And I was too easy on him. We agreed not to mention the fact that he hadn't slept that night. I didn't want the poker game to be brought up."

"He's a good friend of yours, isn't he?"

"Yeah, I guess. But lately..." He stopped, thought. "We shouldn't talk about it. It doesn't concern you." This he said without harshness.

"I know," said Fred. He put his hand on Jack's chest and felt his heart beating beneath the flesh, the ribs. "Any idea where we're going next?"

"Does it matter?"

"No, I guess it doesn't."

"One goddamned Jap island is just like any other," said Jack. He settled onto Fred until the full lengths of their bodies were touching. "They'll be finished with the repairs on the ship in three or four days."

"That soon?"

"They deballasted. Put a list to starboard so the port side damage would be out of the water. When it was done they discovered it wasn't nearly as bad as they thought. A fuel tank got ruptured. Most of the blast was taken up by the blister at the water line. We were really lucky."

"We sure were." Fred knew all about the deballasting, but he liked to hear Jack talk.

"I've never seen so many men working on such little damage before. They're really pushing to get her finished and out again."

"So we're headed somewhere important."

"That would be the obvious conclusion..."

"Hmm."

"There's more. The task groups aren't coming back to Pearl anymore. They've taken a lagoon near Kwajalein called Majuro. It's big enough for the whole damn fleet and they're staying there now instead of coming all the way back here."

"That's interesting." Fred rested his chin in the hollow of Jack's neck and felt the movement of his jaw as the older man spoke. He was thinking that he loved Jack very much but would never find the time, the place, or the words to tell him so.

"Now we'll be closer to the fighting, all the time. We'll never have another chance like this again," Jack said.

Fred squeezed Jack as hard as he could.

"We shouldn't have done this," said Jack.

At 11:15, Duane started from a doze and looked around. Something had arrested his attention. The grass was wet with dew. A nearly full moon was rising. It was impossibly still and quiet. And someone was coming out of Jack Hardigan's room. It was a man, in uniform. Completely dressed. Trusteau.

The moonlight was sufficient for Duane to see Trusteau walk the length of the second-floor landing, hands in his pockets, and stand and look out at the moon and the sleeping air station. No lights came on in the skipper's room. Trusteau looked into space for two or three minutes, then with no apparent haste, made his way down the steps and to a room on the lower floor into which he vanished. Duane was alone once more, half-asleep, half-drunk, wondering what he could do with this information.

41

"Dear Jack: Just a short note to say hi and see how you are doing these days. It's been ages since we talked, or at least it seems that way, and I thought maybe you and I could get together some afternoon soon and recount some good, old times. Please give me a call, Jack, I'd really like to see you again. Yours, Eleanor."

The day after the arrival of Eleanor Hawkins's note and two days before they were due to sail again, the *Constitution* began running its own boats between the naval station at Pearl and the air station on Ford Island. Jack took advantage of the situation to make a call to Eleanor and arrange to meet her at the Royal Hawaiian. Her note implied that she had something specific in mind. He had no idea what that could be. And almost as an afterthought, on the afternoon he was to leave, he invited Fred to accompany him. He cancelled flying at four o'clock, cleaned up at the BOQ, put on a fresh white uniform, and met Fred at the landing. They made the pleasant boat trip with a number of other pilots, caught a bus to the naval station gates, and a taxi to the Royal Hawaiian. Fred had never been there before.

"I spent a week here once," Jack told Fred as they walked through the elegant, high-ceilinged lobby toward the bar.

"When was that?"

"July of '42."

"After Midway."

"Right after. It was the first time I ever stayed in a really fine hotel. I was expecting a bellboy, room service, all that."

"There wasn't?"

"When the Navy took it over they threw out all the nonessentials. No more room service."

"Carry your own luggage?"

"That's all we are anyway—" Jack spotted Eleanor sitting at a table in the rear of the lounge and waved to her. "—glorified bellhops."

Eleanor met them in the middle of the big, padded bar. She was dressed in a summery dress and carried a wide-brimmed hat. Her hair was fixed in layers of tight curls close to her head. "It's a good thing you came when you did," she said. "I've refused eight drinks, four dances, and two proposals of marriage." Jack laughed. "And that was from just one stranger."

"I'd like you to meet one of my pilots," said Jack. He pulled Fred forward by the arm. "Eleanor Hawkins, Fred Trusteau." Fred shook her hand.

"Well," she said, sitting at the bar. "I ask for one but I get two very handsome escorts. This is a pleasure."

Fred glanced quickly at Jack and caught a signal. "You two must want to be alone..."

"Do you mind terribly?" asked Eleanor smilingly. Her voice had an underlying note of seriousness that piqued Fred's curiosity.

"Not at all," he said and turned to go, but Jack caught his arm again.

"Thirty minutes," he said. "Check back with me in thirty minutes."

"Yes, sir. Miss Hawkins." He nodded to Eleanor and left them, going back through the bar and into the lobby.

"He seems like a nice man," said Eleanor.

Jack pulled himself onto a stool, thinking that they should sit at a table but not wishing to tell Eleanor that it wasn't polite for a lady to sit at the bar. "He is," Jack said. He signaled the bartender and ordered a Scotch and water for himself, a Tom Collins for Eleanor. When the drinks came, they sipped together and he said, "You look well, Eleanor."

"Thank you," she said. "So do you." She touched a ribbon on his left chest. "You've added a few new ones since we last saw each other."

"Nothing important. Good conduct." He eased back onto his stool so that no part of them touched and watched her face. How long would it take her to come to the point?

"Thirty minutes," she said, smiling that smile that was

obviously something more. "Is that all the time you can spare for me?"

"We came here together," said Jack. "I like to keep track of my men as closely as possible, especially when we might have to leave on short notice."

"I thought you were just being considerate."

"That, too." He turned to face her squarely. "Now then, what was it you wanted to talk about?"

Eleanor took a drink and set the glass down firmly on the bar. "Well," she said, "I see you want to be direct." When Jack said nothing, she continued. "I'll come right to the point," she said. "I like you a lot, Jack." Her eyes did not waver as she said this. "No, that's not strong enough. I could love you very easily. You're so much like Stan—and he was everything to me."

Jack watched her attentively, not knowing what to say.

"I think I told you before that I might have to find someone else." She paused and Jack nodded. "I guess what I really want to say is that there *is* someone else now and if I know my men at all, he's getting ready to propose. Should I say yes, Jack?"

Her question caught him completely by surprise and it took him several seconds to realize that it had a double meaning: Should she say no to this other man because there was a chance in the future of saying yes to Jack? But he had never even considered marriage to a woman before, even before there was Fred. And yes, impossibly, Fred did have a great deal to do with his answer.

"Do you love him?" It was an automatic response and he instantly regretted having said it.

"Love?" she said, sarcastic and humorous at the same time. "Is that the number one ingredient of a successful marriage?"

"I wouldn't know," he said kindly.

"I would," she said. She took another sip of her Tom Collins. "Need—is sometimes more important."

"Need is sometimes more important," he repeated softly, intrigued with the hidden meaning of those words.

"I know this isn't the correct, traditional manner by which a lady determines the depth of a relationship," Eleanor said, now very proper, "but I somehow feel it *is* important I know how you and I feel about each other before I say yes or no to—the other man." Jack saw, even in the dim light of the bar, that she was blushing fiercely. Nothing else about her face gave away her embarrassment.

"Eleanor," he said, "I'm sorry."

"Don't be, Jack. I just feel that, times being what they are, it just isn't wise to be overly cautious, if you know what I mean."

Jack looked away from her. Fred had come back into the lounge with an older man wearing the shoulder boards of a lieutenant commander. They walked up to the bar and ordered drinks. Jack had seen the man before but couldn't place him.

"I know what you mean, Eleanor. Really I do. Caution was never one of my strong points."

She looked back at him. The embarrassment was gone.

"I'm afraid what I said before still stands," he said.

The lieutenant commander at the bar with Fred was drinking hard and talking loud. Eleanor watched Jack's eyes flicker between herself and Fred. For several long seconds, then, she looked into her drink. She shook her head.

"Okay," she said finally. She reached over and took his hand. "Still friends?"

Jack smiled. "Still friends."

"Did I tell you about the property I have over on the west shore? Sunsets," she leaned back her head and laughed easily, "sunsets you wouldn't believe. If the Army ever gives the islands back to the civilians, I'm going to build the most outrageously expensive house in the world there." Jack laughed with her, keeping an eye cocked toward Fred and his guest at the other end of the bar. For another fifteen minutes Jack and Eleanor talked of trivialities and had one more round of drinks.

Fred literally ran into Lieutenant Commander Deal in the main entrance to the lobby of the Royal Hawaiian. Fred was leaving, Deal was arriving, and both stood aside to allow an army officer with a Wac to use the door first. Then both tried to cross the threshold in opposite directions, at the same time. Only when he had apologized did Fred recognize Deal. His first impression was that Deal had grown ten years older since the last time they talked, nearly eight months before. Deal's rumpled dress khaki uniform heightened the impression.

"Pardon me, sir," said Fred.

"I know you," said Deal, obviously searching his memory.

"Trusteau. Fred Trusteau." They shook hands.

"What are you doing here?" Deal asked.

"Passing time," Fred said. He nodded toward the lounge. "Buy you a drink?"

"Why not? I was headed that way myself."

The two pilots fell into step beside each other.

"I didn't think there were any other air groups around the islands," said Fred. "Aren't you on the *Cowpens*?"

"Yeah," said Deal. They entered the bar. "You?"

"The *Constitution*," Fred answered. "She took a torpedo in the Kwajalein operation."

"Oh, yeah." They reached the bar, pushed aside the stools, and stood like western movie cowboys, feet on the railing, elbows on the bar. "That was tough luck. You seen any action yourself?"

"A little. Nothing important. How about yourself?"

The bartender arrived and they ordered.

"The goddamn brass keeps the little carriers doing the goddamn CAP work while the heavies do all the sweeps," Deal replied. "You should know that."

"Yeah," said Fred. "That's too bad." He had heard that bitch before and tried to imagine what it would be like now in a squadron with a skipper like Deal, as the weeks at sea went by and the squadron did nothing but fly Combat Air Patrol for the bigger carriers. How would the new guys take it? Silver? Was that his name?

"How's Silver doing?"

Deal snorted and drained his bourbon. "Chickenshit. No goddamn guts at all." He pounded on the bar with his palm. "They didn't give my boys a chance. They're still out there flying CAP like a bunch of goddamn trainees."

"They're still out there?" asked Fred. "How come you're..."

"New orders. I'm heading stateside." Deal made the pronouncement as though it were a consignment to hell itself. He pounded on the bar again. "Barkeep," he bellowed. The bartender arrived and refilled his glass, which Deal promptly emptied into his mouth. "A frigging training command," he said. "They're gonna have me teaching kids like you how to find their asses in a cockpit."

"That's too bad," said Fred. He looked over at Jack and Eleanor. They were laughing together pleasantly. He looked back at Deal, thinking that he would like to tell him he had five kills to his credit, but that Deal probably wouldn't believe him.

"You just keep filling that sucker up," Deal was informing the bartender as he received yet another shot of liquor. Fred was only halfway through his first drink and was wishing he had ordered Scotch. Lately bourbon made him want to throw up.

"You take that little action last week," Deal said. "You know, that one with the radar turkey where the two Hellcats clobbered that Jap torpecker formation." He slammed down a fist to add emphasis. "Now that was a goddamn interception! I knew that buzzard Jennings. He's the only one with the guts to do a job like that. I told our CAG we should try a bat team, but he axed the whole frigging thing. Said he didn't have time. The chickenshit coward."

Fred smiled to himself and said, "It wasn't such a good idea anyway. Night ops keep the ship awake when they could use the sleep."

"What do you know about it?"

"Jennings was my group C.O. That was *Constitution's* action."

"Hell. At least it was constructive. Look at the Japs they killed. Ten or twelve at least."

"Five," said Fred, "maybe six." He looked back at Jack and Eleanor. They appeared to be saying good-by.

"It was still something," Deal said.

"It sure was," Fred replied. Eleanor stood on tiptoes and kissed Jack's cheek. The two parted. Jack came toward them. "Yes, it sure was."

Jack arrived and clapped Fred on the shoulder. "How's it going, Trusty?" he asked. "Hello, Deal."

"Hardigan." Deal turned back to his drink.

"Mister Deal's headed back to the States," said Fred.

"Lucky stiff," said Jack. "New air group?"

"Training command," offered Fred.

"You know, Deal, you should have kept this young man here." Jack slapped Fred's shoulder. "You know that night interception last week with the bat team?"

"We were just talking about that," said Fred.

"What of it?" grunted Deal.

"Trusty here was one of the F6s. Got two of the Bettys himself."

"Oh, yeah?" Deal turned and gave Fred an up and down, disbelieving look.

"Added to his previous three kills—"

"Three?"

"That makes him about the hottest damn fighter pilot in the whole fleet."

"Congratulations," Deal mumbled. Fred felt very uncomfortable. It wasn't much fun putting Deal into a spot like this. (But he was sort of glad the skipper had done it.)

"You about ready to head back, Fred?"

Fred drained his glass. "Sure. Let's go."

"Good luck in your new job, Deal," said Jack.

But Deal didn't reply. Jack and Fred left the Royal Hawaiian together.

After an eleven-day layover in Majuro Lagoon in the Marshall Islands, Task Force Fifty-eight sailed again for hostile waters. One task group of three carriers left to cover the amphibious assault on Eniwetok and the remaining nine, with their growing escort of battleships, cruisers, and destroyers, headed southwest at best speed for fabled Truk, home port of the Combined Fleet and the site of strong aerial power. At the time it was not known, even at the highest levels, whether or not Truk would later be seized for our own use. The only thing certain about the mission was that it was the first time carrier air power was being required to neutralize a massive concentration of land-based air strength. Many pilots understandably expected to die, and all expected a fight.

(J.E. Hardigan, Commander, USN (ret.), *A Setting of Many Suns: The Destruction of the Imperial Navy* [The Naval Institute Press, 1962], p. 275.)

Part VII

Combat Three:

Truk

42

10 February 1944: U.S.S. *Constitution*, designated TG 58.3.4, sortied from Pearl Harbor in company with U.S.S. *Oakland* and five destroyers. Air Group Twenty was brought aboard at 1300 hours. Force direction of advance is approximately 210 true although actual destination has not yet been announced. Squadron strength includes thirty-two pilots and thirty-three aircraft. During downwind approach leg, aircraft piloted by Ensign Patrick collided with aircraft piloted by Lt. (j.g.) Smith, losing most of its rudder and forcing Patrick to bail out. He was picked up by destroyer *Harwell* shortly thereafter. Lt. (j.g.) Smith landed safely.

12 February 1944: Aircraft piloted by Lt. (j.g.) Heckman crashed when landing as a result of applying instead of cutting power. Aircraft caught the top of the barrier and flipped, landing upside down on parked SBD of VB-20. Mister Heckman is in critical condition following surgery. Seaman Apprentice Samuel Crabbe was killed instantly. There was no fire.

"Jack." Boom Bloomington, the new air group commander, waved his arms about as if to ward off the evil spirits in his stateroom. "Jack," he said, "what the *hell* is wrong? What the hell is *wrong* with your pilots?"

Jack sat on the edge of Boom's bunk and tried to think of an answer, but Boom didn't allow him the time for one.

"They've caused more fuck-ups since we left Pearl than than I remember seeing for six months. They're not just fuck-ups, Jack. They're killers. They're flying like a bunch of goddamn trainees. What the hell is wrong?"

"Well," said Jack carefully, "I wasn't able to work with them very closely for several weeks while CAG had me flying at night." He was not even satisfied with his own answer.

"That's no reason," said Boom. He was finding his new job grindingly hard. It seemed that the great pools of replacement pilots had lots of new, young lads but there was nary a one experienced enough to take up where Commander Jennings had left off. "Have you seen? Are you aware there's a problem?"

"Yes," said Jack quietly, "I've seen there's a problem. I just don't know where the answer is right now."

"Asper says he hasn't given this many wave-offs since October. It's as if your boys have forgotten how to fly."

Jack sat still and felt the vibration of the deck beneath his feet, a sensation that was quite different from the ordinary feel of the ship underway. *Constitution* was making a good twenty-eight knots through heavy seas, hurrying toward an as of yet unannounced rendezvous with the enemy, burning up three times the normal amount of fuel and battering the hapless destroyers of the screen, forced to keep up, with the pounding waves.

"Any word on where we're going yet?" he asked.

"Not a peep," said Boom. He sat astraddle the single chair in the room. "I hate to say this, Jack, 'cause I know it makes me sound like my worthy predecessor, but I think—"

"My men have the wrong attitude," Jack finished for him. He had been thinking it, too. Since Kwajalein they were listless, careless—dangerous. They needed motivation. Whose fault was all this? "I understand. I'll work on it."

"Do it fast, Jack," Boom said seriously. "Wherever it is we're going, we'll be there in a few days at the most." He stood up and opened the door to indicate the audience was over.

"Sure," Jack said, standing. He was slightly miffed. Boom hadn't offered the usual courtesy of a drink from the hidden bottle of Scotch. Rank and position inevitably changed a man for the worse, Jack reflected. He said good night and left.

It was just past darken-ship time. The labyrinthine passageways of the carrier were lighted dimly in red or not lighted at all. He wandered through an area of pilot berthing, enjoying the nighttime sounds of men left temporarily to their own devices. Many were asleep, stretched out in three-deep bunks with the covers thrown off and the doors open to try to keep the warm, stale air moving. More than a few men appeared to be writing letters. There were no bull sessions in progress, no loud, boasting, speculating pilots jammed into staterooms. That was most unusual.

Jack passed Higgins's stateroom and stood in the open door. He would have put money on the fact that Duane would not be there, and sure enough he wasn't. The lieutenant from the torpedo squadron was in the lower bunk reading a letter. Without looking up, he said, "He isn't here. Big game going somewhere below."

"Thanks," said Jack, not surprised. He continued his stroll, heading in the general direction of Fred's stateroom. The fact that Duane was in another poker game didn't really bother him. He was sure that the uproar and the reprimand over the mission at Kwajalein had put the fear of God in him and there would be no repeat of that fiasco.

Fiasco, he thought. Three men, one of whom you know well, get killed, and you call it a fiasco. What would be a tragedy under any other circumstances was merely a fiasco under the auspices of war.

Jack dodged a steward hurrying in the opposite direction. Why, he asked himself, did they design the passageways to twist and turn this way? Why aren't they straight? He pounded his fist against a bulkhead and tried to imagine what was on the other side. He remembered a true story about another *Essex*-class carrier where a fully equipped metal-turning workshop was inadvertently walled off, and had gone undiscovered until six months after commissioning.

He came to Fred's compartment, but it was empty. Fred's bunk was tightly made. The others were messy. Jack smiled to himself. That was how Fred kept his life: orderly, well made.

He left the small stateroom and headed topside, trying to arrive at a word for how he felt about Fred. All this time, all these things we've done together, he thought. And still it eludes me.

The hangar deck was dark and quiet, swept by the ocean air that found its way through openings in the sides of the ship and eddied about the propellers, wings, tails of the silent aircraft. Picking his way through them, Jack found the deck edge elevator and stepped out onto it. The wind was too strong there though. He retreated to a sheltered spot near the forward part of the great square opening. There in the shadows he gently collided with someone else.

"Fred."

"Skipper."

"Small ship, isn't it?"

"Gets smaller every day." The two men pulled back cautiously until no part of them touched. Then both leaned back against the hard steel and looked out at the blackness of ocean, the cold blaze of stars.

"It's been a while since I saw you here," said Jack. Whenever they talked aboard ship, he felt as if someone were listening to every word they said. He noticed it this time, too.

"I haven't been up here for a while. It's nice," said Fred.

"Windy."

"For sure." The conversation petered out. Jack reached out and, in the darkness, placed the palm of his hand in the small of Fred's back.

"Fred, you see things differently from where you are."

"Yes, I suppose so."

"What's the matter with the squadron?" Fred shifted uncomfortably. "How come things look so sloppy?"

Fred didn't answer immediately.

"What do they talk about?"

"They, uh, don't talk about much at all." Fred sounded uncertain.

"Of course they do. Come on, help me."

"They talk about Mister Higgins and the guys we lost at Kwaj."

"Still on that one?"

"They're about evenly divided. Half of them think you did the right thing. The other half think he was unlucky and you were wrong."

"That about says it, huh?"

"They're also talking like they'll never make it through the war. The way they see it, the pilots do all the dangerous work. Sooner or later the Japs'll catch up with you. There's no end to it."

Jack withdrew his hand and sighed audibly. He could depend on Fred to answer him honestly, even if he didn't want to hear the answer. It made sense, unfortunately. He changed the subject. "I still haven't decided who I want to write the Diary. Have you any ideas?"

"Sure," said Fred. "Me."

"No, you've done enough."

"But I want to. Makes me feel like I'm contributing something."

"Why is it I can never argue with you?"

"I'm still thinking about your book," said Fred.

Jack laughed. "You think about it more than I do. It'll probably never get off the ground."

"You mean out of the water."

"Whatever."

Behind them, from the depths of the hangar deck, the address system growled to life and echoed hollowly around the great enclosed space. "Now hear this. Now hear this."

Jack nudged Fred and the two men moved further into the shelter of the hangar deck, out of the wind.

"What time is it?" asked Jack.

Fred consulted his watch. "8:15."

"I wonder . . ." said Jack, but he was cut off by the voice of the captain.

"This is the Captain speaking. I want all hands to know that fifteen minutes ago we received by radio broadcast the information we have all been waiting for. I'm passing it along to you now because I'm tired of hearing rumors that we're headed for Tokyo again." He paused as if to let the laughter subside. "Our target is the island base at Truk in the Caroline Islands approximately six hundred miles west of Kwajalein. The day after tomorrow we will rendezvous with the rest of Task Force Fifty-eight and head into the target on the morning of the seventeenth. I have every confidence that when we leave the area on the eighteenth the Japs will know they've been repaid for Pearl Harbor. That is all. Carry on." The address sytem gave a final burst of static and clicked off.

Jack exhaled the breath of air he had held since the captain had first said "Truk." He and Fred silently stepped to the edge of the elevator.

"Truk," said Fred.

"Why not Tokyo?" Jack sounded bitter. "Maybe what the guys are saying is right. If they try hard enough, they just might manage to get all of us killed."

"We're up to it," said Fred simply. "Like you said, if it's not one Jap island, it's another."

Jack stood helplessly for a minute, feeling the wind search his face and clothes. "I wish I had about a dozen more of you," he said. Then, "No. I don't know what to do with one of you. What would I do with more?"

"You'd have a well-written War Diary."

Jack laughed. "I'm going to bed," he said. "I've had enough for one day." He tousled Fred's hair playfully, and the two left the elevator and headed below.

Before they parted, however, Jack asked Fred if he had the will in a safe place, and Fred said that he did, but that he would never have to open it. Humorlessly, Jack told him not to bet on that.

Duane screwed up his courage one last time, knocked on the door of the squadron office, and entered without waiting for an answer. Jack was at the desk, writing with his fountain pen. He looked up to acknowledge Duane, then continued to write. Duane seated himself and cleared his throat, waiting for Jack to finish.

"Yes?" said Jack evenly, still writing. "What can I do for you?"

"There's something we have to talk about," said Duane.

The way he said it made Jack stop writing and cap his pen. "And what would that be?"

"A couple of things." Duane was sweating, not heavily, but enough for Jack to notice. "First off, there's something I have to clear with you. It's just a formality, really..."

"What is it?"

"I've decided to get married."

Jack broke into a sardonic smile and leaned back. "Is that right?" he said.

"That *is* correct, isn't it? I mean, you have to approve of it?"

"You were right. For someone like you, it's just a formality. I'll pass it along to Commander Bloomington and that's as high as it goes." Jack continued to smile. "What made you decide to take the plunge?"

"Nothing in particular. Just thought it was about time to do it."

"And who's the lucky girl, if I might ask?"

"You sure can," said Duane. He had practiced saying this again and again, trying to find the most effective way to get the point across. "Her name's Eleanor." Jack's eyebrows went up a notch. "Eleanor Hawkins." They went up another notch. Silence reigned for several seconds. "We'd like to do it as soon as possible." Jack's expression remained unchanged. "I mean as soon as we get back, or the first opportunity..." He didn't understand. Jack was supposed to be upset, shocked, something. It wasn't working right. Jack just sat there, the beginnings of a smile pulling at the corners of his mouth. "I've been seeing her for a couple of months now..."

Jack gave a sound like a chuckle, only it came out derisive and hard. "Son of a bitch," he said.

"You have no objections?" Press him, thought Duane, press him into admitting...

"I wish you every happiness," Jack said. He sat forward, uncapped his pen, and began writing again.

Is that all there is? Duane thought. No rantings, no ravings? "Thank you," he said formally. "You're invited to the wedding, of course."

"Of course." Jack's head bobbed slightly. "By the way," he said, "I was just working out the schedule for the strikes tomorrow. Tell me what you think of it."

Jack turned a piece of paper around so Duane could read it. The *Ironsides's* contribution to the first strike—a massive fighter sweep drawn from seven carriers—was being led by Hardigan and wingman Trusteau. The second strike, late in the morning, composed of bombers and fighters, was being led by Lieutenant Schuster. Duane looked for his name and found it; he was second division leader in the first strike. He contemptuously sailed the single sheet of paper back on the desk. Jack made no move to touch it.

"Don't want me leading a strike again, huh?" The blood was rising to Duane's face.

"Not this time," said Jack.

"Why don't you just demote me to ensign and let me fly wing on one of the new guys?"

"I thought I was doing you a favor."

Duane snorted. "Thanks," he said. "There's someone else you can do a favor for."

"Who's that?"

"Why don't you make Trusteau a section leader? Or a division leader? I think he's ready for it." By the look on Jack's face, Duane could see he'd touched a sensitive spot.

"Trusteau flies wing on me," said Jack.

"Hell, he's got five kills. All the guys look up to him."

"Trusteau flies wing on me. The matter isn't open to discussion."

"I know he flies wing on you," said Duane hotly. "What else does he do for you, Mister Hardigan?"

"What do you mean by that?" snapped Jack.

"I mean you and he are pretty damn chummy when you're off duty, after lights out..."

Jack's chair crashed to the deck. His tight, white-knuckled fist hovered under Duane's nose.

"Get out of here." The command came from a throat rasping with barely controlled rage.

Duane slid back his chair and stood to go. He stopped at the door, as if to speak again.

"Get out of here," Jack said again.

Duane left, closing the door behind him. As he made his way through the bustling passageways, to nowhere in particular, he kept thinking: I didn't even have to mention that night at the BOQ. It's true, by God, it's true.

Fred Trusteau sat in his chair and played solitare while the tension in the ready room, packed as it was by nearly all of the squadron's men, gathered like storm clouds. The ship was operating a two-plane CAP and no ASW searches, a puzzling format considering how close they were to Truk. By careful reasoning, he deduced that the wind was wrong for flight ops and high speed along their direction of advance at the same time. In the morning they had to be in position for the launch of the dawn fighter sweep over the target, and since they were making an amazing twenty-eight knots, any deviation from the charted course, even for flight ops, could throw them seriously behind schedule. So they operated a minimum of aircraft and kept the rest on alert, ready for immediate action should the need arise. But the need had not arisen, and the storm gathered.

The skipper had been in and out of the ready room several times, never once stopping to talk to him. Fred could see that Jack was seriously agitated. He wore a scowl, talked in grunts, and seemed to avoid anyone who didn't have important business.

The skipper's irritation seemed to be catching. Just five minutes earlier Higgins had broken up an argument between Rogers and Jacobs before it reached blows. Higgins went back to a card game in the rear of the compartment. Jacobs and Rogers sat and sulked. Fred dealt himself another game of solitaire and listened to the conversations around him; he kept an eye on the skipper sitting in the front row, growling to himself over a bundle of papers.

Fred could hear Schuster talking conspiratorially with one of the two new men, a wistful youngster named Horace. Schuster was trying to sell the kid one of the giant Japanese rubbers, complete with the line about the Emperor's personal pilots and their manly qualifications. Horace wasn't buying it, though not for the obvious reason. He kept saying that after tomorrow he wouldn't have any need for it because the Japs never took prisoners.

Fred laid out his cards in a pyramid—one at the top, two covering the one, three covering the two, and so on, down to a line of seven at the bottom. Then he began turning over cards from the remaining pack and matching up cards that totaled thirteen—sixes and sevens, fives and eights, fours and nines, threes and tens, deuces and Jacks, Aces and Queens, Kings by themselves. He worked the pyramid down to the point at which he could match no further without cheating, then started over.

"Come on," said Jacobs to Bracker, "he's here now, we can ask him."

"No way, fella," said Bracker. "I don't wanna ask the skipper."

"Come on, trade with me. I want first crack at them Nips this time." Jacobs was in the second strike, escorting the bombers. Bracker was a member of the sweep.

"I won't do it," said Bracker. "I don't want to, anyway."

"Why not? Everyone says it's supposed to be a suicide run."

"Who says the second strike'll be any better? I just want to get it over with as soon as possible."

Fred began matching thirteens again and worked the pyramid down to three cards at the top before he was stymied. The skipper had heard that exchange, he was sure. He set up another hand.

"Hey, Trusty," said Patrick, sitting in the chair next to his. "How do you spell 'funeral'?" He was writing a letter.

"F-u-n-o-r-a-l." Fred took out a King and matched the Jack of hearts, the familiar Jack of hearts, with the deuce of clubs.

"Thanks," said Patrick.

"Don't mention it."

Bagley and Levi came into the ready room from outside, dangling their flight gear, talking about the LSO.

"That jerk," said Levi, hanging up a Mae West. "Three goddamn wave-offs. He must be blind as a bat."

"Nah," said Bagley. "Just a grounded flyboy. Jealous of the fighter pilots."

"Tell you what," said Levi. "I'd trade with him in a second right now. After tomorrow he probably won't have much of a job."

Fred glanced up. The skipper had heard that one, too. Bagley and Levi continued undressing, then settled comfortably into their chairs. All the pilots were here now. The tension was palpable.

"Aw, shit," said Duggin loudly, "we don't stand a chance. The Japs'll make mincemeat out of us."

"Now all pilots except the duty section stand down from flight quarters," said the address system. "Now all pilots except..." The remainder of the message was drowned out by the noise of pilots rising, stretching, talking, heading for the door. Almost immediately another voice, a very harsh one, stopped them in their tracks. It was the skipper. The storm had broken.

"Take your seats, gentlemen," said Jack Hardigan. He blocked the path to the ready room entrance.

Since Fred was in the duty section, he hadn't moved, but he noticed that Higgins had somehow been closest to the door and thus was now closest to the skipper. The men found their ways uncertainly but quickly to their seats. Higgins merely sat in the one nearest him. The skipper tossed the bunch of papers into his chair. A move that eloquently displayed his displeasure.

"Mister Duggin. Stand up," he said.

"Sir?" said Duggin in a high voice.

"I said stand up!" The last words rang out like artillery shells. Duggin got shakily to his feet. For a moment silence hung like a shroud.

"Mister Duggin," said Hardigan, "if I hear you just one more time, *one more time,* make the slightest remark downgrading the fighting men in this outfit," a pause for emphasis, "I will have you in hack so fucking fast it'll make your head swim."

Fred felt sweat on his upper lip but made no move to wipe it off. Around him he could feel, could sense the eyes of the other men moving, looking, each man glad he wasn't in Duggin's shoes.

"Do I make myself clear?"

Duggin broke the almost hypnotic gaze the Skipper had leveled on him and looked down at his feet. He mumbled something.

"I can't hear you," said Jack in a voice that cut right to the heart of everyone who heard it.

"Yes, sir," said Duggin clearly, still studying his shoes.

"Sit down," said Jack.

Fred exhaled, unaware that he had been holding his breath since the exchange began. The skipper was very mad—so mad he had sworn, something Fred had never heard him do in front of the men. And if he'd only been pretending to be mad, he should be nominated for an Academy Award.

The skipper glared at them for a long moment with dark eyes that shone like polished rocks. His forehead glistened.

"What the hell do you want?" he began. "What in the name of

God do you expect?" He paused at the end of each phrase, as if to choose his words carefully. "You fly the best goddamn fighter in the world. You've spent more time in training than any pilots in history. You've got the best food, the best mechanics, clean sheets, and stewards to make your goddamn beds every morning. What in hell do you want? Do you want the Japs to surrender? Just like that?" He snapped his fingers.

Then he broke his stance and turned his back on them. He picked up the wooden pointer leaning against the status board in the front of the room. He faced the pilots again, and the pointer carved out a swath of air, like a sword. It struck sharply against the back of a chair. "I've listened to your bitching for a week and I won't listen anymore." He flexed the point like a riding crop, and it broke with a snap. "I won't ask, or request, or suggest—anymore. You can consider this an order, gentlemen." He held the two pieces of wood in his right hand and stabbed at the air. "Every pilot who leaves this ship in the morning will come back aboard with at least one confirmed kill or he'll stand in front of me tomorrow evening and tell me in detail why he didn't. Is that clear?" He waited in silence for several seconds, then bellowed, "Is that clear?" A smattering of voices hesitantly replied, "Yes, sir."

"I can't hear you!"

"Yes, sir!" The ready room resounded with a single voice. Jack Hardigan looked up, as if for divine guidance, then back at his pilots. "I've spent one year, gentlemen, twelve months, trying to turn you into fighter pilots. I didn't invest that much of my time just to have a whining bunch of momma's boys call themselves Fighting Twenty. Truk." Jack swung the arm with sudden violence and the pieces of pointer clattered into the corner. "Fuck Truk! If you think the Japs at Truk are going to give you a hard time, you haven't reckoned living with me if you blow this mission. And if you blow this mission, gentlemen, you know where to lay the blame. Not on me. Not on the aircraft. Not on the goddamn stewards. But on yourselves. No one else." He looked one more time at thirty unmoving, scarcely breathing men, then strode to the door.

Duane Higgins stood suddenly in his path, but Jack pushed up to him, face to face, his head shaking slightly as if it were difficult to control himself any longer. "Don't cross me," he said to Higgins, just loud enough for the entire squadron to hear, and was gone.

The skipper's footsteps had faded away in the passageway outside before the numbing spell began to wear off.

"He's right, you know," Bagley said simply.

Higgins bolted through the door and disappeared.

Slowly, quietly, the rest of the pilots pulled themselves to their feet and shuffled out. When all were gone except the four pilots of the duty section, Fred got up and carefully gathered up the skipper's papers. He straightened the pile and left them in the chair. Then he sat back down, dealt himself another hand of solitaire, and began matching the thirteens.

43

Fred Trusteau sat suited and ready in his chair, marveling at the change that had come over the men of Fighting Twenty. They were as hot for combat as he had ever seen them. Again and again he would hear repeated the skipper's remark from his now-famous pep talk: Fuck Truk. Jack Hardigan was in front of them now, giving the final briefing in as businesslike fashion as was possible. Much of the information he was giving was repetitious—course, speed and altitude to the target, expected opposition, launch time—but most of the details reflected the urgency of the moment.

"Two miles on the launch heading will be a can with a white truck light. Do a standard group grope to the right and join up by divisions. We still stay at one thousand feet until thirty miles from the target, then circle twice to fifteen thousand. We'll be over the target at 7:45."

There were no surprises, only a comforting sort of security in routine practices. Fred took it all in and wondered ...

He wondered how everyone had changed so since yesterday. Patrick—of his three bunkmates the only other fighter pilot—was up before reveille. He woke Fred with his shaving and humming and told him that he wasn't writing home until he got back that afternoon and could give his parents the news that he had his first kill. Fred lay in his rack until Patrick was finished with the sink, then as he was brushing his teeth, Patrick casually remarked, without malice, that Fred didn't know how to spell. They went to breakfast together.

At breakfast in the wardroom, the twelve pilots of the first sweep ate together at the same table in high spirits. The skipper came in last and was welcomed by all but Duane Higgins, who got up and left before he had finished his steak—only Fred seemed to notice that. The skipper said he'd been back to sickbay to see Heckman, who was awake at this ungodly hour and wishing the squadron well. It was a nice touch, the skipper checking up on his men. It sat well.

"The Japs have five airfields at Truk," Jack was saying now, "scattered through the various islands. Intelligence says they have a total of 185 aircraft there, maybe half of which are fighters. We'll be coming in with about eighty Hellcats with tactical surprise, so pickings should be pretty damn good."

A cheer went up from the men, punctuated with several "Fuck Truks."

"Attack whenever you get the chance. We're under no escorting constraints. Just clear the air of Jap planes. And don't get caught alone."

Duane Higgins stood by himself off to the side of the ready room, fingering the heavy black pistol holstered under his left armpit. Fred and Higgins had never been all that friendly, but recently the executive officer had been positively rude. And now Higgins was going in with the first sweep, instead of leading a subsequent strike. Fred figured that either the skipper was cautious about letting him lead another strike so soon after the disaster at Kwajalein, or he wanted his best pilots in what would probably be a monumental fighter battle.

"We're making the trip in at 180 knots, so we'll have plenty of time over the target. Rendezvous on command or at the latest at 8:30, and don't get caught alone..."

An enlisted petty officer came into the ready room and handed Jack a cardboard chart covered with crude airplane outlines and scribbles. "Okay," said Jack, "looks like we're spotted in launch order with one exception. Mister Higgins is still on the elevator with a couple of SBDs in front of him. But they'll work that out as they clear off the deck. Check the chart on your way out, gents." Fred glanced at Higgins and thought that the uneven spotting of his fighter was an omen, and he would be killed over Truk, or worse, captured by the Japanese. It was nonsense, and he quickly felt ridiculous for thinking it. But Higgins was still acting strange this morning.

"The time is now 0615. Launch is at 0640. Don't be late, gentlemen." A scattering of laughter swept the ready room and the briefing ended. Fred sighed, resigned to the waiting, and took out his deck of cards for another game of solitaire.

Duane Higgins found his fighter in the dark without trouble. It was squarely on the number three elevator with two Dauntless dive bombers parked in front of it. He didn't wonder how it had come to be that way; that was not his problem. As the planes were launched in proper order in front of him, the deck crew then would push the other two out of the way so that he could taxi forward to the flight line. He climbed up the wing root and lowered himself into the cockpit, immediately making the radio connection and adjusting his parachute pack until it felt moderately comfortable. Goddamn, but it was dark.

He had known the skipper for what seemed like a lifetime. How could he think of him as anyone but the man whose life he had saved at Santa Cruz, who had saved his life more than once at the 'Canal and Munda? Dark shadows hurried around his aircraft. A faceless figure appeared beside him and checked him out, tugging quickly at the straps, then disappearing. An amplified voice boomed out: "Pilots, start your engines." Duane flipped the power switch. The instruments glowed. He tapped the fuel gauges and the needles rose quickly to the "full" position. He primed the engine and hit the starter button.

The ear-splitting roar of engines in front of him drowned out everything, even the noise of his own engine as it caught, sputtered, turned over, caught again, vibrated into steady running. The r.p.m. indicator danced, fuel and oil pressure rose, cylinder head temperature began to climb. Duane stood hard on the brakes and revved the engine, satisfied that all was in order.

What had Jack been trying to accomplish yesterday in the ready room? Did he actually believe that a routine like the angry speech he had given would help their chances on a mission like this? Duane cursed to himself because he was behind most of the launch, and the exhaust gases swirled around his plane and entered the open cockpit. Ahead of him lighted wands began directing planes forward. He checked his watch. It was 6:35, almost time to go.

Eleanor Hawkins popped into his mind—incongruously at such a time. It disturbed him to think he had won her without a fight, that Jack Hardigan didn't care whether he married her or not. That maybe he was even glad Duane was doing it, to get her off his back, as if she weren't a good-looking, desirable woman.

But maybe Jack didn't find *any* woman desirable. But that was as hard to believe as his finding Fred Trusteau desirable. Duane had tried to imagine what the two men could have been doing with each other in the darkened BOQ room, but it was so bizarre that he couldn't visualize it. How could that same man be leading this fight of Hellcats toward the Japanese equivalent of Pearl Harbor? It didn't make a particle of sense.

They were launching the first aircraft ahead of him. The rumble of engines increased as the lighted wand circled, then fell as the Hellcats accelerated down the deck and climbed into the air. Two, three, four more fighters followed in rapid succession. Suddenly one of the two Dauntlesses moved magically away from in front of him, and Duane saw a man scamper under his wing and emerge with a chock. A light wand directed him forward. He taxied slowly off the elevator and stopped just short of the island. Two more aircraft roared down the deck and took to the air, then it was his turn. The conical wand bade him run his engine up. He ran it up to twenty-seven hundred revolutions. The tail tried to rise in the whirlwind produced by the propeller. He strained to hold the brakes down and the stick forward. The instruments blurred in the vibration. Duane leaned out and checked for the hooded deck lights, the wand snapped downward, and he was off, snatched away by the thundering engine.

When the accelerative forces released him, Duane searched vainly for a horizon to fly by, couldn't find it, and turned to his instruments. He climbed at a shallow angle to five hundred feet and began looking for the rendezvous light. In a minute it appeared reassuringly, and he flew directly over it, turning right, and climbing slowly. Tiny, starlike lights were moving against a background of real stars, and he knew he had found the main body. He moved in cautiously, constantly checking his artificial horizon to make sure he was in the proper attitude. He joined up on two Hellcats he hoped were the other half of his division. Moments later another dark shape glided in on his left and edged into a wing position. A few more minutes of circling and they were ready. As if on signal, the white turtle-back lights they had used to join up were extinguished, and the whole formation turned ponderously onto the heading for Truk.

The twelve *Ironsides* fighters leveled off at one thousand feet in tight formation, without the aid of radio. Duane accepted the fact casually, without thinking of the difficulty involved. It was what they were trained to do, so they did it. What concerned him now was the coming fight. Maybe it was better the skipper had brought him along on the first sweep; they were sure to find opposition and the ugly blot against his record from Kwajalein could be expunged. He didn't care now if Jack Hardigan went to bed with left-handed, cross-eyed gorillas. He would show him, and his ace-hero wingman Trusteau, that he could fly and fight as well as or better than both of them put together. Duane Higgins settled his body and mind and grimly composed himself for combat.

The first intimation that something was wrong came to Jack just as the sky was beginning to brighten. They were climbing steadily as planned, and the encircling reef of Truk Lagoon was plainly visible ahead of them. But just as they were reaching five thousand feet, Jack noticed Fred Trusteau, on his left wing, gesturing frantically and pointing over his shoulder. Jack looked back, straining hard to see into the eastern sky, and was shocked to find only emptiness. The four aircraft of Division One—he and Fred, Hughes and Fitzsimmons—were quite alone. He turned back, rubbernecked rapidly in all directions, but the others were nowhere to be seen. He looked across at Fred and shrugged exaggeratedly, implying that there was nothing he could do about it. Fred's masked face nodded agreement, and the four Hellcats flew on toward the enemy. Jack checked his clock. It was 7:40. The lagoon, the humpbacked green islands of Truk itself crawled across the face of the dark sea until they were directly below. Spotty clouds, brightened by the first rays of the sun, drifted across the target. Jack led the division in a wide circle to the left, thinking they were a few minutes early, that surely the rest would be along shortly.

Higgins. It was Duane Higgins again. Although he didn't want to judge Duane before knowing all the facts, Jack still realized that his Exec had been leading the Second Division, and the Second Division led the Fifth. It was quite possible that they had become separated as they climbed to altitude in the dark and passed through clouds on the way up.

But nothing could change the way Duane had acted for the past two days. His veiled accusation about himself and Fred left Jack feeling very cold.

"Bandits." The single-word transmission caught him by surprise, made him jump. "Nine o'clock low." It was sharp-eyed Fred. Jack looked to the left and found the enemy—Zekes, still far away but climbing straight for them. He counted five, nearly invisible against the backdrop of dark green island and early morning shadow. As he looked, several more, strung out behind as if they had just taken off, straggled into view. And Jack knew that if Duane and the rest of the squadron didn't show up soon, they'd be outnumbered at least two to one. Their best choice now was to attack without delay, while speed and altitude were on their side.

"Let's take 'em, guys," he said. "One fast pass, then take it back up. Stay together." He leaned the stick over and started down, still looking for the rest of his squadron. His speed increased quickly and he checked on Fred, satisfied that Fred could follow him anywhere. Fitzsimmons and Hughes moved away to get flying room, then went down, too.

Nose high, the Zekes struggled for altitude. Jack figured they could flame a few before the rest closed in and forced them back up. It would be extremely dangerous, almost certain death, to get below that many enemy fighters, even though the Hellcats could outclimb the Zekes without difficulty. He lined up the head formation, three greenish brown planes in a backwards V. His speed climbed to 350 knots. Black puffs of antiaircraft explosions began to spot the sky around him. A messy explosion boiled up on one of the islands below. The battle was being joined.

The leading Zeke was turning toward them, still climbing, and his wingmen were following. It would be a head-on pass at extreme speed. Jack checked on Fred again, centered the rapidly closing target, and squeezed off the first burst. Then suddenly he'd passed through the enemy formation. Without being able to observe the results of the pass, he pulled up and around in the tightest turn he could manage. Enemy planes, islands, water, and sky flashed before his eyes until he could haul the fighter around and level it. He had time to see a Hellcat (was it Hughes?) twisting tortuously to stay on the tail of a Japanese fighter, while another Zeke twisted after the first Hellcat and another Hellcat followed the second Zeke. But he had no time to watch.

The Zekes they had attacked were racking around and coming for them. Jack chandelled up five hundred feet, throttle wide open, rolling out on the tail of a turning Zeke and snapping off a burst before losing him. Again he was unable to observe the results; again he checked Fred; he was still there, as before. Up to this point they'd had it easy, with speed and altitude to their advantage, but now things were different. The Zekes were on their level, closing in, lining up for passes. Jack counted five. Far ahead of them, to the east, he saw aircraft going down in fire and smoke and wondered briefly if that could be the other divisions of Fighting Twenty or perhaps Hellcats from another ship. But they were too far away to help him and Fred. Jack pressed his throat mike. "Weave," he said, "cover each other."

"Roger." Fred's Hellcat abruptly left Jack's wing and soared out to the right. Jack banked sharply to the left, checking Fred's tail, just as he knew Fred was checking his. It was a standard defensive maneuver: If enemy fighters were closing either Hellcat from behind, the wingman would be in position after a simple turn to hit the attacker with a deflection shot. At the limits of the weave, both fighters turned back towards the center, crossed over, and repeated the pattern. On the second weave, a Zeke turned onto Fred and came under Jack's guns. He snapped off a quick burst, trying to conserve ammunition, and the Zeke dove away below. Jack resisted the temptation to follow him down—the Hellcat was heavier and could catch up with ease—because the Japanese pilot's comrades were now on three sides and high. Goddamn it, where was the rest of the squadron.

"Behind you, Skipper." Jack looked and saw the two clean little fighters curving in behind him. He moved stick and rudder to turn toward his wingman. When he did, he saw that another Zeke was closing Fred from behind. There were just too many...

"Behind you, Trusty." Jack had time for a single burst, then hauled it around to try to follow the Japanese fighter. Damn the Zekes on his tail! He would take his chances with Fred's shooting. Jack lost sight of his wingman as he followed his target down and away. The enemy pilot was fatally inexperienced. His turns were rough. Still he headed down. Jack centered him in his sights, squeezed off a burst. The tracers seemed to arch out ahead. He fired again, holding it down. A puff of black smoke chuffed back. He hung on grimly, firing continuously. The Zeke started burning. Debris tore off, fluttered back. An explosion! His victim collapsed into a falling tangle of burning junk, and Jack racked his heavy fighter around and up, looking for Trusty—or a friendly aircraft of any kind.

A burning Zeke was falling, a parachute was blossoming, and Fred Trusteau was hot on the tail of another. The two aircraft twisted through the air in a strange and deadly dance. As he watched, the enemy fighter trailed flames and smoke, fell off on one wing and headed down. Jack turned for Fred, trying to join up again.

"Join up, Trusty, let's get out of here," said Jack. He saw

Fred turn toward him, in an elegant, plunging roll. His wingman was flying like the ace he was.

"Look out—" Tracers zinged past his canopy, slugs chewed into his wingtip, and Jack snapped into a roll without thinking, acting purely on instinct. Suddenly they were all around him, looping, rolling, firing. Jack lost sight of Fred then as he fought for his life, not flying level for more than a few seconds at a time, evading the Zekes only by virtue of his experience and his desperate need to survive. He lost altitude steadily, never able to climb long enough to get safely back above them. He was almost to sea level, out of flying room and time when the rest of Fighting Twenty arrived.

He would remember those minutes of combat for the rest of his life, as though they were a strange and marvelous dream burned too deeply into his mind to forget. He leveled off one final time, below the tops of the trees on the islands. Above him, the rising sun painted the fluffy clouds pink and gold. All around him were deep green islands and blue waters—and drifting black columns of smoke. He knew he could go no further, that it could be minutes, even seconds, before they closed in on him and killed him. He had done his best, and it just wasn't good enough. Fear, though, made him look over his shoulder to see how close they were, to see how long he still had. What he saw, to say the least, was far more comforting.

The big blue fighters cut down on the Zekes with unmatched ferocity. Even as he watched, two Zekes exploded in flames and tumbled down. As a third caught fire, the rest turned to meet the new threat from above. But it was too late. Jack circled and climbed and watched the slaughter. A fourth Zeke stonewalled with the water, a fifth landed in a bloom of flame on a nearby island. Parachutes began to drift down, as a sixth and then a seventh Zeke went down. Amazed, awed, Jack lingered and watched two more Japanese planes destroyed, and then he remembered Fred.

It seemed like hours since he had heard from him. He went to his throat mike. "Trusty, where are you, Trusty." There was no reply.

A pair of Hellcats crossed in front of him; the pilots waggled the wings and held up their fingers showing the number of kills they had. Jack ignored them, then realized with a start that he couldn't hear anything on what had to be a cluttered circuit.

He tried again. "Any Banger aircraft respond. This is Banger Leader, come in please." Nothing. Jack wrenched around in his seat and looked at his antenna, a short stubby mast aft of the cockpit. It was gone, shot away. Fine, he thought. Where would he go?

He checked the time. 8:20. Rendezvous would be in ten minutes. Maybe Fred was already there. Jack looked around quickly, getting his bearings by the morning sun climbing above the horizon, and headed back the same way they had entered the lagoon area. Antiaircraft fire followed him, but he didn't notice. One thing alone occupied his mind.

What was the reciprocal course on which they had come? Subtract one eight zero from two four zero. Zero six zero. Jack increased speed, turned to zero six zero as he crossed the reef and headed out to sea. He had to be here. He flew for five minutes, nearly losing hope, before he found the Hellcat.

It was at one thousand feet but slowly losing altitude. As he approached, he saw it was streaming smoke, a wispy white trail that hung in the air behind it and drifted with the wind. Jack increased throttle to come alongside. His heart rose into his throat as he realized who it was. The Hellcat was missing part of its rudder and left elevator surface. An aileron was gone. Oil oozed from the engine and smeared the fuselage and canopy. As he came abreast, he saw the pilot—grimly staring straight ahead, seeing nothing. He held the stick in both hands. Jack had found his wingman.

Duane and the seven Hellcats following him lost the First Division in the circle and climb to fifteen thousand feet, halfway to the target. The mix up was partly his fault, partly sheer chance.

When the time came to make the circle and climb, Higgins noticed that Second Division had joined up completely wrong. It was barely light enough to make out numbers on adjacent aircraft, and he saw with a start that he was escorting the last section of Hardigan's division, Fitzsimmons and Hughes. He signaled his wingman, Bracker, who saw and understood what had happened, and was about to signal the rest when they entered the turn. Hoping the rest of the flight would see what he was doing, Higgins dropped back to allow the First Division to pull ahead, and the rest of his division to catch up. As he and Bracker fell out of formation, the second section of his division pulled alongside and passed them, causing Duane to curse helplessly at their oblivious manner of flying. He then led Bracker down and under the second section of his division to come up on the correct side of them, turning and climbing all the while. Just when he thought they should be moving into the correct configuration, they passed through a thick layer of clouds that had them flying nerve-rackingly in the blind, still climbing and turning, until they were out of it.

When they were in the clear again, Duane checked around in the growing light and found that all eight aircraft of the Second and Fifth Divisions were nicely in place, in perfect formation. And then he checked on the First Division. They were nowhere to be seen.

It took him ten minutes of flying in the wrong direction to discover that he had leveled off at fifteen thousand feet on two six zero instead of the correct heading of two four zero. He cursed again, this time at his own stupidity and the blithe way his squadron mates had of accepting his error and following him off into the wastes of empty ocean. Knowing that the Skipper and his division would now undoubtedly arrive at the target many long minutes before they would, Duane turned back toward Truk, to two three five—five degrees short of the original heading of two four zero. He increased speed to two hundred knots, hoping his dumb followers would have the sense to keep up. Screw them, he thought. He, at least, would not leave the skipper to tangle with God knew how many enemy fighters without assistance. He hoped almost desperately that he wasn't too late, remembering another time, at Guadalcanal, when he and Jack had lost the main body of a flight and gone in alone against dozens of Zeros, and had almost been killed. He wouldn't let that happen this time. The eight Hellcats arrived over Truk fifteen minutes late.

His first sight of the breathtaking beauty of the atoll and its mountainous islands included a flight of six or seven Hellcats chopping a formation of Judy dive bombers into flaming ruin, low on the water to the northeast of the reef. He led his eight fighters past the fight, knowing that it couldn't be the Skipper. Next he sighted falling planes near the center of the atoll amid spotty flak. He hurried toward them, increasing speed to be ready for whatever turned up. What did turn up was a gaggle of Zekes chasing a single Hellcat around and around, dropping close to the water and swirling back up again. Had he had time to observe, Duane could have determined that it was indeed the skipper. Now he could see only that the lone fighter needed help. They tallyhoed and went down.

Never in his life had Duane seen such a battle. The Zekes were well trained and aggressive, but the heavier, faster Hellcats fell on them recklessly from above. Duane got his first with a simple six o'clock shot. The enemy fighters burned quickly, alerting the others—too late—to the danger from above. He reeled in another with a short burst that sent the lithe little fighter into a desperate split-s at five hundred feet. Duane almost followed, but instinct held him back, and he watched the Zeke dive straight into the water from a doomed maneuver. When he had time to catch his breath and look around, he found not another Zeke in the air. Two of his Hellcats cut victory loops in the sky over the lagoon. Then someone was calling on the radio that millions of Jap fighters were taking off from an airstrip near the northern edge of the reef. The Hellcats around him stumbled over themselves to find the action, a deadly, rampaging gang of killers. Duane almost followed them, but instead he found the skipper.

Duane saw the zero two on the fuselage as Jack Hardigan's plane flew right across his nose, at lower altitude. He curved in behind him, calling repeatedly on the radio but getting no answer. Hardigan was flying fast, leaving the area on the return heading, and Duane tried but could not catch up. He followed at a distance, a little mystified. Five minutes after crossing the reef another Hellcat appeared ahead, trailing smoke and descending. Duane watched the two fighters join up and continue toward the task group, and he wanted to stay with them, but the chatter from the radio said that another rhubarb was forming up over the airstrip on Eten Island. He got close enough to determine that the damaged Hellcat was Trusteau, and then he peeled off and headed back. If anyone could help Trusteau, it was the skipper.

Back over Truk again, Higgins found the battle and eagerly joined in, adding another kill to his growing score. The rest of the squadron added another seven. It was, as Bagley would say later, a field day....

After the fight over Eten, Higgins gathered the elated pilots, including Hughes from the First Division, and headed for *Ironsides*. His own personal bag of three and the excited bragging of the other eight men made him think that everything was all right. But he discovered when he landed that an error of his had again caused the loss of three pilots: Fitzsimmons, Trusteau, Hardigan.

Fred killed the first Zeke as it tried to walk up on the skipper's tail, with a low-degree deflection shot that was just like shooting at a towed target sleeve. The enemy pilot had shown a fatal lack of attention by letting Fred get that close in perfect firing position. It took three seconds of shooting. Every shell seemed to hit; the great greenhouse canopy was smashed and one wing was torn off completely. He had time to notice that the pilot was bailing out and hoped he could be that lucky if the time ever came. Obviously, the stories of Japanese pilots jumping without parachutes were not completely true. The second Zeke had come at him from ahead and above and it missed; then stupidly it had tried to outclimb the Hellcat. Fred simply followed him into a well-executed Immelmann, rolling out at the top of the half-loop to find himself in perfect position. He exploded the Zeke's fuel tanks with a single long burst. Then he split-s'ed back to his previous altitude in time to see the skipper begin tangling with five or six more Zekes.

He wanted badly, desperately, to help, but it was impossible. The enemy pilots that came at him now were obviously better trained than the others; nothing he did could shake them, and they were steadily shooting him to pieces.

The first one scattered machine gun bullets down his right wing like a handful of rocks, leaving a random pattern of little holes. Another sawed off several inches of wingtip and put a very ominous, single small hole in the engine cowling. In minutes the overheated engine began to throw oil, obscuring his vision forward just when he needed it the most. After a particularly violent maneuver in which he climbed vertically until he stalled and then fell like a stone for five hundred feet before regaining control, a pair of deadly Zekes hit him hard somewhere in the rear. The rudder controls became very sluggish. Once during the struggle he saw a Hellcat locked in another tangle with several Zekes and thought it might be the Skipper, but he couldn't be sure. They had him trapped and almost done for when he heard someone tallyhoing. It sounded like Duane Higgins. Hellcats dove past him and burning Zekes began falling like so many autumn leaves. But the last enemy pilot, as if giving him a parting shot, hit him hard and very nearly killed him.

It was a single twenty-millimeter cannon shell, he was sure, that slashed through the canopy just above his eyes and exploded outside of the aircraft with a tremendous *whomp* that tore the stick from his hand and blinded him with its flash. When he could see again he was almost on the deck, fishtailing erratically and barely flying. But calm instinct took over and he trimmed the plane. He began to climb, dimly aware that something was very wrong. It was then that the pain hit him.

The pain was like a living thing surging up through his arm and side and wrenching control of his own body away from him. It overwhelmed him and he nearly blacked out. He came to only by the strength of sheer terror and shock, and then he knew there was no time to lose and that he must get back to the ship. When he tried to climb again, he realized that something was wrong with his right hand, the hand on the stick. When he moved it, the pain shot through his arm and washed in waves over his heart. He grabbed the stick with his left hand, and the pain eased somewhat. Forcing his mind to work, he remembered the course back to the task group and shakily turned to zero six zero, crossed the islands and the reef and headed out to sea. He flew mechanically, totally oblivious to the blood slowly saturating the right side of his flight suit.

In a few minutes, his engine began to run rough and trail smoke. The idea that he might not make it back penetrated his barely functioning mind. He looked past his bleeding hand to the instrument panel, saw that oil pressure was nearly gone and engine temperature was far into the red. He began to lose altitude in order to ditch. He took it down to one hundred feet before decreasing the throttle, knowing he couldn't reach it with his throbbing right hand, yet unable to take his left off the stick and face the pain that would inevitably follow. Finally he could wait no longer. For a moment he clenched his teeth, then shouted deliriously when the weight of flying again hit the damaged hand. But he cut back on the throttle, even lowered the flaps some, before taking the stick again with the left hand. Concentrating grimly on the task at hand, unaware of anything else, he mothered the sinking fighter to the surface of the water, flared to drag his tail portion first, hit hard, bounced once, and nosed over to a crashing stop. At the final contact, the straps on his right side tore loose and his body was flung into the instrument panel. His head crashed into the gunsight.

Strangely, he was feeling no pain as he calmly pushed himself back into his seat, reached up and slid the canopy back. The sudden quiet after hours of continuous noise was somehow comforting, and he disentangled the straps on his left side and tried to hoist himself out of the cockpit. When his right foot found a step on the seat, his leg collapsed and he dropped back. "Damn," he said out loud, and he began again to crawl out of the sinking plane, pulling himself with his left hand and pushing with his left foot. He rolled onto the wing like a sack of potatoes, slid head first into the warm sea water, and quickly pulled the handle on the Mae West to inflate it. It whooshed up around him and he bobbed, contented. He was alive.

Relaxed, Fred suddenly felt half-asleep. The sea water and the quiet lapping of small waves against his life jacket seemed to ease the hurts, and he thought, I'll just take a little nap, then head back to the ship. Things will be all right then. I can have dinner with the guys and the skipper, maybe take in the evening movie; then I'll hit the sack and get a good night's sleep. It will be nice. Everything will be all right.

He slept.

Jack watched Fred's Hellcat sink. Then he saw the tiny figure of the pilot floating on the water like a piece of debris. He slowed to minimum speed, lowered flaps, and drifted over at fifty feet. Fred was alive. He had to be. How else could he have gotten out? Or inflated the life jacket? Jack circled and flew over once more, torn between staying near Fred or flying away and leaving him. If I leave him, he thought, he'll die. There could be no other end. He checked all around him, seeing only empty sky. His aircraft seemed in good shape. The engine ran smoothly. On the horizon, delicate smoke rose from the islands of Truk.

He ditched almost casually, nearly losing sight of his wingman on the final approach. Then for a horrible second he thought he would run over him in the water. But the Hellcat mushed in and stopped short of the bobbing figure by a good hundred yards. As though it were an everyday experience, Jack lay back the straps and turned off the power switches just the way he did when he left the fighter on the deck of the *Constitution*. He stepped out, reached back in for the seat-cushion raft, and plunged into the water. He inflated his life jacket first, before his heavy flight boots could draft him under. Then the life raft was blown up and he struggled into it. The little folding paddle and the first-aid kit were right where they were supposed to be. Jack took out the paddle and began to row.

One hundred yards in a rubber doughnut proved to be almost more than he could manage, and it took him an agonizing thirty minutes to reach Fred. When he did reach him, he was so motionless in the vinyl pillows of the Mae West that Jack thought he was dead. The water around him was brownish with blood.

"Fred." Jack tucked the paddle under his feet and grabbed Fred's collar. "Fred, wake up." He shook him.

"Hi, Skipper."

Jack heaved a deep sigh of relief and tried to pull Fred's inert form into the raft. "Help me here, Fred. Please." Jack reached out and removed Fred's goggles; then he saw with shock that Fred's eyes had been forced shut in his black, swollen face. "Come on, Fred. There's room in the raft. Come on."

"Sure, Skipper," said Fred. Sluggishly, he placed both hands on the side of the raft. Jack saw that one hand was bleeding. He grabbed Fred by the back of the flight suit and tugged with all his strength. The raft nearly foundered, but when it settled, Jack had Fred halfway in.

"Come on, Fred, help," he pleaded. Fred groaned, began to crawl painfully. Working together, they inched his body into the raft. Jack turned him over, holding him like a baby.

"Oh, Jesus," said Fred, and was quiet.

Jack looked at him carefully, afraid that he'd stopped breathing, and put his head on Fred's chest to listen to his heart. He couldn't hear it but felt his chest expanding and contracting. He lifted Fred's right forearm and pulled off the glove. The ring finger tore off and stayed in the glove and a fountain of blood poured out. Aghast, Jack fought to keep control and scrabbled for the first-aid kit. Fred came to again and began thrashing and moaning as Jack broke open the little package, found a bandage, and tried to stanch the flow of blood. Fred passed out again, thankfully, and Jack wound the bandage around the hand and nub of finger, then took out the second and last bandage, wound it into a strip, and tied it as tightly as he could around Fred's upper arm. He hoped it was enough.

Fred moaned, delirious. Morphine. That would help. Jack searched through the kit and found five Syrettes. Shaking uncontrollably, he broke one open, uncovered the needle, pulled back the left arm of Fred's flight suit, and jabbed it in. He had to try several times before he found a vein, but Fred almost immediately calmed. Breathing easier, Jack dropped the Syrette overboard and began to search the rest of the body.

Halfway down Fred's right side was another surprise. He caught his finger on something sharp and jagged, then rolled him over to get a better look. A three-inch piece of aluminum was protruding from his side. He touched it gingerly, finding it solidly wedged in between the ribs. There appeared to be little blood, so he left it. He searched some more, and found an ugly, black-and-blue, knobby fracture in the right leg below the knee. He took his hands away, grateful that there was nothing more to find, but still overwhelmed by the nature of the wounds. He could no more help Fred than he could get them both back to the ship. He drew a shuddering breath and exhaled it. He felt very helpless.

"Not time to go yet," said Fred, distinctly.

"No, Fred," said Jack. He tried to hold him close. "I won't leave you."

"Champ," said Fred, "and don't you forget it."

"I won't," said Jack.

"Skipper wouldn't like it. No more doping around."

"Don't worry. You'll be all right."

"Me and Heckman."

"Yeah," said Jack. "You and Heckman."

Then Fred was still, and Jack held him all through the morning while the sun burned down on them. A strike force of bombers and fighters passed overhead. Two of the fighters stopped to circle. Jack waved frantically, but the fighters left, and they were alone again.

Some time in the early afternoon—Jack couldn't tell exactly when because his watch had stopped—Fred came to. The morphine was wearing off. For a few minutes, before the pain became too much, he was lucid.

"How'd you get here, Skipper?" he asked.

"I flew," said Jack. "Don't talk. You'll be all right."

"I'm getting pretty good at this ditching business."

"I'd say you got it down pat."

"I never got to show you how to tie a knot in a cherry stem."

"No, you didn't."

"Got a cherry on you?"

"'Fraid not, Fred. I'm sorry."

The sea rocked them gently and the piece of aluminum bore into Jack's stomach. "Looks like the guys did pretty good back there," said Fred.

"I knew they would," said Jack.

"If only they'd gotten there a little sooner."

"Yeah."

"What time is it?"

"Two-thirty." Jack didn't even look at his stopped watch.

"Already?" Fred chuckled, his eyes squeezed shut by the swelling. "Were you really mad at us yesterday?" he asked.

"Nah," said Jack. He was looking for another Syrette. "Not really. Not at you anyway. But I had to do something."

"Well, it sure worked." Fred's ugly black face contorted into a grimace of pain.

"Yeah, it worked." Jack found the morphine, injected it, and his wingman drifted away. The afternoon sun beat down on them, burning Fred's lips until Jack covered them with his handkerchief. Feeling hopeless enough for prayer, Jack tried and could remember only part of one, from his boyhood days in church: We have left undone those things which we ought to have done, and done those things which we ought not to have done. And there is no health in us.

The sun sank low. Jack's body hurt from the cramped position he had held all day, from sunburn and hunger. When it was nearly dark and Jack was sure Fred would never last through the night, a submarine named *Searaven* grumbled and smoked over the horizon and plucked them both from the sea off Truk.

Although postmission analysis reduced Fighting Twenty's claim of thirty-six kills over Truk on 17 and 18 February to a more modest twenty-four, it still stands as the highest score for any squadron engaged.

Jack Hardigan led Fighting Twenty with an iron hand for another four months of unremitting action, culminating in the incredible fighter victory of the Turkey Shoot off Saipan in June, 1944. Under another C.O. the Jacks fought in every major action up to and including Okinawa, emerging in the top three wartime squadrons for most confirmed kills.

Without reservation, it can be said that Fighting Twenty went to Truk a dispirited, hard-luck outfit, and emerged two days later a striving, deadly squadron satisfied only by excellence. To the skipper must go the credit...

(Lt. Cmd. James R. Bagley, USN: "Jacks Over Truk: The Metamorphosis of Fighting Twenty," *Sea Power*, Vol. VI, no. 6, June, 1953.)

Part VIII

Scrapbook

44

Naval Hospital
Pearl Harbor

April 15, 1944

Dear Skipper:

Just a little note to catch you up on things these days, even though there isn't a whole lot to tell. I haven't been doing much of anything outside of lying around and, as the doctors say, getting better all the time. They took the finger off completely down to the knuckle, and I haven't really gotten used to looking down and finding one gone. Also, they've been taking x rays of my back and neck like there was something wrong there, although it feels all right with me. The leg has mended just fine.

Admiral Berkey was in the hospital for a while back in March. When I asked one of the doctors where he had gone, she said he died of cancer. It was too bad. He was a nice person.

How's the squadron doing? Fine, I hope. I really miss being back with you and all the guys, doing something important, but they won't tell me when they think I'll be ready to return. Typical Navy doctors, all of them. I hope the censors leave that part in.

Well, there isn't much more to say right now, so I guess I better sign off. It's just before noon here on Saturday,

and this nurse I know pretty well keeps asking me to go
down to the beach with her, so this time I guess I'd better
go. It's all for the war effort, you know. Maybe she'll put
in a good word for me and get me back to the ship where I
belong.

Write soon and catch me up on things. Take care of
yourself.

Sincerely,
Fred

P.S. Just heard that they are giving me another medal and
that you had something to do with recommending it. I was
having enough trouble keeping the nurses off my back,
now they won't leave me alone. Thanks for everything.
Regards, Fred (Old Nine Fingers)

USS *Constitution*
Somewhere in the Pacific

30 June 1944

Dear Fred:

Got your letter last week and had a good time reading
it and showing it to a few of the guys. They seemed to be
amazed at how far things have gone—now the gals ask the
guys to go to the beach. Or is it just your irresistible
personality? Whatever it is, as Jim Bagley says, "Trusty
strikes again."

As to news of the squadron, there's quite a bit to tell,
most of which I can't say in a letter. Suffice to say that
we've been busy, ending up a week or so ago with the big
action I'm sure you've read about in the papers. The whole
air group was involved there, and I got another one added
to my score as did most of the other old-timers. We've got
a lot of new men and they are all right as far as that goes,
but they'll never be the same as the good old bunch we
started with. By the way, Dave Peckerly was lost on a
training flight last month. We don't know what happened
to him.

Duane Higgins will be detached sometime next month
and will head back to the states to form a new squadron.
He'll be upped to lieutenant commander, too. I
recommended him highly for the job and feel he deserves
it.

Now for the big news. After this last action I was

recommended for a decoration (Navy Cross), and now they want to rotate me back to the States to help sell war bonds for a while and then maybe head up a new air group. All of this will happen in the next month or so, as soon as I break in the new skipper. I tell you all this because I'll be coming through Pearl on my way stateside and maybe we could get together for a few drinks and talk over old times. That is, if you haven't left for a new squadron yourself by that time. Write me and keep me up to date on your latest address.

Well, it's time for the evening movie, so I guess I'll close for now. Don't forget to write, and take care of yourself.

Sincerely,

J. E. Hardigan

Bachelor Officer's Quarters
Pearl Harbor Naval Station

August 2, 1944

Dear Jack:

Here it is August already and I guess I put off writing until there was some news to pass on, but before we get into that I want to say that I had a great time when you came through Pearl last month. I apologize for the lack of room, there being more brass in the islands these days than swabbies and mere lieutenants like myself. Yes, they kicked me up to lieutenant. More on that.

It seems they kicked me up a grade as a sort of consolation prize, to make up for the fact that they're kicking me out altogether. Out of the Navy, that is. It came as a surprise. I know that a man can't fly a plane with 10 percent of his digits gone, but I was still hoping for something else to come along. Until last week, that is. I was having some minor problems with my eyes and I didn't think it was serious, but then they looked real close and found a sliver of steel in my left eye. It's been there since last November, I think, when I got the three Kates. I wasn't wearing my goggles then. Anyway, they've also decided that one of the bones in my neck is cracked or bruised or something and could cause trouble later on. Therefore, it's civilian life once more.

Well, I've been talking all about myself and not about you. How's the bond drive going? Are things really that short on the mainland? I heard someone say that you have to stand in line to buy a tube of toothpaste. I can't believe it's that bad.

My separation orders will be coming through sometime next month, and then I'll go to an outfit in San Francisco for final processing. After that I guess I'll go home to San Jose. If you ever come through there, I certainly hope you'll come by and say hello. It would really be great to talk to you again. Write soon.

Regards,
Fred

Naval Air Training Command
Washington, D. C.

14 January 1945

Dear Fred:

Where does the time go? It seems like I've been here for only a month or two, though it's been more like six. I appreciate the letters you write, if only because I don't get very much other mail. I'm close enough to home to fly up there (Maine), and I do every couple of months, but it's no fun when all you hear is, When are you getting married?

I seem to have gotten a little rusty since last June, and I'm not sure if I'll ever get into action again. I can't imagine the war lasting much longer, what with the pasting we gave them last October.

Congratulations on your new job. Running a hardware store may not sound like an important thing right now, but I have a feeling that after the war things are really going to boom and that will be as good a place to make a name for yourself as any.

Did you think the old *Ironsides* was a big ship? Well, they're building another class of flattops that make the *Ironsides* look like a ferry boat. I've done some of the original air group planning on them. Who knows, they might offer me a squadron on one of them, which would be a mixed blessing. I can't say more on that subject.

By the way, I'm considering flying out to the coast for training (and to keep the extra pay) sometime this month. Moffet Field would be a good choice. You could show me that store of yours and maybe we could wow the kids on the block with some sea stories. What do you say?

Write soon, and don't take any wooden nickels.

Sincerely,
Jack

USS *Bon Homme Richard*
Somewhere in the Pacific

August 6, 1945

Dear Fred:

How about that? I guess I was just premature about it all. The war isn't over yet and here I am, back at sea. Although I was expecting an air group, it seems they've got too many CAGs around these days, so it's old Squadron Leader Hardigan again. All the pilots are experienced now, not like back in '43 when three-quarters of the squadron were bare-faced ensigns, yourself included. I ran into Duane Higgins on the way out. He's got the fighters on the *Ticonderoga*. We only had time to say hello in passing, and he didn't seem very friendly. I guess we had little to talk about anyway.

You can tell that things are going well for us out here now, except we don't quite know what to do about the suiciders. It's something that one can't quite understand or explain, these pilots killing themselves that way. It just doesn't make sense, when you think that they must be as tired of the war as we are. Why don't they just quit? I've been thinking about your offer of going into the hardware business with you when it's over, and it sounds better all the time. I think I'd like counting nuts and bolts better than counting kills.

Well, I've just got time for this short note. We're actually not far from enemy airfields right now (hope the censors leave that one in), and we're maintaining an eight plane CAP during all daylight hours. Keep up the good work and write soon.

Sincerely,
Jack

San Jose *Mercury News,* March 21, 1946

The son of the late owner of San Jose Hardware announced today the opening of a new and bigger hardware store in downtown San Jose. Frederick Trusteau, the son of Robert Trusteau, who passed away last month after more than thirty years in the hardware business, says that the new store will occupy an entire city block on First Street between Taylor and Jackson and will be open for business the first day of October.

Trusteau's partner in the venture will be former Commander Jack Hardigan, a much decorated naval officer and shipmate from the war. The new store will be called "Trusty's Building Supplies," and will handle a number of new lines including lumber, roofing materials, and flooring products.

The announcement is concurrent with the latest figures on the building and commercial development surge which the Bay Area, and San Jose in particular, is experiencing...

San Francisco *Chronicle,* March 21, 1948

Shown above is Miss Erma Badger, cutting the ribbon on the new Trusty's Building Supplies Store on Shattuck Avenue in Berkeley. To the right and left respectively are Frederick Trusteau and J. E. Hardigan, major stockholders in Trusty's Incorporated, which now boasts three stores in the Bay Area, the other two being in San Jose and San Bruno. Mr. Hardigan states that the board of directors is considering the placement of another store in either the Los Angeles or Sacramento area...

From the Desk of Frederick Trusteau.

March 21, 1951

Jack—Sorry I missed you in the office today. The final figures for the L.A. store are in and do they look good. I put them in your box which means you've probably already seen them.

I have a doctor's appointment at ten, and after that Bob Gilardi the real estate man is going to show me some parcels in the Willow Glen area. I'll make it back in time for the manager's meeting this P.M. See you later.
Fred, 9:15

U. S. Naval Air Station
Yokosuka, Japan

August 9, 1952

Dear Trusty:

I have to thank you for the fine letter of last July. Your reminiscences of the old squadron were right on target, especially the parts about the skipper. I'm just sorry we couldn't get together and talk in person, but we're both pretty busy these days. I thought maybe they'd bring back the old *Ironsides* like they did so many of the other Essexes, but it looks like they never will. These jets are really something, but every once in a while I wish I could see the old Hellcats again.

I wish I had time for a longer letter, but the baby's crying and Darlene wants to get dinner over with so we can have a little time to ourselves this evening. I'll be leaving in the morning for another cruise off South Korea. Rough business, this flying, that keeps a man away from his wife and kids. But that's something you don't have to worry about, is it? Thanks again for everything.

Sincerely,
Jim Bagley

P.S. I've already found a publisher for the article. Magazine called *Sea Power*. (*The Proceedings* didn't want it.) I'm calling it, "The Metamorphosis of Fighting Twenty." Snazzy, huh?

Jimbo

Christmas, 1956

> *A Christmas note of warmth and cheer,*
> *To say, "God Bless," I'm glad you're near.*
> *On such a fine day*
> *It's easy to say*
> *I wish you the best all through the year.*

Fred:

Ten years is a long time to be in business. To show my appreciation for all we've done together, you'll find something in the driveway that almost says it all. Hope you like it.

Jack

Ready Man Real Estate
San Jose, California

May 10, 1957

Dear Mr. Trusteau:

It is my pleasure to thank you sincerely for the long and fruitful association we have enjoyed. It is always a pleasure doing business with a man who knows exactly what he wants, and one who is possessed of such high standards of professional ethics as yourself.

The final papers on the Los Gatos estate will be arriving by mail in several days at the latest. May I compliment you again on your choice of location? I'm sure it will bring you and your family many years of comfort and joy.

As per your attorney's instructions, the deeds and title will indicate joint ownership with one J. E. Hardigan, business associate of yourself. I hope sincerely that should you have any real estate needs in the future, you will come again to Ready Man. Again, thank you.

Sincerely,
Robt. A. Gilardi, Sales Representative

TO: JACK E. HARDIGAN, M.S. EASTWIND, ENROUTE GUAM MARIANAS PROTECTORATE

FROM: M. HARDIGAN, PORTLAND, MAINE

MOM NEAR DEATH STOP BAD OFF STOP PLEASE COME IF ABLE STOP

MONTY
23/11/581202Z

Message from the Front Desk
Jessie Beck's Riverside Hotel and Casino
Reno, Nevada

September 12, 1961

Mr. Jack Hardigan, the California Suite:
Please call Erma Badger at your earliest opportunity. She says she has good news about your book.
A. G., 1:45 P.M.

Medical Associates
15000 Comstock Boulevard
Denver, Colorado

February 26, 1963

Dear Mr. Trusteau:
We have received and looked over the medical records and x rays sent us by your personal physician in San Jose. We are indeed interested in seeing you and examining you personally with a view toward possible treatment of your spinal condition. However, we must in all honesty reserve

judgment as to the treatability of your condition. As in most instances of spinal and neck vertebrae injury which are not immediately crippling, as in your case, it is quite often safer to do nothing. Surgery in this area of the human body can have risks which do not justify the gain. We will be able to tell you more after we have seen you.

Incidentally, in the single set of x rays of your right rib cage area, we spotted a small, triangular-shaped object, undoubtedly metallic, lodged inside the thoracic cavity interior of the fourth rib. Since no mention of this object is made in your records, may we recommend that at the earliest opportunity (if you are unable to come to Denver soon) you have your present physician investigate this?

You may schedule an appointment with our admissions desk at any time. We look forward to seeing you.

Sincerely,
A. M. Duckworth, M.D.
AMD/cc

San Jose *Mercury News*, November 5, 1965
    ...elected to the City Council of the Incorporated Town of Los Gatos was Jack E. Hardigan, part owner of Trusty's Inc., and long-time resident of Los Gatos, to a two-year term to become effective January 1. Reelected was the incumbent...

From the Desk of Fred Trusteau.
Mr. T—We've been trying all afternoon to get hold of you. Sally is putting this note on your front door and I'm leaving another on your desk. Mr. Hardigan has been taken to Lakeside Memorial with bad chest pains. We don't know what to do. I am with him. Please come as soon as you can. Erma, 10-6-69, 2:15.

Epilogue

45

The day of Jack Hardigan's funeral was one of those pristine California days when the illusion of fall is in the air—autumn in California existing only in the minds of those who come to the state from Maine or Georgia or Ohio where the leaves turn red and yellow and frost touches the ground in the mornings. It was a temperate day. Short sleeves could have been worn without discomfort. But the occasion called for coat and tie. The altar arrangement in the chapel of the funeral home was correctly though incongruously done in the orange and brown colors of harvest. Under other circumstances, Fred might have admired them.

The group of mourners that accompanied the hearse to the Peaceful Hills Cemetery in south San Jose was large when one considered the fact that Jack had left no immediate family except his married sister, who had flown out alone from Leeds, Ohio. Most of the mourners were from the company. Fred and the married sister occupied the front row in the chapel, with the corporate secretary Erma Badger, who had been with the company since 1948. Three of the pallbearers were from the funeral home. When the short service at the grave site was over, the group dispersed slowly, perhaps reluctant to leave the gently rolling hills and manicured lawns, the gorgeous foliage of the cemetery. Fred was almost to his car (Jack had picked it out scarcely a month earlier) when a familiar voice from many years back stopped him. It was Duane Higgins. Fred's red eyes and drawn face made Duane look away when he spoke.

"Trusty?" That name, thought Fred, would he never lose it?

"Duane. Duane Higgins." They shook hands as warmly as the occasion allowed, mutually surprised at the aging effects of the passage of over twenty-five years. "It's good to see you again."

"You, too, Trusty."

"No one's called me that in years." He hoped Duane would understand and stop using the name, although it seemed as if there was nothing anyone could say or do at this particular time that would penetrate the thick mantle of fear and isolation that had settled over him.

"He meant a lot to you, didn't he?" Higgins said.

"How did you hear about it?" asked Fred.

"I was in town on business and I saw it in the paper yesterday. Figured I had to come out and see the skipper off . . ." Another name from the past, almost forgotten.

"No one's called Jack that in years . . ."

A car scratched by on the gravel road, and Fred saw Erma Badger and two of the office workers inside. She slowed down as she passed, halting when Fred motioned with his hand. "Put a note on the doors, would you, Erma? Just say that we'll be closed until next Monday. You and the rest can take the week off." Erma nodded wordlessly, and the car pulled away down the hill toward the cemetery gates.

"Look," said Duane suddenly, glad for the interruption. "Let me buy you a drink. Maybe we could catch up on some old times." There was a hint of pleading in Duane's voice.

"Sure," Fred said. "I know a place close by. Can you follow me?" He walked around the front of his car and opened the door.

"Yeah," said Duane. "I'm driving that blue Caddy down there."

Fred got in his car and swung the door shut, glad to be alone. But the new car smell was mingled with the aroma of Jack's cigars, and he remembered again what he had lost. He turned the key, felt the engine come to life, waited until Duane reached his car and got in. Then Fred drove slowly down the hill, away from Jack's final resting place, leaving a great, irreplaceable part of himself there, too.

When they had taken a booth in the plush little cocktail lounge and ordered their first round, Fred asked Duane what he had been doing for the last quarter century.

"You make it sound like such a long time," said Duane.

"It is a long time. You haven't spoken to Jack since 1945." The lounge was a world away from the chapel, the muted organ music, the gentle sobbing of the corporate secretary at the graveside service. Fred was finding it easier to talk.

"I'm in real estate," Duane said. "Office in Santa Barbara. Doing right well, I have to admit." He took out a cigarette pack, offering one to Fred. Fred shook his head. Duane patted his pockets for a match. "Damn," he said.

Fred took out the Hornet lighter which he often carried and struck a flame for Duane. As he lighted the cigarette, Duane caught sight of the insignia on the case.

"Look at that," he said. "May I?" He took the lighter from Fred's hand and examined it closely. "Boy, that sure brings back the memories."

"Jack gave that to me back in '43. On the *Ironsides*." The drinks arrived and Duane handed the lighter back to Fred, wiping his hand on his lapel as if it were dirty. For the first time Fred noticed a wedding band on Duane's hand. "You're married?" he asked.

Duane laughed nervously and tugged at the ring. "Divorced a year ago," he said. "Can't get the damn thing off." He stopped tugging and took a sip from his drink. "Three boys. The oldest one's a law student at Berkeley."

"That's nice to hear. I'm glad you've done well."

"I guess I have." Higgins lapsed into self-conscious silence. With rising anger, Fred thought: Here it is again, the same old game. Hide-and-seek. Goddamn, I wish I could just talk and be myself.

"Neither Jack nor I ever married," he said.

"Look, Fred—" (Thank God, thought Fred, he's quit with the Trusty thing.) "If you don't want to talk about it, it's all right."

Fred looked at him hard and unconsciously fingered the great gap on his right hand. Duane couldn't help but notice. "You're the one who wanted to talk," he said.

Duane sipped his drink slowly. "You know," he said, "after you left he was a different man. I mean really different. Man, he drove us. But he sure as hell made an outfit out of Fighting Twenty. Damn, we were good. It was like old times there after a while. . . ." Fred said nothing, and he continued. "But there was something that really bothered me then, and since yesterday I've been thinking about it again. I know it sounds kind of dumb, but I really have to know . . ."

"Know what?"

"Well, do you remember that first raid on Truk? The sweep?"

Fred held up his disfigured hand, touched his side. "I'm still carrying a piece of my plane. How could I forget?"

"Look," said Duane, becoming almost animated. "I saw Jack leave the target in a perfectly flyable aircraft—"

"Yeah?"

"What I want to know is this. Did he ditch just—because of you?"

Fred stared numbly at Duane. Jack had never mentioned the ditching. To find out something like this after all these years, to know that Jack had risked his own life to save him, putting his Hellcat down in the hostile sea with no real hope of being picked up...

"I don't know," he said wonderingly. "We never talked about it." Oh, Jack, he thought, did you really do that? Why didn't you tell me?

"I just had to know," said Duane. "I don't think anything less of Jack for what you and he—"

Fred pushed his drink aside. "Why don't we get it out in the open? I'm not afraid of anyone any longer, and I've got nothing left to lose."

"Fred," Duane began, but stopped as if he had lost his train of thought.

"Jack and I were a lot more than just wingmen. For the last twenty-five years we've been a lot more than just business partners."

"I know," said Duane quietly. "I knew it then. I've seen your pictures in the papers every now and then. I'm not stupid."

"He spoke of you before. He said he loved you like a brother and you saved his life once. But there near the end you really scared him bad, made him think that everything was going to pieces." Fred's voice lost its edge and he took a drink from his glass. "The way you acted, you really scared him."

Duane was sweating slightly. "How did he die?"

"Heart attack. It took him three days to go. He was in a lot of pain." Fred almost choked. He passed his hand over his eyes, embarrassed at his loss of control.

Duane finished his drink and signaled the waitress for another round. "When you think about it," he said after a moment, "we were together a pretty short time. But it seemed like years. He was so goddamned strong. You know what I mean? He could handle anything that came along no matter what it was. And you know, I tried like hell to measure up to his standards. But I just never made it."

The drinks arrived and Duane paid.

"Then for a while there, after Midway, you know, he was different. I didn't know what the hell was wrong. I just thought it was the war and things. Then I watched you and him for a while and it started to scare me, too. You know? I didn't know what the hell was going on. You can't blame me, can you?"

"At first, he was like a father to me," said Fred, as if to himself. "The only one I'd ever had."

"Me, too, I think," Duane said, not quite understanding. "Or a big brother, maybe." Duane's hand went to his collar, loosened his tie. "It isn't easy to say, Fred. But I loved him, too. I really did. I tried to live the rest of my life the way *he* did those first six months I knew him." He tugged at his collar. "I was never the man he was. He could handle anything."

Fred drank his cocktail and thought about the man he had shared his life with. He wasn't about to tell Higgins what it was really like for Jack: The ever-growing paranoia, Jack's fear that he and Fred would be found out, ridiculed, cast out. The creeping mental confusion brought about by the continual battle between his love for Fred and the knowledge of the danger that that love represented. And how in the last years that confusion had reduced Jack's sharpness and wit and decision-making abilities to a constant state of apprehension, always looking over the shoulder to make sure he wasn't followed. Fred suddenly realized that in all their years together, they had never taken a vacation with each other....

"Yeah," he said. "Jack could handle anything."

"Another one?" asked Duane, holding up an empty glass.

"No, thanks."

"Well."

"I imagine you have to be getting back."

"Yeah. It's a long drive down the coast."

"Next time you're in the area..."

"I'll give you a call. Maybe we could have dinner, talk over old times."

"Sure. Drop by."

"Take it easy." Duane Higgins left a dollar tip on the table and left, without having said once that he was sorry. Fred never saw or heard from him again.

After Higgins left, Fred went out to the car that Jack had chosen and sat in it, enjoying the warmth of the sun and the smell of Jack's cigars. The two drinks had sapped his strength. He didn't feel like doing anything, and he particularly didn't want to drive home to the great empty house. Pressing items awaited him there: a hefty life-insurance claim was one; the company, which he had already decided to sell, was another. The world was no longer the same without Jack. Fred drove over the mountains to Santa Cruz to watch the sun set into the Pacific Ocean, and for the second time in his adult life, he cried.